Out of the Gray Zone, Heading South

By LJ Sinnott

ISBN 9781479383139

COME WHAT MAY, THANK YOU ALL.

Charles Campbell Ph.D., Mark McCollum, Nancy Wilds,
James Middleton, Roger W. Roosa, Victor B. Cauffman,
Sharon Bakken, Virgil Bakken

ACKNOWLEDGMENTS

Dawn Smith   Cover Art

TABLE OF CONTENTS

LIST OF MAIN CHARACTERS

Matt Lovell
Bill Lovell – Matt's Uncle
Brent Chandler – Bill's best friend
Eric Ericson – Matt's best friend
Abby Lassiter – Matt's girl friend
Juanita – Professional Soldier
Rose – The girl next door

Montana (Juan Torres)
Moalim – Montana's partner

CHAPTER 1
PART 1

Matt Lovell's heart rate increased to keep pace with the fast talking anchorwoman on the ten-o'clock news.

A new report by field correspondent Rusty Macintyre claims the elderly are afraid to open their doors or answer their phones or even open their mail. Many, however, have found new hope in the Brotherhood Church for the Elderly who promise protection by God and Clergy if congregants will sign over their mortgages to the church; due upon their passing. The church also offers financial help for those who are struggling to pay their mortgages.

Parasites, thought Matt, relaxing his shoulders and lowering his chin and breathing in deeply through his nose and exhaling slowly through his mouth. One-thousand-and-one, one-thousand-and-two, one-thousand-and-three, he counted, staying true to the ritual that his Uncle Bill had taught him over thirty years ago. "It will relax your whole body and calm your nerves," his uncle had promised. And back then, when Matt's mother went off the deep end from too much alcohol, too many pills, and too many all-nighters, this simple ritual had been a life-saver. These days, however, Matt equated the process with tuning the high "E" string on his guitar; both are lessons in futility. These days, he seldom feels free of stress, and the "E" string on his guitar seldom stays in tune.

In other news, ten-year-old Melisa Martin's body has been recovered from Dawson's Pond, six weeks after she went missing on her way home from school. The police are looking for a 16 year old neighbor...

When they find him, he thought, they should nail his dick to a tree with a sixteen penny nail and hand him a dull, rusty butter knife. Most likely he will get off with a slap on the wrist because he's under age.

"Everything," he'd recently lectured his best friend Eric, "should be as fundamental as, is it *right* or is it *wrong*, but everything falls into the *Gray Zone*. Everything is just a little bit right and a little bit wrong. It's a crock of shit, my friend. Different people, different towns, and even different countries, but it's always the same bad news: murder, rape, pedophilia, drive-by shootings, religious extremists killing in the name of their one true God, corrupt politicians...." One-thousand-and-one, one-thousand-and-two, one-thousand-and-three.

At 10:30 p.m., Matt Lovell picked up his stainless steel Colt .45, flipped off the television set, and walked silently to his bedroom down the hall. One-thousand-and-one, one-thousand-and-two, one-thousand-and-three.

*****

Thirteen hundred miles to the south, a van driven by a tall lanky cowboy named Montana, alias Juan Torres, is about to cross the border at Nogales, Arizona, with four passengers.

Montana glanced quickly at the passenger sitting next to him and then into his mirror at the three in the back seat. He is confident that they will cross, once again, without incident and snickers at the corruption at the border. Money really can buy anything and anybody, he thought. Everyone has a price and he was no exception.

He leaned onto the steering wheel and thumped his thumbs to the beat of a song that only he could hear. As they waited patiently in the sweltering heat, the smell of pan-fried corn tortillas wafted in through the open windows, and bringing with it the nightmare of his eighth birthday.

*****

He was born in a small village on the U.S. side of Nogales, Arizona, to the parents of legal immigrants. His father, Marcos Torres, also an alias, was a dark skinned, stout man who had immigrated from Iran but passed for Mexican. He had come to the United States legally and had never caused a problem; he'd even converted to Catholicism. His mother, Maria, was a tall, thin, fair-skinned immigrant from Mexico, and as far as anyone knew, Juan Torres was the legal son of legal immigrants from south of the border.

On a muggy Friday afternoon in August, a senior clerk at the Nogales substation for Home Land Security came across the files of one Mohammad al-Hadadi. Curious, he opened the file and discovered that Mohammad al-Hadadi and Marcos Torres were one of the same. Shocked with disbelief at learning that his neighbor was a fraud, the bigoted officer turned to his colleagues with the news, and that very evening, in frenzied hatred, he and a band of nine sweaty, dusty, and angry cowboys stampeded through the gate of Marcos Torres's ranch and began accusing him of being a spy and a jihadist.

They tried hard to beat a confession from him, but he had nothing to confess. Incensed and enraged, they beat and tortured him until his naked body looked as if it had been skinned from head to toe. Near death, they tied his hands behind his back and hung him by his neck from a tree in his front yard; just high enough off the ground for him to balance on the tips of his bloody toes and watch through swollen eyes as they stripped Maria and took turns raping her; again, and again, and again. At first she screamed and fought hard to resist, but her eyes soon glazed over and she became a rag doll in the hands of her attackers until she passed into darkness.

2

Juan had recognized all of the men as local town folks and neighbors, and was at first elated to see them, mistakenly believing that they'd come to help celebrate his birthday, but when the trouble began, he ran and hid in the creosote bushes surrounding his house and watched in horror until the end. When one of the men called to him, Juan quietly scampered like a lizard into the desert to the secret underground sanctuary that his father had dug into the desert floor.

"This is where you will hide if the need should ever arise," his father had told him with no further explanation. Juan sat quietly amongst the jars of preserves and sacks of dried beans and held his breath. He sat very still and prayed as they trampled on the hard desert floor above his head and beat through the desert bushes, searching for him and calling his name.

"Juan, we just want to talk to you. Come on out, we won't hurt you. "

Even at eight, Juan knew what his fate would be if they found him. After what seemed like hours, a familiar voice yelled, "We know you can hear us Juan. If you want to live, keep your mouth shut."

Juan stayed very still and listened as the footsteps retreated, and soon he was alone in the silent darkness of the underground cave. The smell of his mother's corn tortillas seemed to be in the air, and he wondered if God had answered his prayers and all was well. But wary of his senses, he stayed hidden in the bunker the rest of the day and all that night, and all the next day. He stayed until nightfall, then quietly slipped out into the darkness and returned home. Peering through the brush, he saw that the bodies of his father and mother were gone. All evidence of the crime had been wiped clean; all except for the images that were etched forever into his memory.

When the police arrived he tried explaining to them what had happened, but they would not listen. Without evidence of any wrong doing, the authorities filed a report of abandonment, and on that very day they made him a ward of the state and shipped him off to Saint Mathew's Orphanage, where for the next ten years the nuns force-fed him the catechism. During his detention, hatred grew exponentially inside him like an alien cancer. Someday he vowed; he would get even with them all.

On the morning of Juan's eighteenth birthday, Father Benito called him to his office.

"It's time for you to go out into the world and make a living on your own," he'd said stoically and without preamble. "You can't stay here any longer," he repeated harshly. He stood like a statue in front of the troubled teenager, looking as anxious to be rid of Juan as Juan was anxious to be rid of him. "It's policy." And without further ado, the old priest walked him to the front gate and handed him a tattered cardboard suitcase with one clean change of used clothing. He also gave him a wrinkled, used envelope containing just enough money for him to get somewhere and find a job doing something. "I'm sorry we can't give you more," he said with dubious detachment, "but as you already know, your parent's estate was sold off to cover your room and board here at Saint Mathews. There is nothing left." Nothing had been said about the days, weeks, months, and years that Juan had worked scrubbing floors, painting and repairing stucco walls, or cooking in the kitchen, and as soon as he walked through the arches of Saint Mathews, the old priest quickly closed the gate to the orphanage and disappeared.

For the next three years, Juan drifted around the country looking for a place he could call home. It was somewhere in South Dakota that he'd changed his name to Montana, hoping that a name change would help him to fit better into a part of the country where dark skinned people were looked upon with suspicion. He stayed just long enough to beg, borrow, and steal enough money to catch a ride back south to a warmer climate and friendlier people—to a place where dark skin was the norm. He drifted from border town to border town, picking up odd jobs along the way, then somewhere on a long stretch of highway in a run-down bar, next to a run-down truck stop in southern Texas, he met Bill Lovell, who was driving to New Orleans for Mardi Gras.

"Hey, that's where I'm headed," lied Montana. "Mind if I tag along; I've got gas money?"

"What the hell. Why not? I could use some company." And after a few more beers the two became like brothers who hadn't seen each other in years.

After Mardi Gas, plus a few more weeks of hangin' together, the thrills wore thin, and one rainy morning in March after a handshake and a promise to keep in touch, Bill hoped into his truck and headed north to Washington State to see his sister, Brenda, and his nephew, Matt. Montana put out his thumb and headed back to Nogales, where he began smuggling pot across the Mexican border.

One day while sitting in a bar on the Mexico side of Nogales, two men approached Montana and asked for a ride across the border. Although they were dark skinned, their features were strikingly similar to those of his late father's, and Montana knew immediately that they were not Mexican. He asked to see their passports, which they quickly produced, and when he opened them to the identification page, he found ten, new, one-hundred dollar bills in each. Paying for a ride across the border was not unheard of and was certainly not against the law, but a grand a head was ten times the going rate, which got Montana to thinking that something fishy was going on.

The passports identified the two men as native Mexican and looked official, but Montana knew they were forgeries. But, he did not care. If he encountered a problem crossing over into the United States, he would simply tell the guards he was just doing the hitchhikers a favor. For this reason, he did not ask them their real names nor did he offer his.

Time moved slowly in the thick heat, but finally the car in front of them was waved through the gate and they were signaled to pull up to the guard gate, and after a show of papers, they too were waved through the gate.

Montana drove with caution and soon settled into a comfortable pace with all the tourists that were coming back from south of the border with meds and souvenirs. The feds in and around Tucson didn't take kindly to drug traffickers from south of the border.

"I'm heading to Tucson," said Montana, breaking a long silence, and then I'm heading west to Oregon. Where would you like to be dropped?"

"If you don't mind, Tucson, perhaps."

Hot desert air raged in through the open windows of the van, swirled around and then found a way out to make room for the next gust. It felt good to Montana, who always preferred the heat over the cold and never used the air conditioning.

Montana kept pace with the traffic rolling up Highway 19 towards Tucson, and no one spoke for a long time, although the passenger sitting next to him, turned in his seat to face his comrades in the back seat more than once. It seemed to Montana that they were having a silent conversation and after some time.

"How would you like to form an alliance with me," asked the man in the passenger seat. "You will make a lot of money."

Matt thought it an odd conversation opener, but decided to go along to see what was up. "Money's the name of the game," answered Montana, coolly. The passenger continued as if they were old friends talking about a recent sports event.

"If you bring four riders across the border at a time for me, you can make four thousand dollars a trip. There will be many trips and a lot of money."

Montana had a good life shuffling pot across the border; he'd paid his dues and the men who assured his safe passage, and if he didn't do anything stupid, his chances of getting caught were slim. He silently weighed the pros and cons of transporting drugs as opposed to illegal aliens. If he got caught with a load of marijuana by someone who could not or had been bought, he faced a long time in the slammer; however, if he got caught bringing illegal immigrants across the border, he was just an innocent tourist with a pocket full of franklins. It would be easy money and safer than what he was doing. He would do it, but before he committed aloud, he wanted to make it clear to his dark skinned brothers that he was his own boss and that no one was going to order him to do something he didn't want to do. Those long-suffering days of taking orders were as far behind him as the slamming of the gate at Saint Mathews.

"What's your name," asked Montana.

"Mohamed Moalim," the passenger answered without hesitation. "Please call me Moalim. And this," he pointed to one of the men in the back seat "is Sahib. We are from the Middle East," he said confirming what Montana already knew. He did not introduce him to the other man.

He looked into the rear view mirror at the men in the back seat and saw that Sahib had let his jacket fall open to display a large caliber hand gun slung from a shoulder holster under his arm. The man was not smiling and his stare was cold as black ice. Montana wondered why the intimidation card was being played; these boys wouldn't do anything stupid on Interstate 19 with a hundred cars around, would they? He eyed the side panel of his van where he kept his own revolver and wondered how fast he could get to it if it became necessary. The mood inside the hot van had just become a bit more serious.

"What's your name?" asked Moalim.

"Montana."

"I mean your birth name. You have the features of a *brother*," he added, lighting a cigarette, which he handed to Montana. "Are you from the Middle East, too?"

No one had ever asked him that before, and it caught him off guard, but after a long exhale of smoke, he answered.

"I'm not from the Middle East, but my father was from Iran and my mother was from Mexico; I was born in Nogales," he said all in one breath, not knowing for sure why he was spilling his guts.

"Where are your parents now," asked Moalim.

"They're dead." It was the only answer he'd ever given and all he'd ever told anyone. This time, however, he felt compelled to continue. Maybe because of the heritage they shared, maybe it was the dry heat of the desert, he didn't know, but the story of his life poured from his mouth like water over Niagara.

"They were murdered on my eighth birthday," he started, and for the next thirty miles, Montana relived the story of the slaughter of his parents and how he'd escaped by hiding in the underground shelter that his father had built. It was the first time he'd ever told anyone since he'd told the police, and when he finished, silence hung thick in the car like muddy swamp water.

"I'm very sorry for your loss, my friend. It must be very hard," said Moalim after some time had passed. "If there is anything we can do to help ease the pain," said Moalim, "please do not hesitate to ask." Montana was silent, but he was thinking how just a few hours ago he was smuggling pot across the border and how in that same amount of time, events had escalated to smuggling illegal immigrants, who may have just implied they were willing to help him get even for the injustice that had been done to him. His head was actually spinning and he wondered if he were reading more into Moalim's last statement than was really there.

"Four thousand dollars a trip is a whole lot of money," said Montana, changing the subject. "How many...."

"No questions," interrupted Moalim. It will be better the less you know. It will be easy. I will contact you when there are passengers and you will bring them across the border. We have been watching you for some time, my friend, and after we were satisfied that you could cross the border without incident, we approached you." Silence ensued once again, and finally Moalim added, "And there will be many trips, my friend. You will become a very rich man. You will be able to give up this childish pastime of smuggling drugs," he said, tapping the side panel of the van.

"So, you've been spying on me?"

"Observing you, my friend. "It appears that you have contacts and so bringing our friends across the border should be as simple as it was today."

Montana flipped on his blinker and pulled over to the side of the road. In the mirror, he noticed that the bodyguard had moved his hand to the butt of his pistol.

"No need for that," he said to the reflection in the mirror as he slowed to a stop. "I'm in," he said, extending his hand to Moalim. "Tell me what you need me to do," he said, looking Moalim straight in the eye but not letting go of his hand. He deliberately looked over his shoulder at the man in the back seat, and when the body guard moved his hand away from the butt of his gun, Montana let loose of Moalim's hand.

Moalim and Sahib disembarked in Tucson but not before getting Montana's contact information.

"We'll be in touch real soon, amigo," said Moalim, grinning.

*****

It had been nearly ten years since that day, way back then, when an enterprise had been formed, and before Montana's first job, the partnership had been consummated in blood. With the help of Moalim and a half-dozen cold-blooded assassins, Montana's promise of revenge for the killing of his parents had become a reality when nine, sweaty and angry redneck cowboys and their families, and one immigration officer and his family, all died horrific and painful deaths. In all, there were forty-eight related and unsolved killings in one night. A long time ago, thought Montana.

How many killers he'd brought into the states since then, he'd lost count of years ago. Where they went or what they were up to, he was never privy to. But this trip was different, and he had a bad feeling in his gut that things were about to change.

*****

Matt and Eric hurried through the milling mass of shoppers in the mall. They were on a mission to find a pair of boots for Eric's upcoming romp in the woods of western Washington. Eric, a computer geek, had picked up a side job installing surveillance cameras on Brent Chandler's property, and his high priced leather penny-loafers were not going to cut it in the soggy rainforest that hid Brent's cabin from view outside Monroe, Washington.

Brent Chandler, a native Washingtonian, has been Matt's hero since childhood, and when the 5'-9", 160 pound mountain man spoke to you, he looked into your eyes with a probing gaze that searched your soul for anything that did not show on the surface. His brown curly hair was neither long nor short and matched the color of his bushy, handle-bar mustache. Brent Chandler is a handsome, easy-going guy with a smile that is as catching as his laugh. He believes a state of anarchy is inevitable, and that life in the United States will, one day in the not so distant future, become a matter of survival. Brent Chandler is also a gun-for-hire.

"Folks with land, well-water, a truck load of guns and ammunition, and a gang of warriors to defend it will survive, and those without will perish," he'd preached to Matt on more than one occasion. Brent Chandler was the ultimate warrior and survivalist, and there was little doubt in the minds of anyone that knew him, that *if and when* anarchy became the order of the day, Brent Chandler would live to see *the* new beginning.

Eric Ericson contrasted with Brent Chandler like ice to fire. Eric was shorter then Brent, thin, and un-muscled. His short blonde Ivy League haircut was never mussed, and his teeth were perfectly straight and as white as a swan's feather. He wore designer cloths and drank cocktails. To say he was naïve as to what was going on in the world outside his up-scale condo, which hung on the side of the cliffs overlooking Lake Washington, would be an understatement.

He graduated from the University of Washington with a post-graduate degree in computer science and would be a good candidate for "Phone a Friend" on *Who Wants to Be a Millionaire*. He works for a software company that develops games and is not at all into the whole survival thing like Matt and his friends. He believes that if all the guns were collected by the government, gun related crime would decrease as well. He loathes violence and is the quintessential upper middle class citizen, who cannot grasp the concept that if the government outlaws guns, outlaws will still have guns.

It was the combination of being a computer geek, and being friends with Matt, along with a good recommendation from Uncle Bill, who had had Eric install surveillance equipment in his garage, that got Eric the job at Brent's. "Keep it in the family," Uncle Bill and Brent had agreed, "even if he is a geek."

"I have never been in the Boy Scouts or even the Cub Scouts," whispered Eric, who was following a half step behind Matt, dodging here and there trying to keep up without bumping into other shoppers. "I've never even been camping," he confided softly. Despite Eric's brilliance and rank in society, he had a low self-esteem. Maybe it was because of his small physical stature or maybe it was because his head was just a tiny bit too big for his body, or perhaps it was his lack of worldly knowledge, or that one eye was just a little bit crossed, Matt didn't know. "Get over it," was Matt's response to anyone, including Eric, who whined about their lot in life.

"You'll do fine," said Matt, with no further words of encouragement. And after analyzing and trying on numerous steel toed boots, water proof boots, canvas boots, and rubber boots, Eric finally decided on a pair of ankle high, water-proof, canvas boots, and none too soon for Matt, who had become as antsy as a five year-old waiting in line to use the toilet.

Eric paid with an American Express credit card, and the two friends were soon back in the main corridor of the mall where a myriad of scents coming from the Food Court, Macy's, Penny's and the rest of the tiny roll-up shops, that lined the center isle of the mall, accosted Matt's olfactory senses, bringing with it a tide of nausea. He needed air. Even city air was better than the stench inside the mall. As they approached the sliding glass doors that enveloped the gargantuan concrete and glass structure, Matt unexpectedly and abruptly stopped short, turned slightly and stiff-armed Eric who was a few steps behind, bringing him to teetering halt.

"What the hell is wrong with that metal-head, dip-shit?" Matt said, pointing with vigor. "He just tossed his fucking wrapper on the ground. Probably shits in his living room too," he added more loudly. "Hey! Pick that up and put it in that garbage can," Matt yelled. "The trash can is a whole three fucking feet to your left," he said, pointing and yelling loud enough to draw the attention of passing mall-shoppers, some of whom stopped to see what all the commotion was about, while others hurried on their way, not wanting to get involved.

At first, the stunned metal-head looked as if he were going to ignore Matt or flip him off and keep on walking, but instead, he stood perfectly still like the hands of an electric clock when the plug has been pulled, and stared into Matt's steely eyes. The instantaneous transformation from metal-head tough guy punk to weak wimp verged on the uncanny, and resulted in a quick retrieval of the wrapper and an even quicker disposal of it.

"Asshole," Matt said, glaring at the punk who was holding up his pants by the waist band to keep them from falling to the floor. The two comrades watched for a moment as the litterbug waddled, bow-legged, off into the heart and stench of the mall. "I hate those fuckers," said Matt, as the punk disappeared into the crowd. Eric let out a long deep sigh of relief. His buddy had become a loose cannon, and hazardous to be around.

*****

Abby Lassiter's long blond hair danced in a sudden gust of warm air, as she closed her door and waited on the balcony for Matt. They have been friends with benefits since she moved to Seattle four years ago from Cave Junction, Oregon, where her parents took early retirement on 250 acres of wooded land bordering the Illinois River.

"Good mornin', darlin'", he said, looking over his shoulder while locking his door.

"Good morning Matt. It's a beautiful day," she said.

They walked in silence, enjoying the sunshine and warm weather. Their destination was the library to return a video. Usually, one or the other would drop it off depending on who was going in that direction. Today, however, she has an agenda. She wants to talk to Matt about his new volatile personality. She plans to make it clear that if he wants her in his life, that he is going to have to go back to being the good ol' boy he used to be. His new aggressive and tenacious affinity with righting all wrongs is more than she can deal with, and she plans to tell him just that, again.

She has rehearsed what she is going to say and was just about ready when they reached the red brick library. The concrete walk narrowed in that particular spot, forcing Abby to step in front of Matt where she continued walking towards the drop-box. She would wait until they could face each other—just a few more minutes, she thought, taking a deep breath.

Sitting on the brick planter in front of the drop-box, puffing the last of their filter tipped cigarettes, was a skinny flat-chested, pimply faced girl and a long haired shaggy looking boy.

"Excuse me miss," said the girl, tilting her head and squinting into the sun, "do you have any spare change?"

"No. I'm sorry," Abby answered, smiling. The shaggy boy, not much taller than Abby, dropped his cigarette butt onto the sidewalk next to Abby's foot and then stood up and ground it with attitude under his dirty and tattered tennis shoe. The pimply-faced girl just dropped her smoldering butt and let it lie. Abby cringed, knowing all too well what was about to happen.

"Hey! Pick those up and put them in the trash," Matt yelled, snarling like a caged bull as he moved up quickly, getting into the faces of the young beggars. The morning sun, still low in the blue sky, shone just right so that Abby could clearly see spittle spewing from Matt's mouth. The two ragamuffins looked at him in bewilderment. Abby, for the third time in as many weeks, stood stunned by Matt's verbal assault.

"Pick them up, or I will call the cops!" he ordered loudly, pulling his cell phone from his pocket and flipping it open. The dirty little urchins, now probably coming to the conclusion that he was crazy, indolently bent down and picked up the butts and started for the trash can a few feet away. But Matt was not finished. He quickly stepped in front of them, blocking their path.

"What the hell is wrong with you, you stupid little fuck?" he continued, bending down and getting within a few inches of the boy's face. "You want to kill yourself with tobacco, that's your business, but tossing your butts on land that my taxes pay for is my business," he lectured. "And you, ya little...tramp, are you so dumb that you don't know you could have started a fire?"

When it became obvious that neither had anything to say, he moved aside and let them pass, but watched intently from behind his dark Ray Ban sun glasses as they ambled to the city garbage container to toss their butts.

Matt had become so bitter and hostile and so full of hatred over the past few months, that Abby was afraid to go anywhere with him. He was right, of course, about tossing cigarettes onto the ground, but his manner of getting his point across was scary, at best. After dropping off the videos, they walked back to the apartment in silence.

"I have some laundry to do, Matt. I'll see you later," she said, dismissing him when they stepped up to her door.

"Figures."

"Well what do you expect, Matt. I told you I don't like that kind of crap," she scolded."

"Well, someone's got to tell them, Abby. Hell, what they did was wrong in every way. Hell, Abby, it's the middle of summer, they could've started a fire, for Christ's sake." He used to apologize for his outbursts, these days, however, he just rationalized.

"Whatever. I'll see ya later," she said."

"Whatever," he shot back.

Matt reached for the key to his door and Abby reached for hers, and as if choreographed, they opened their respective doors at the same time and entered and closed them at the same time, as well.

Once inside, Abby leaned against her closed door and exhaled deeply, wondering, *again*, if Uncle Bill knew about Matt's new Jekyll and Hyde personality. She made a mental note to tell him the next time she saw him, probably on the 4th of July.

It was the middle of June, and the big shindig was only a few weeks away. It was by invitation only; Uncle Bill's invitation. If you were not personally invited, you had better not show up.

Uncle Bill's 4th of July party was in no way your run of the mill, upper-middle-class American barbeque, where men wore Bermuda shorts, polo shirts, and sandals, and women donned new perms, white slacks, flower-print blouses, and flats. In fact, it was forbidden to refer to "*The Party*" as a barbeque at all; it was a *4th of July Party* for Uncle Bill's outlaw friends who he'd met and had kept in touch with over the years; bikers, cowboys, and warriors, all of whom drank beer and whisky and ate steak and ribs.

"No salad boys allowed," Bill joked that first year when one of the gals mentioned salad. "Salads are good for feeding cows so they can grow up big and strong to produce good steaks."

Abby was looking forward to the party, but she wasn't looking forward to going with Matt. She was at the end of the line with his cynical talk and contemptuous attitude, and one way or another, change was on the horizon.

*****

Moalim seldom accompanied Montana when he picked up passengers. This time, however, he rode shotgun. Montana was thinking that there was

11

something very different about this trip. Something was certainly different about the three passengers cramped into the back seat. They all seemed to be in deep thought—heavy thought. They seemed more calloused, maybe, or more serious, more aware, more alert, more dangerous, and the stink of perspiration was nauseating. Whatever was coming down, Montana felt uncomfortable from the moment they had climbed into the van.

They'd been working together for close to ten years, now, and it was Moalim who gave Montana his limited instructions: which border crossing to be at and when, how many passengers there would be. Montana had long ago given into the fact that he took orders from Moalim and that he was no longer in charge of his own destiny. He was in as deep as anyone could be, which disturbed him because he had never told why he was doing what he was doing. He had an idea, but it had never been confirmed. The agonizing silence inside the van was becoming claustrophobic.

"There will be a motel on the right in about a mile," said Moalim. "Pull into the parking lot and stop, but do not turn off the engine. And leave the headlights on."

Montana pulled onto the gravel parking lot and stopped next to one of the big rigs that was parked there for the night. It was a shabby motel on the outskirts of Tucson and they were only there long enough to drop off one of the passengers. Within moments, they were back on the highway.

The miles and hours passed slowly and with minimal conversation. Even the radio had been forbidden. At last the city lights of Grant's Pass, Oregon, a small town near Cave Junction, came into view on the night horizon.

"There will soon be a Motel called the Shady Rest on your right," said Moalim, "pull into the parking lot, stop, but do not turn off the lights. Keep the motor running."

As soon as Montana came to a stop, another of his passengers prepared to disembark. His orders, Montana had overheard, were to wait until Moalim contacted him before making his way to the Lassiter ranch in Cave Junction. He was guaranteed that it would not be too long of a wait, *Insha'Allah*. His exact assignment was not discussed and Montana's angst red-lined.

Whatever was going on was not good, and Bill Lovell, who had introduced Montana to the Lassiters way back when the two of them had gotten together for a reunion just before one of Bill's parties, was not going to like whatever it was. Not that he cared much, but he could see trouble coming. He suddenly realized that Moalim was speaking English instead of Arabic. Arabic had always been the vernacular of choice when Montana was around. More than once he'd walked in on a conversation that was in English but quickly changed to Arabic when his presence had become known. It was SOP, which Moalim sardonically pronounced *sap*, and it was a term Moalim used when Matt asked a question Moalim did not want to answer. "It's sap, my friend, but you will know soon enough." Montana had been hearing it for 10 years! His claustrophobia became stifling, as goose bumps made their way up the back of his neck. Something heavy was about to go down, he was sure.

After his orders, the passenger quickly exited the van with his oversized duffle bag and briskly walked towards the neon 'welcome' sign in the window of the run-down office. Moalim did not give the order to drive on until after his comrade had entered the office. "Drive through Grant's Pass and stop at the Clear View Motel. It will be on the right, as well," ordered Moalim.

The horizontal wood siding on the motel needed new paint, but the three-star joint was in better condition than the previous two. It was the type of place where secret lovers could go and not be discovered. Parking was in the rear, out of sight of passing traffic.

There were two queen size beds, only, and Montana tossed his bag on the one closest to the door and said, "dibs," to which there was no response. He then pulled his kit from the bag and headed towards the bathroom to take a much needed shower. Moalim and the last passenger waited there turn and when Montana came back into the room, he was told to order pizza, which he did. While he waited in silence, paging through a tattered and stained TV guide, the other two took turns in the shower. Only after the pizza arrived, and the three bolts on the door had been secured, did any of them relax their guard.

"Moalim," Montana said, carefully, as he pulled a cheesy slice of soggy pepperoni pizza from the greasy cardboard box, "what's going on? Why is your man going to the Lassiter ranch?" Moalim set his pizza down on the lid of the box.

"About a week from now," began Moalim, with no hesitation and no preface, "there's going to be…well, let's just say for now, an *interruption in the infrastructure* here in these great United States, of yours, but before that happens, we need you to do us a favor." Montana looked on, straight faced and waited for Moalim to continue. "We need you to get a room for Ali in Seattle." He nodded towards the last of the riders who was sitting at the round table by the sliding glass doors, that led to the balcony. "His face is well known by Interpol, and it's too close to payoff time to take the chance of him being recognized." Moalim locked eyes with Montana and waited for his reaction, and Montana knew, as if the words had been spoken aloud, that if he did not go along, he was probably not going to leave this room alive.

Montana, for some reason, suddenly felt very threatened. Hadn't he paid his dues a hundred times over? Wasn't he part of the Middle Eastern brotherhood? Sometimes, it seemed, that Moalim separated him from them, as if he were an outsider; nothing more than a convenience, a means to an end.

"Sure, Moalim, whatever you need?" he said, after swallowing a prolonged chew of pizza. "Hell, I didn't guess y'all were coming to the US of A to start families, for Christ's sake. What's up? What do the Lassiters have to do with any of this?" he asked again, "and what exactly does 'interruption in the infrastructure' mean?"

"I think you know, Montana. Even though I have not told you exactly, I think you probably know why you have been bringing all our brothers across the border. What you don't know, my friend, is how extreme the *interruption* is going to be. So, let me tell you. It's going to shut your country down."

Montana felt like he'd forgotten to dry off after his shower. He was soaking wet, and it showed. Talking the talk was one thing, but walking the walk was another; especially when his boss was talking about *shutting down the United States of America!*

"You appear to be a little uneasy with this," said Moalim. "Hell, Montana, no hard feelings if you want out," continued Moalim, now standing and pacing, not giving Montana a chance to answer. "No problem," he continued, gesturing with his usual palms up motion. "If you want out, you can go your way and we'll go ours."

Montana had no intention of bailing, but he knew better than to believe that he would leave this room alive if he decided to run. He knew too much. He knew he was a dead man if he chose to bail. It would be an act of stupidity to leave behind a loose end, and Moalim was not a stupid man.

"Damn Moalim, we've been partners for a long time. You know I'm in for the long haul. And you *know* the reason why. Of course I'm in—always have been. I'm as much a part of this as you or him," he said, pointing to the man sitting at the table. "You just caught me by surprise, that's all. Damn, bro, it's a lot to process, but you know I'm in. Why even ask?"

"No problem with the Lassiters?" Moalim asked, holding a steady eye on Montana and not answering his question.

"I hardly know them. Hell, I'd be more concerned about Bill Lovell, if I were you."

"I've thought about that, and I think it's time I met this old friend of yours, *Bill Lovell*," he said smirking. "What say we drop in on his infamous 4th of July party you've told me so much about? After we drop Ali off in Seattle, that is."

"Sounds good to me," answered Montana, feeling more ill-at-ease than ever.

"Could get ugly," said Moalim. "Any problems with that?"

"No," answered Montana, smoothing back his long hair with both hands.

Moalim and Ali exchanged glances as if communicating via mental telepathy, and quickly nodded in agreement, which Montana took as a nod of approval—or maybe a rite of passage of some kind.

"Okay, Brother," said Moalim, squaring his chair and shoulders up to face Montana. Locking eyes, he began explaining. "Sometime in the next few weeks, at an exact and coordinated time, thousands of strategic targets in this country will be neutralized. The intent is to disrupt the infrastructure to such a degree that America will be cast into a state of anarchy, overnight." Montana kept his eyes locked on Moalim's black steely eyes but did not respond. He'd thought it, but hearing the words was like a smack in the head with a sledge hammer. "After it's all over, a *New State* will rise up from the ashes, Insha'Allah," said Moalim, looking at Ali. Montana swallowed hard, but all he could say was, "damn."

"So then, Montana how does it all sound? Will it work? What are your thoughts, brother?" asked Moalim. Montana only heard parts of the question, but knew what he was being asked. Jihad was on the doorsteps of America and Montana had played a very big role in making it happen.

"It sounds good," was all he could utter.

"*Good*?" teased Moalim, laughing menacingly. "That's all you can say? It sounds *good*?"

"Yeah, Moalim, it sounds good. It sounds like it will work. What the fuck do you want me to say? Fuck, man, I need time to digest this, for Christ's sake. How are you going to do it, what kinds of weapons do you have, how many people are involved, where are you going to strike. Shit-hell-fire, man, it's a lot to digest," he repeated.

"We'll talk again in the morning, brother, after you, what do you say in this country, sleep on it?" he said, dismissing Montana as if the final class bell had rung.

Montana lay in bed shaking, not from the cold, but from all he'd heard. He fell asleep wondering what role a non-Muslim was to play in a New State. He wondered too, if he would wake up at all.

*****

Eric picked Matt up early Saturday morning for the drive to Brent Chandler's place to install video surveillance equipment. He hadn't seen Matt since the incident at the mall and was a bit apprehensive about the trip to Brent's, but had decided to stay positive and make the best of it. Keep it light and stick to business, he kept repeating to himself. He had never met Brent but Matt had told him that Brent was a survivalist, nothing more. He hoped that Brent and Matt together were not a combination of gasoline and fire.

There was a lot of work to do: wires to run, cameras to mount, software to install, and monitors to hook-up and test, but it was early and he had all day to get it done. It was not going to be a problem if he could get right to it and if he didn't encounter a lot of unknowns, like bears or mountain lions, or snakes, thought Eric, snickering to himself.

It would not be a big payday but the bonus was huge! If all goes well, he is guaranteed an invitation to Uncle Bill's 4th of July party. He wasn't supposed to know, but Matt had told him, and he was stoked but apprehensive, causing an anxious excitement that he seldom experienced in his day to day structured life. Finally he was going to get an invite to the party he'd been hearing about ever since Abby had introduced him to Matt four years ago.

Eric was once secretly in love with Abby and wondered how she was doing with Matt's recent personality change. He hadn't talked to her for a few weeks. Work, it seemed, always got in the way of hanging with friends, and he was a bit giddy at the prospect of seeing her on the 4th.

Erick cruised south in his new, pearl white, Cadillac Escalade, listening to the cranked up tunes of John Fogerty on the surround sound which was being piped in from a satellite someplace 200 miles over their heads. The traffic was light, the sky was blue, and the greens and reds of the flora were intense through his Maui Jim's. It was another exceptionally fine spring day in the Great Northwest, and Eric was in a cheery mood.

"Fucking traffic is getting worse every fucking day," complained Matt. "Crazy fucking feds are always adding another fucking lane. They use our tax dollar to put a bandage on a mortal fucking wound. I hate those fucking morons. More lanes, more fucking traffic. It's never going to get better. Only worse. I need a fucking beer. Want one?"

Eric did not turn down the stereo to listen to his friend. He'd heard enough of Matt's incessant bitching over the past few months in regards to everything from pedophiles to the corrupt judicial system. Eric was not a prude, but Matt's language lately consisted of "fuck" used as an adjective, a noun, a verb, a pronoun, an adverb, and every other part of speech possible.

"Don't you think it's a little early to be drinking beer?" he finally said.

"Do you want one or not?"

"For the millionth time, I don't drink and drive," he yelled over the blare of the radio. Matt had a small six-pack travel cooler in his hand when Eric had picked him up earlier. Eric, checking his rear view mirror, pounded himself mentally for not saying something then.

At the same time that Matt popped the tab on his beer can, a small, silver Honda Civic, the kind with loud glass-pack pipes that are so popular with street racers, sped up on his right and paused just long enough for Matt to look over and see the greased back, black hair of the young dark skinned driver.

Eric had seen the car coming down the onramp, but having a considerable lead, he'd figured the driver would pull in behind him. Instead, the tiny noise maker suddenly floored it and sped past Eric cutting him off just before the onramp lane ended at a concrete wall, forcing Eric to check his mirrors at lightning speed before hitting his breaks to avoid a collision.

"That fucking bastard," yelled Matt, putting his spilt beer on the floor boards between his feet and wiping his hands on his jeans. "Pull up next to the faggot," he yelled at Eric, as he pulled his .45 from the holster on his belt.

"What are you doing?" yelled Eric, scowling like a gargoyle. "You can't shoot the guy. Put that away!" Matt turned just enough to give his buddy a wicked smile.

"I'm not going to shoot the bastard, Eric. I'm just going to scare the fucking crap out of him; pull up next to him," he urged again. "Don't worry;

I'm not going to shoot the fucker—just scare him back across the *Rio Grande* where he belongs," he said, smirking.

"I'm not going to pull up next to him, for Christ's sake," said Eric, losing his patience. "Jesus, Matt, you don't know he's Mexican," he argued for lack of something better to say at the moment. "Put the fucking gun away," he said more loudly, reaching for the knob on the radio to turn it down.

Eric didn't normally swear, or even raise his voice, but he didn't know what Matt was going to do these days, and this whole scene was moving in a direction he did not want to go. He wondered, as he had many times in the recent past, how he'd ever gotten mixed up with Matt in the first place; after all, they really didn't have much in common. He watched as Matt holstered his gun, silently blaming Abby for introducing them.

"Of course he's Mexican, Eric. They all drive the same stupid kiddy-car. I hate those ratty-ass noise-makers."

Eric alternated between watching the road, Matt, and the Honda Civic which was now four or five cars in front of them. Matt retrieved his beer from the floor boards and finished it off in a few big gulps, crushed the can with one hand and tossed it into his travel container, and retrieved another. "Sure you don't want one?" he asked, shoving it in the direction of Eric, still keeping an eye on the little Honda Civic.

The driver of the Civic had slowed to below the speed limit, and Eric, wanting to get as away from him as possible, decided to move to the transit lane, and so he moved to the right, one lane. He wanted to move over one more lane but a transport truck hauling a loader dozer was now alongside of him, and in front of him was an SUV and another SUV was hot on his tail. He was boxed in, and he was being forced forward and soon he would be right next to the Honda.

He glanced quickly into his rear view mirror and freaked when he saw the woman with the black scarf over her head tailgating him in the oversized black SUV. He could see enough of her to know that she was wearing an abaya, the traditional dress of Arab women from Saudi Arabia, and silently prayed that Matt would not notice.

Matt had recently been on an, "all Muslims are al-Qaeda terrorists and should be gathered up and shipped out," rage. "They're a cancer to our country, our history, our heritage, and our religion," he'd said, emphasizing heavily, *country, history, heritage,* and especially *religion.* "Destroy a country's religion and destroy the country. It's a fact." At the time he'd presented this argument, he'd backed it up by saying it was something he'd read in the Sierra Times; however, that was then, these days he no longer bothered to back up his arguments with references, he just vented, and often times, it seemed to Eric, that Matt confabulated the issues to make his point.

Eric wanted to move but it was impossible and he soon found himself next to the Civic. Matt used the international middle finger sign language to address the driver of the Honda. In response, the driver, who was slouched low in his seat, casually responded with the same, but with both hands, laughing while steering with his knees.

Quick as the glint of a diamond in the sunlight, Matt retrieved his gun from his holster and pointed it out the window at the dark skinned driver of the Honda. A look of terror quickly replaced the bullshit sneer on the driver's face when he saw the gun, and he stepped on his breaks causing cars behind him to do the same.

"Pull over in front of him and take the next exit," ordered Matt, leaning forward to watch events unfold in his side view mirror. "We'll take the back roads the rest of the way. Fucking asshole. I hate those arrogant bastards."

"Don't ever do that again while you are in my car, Matt, or so help me you will be walking! Friend or not! What the fuck are you thinking, anyway? You can't pull a gun on someone just because they cut you off. Jesus! You scared the shit out of me."

"Scared the shit out that jerk-off bastard too," said Matt, tucking his gun in his waistband instead of replacing it in the holster. He looked over at his friend and smiled. "Time for a beer yet?" Eric shook his head in a way that implied, "unbelievable" as he quickly drove onto the exit ramp in search of the back roads to Brent's.

The installation of the surveillance equipment went well and the job was finished early and they were on their way home before dark. He was going to be glad to be rid of Matt, and he was definitely going to talk to Abby about her out-of-control boyfriend.

*****

The 4th of July snuck up like a 50th birthday. Tomorrow was the party, and Matt and Abby were gathering up last minute supplies. In spite of all that had happened recently, they were still going to the party together. Abby was looking forward to seeing all the gang—especially Brent Chandler, and she was excited for her friend Eric, who was getting initiated. She was not, however, looking forward to going anywhere in public with Matt Lovell! He was too off balance. His verbal attacks on people were increasing and becoming more venomous, and it was just a matter of time, before he got physical.

"Got to have greenbacks in my pocket," he said, springing into the cab of his truck, "so the first stop will be the handy-dandy bank-a-roni," playfully giving Abby's knee a squeeze, making her jump.

He seemed like his old self, and Abby hoped it would last the day. "After the bank, we'll go rob Fred Meyers," he said jokingly.

They went into the bank together and stood in line waiting for the next available teller. When she motioned Matt to come forward, he stepped up and presented her with a check to be cashed. Matt kept his money at home because he didn't trust banks. He only kept a trivial amount in Bank of America so that he could cash checks without a hassle.

A tall woman with long brown hair and moderate makeup took the check and began processing it. Then, out of nowhere, a man stepped up beside Matt and leaned over into Matt's space to get the teller's attention to ask a question. He spoke a foreign language that sounded like Russian to Abby, and she shivered when the teller quit processing Matt's check to answer the man's question.

"What the fuck is this?" Matt said, moving back a step and pointing his finger, first at the man and then at the teller and then back at the man. "Can't you see there's a fucking line here? We wait our turn in this country. Or are the rules different for foreigners," he blurted, looking directly at the stunned teller and talking loud enough to attract the attention of the floor manager as well as everyone else in the bank. The floor manager moved quickly to stand behind the teller.

"Is there a problem here?"

"Damn straight there's a problem here," answered Matt, not waiting for the teller to explain. "This guy, here, thinks it's okay to crowd to the front of the line because he's a foreigner, I guess," said Matt, pointing to the cowering man who probably wished he were anywhere but where he was. And before the floor manager could respond, Matt added: "And the teller here," pointing now at the tall girl, who had turned as red as the stripes on the American flag pin she wore on her lapel, "thinks it's okay to quit working on my transaction and take care of whatever the fuck his business is," pointing to the man next to him again.

"I am sorry, sir," the manager said to Matt and then turned to the two violators and addressed them in the same foreign language they had spoken to each other. The man nodded and smiled and moved away and the teller began processing Matt's check, again.

"I hope this is satisfactory, sir," the manager said in broken English.

"Yeah, it's fine," Matt said with a look of exasperation smeared on his face. "But you should let *these people* know they need to follow the rules and laws of our country if they want to live here." It was quickly turning into a lecture, and Abby wished she were invisible. Before the manager could reply, a bank guard, with one hand on his weapon, had moved up next to Matt.

"Is everything okay here?" looking first at the manager and then at Matt, where he rested his gaze, waiting for a response.

"Yeah; Fine," said Matt, taking his money from the teller and turning around, smiling a forced smile at the guard who was a Mona Lisa of seriousness. Abby could tell by the look on Matt's face that he wanted to take the guard's gun away from him and beat him with it, which she knew he could probably do and relieved that he didn't.

She had tried talking to Matt about his temper and his attitude, but he always had the same response. "Someone's got to stick up for what's right and what's wrong. Shit! Let the assholes walk on you once and they think it's acceptable. I hate their fucking arrogance! They need to learn that if they are going to live in this country that they have to follow the same rules that we do. If they don't want to assimilate, fuck 'em; send 'em back to wherever the fuck it is they came from."

They left the bank accompanied by the guard and walked in silence to the truck; Matt, proud and arrogant, Abby mortified and distraught.

"Okay, then," said Matt, climbing into the cab of the truck, "it's off to Freddy's." Abby wondered how he could switch from being a nice guy to being monster and back from one minute to the next. It was too much.

"I want to go home, Matt. I can't take any more of this. You act like you're about to kill someone. It's scary, Matt."

"Well, Abby, I'm not going to kill anyone," he said quietly, almost whispering, "but like I said, someone's got to stand up for what's right and what's wrong." He started the engine not expecting a reply. "It's not just me, you know," he said as he put the truck into gear and checked the mirrors before pulling out into the traffic. "There's a whole lot of people in this country who are fed up with the belligerence of foreigners. They are so disrespectful, Abby. I am not wrong about this. Someone has got to take a stand."

"Maybe you're right, Matt. In fact, let's just say you are right, but the way you make your point is scary." She was shaking and on the verge of tears. "Please – just - take – me - home." Matt shook his head and turned the truck back towards the apartment.

"It's meant to be scary. What do you think I should say? 'Excuse me, but the line forms at the rear.'"

"I don't know—I don't know. I just want to go home, she whined. "We can pick up whatever else we need in the morning, on the way. Or you can go shopping by yourself. You can go the party by yourself, for that matter. I can drive my own car."

"Okay. I'm sorry I upset you. I'll take you home and we can go shopping in the morning," he said, ignoring what she'd said about driving herself. "See you tomorrow," he said, as she climbed out of the truck.

"Yeah," she said, closing the door softly and walking briskly away, thinking it was time, *past time*, she spoke to Uncle Bill.

CHAPTER 2

Matt Lovell had been brought up differently than his school mates and peers. Until he was ten, he'd been raised by his mother, Brenda. Must be, he figured when he'd gotten older, that he'd been taught to call her Brenda from the day he was born because he had no recollection of ever calling her mom or mother or even mommy. He didn't know his father, and Brenda hadn't made one up for him. She didn't tell him that his father had been killed in the war or had run down by a drunk driver.

"I don't know who your father is, kid. Life's a bitch and then you die. Get used to it," was the explanation he'd received the one and only time he'd asked.

Brenda slunk from one dingy apartment to another, but never changed zip codes—never moved out of the slum part of town. Although she didn't have a job, she was seldom at home; sometimes gone two or three days at a time. As a result, Matt, from a very young age, pretty much depended on his own ingenuity to get by from day to day. He learned to fend for himself—street smart before his time—sort of like a modern day David Copperfield. He lived on bologna sandwiches, milk and apples, of which, there seemed to be an endless supply. He had few memories of his childhood, and the ones he could remember played in his head like scenes from a cheap 'B' movie.

He remembered a tiny second story apartment over a rowdy cowboy bar. He remembered the smell of stale beer that emanated from the stained orange shag carpet that covered the small living area, and the constant drip, drip, drip of water in the sinks and tub, and he remembered the dark rust stains that were the color of poop.

It had been an unusually hot and sultry night in September. He remembered the month because his birthday was in September. Not that his birthday was much to look forward to, other than the fact that he was one year closer to being able to leave home. He didn't expect a birthday present or a card from Brenda. He didn't even expect a verbal, "happy birthday," although he'd secretly hoped.

He had been sitting at the table in one of the two painted and chipped wooden chairs that had come with the apartment, and staring through the open window 8 feet away, and longing for silence and freedom. Outside, hanging from the side of the building, two feet away, flashed the bright red neon letters *…D's BAR A….* The whole sign read, *FRED'S BAR AND GRILL*, but the letters were too big to see the whole sign from inside the apartment. The breeze coming in through the open window was warm and smelled of greasy deep fried food which came from the exhaust fan on the side of the building, probably from the kitchen in the tavern below, he figured.

The floor was vibrating from the honky-tonk band below that was belting out an old Hank Williams cowboy ballad. Something about a cheating heart. Brenda was agitated and was prancing back and forth in front of the open window and the flashing neon sign. She had been dressed only in a skimpy, thin black bra and red panties. She was very drunk and was swinging her arms and hands in an exaggerated cartoonish fashion. Ashes from her cigarette onto the dirty carpet, and beer spilled from the can she waved. Every other word was a curse word—most he'd heard hundreds of times before, others he'd never heard at all. She was raving on and on about the feds. He wished she would pass out.

"The fucking feds don't pay me enough to pay the fucking rent and buy groceries, let alone raise a fucking kid," she shrieked.

For Matt, there was no escape. There was no TV or radio in the tiny two room apartment, and he was too young to stomp out the door, so he sat as stiff as a board, trying to block it out by thinking about life after he was old enough to run.

"Why don't you get a fucking paper route and help out around here?" she screamed, standing right in front of him, staring down at his tiny upturned face. He'd heard it all before and wished he *was* old enough to get a paper route and help out, but his mother was unaware of his feelings or wishes. Spittle blasted from her foul smelling mouth as she leaned down to within a few inches of her son's face staring blankly into his innocent eyes.

Even at his young age, Matt had realized how disgusting and hideous his mother looked as she staggered back and forth in the shadows of the small stinky apartment. Her bright red lipstick had smeared around her lips reminding him of a clown—a scary clown. And her mascara had streaked down her face, following the flow of tears of self-pity. In the glow of the flashing neon light from outside the window, his mother continued to rave about the feds until she finally passed out on the couch, and as he often did, Matt covered her with an old brown army blanket and then went to sleep, in his clothes, in a chair in the corner, five feet away. Matt's second real memory was of his Uncle Bill.

Matt's Uncle Bill, Brenda's brother, had been a drifter in his earlier days, and Matt didn't remember much about him until he started showing up when Matt was about seven or eight years old. His uncle would stop by his sister's house when she was gone, which was most of the time, and sometimes he'd pick Matt up from school and take him to McDonalds or Denny's. It was such a big deal to Matt to see his uncle that he looked for him every day and was disappointed when he didn't show. When he did show up, which in the beginning was only about once a month, it was like a party because he always came with a brown paper bag full of groceries and other surprises: a new football, new underwear and socks, books on camping and how to survive in the woods, a pocket knife, a compass, a new baseball cap.

"Here, put these in a hiding place," he'd say, handing Matt a bag of groceries containing sardines, crackers, candy bars, chips—and books.

He remembered spending time at his uncle's house and wishing he could just stay there and never go home. His mother would drop him off at the curb in front of his Uncle Bill's house with a paper sack containing a pair of socks, a pair of underwear, and a spare shirt—sometimes clean sometimes not, and drive off without so much as a goodbye, see you later, or I'll be back—whenever. He always stayed for at least one night and sometimes two or three.

On one particular day when she'd dropped him off, the routine changed. Instead of just dumping him out and speeding off down the road, she'd gotten out of the car and came around to the passenger side where Matt was standing, holding his paper bag. She stooped down and gave him a hug and then a kiss on the cheek. When she stood back up, he remembered seeing tears in her eyes. Not tears of self-pity that he was so used to seeing, but tears of such sadness and sorrow that they touched Matt's heart like nothing ever had done before, and he began crying, too. He stood on the sidewalk, shaggy and unkempt with the wrinkled up brown paper bag held tightly to his chest and watched as Brenda drove off in a cloud of blue smoke. It was the last time he'd ever seen her, because she never came back to get him.

After a few weeks had gone by, and then a month and then two months, and still no Brenda, word spread in the 'hood that foul play was behind her disappearance. Most people, however, including his uncle, were pretty sure she had just flat abandoned the kid. Whatever happened to Sweet Brenda, as she had been known about town, has remained a mystery.

The relationship that developed between Matt and his uncle was not that of father and son, but rather that of mentor and student, friends, best friends. Matt felt grateful to his uncle for taking him in. He felt, even at the young age nine, that he was much better off being raised by the firm hand and the guidance of his uncle than trying to figure it all out on his own. Uncle Bill believed a solid smack up-side the head was the best way to get a kid's attention. The Spock Methodology of raising children was not an option, and Attention Deficit Disorder as an excuse for not paying attention was handled with the same smack up-side the head, and it did not take many *smacks* to get the young boy on the right track. Matt liked living with his Uncle Bill and his uncle had adjusted to having a child in his space. It was good—all of it. And like the light of day fading into the darkness of night, Matt's memory of Brenda began fading with each passing day.

"Just plain Bill," his uncle had insisted from the start. "I would prefer, Matt, that you just call me Bill." But it never took; and in time, all of Bill's friends were calling him "Uncle Bill," as well. It was pretty funny how that worked out, and it's still a chuckle to hear Tiny, a three-hundred pound biker, who hails from Bellingham, WA, call him Uncle Bill.

Matt had learned to survive by living with his mother, but he'd learned to be a *survivalist* by living with his uncle. Uncle Bill's outlaw friends were survivalists to the core and in the real sense of the term. They stocked water and rations, guns and ammo, and they believed strongly in the Bill of Rights and in particular the Second Amendment to the Constitution; "*...a well-regulated militia, being necessary to the security of a free state, the right of the people to keep and bear arms shall not be infringed.*" Some of them were more prepared than others, but all of them believed in being ready. Matt had learned how to hunt, fish, start a fire with nothing but what he could find in the woods, build a shelter, and find water. His uncle had taught him how to live off the land, but it was Brent Chandler who had taught him about weapons and self-defense, one of Brent's mentors being, Michael Echanis, a student of the martial arts who'd taught self-defense to counter insurgency Nicaraguan National Guard.

Matt learned that life was not always fair, that the world outside the walls of home was hard, and, if a person was going to survive, he had better be prepared to take care of himself. He'd learned about *life* from his uncle's friends, a *wily gang of outlaws* who had taken Matt under their wings. They became uncles and aunts, and each treated him as if he were their own personal protégé, refining what he already knew, testing him, and teaching him new methods of survival and self-defense. The group of outlaws had become the family he'd never had, and he loved them all as if they were blood. As he grew into his teenage years, he started calling them by their nick-names: Tiny, Snake, Scar, Cowboy, Slim, Montana, Rose, Thunder Thighs, and more. And although *they* all had nicknames, Matt remained Matt.

He wore second-hand clothes bought from the surplus stores that lined the streets of the old part of town. "No sense in paying a lot of money for clothes you're going to outgrow in a month," his uncle had told him. Although they were second-hand, they were better than anything he'd ever had while living with Brenda. He'd developed a new sense of self-esteem. He started to gain weight and he looked and felt better than he ever had. He'd become a fitness freak and his skinny, undernourished frame began to fill out as he started lifting weights and chopping cord wood for extra money.

He went from wearing tattered tennis shoes and plaid pants that were far too large for him, to wearing T-shirts, jeans, cowboy boots, and black leather jackets. On the 4th of July, however, he wore a colorful, flowered Hawaiian shirt in remembrance of a real cool biker dude named Flathead Fred, who went down doing what he liked doing best, as the tattoo that spanned his entire chest attested to, *Live to Ride, Ride to Live*. Matt learned about mortality at an early age and learned to cherish life, and he looked forward to each new day, and he was thankful to God for his Uncle Bill. In spite of his time with Brenda, he'd turned out to be a good kid.

Because of the way he'd been brought up by his uncle, and because of those who mentored him, he was more knowledgeable about what made the world go around than his peers. He'd been the first in his fifth grade class to know the facts of life, for example, and although he didn't quite understand it all, he had taken pride in spreading the word on what little he did know. What he'd told the other kids wasn't much more than a verbal description of the differences between male and female anatomies, and the basic functions they played in producing offspring, but for a few short weeks he was the big shot in the school yard. He was riding high with attention from the girls as well as the guys until Uncle Bill started receiving phone calls from horrified parents who'd listened to graphic descriptions from their children, passed on from their new mentor on the playground. It was the summer after, between the 5th and 6th grade, that he'd met Rose.

Rose lived next door to Uncle Bill and was getting ready to start the 9th grade. She reminded Matt of the red-headed woman with dark red lipstick and red eye shadow in the poster in Uncle Bill's garage. Rose didn't hang with the outlaws back then because she was too young. Jail bait, he'd heard her being called, not knowing at the time what it meant. Eye candy, the guys had called her, which when explained to Matt, by Lip, made perfect sense. And although Matt knew the basics about the facts of life, he never really considered doing anything about it. Not back then. Not in the fifth-and-a-half grade, anyway.

It was in the last week of August when he was gearing up to start the sixth grade. The sun was still high in the sky and there was a strong, sweet scent of rose blossom in the air. She'd come outside to empty the garbage wearing the shortest turquoise mini-skirt he'd ever seen. It matched the color of her tight turquoise halter top that encompassed her breasts and hard nipples, which were covered, but visible. He watched as she reached up to open the lid of the garbage bin and had caught a glimpse of her white panties. When she'd caught him looking at her, Matt blushed and told her that she looked real pretty. She looked down at the ground in front of her and only lifted her eyelids to look back at him. At first Matt thought she was going to scold him, but then she raised her head and smiled the prettiest smile he'd ever seen. "Thanks, Matt. Would you like to come over for a cold glass of lemonade?" Her words floated through the hot summer air like the melodic call of a Siren, and he flushed and felt weak in the knees at the prospect of sharing a glass of lemonade with the gorgeous girl next door.

That summer, he experienced his first dip into the legendary *lotus flower*. Indeed, it was Rose, his uncle's next door neighbor, who had taught him that he could do something more with his penis than just pee. After that summer, he understood much better what his uncles meant when they talked about women and that sweet *"thang"* between their legs.

When he ponders that night, he can still smell the roses, and every time he actually smells a rose, he remembers, Rose, the girl next door. But that was a long time ago. The world has since turned dark and cold and the future looks bleak. And the smell of rose in the air has all but dissipated into low hanging, pungent, gray smog engulfing the city.

*****

Matt knew that he'd been making everyone around him nervous and anxious with his, "let's start shooting the bastards," talk. He tried hard to stay calm and turn a blind eye, but he'd become preoccupied with all that was wrong in the world, and the fact that he couldn't fix it like he could fix a broken engine was gnawing at him; eating away at his gut like so many maggots consuming the carcass of a dead rat.

He'd been raised not to judge people by their color, culture, race or religion, and on the one hand he believed it; but on the other hand, it seemed that those were the very features that distinguished the good guys from the bad guys and were often stable indicators of a person's expected behavior. He used to judge people by their actions, but now, more and more, he'd begun judging them on sight. "I know it's politically incorrect," he'd told Eric, twitching his index finger and his middle finger on both hands indicating a quote, "but there is logic in profiling. The old adage, 'if it looks like a duck, walks like a duck, and quacks like a duck, then it's probably a duck,' is a truism, especially in this day and age," he'd argued.

*****

Montana drove into Washington State on I-5. Moalim gave him directions to an upscale hotel in downtown Seattle that was accustomed to international travelers and the significance of privacy. Montana went in and registered for a room under a false name, using false I.D. Moalim had given him. When he returned to the van, he handed the keycard to Ali who, after quietly speaking to Moalim in Arabic, quickly departed.

"What was that all about," asked Montana as they pulled back into traffic.

"Ali said that all will go as planned, Insha'Allah." Montana knew the Islamic saying meant, God willing, and nodded his head. "We will now go to Everett to a safe house that has been set up there. There are supposed to be a lot of cowboys and, what do you call them, cowgirls?" he said with a laugh. "you must admit, my friend, those are funny names," he said, still laughing. "Tonight we will make plans to visit your friend, Uncle Bill, at his 4th of July party. We need to assess the enemy's strength and determine if they will be a threat to the Cave Junction connection."

Montana told him about the invitation rule, but Moalim shrugged it off. "You told me you have been there many times and that you have an open invitation; is it not true?"

"Well," started Montana a bit uneasy, "I used to have an open invitation, but me and Bill sort of had a falling out awhile back, and I was asked not to come around for a while. I've been back a few times, but it's always been a bit awkward. It's been a while, so it should be okay for me, but I don't know about you."

"No matter," said Moalim, "he would not be foolish enough to start trouble when lives could be lost, I'm sure. Most people are not. And besides, it won't be a surprise and we won't be alone. Our cowboy and cowgirl friends will be accompanying us."

"You don't know these, guys, Moalim. They're real bad."

"Thanks for the warning, but orders are orders, and Ali said to check it out. Do you think it will be a huge problem?"

"I don't know," said Montana, realizing for the first time that Ali was Moalim's boss.

"Well then, Montana, we'll just play it by ear," said Moalim, turning towards the window to see the sites.

"Sounds like fun," said Montana sarcastically "Giddy-up!"

"Giddy-up," laughed Moalim. "Giddy-up."

CHAPTER 3

A heat mirage floated a few feet above the black pavement in the parking lot of Iverson's Market, and lines of cars sat idling in the hot July sun, as drivers waited patiently for others to back out so they could pull in.

Matt and Abby had just finished picking up some last minute supplies for the party and were on their way back to Matt's truck, which was parked at the far, far end of the parking lot. They had just stepped off the sidewalk into the parking lanes when suddenly, like an unexpected flash of summer lightning, the driver of a shiny red BMW sped past a line of waiting cars and quickly maneuvered into a spot clearly marked for the handicap, and just as quickly jumped out of the car, with ease.

"Hey! You can't park here," hollered Matt at the lady in black. Ignoring him, she began searching for the button on her remote that would activate the security system on her car.

Fury raged inside of Matt like hot lava ascending from hell, and his words were venomous, as he spat more loudly, "This is a handicap zone, and you don't have a handicap license plate or a sticker, and you sure don't look crippled," he protested, as he pounded with the heel of his closed fist on the *Handicap Parking Only* sign directly in front of the bumper of her car.

Abby moved quickly away as he continued to berate the criminal for her flagrant disrespect for the law. "My taxes pay for this parking spot," he yelled, jabbing his middle finger towards the spot where the BMW was parked. The lady in black jerked her head up and sideways, pausing for just a moment at his sudden movement, and from behind her thin black veil, dark piercing eyes quickly sized him up before looking away and ignoring him, as if he were a child throwing a tantrum. Without a word, she started walking towards the large sliding glass doors of Iverson's Market; her black gown billowing behind her, producing the allusion that she was gliding like the wicked witch of the west.

Over the past six months, Matt had become more irritated and more exasperated with immigrants who took advantage of the broken judicial and the government that catered to them. Their contempt went beyond pompous and arrogant—it was treasonous, and what he once only thought about saying had of late become verbal reproves.

Abby slowly lowered the overloaded plastic shopping bags to the simmering asphalt. She wanted to walk away, but the combination of Matt's tirade and the stale smell of deep fried chicken from the kitchens of Iverson's Market, mixed with the thick stench of exhaust fumes and hot tar, had made her nauseous.

"Hey! You can't park here!" Matt yelled again, his face red with rage and contorted into an evil likeness of a wrinkled gargoyle. People began to stare, some applauded his efforts while others, not wanting to get involved, turned a blind eye; but the lady in black just kept walking.

He wanted to smash out the black tinted windows of her car with his fists. He wanted to rip the black, silk veil from her face and expose to the world that a pompous and egotistical demon lay hiding behind the opaque disguise. He wanted to make her listen, to obey; but she just plain ignored him.

"You fucking pig!" he yelled more loudly. "I'm calling the cops! They're going to tow your piece of shit car, you fucking bitch," he screamed at the backside of her black silk gown as she glided through the glass entrance and disappeared inside. His heart was pounding like the heart of a jack-rabbit on the run, and sweat dripped from his temples as his words fell on deaf ears. His last outburst was enough to make even those who agreed with him quickly disperse.

When Matt finally realized that there was nothing he could, he sneakily keyed the entire length of the red Beamer as he walked to where Abby was waiting.

Abby, still nauseated, picked up the heavy bags from where she was standing and waited, straight-backed, for Matt to step up to her. She looked up at him with harsh, cold eyes and tight lips that revealed the disgust she felt. She shoved the cumbersome bags into his mid-section and quietly said, "Let's go."

But before she turned to walk away, she leaned into him as if sharing an intimate secret, and quietly added, "You can't just start screaming at people like that, and you sure as hell can't "key" everybody's car that pisses you off."

"What she's doing is wrong," he said in his defense. "That spot is for disabled vets and...."

"Let's just go," she said sternly and more loudly, cutting him off. "*Your friends* are waiting for us at your uncle's." Matt had noticed that when Abby was upset, which was quite often these days, she referred to Uncle Bill and his friends, as *your friends,* instead of, *our friends,* despite the fact that Uncle Bill and Abby's parents have been best of friends since before Abby was ever a gleam in her father's eye.

Matt fell into line behind Abby and followed as she led the way back to the truck. He had no problems with what he'd done, but he was at odds with the way Abby was treating him. She didn't seem to understand, for example, why it was wrong to park in a handicap zone when you're not handicapped, or why it's wrong to toss cigarette butts and garbage onto the streets? He wondered why she was so passive or how she could act as if everything was just fine. Why couldn't she understand how much he detested blatant contempt for what is right and what is wrong? Why couldn't she stand behind him and support him? Before they got to the truck, Matt stopped and put the bags down. "Wait!" he demanded.

Abby stopped and turned to face him.
"What?"

He looked hard into her light blue-gray eyes. "Why can't you understand that I despise that woman because she is spitting in the face of the very system that created the laws that made it possible, legally or illegally, for her to be in this country to begin with. I hate her total lack of respect, Abby."

Abby listened, but did not respond, which irritated him even more. He wished she would agree with him. Tell him that she understood and that he was right. But she didn't, and he hated it.

"Well?" he asked, raising his eyebrows and putting his hands out, palms up, waiting for a response.

"What can I say that I haven't said before, Matt? Right or wrong, you can't just start screaming and swearing at people, and calling them names." She then turned away and continued walking towards the truck. Matt, not wanting to beat a dead horse, just shrugged his shoulders, shook his head, and let it go. She just doesn't get it. When they got to the truck, they loaded the supplies into the bed without speaking and headed for the party at his Uncle Bill's.

Abby's coconut perfume was seductive and wafted through the cab of Matt's truck like a butterfly flitting over a grassy meadow. Wisps of her blond hair floated and shimmered in the wind and sunlight of the open window. She tapped her foot to the music, causing her breasts to jiggle, just a bit, and in some odd way it pissed him off that she seemed to have put the whole scene with the lady in black behind her. She was looking her best for the yearly shindig, and he wanted to tell her so, but he just couldn't bring himself to say the words.

Matt drove slowly through the deep pot holes in the dirt access road to the back-side of his uncle's property. Abby sat quietly, trying desperately to prepare her mind for the party. It was undeniably past time she talked to Uncle Bill about his nephew.

*****

Uncle Bill grew up in a time when people were afraid of the Reds, Communism, propaganda, and the A-bomb. He *did not* grow up in a world that feared terrorists, gangs, and airplane-bombs. The world in which he and his peers had grown up was sinking like an elephant in quicksand, and a new world, less civilized, less caring, and less compassionate was taking root, but Bill Lovell no longer wanted to sign petitions, march in rallies, or argue politics. He had become quite content with his life as, Uncle Bill.

Turning wrenches was his trade. He specialized in the restoration of carburetor powered muscle cars that were built in the 50s, and since his work was his hobby, he never considered spending ten, twelve, fourteen hour days in his garage as work, at all. He loved what he did and took enormous pride in the finished product, and he faithfully lived by the epigram that he'd coined, "*If you don't like what you're doing, quit doing it.*"

The inside of his garage, unlike the outside, was immaculate. When Matt was growing up, he believed that his uncle had also coined the phrase, *"there's a place for everything, and everything has its place."* The floor was wall-to-wall smooth concrete with a special light blue, oil resistant, epoxy paint that was as clean as any plate coming out of the dishwasher. Snap-On tool chests, one of them, as big as a small car, lined the walls. Shelves were filled with boxes containing generators, carburetors, headlights, brackets, linkage, gaskets, and parts and pieces from dozens of vintage cars. There were fenders and hoods hanging by hooks and nails, and a ladder led up to the beefed up ceiling joists where sheets of plywood had been nailed to provide even more storage space.

A radio tuned to his favorite country station was always on at low volume. Marilyn Monroe held down her famous white dress in a pin-up on one wall, and some girl with long red hair and the biggest knockers in the world was on another, her nipples smeared black with finger prints of dreamers.

He had installed an air conditioner for summer and a wood stove for winter, but his favorite amenity, donated as a *garage-warming* gift from Brent, and always the focal point of conversation, was the urinal.

A window was centered on the wall directly behind the urinal, and since the window was always open during shindigs, the party goers could see whoever was *leaving* a pee, which always elicited jeers from the crowd, and there was always at least one gal at every party who would trot off to the garage for a stand up pee, to which everyone, including the women egged her on with hoots and hollers, claps and whistles.

Uncle Bill was never sure how everyone would get along on the 4th, but he knew they all pretty much had the same ideals. In the old days, there was always at least one fist-fight, but as everyone grew older and wiser, stories of busted lips and broken noses took the place of the actual thing. Still, no one ever knew quite what to expect, and there was always some newbie that felt the need prove himself or herself. It was Uncle Bill's favorite holiday. In fact, the July 4th holiday, *an eloquent statement of the American colonies intention to become an independent nation*, was pretty much the only one he and Matt celebrated.

His warrior friends, the most intimidating of the outlaw gang, mostly made their livings as mercenaries and body guards. They were a downright scary bunch, and they were Brent's Chandler's tightest comrades, many of whom camped permanently and discreetly on Brent's property.

As he looked around at the women, he couldn't help but smile. They were all, even the warrior women, a bit on the trashy side. Just the way I like them, he thought smiling. The years didn't seem to haunt the women like they had the men. The men got older and their hair and their beards grayed, and their leathery skin wrinkled from the sun, but age on his outlaw women friends looked good—mostly.

Today, his redheaded neighbor Rose was wearing all turquoise; turquoise halter top, turquoise ribbon in her hair, and turquoise finger polish. Turquoise was her signature. The skin above her turquoise cowboy boots to the hem of her short turquoise mini-skirt was translucent white, as were her arms. Her face, however, was painted with a dark cover-up that contrasted with her white neck and chest; her eye liner and eye shadow were turquoise, and her lipstick was blood red and shiny and had little sparkles in it. And although she dressed oddly, she was a good looking and provocative girl and everyone liked Rose—and loved her if given the chance.

He saw a pattern to the women who attended his yearly party. The first year they were shy and dressed predictably, but every year thereafter it was less clothing and more skin, new tattoos, shorter skirts, and more cleavage.

Both men and women wore earrings, but none had face piercings. No nose rings or cheek rings or lip rings. At some past party, Tiny, in casual conversation with a new biker dude, who was in his early twenties and who was wearing a lip ring, asked, "Does that lip ring hurt?" The newbie squinted and lifted his chin and answered "no". Tiny, fast as lightning, punched him so hard in the mouth that blood spattered five feet in all directions. The ring split clear though the new guy's lip, and the punch knocked loose a tooth. When the shocked newbie fell to the ground holding his hand over his bloody mouth, Tiny said, "How about now?" which brought applause from all the blood splattered witnesses. The newbie wisely let it go.

Uncle Bill looked around and spotted the victim who had learned a lesson the hard way on that fateful day way back then. He had earned respect by not leaving that day and by returning every year thereafter. He also accepted his new nick-name, Lip, due to the righteous scare that left his lower lip noticeably jagged. Uncle Bill nodded his head as if he were talking to someone besides his own self; Lip had become a dependable and trusted outlaw friend to Brent, Uncle Bill, and the rest, and had become tight buds with Tiny.

Careful observation revealed concealed and not so concealed weapons, and since the 4th was sort of a dress-up day, special guns and knives were on display.

Uncle Bill looked around and smiled and recalled Matt's first 4th of July party. "These are my friends, my family," he'd told Matt. "This is my nephew, my blood," he'd told his friends. "Please watch his back like you watch mine." And so it began.

*****

Matt drove over the hard-packed dirt, loosely referred to as the back yard, and pulled into his private parking spot next to the garage just as Uncle Bill was tossing a big chunk of alder into a huge barbeque pit that had been dug into the dirt. The smell of burnt alder filled the air as a thick cloud of gray smoke rose above the deep bed of burning red-hot coals that surely equaled the temperatures of Dante's hell. So intense was the invisible heat, that the small branches, still attached to the log, burst into flames before the log landed on the coals, sending up a plum of burning ambers that looked like ten thousand fire bugs swarming into the sky. Brent Chandler, evidently mesmerized by this phenomenon, sat to one side, well away from the extreme temperatures, and stared, mouth half open, as if he were in the front row at the theater.

Uncle Bill turned and waved to Matt and Abby as they pulled into the back yard, which once a year during the 4th of July party resembled a parking lot at the county fair. Matt parked his truck in *his* spot right next to the two car garage that was painted the same battleship gray with black trim as the house. His parking spot was well away from the six large Granny Smith apple trees and the dozen or so fir trees that provided shade on the lot. It was his spot and there was a sign that said so.

THIS SPOT IS RESERVED FOR MATT LOVELL
VIOLATORS WILL BE SHOT WITHOUT WARNING
SURVIVORS WILL BE SHOT AGAIN

The sign had been made by his uncle and was Matt's prelude to his 16th birthday present. Matt had started working for his uncle when he first moved in, first as a general clean-up boy and eventually moving up to twisting wrenches, one bolt at a time. He was a natural and learned quickly. Six months before his 16th birthday, his uncle had taken in a beat-up 1955, F150 Ford pick-up truck for restoration. He gave the job to Matt as his first ground-up, outside and inside restoration.

"The owner says spare no expense, so go for the gusto and let's see what you got." Matt chose to power it up with a 351 built-up Cleveland engine with a 4-speed transmission atop a newer 4x chassis, and when finished, it was a real show piece. When his uncle told him the truck was his birthday present, Matt was so choked up he couldn't talk for ten minutes.

He stepped out of his cherry-black pride and joy onto the dusty, cracked dirt in the back yard and said, more to himself than to Abby, "looks like another wild one." It didn't much matter if he'd said it or just thought it because she wasn't paying attention to him anyway. "I'm going to go 'leave' a pee," he said a little more loudly, but still not expecting a response.

"Yep, looks like a good one," she said pushing open the door, preparing to disembark.

*****

Motorcycles, leaning on kick stands, lined the high wood-slat fence at the west side of the property. Small groups of bikers and cowboys were hanging at cable-spool-tables, scattered around the yard, talking shit, drinking beer, and chomping on junk food. There were two tattered weather-stained and beer-stained lounge chairs placed near the barbeque pit that should have been hauled off to the dump years ago. The beat-up *'relaxers,'* a nickname Matt had given them when he was a kid, were kept under a black plastic tarp next to the garage and hauled out every spring and put back every fall. Fenders, trunk lids, hoods, broken windshields, car seats, stacks of old tires and wheels, a few exhausted engines, and all sorts of other miscellaneous car parts added to the junkyard landscape.

The party started on the 4th, and party-goers started showing up right at midnight on the 3rd. It continued all day and all night and officially ended at precisely noon on the 5th. It was the way it was and everyone respected the rules.

Uncle Bill had a personal relationship with everyone who came, and there was a story behind the camaraderie of each one—how they'd met and the journey they'd shared that bonded their friendship. And once a year they all showed up for the annual 4th of July party, where old bros from all over the country rolled in to rock and roll and resuscitate tales from the past. No cares, no worries, and no problems that couldn't be resolved.

*****

Montana and Moalim stayed in Everett for two nights and then drove out to Monroe to hang at Brent's for a day and a night before heading out to the party. "Reconnaissance," Moalim had said when Montana asked why it was necessary. "We need to know how serious these American friends of yours are. Do they just boast of their camaraderie or are they willing to die for a cause."

"They are no longer my friends, Moalim," snapped Montana, "and I can tell you that they are damned serious, and as willing to die for a cause that they believe in as *we* are willing to die for the cause *we* believe in," emphasizing *we* by moving his index finger back and forth between himself and Moalim.

"I'm sorry my friend, I have no reason to question your loyalty after all this time," said Moalim, not missing Montana's agitation. "I hope you can forgive me," he said smirking out the side window.

Montana *had* been loyal and it irritated the hell out of him when Moalim continually sliced away at him with cutting jabs, like 'your friends' and 'your country'. He referred to Montana's friends as infidels, and he referred to America as 'the *real* evil empire. He needed a drink! No. He needed a bottle!

On the other hand, Montana felt uneasy hearing his old friends continually being referred to as, *the enemy.* He had killed in the name of revenge but he was not a cold blooded killer. There was a difference. He knew what was on the horizon and what would be required of him and he was ready for it, ready to kill people he didn't know for a cause, like Jihad, for example, but if it came to gunning down his old friends, no matter what their differences, well, he hadn't really come to terms with that and hadn't given it any real thought until the other day when the Lassiter ranch in Cave Junction was brought up. He was able to get his head around the possibility of eliminating the Lassiters because he didn't know them all that well, but when it came to rationalizing the killing of Bill and Matt and the rest, he really wasn't sure, and maybe Moalim could read this weakness in his character. Maybe there was a certain look or characteristic that illuminated like the beacon of a buoy in the bay that showed up on cold blooded killers that only other cold blooded killers could see. Maybe he was missing some sort of evil glint in his eye or a telling tone in his voice or a surreptitious gate to his walk—maybe a cold blooded killer could distinguish a cold blooded killer from someone who was not or could not be a cold blooded killer. Maybe that was why Moalim had always kept him at arm's length.

To the sentries at the barricade to Brent's property, Moalim passed for one of Montana's, pot-dealing, Mexican friends. When asked for ID, he produced the same passport he had used many years ago when he first crossed the border with Montana. After passing through the gate, Moalim said, "Americans are so naïve. They have no idea what is going on in their own country. Their pretentious ways will be their downfall."

The next morning, Montana and Moalim rose up early and were ready to roll in short order.

"We are going to meet up with those cowboys and cowgirls," said Moalim. "They are going to be watching our backs," he said, laughing. "It's another odd American phrase, don't you think?" Moalim said laughing, "watching our backs."

*****

Abby climbed out of the truck and waved to Uncle Bill and the small gang of outlaws that was hanging around the 'party' pit. The next person she focused on was Brent Chandler, part biker, part cowboy, but mostly *the* ultimate warrior and survivor. He was also Uncle Bill's best friend since before Matt was born. When he looked up and saw Abby getting out of the truck he smiled that irresistible smile that had charmed Abby from the first time she'd met him. He still had the charm, and despite the age difference, she still got a bit damp whenever she was around him.

When Abby first met Brent, she immediately saw the similarities between him and Matt. Brent had been Matt's main mentor since Matt was first came to live with his uncle, and he had picked up some of Brent's mannerisms and had heisted some of his sayings. They were so much alike in so many ways that Abby often wondered who really raised Matt. She was bending over the sideboard of the pickup retrieving a bag of supplies when Brent let loose.

"Who's the good looking broad with the nice butt?" he hollered across the yard as Abby pulled a bag of goodies from the back of the truck. She turned to face the cat-calls and whistles that followed Brent's "hello" and froze. In the next moment, she regained her composure and started the trek across, what seemed to be, five miles of back yard towards Brent and Uncle Bill.

She remembered a few years back when she'd mentioned to Uncle Bill, after a few more than a few shots of tequila, her favorite drink, how sexy Brent, the mountain man, was. "He seems a whole lot younger than he is," she'd said, with a dreamy look in her eyes. At the time she'd said it, she'd had a pretty good buzz going but remembered trying to take it all back the moment the words escaped her loosened lips. "Darn! I wish I hadn't said that. It must be the tequila talking. I was just kidding around. You better not tell him I said that, Uncle Bill. Please," she pleaded, smiling and adding a hiccup for affect.

Uncle Bill just laughed and toasted her with his drink. She always wondered if he ever told his best friend that he had a secret admirer, but knew in her gut the answer without having to think on it too long—it would be good garage talk amongst the men. She had learned a very valuable lesson that day—'lip will get ya.'

She was as red as the bandannas that the cowboys were wearing, but she couldn't help but smile, thinking, the guy really knows how to force an entrance. What a hunk.

*****

She continued her "pageant stroll" towards Uncle Bill, weaving here and there around tables and chairs and some tough and gnarly looking characters who were winking and panting and giving her the once over. When she stepped up next to Uncle Bill, in a waft of coconut perfume, he flashed back to when she was born to two of his oldest and closest friends, Jake and Karla Lassiter.

"You're looking good, sweetheart. How about a hug for your old Uncle Bill?" he said, opening his arms. Abby set down the bags near some ice coolers that were lined up against the house and turned to Uncle Bill, and during the short fatherly hug, she had just enough time to whisper in his ear.

"I need to talk to you, alone. No hurry, but before the sun goes down, partner," she said with a chuckle. Brent pushed his lean and mean frame out of the relaxer and opened his arms.

"Next," said Brent, grinning a smile as big and as wide as his full, handlebar mustache.

"Hello Brent," she said, with a shy smile, turning loose of Uncle Bill.

Brent was wearing a brown leather vest with no shirt. A silver chain necklace with a huge claw from a black bear he'd killed with the ivory-handled Smith and Wesson .357 magnum, which he was wearing in a custom made, leather, cross draw holster that looked as bad-good as Brent did himself. "Emptied my gun on the fucker and hoped for the best," he'd told her.

Flexing her chest, she said, "you want some of this?" and turned red all over again as she instantly realized that her playful gesture of trying to look tough was taken completely the wrong way. Brent smiled through piercing blue eyes but didn't say what he was thinking. After a hug that lasted longer than hugs usually do, and for a silent moment before turning her loose, he looked deep into her sparkling eyes, deep into her soul, and made her heart skip a beat. When the trance faded, he held her by the shoulders and dropped his eyes, just for a second, to her breasts, just long enough for her to notice.

"Yep, you are most definitely looking good little momma," he said, sucking air in through his teeth.

"You're disgusting," she said, turning red all over again and backing away. She waved off the others who were jeering "me next" and "pass it around, momma." It was too early to start shouting, "show us your tits," but the day was still young. Uncle Bill, who was standing close by, shook his head and continued to stoke the fire.

Abby was attracted to Brent in a lusty, animal way—a rip off your clothes and get to it sort of way, which she never felt with Matt. She couldn't help it; he touched her deep inside her soul. Her licentious thoughts brought a new shade of red to her skin as she wondered if a big difference in age was a big deal in a relationship. She took refuge in knowing that no one could read her mind, because what she was thinking was surely X-rated. A slight shiver engulfed her body as she concluded that a lusty *bang* was different than a relationship, in which case, age could not possibly be a factor. It's an animal thing, she thought, feeling a small bead of sweat tickle its way down her cleavage, and she smiled at the way she reasoned, reasonable or not.

"You got a date for the dance, sweetheart?" asked Brent, breaking the silence after what seemed a lifetime but was in fact only a few seconds.

"I've always got a spot on my card for you, cowboy," she said with a wink, regaining her composure. She felt good for the first time in weeks and she felt proud of holding her own, despite the fact she wasn't brought up around these kinds of folks, and if the truth be known, she felt intimidated by most everyone there.

She felt different today. She was suddenly at the top of her game. She felt brave and in charge and she was talking shit, which was not at all the norm for her. She was on a natural high and loving it.

Lip, a short slim cowboy with a very noticeable one inch, vertical scar on the right side of his bottom lip came up and stood next to Brent but was looking at Abby.

"I guess you heard about that judge back east turning that baby-raper loose because the scumbag immigrant couldn't speak English," he said, as if he'd been part of an on-going conversation. "Some people just don't deserve to go on living," he added. Brent and Uncle Bill both gave him the, 'where the fuck did that come from,' look but said nothing. Abby had already heard all about it more than once from Matt and wasn't interested in revisiting the scene of the crime. Although she liked and respected Lip, her glow disappeared like the sun dropping behind the back side of Mt. Rainier, and her voice became stern and hard.

"You're right about that, Lip. It's strange for sure, and it's not right at all. Good to see you again, Lip. I think I'll walk around for a while," she said, turning towards Uncle Bill.

"Okay, sweetheart, but be careful out there," he said, tipping his head towards the yard. "Holler if you need something. Lots of perverts lurking in the shadows in these here parts," he added, nodding his head towards his buddy Brent. She smiled at Brent and Lip and then strolled off towards a group of girls she recognized from past parties.

"Something I said?" asked Lip quietly looking at Brent and holding out his hands as Brent watched her walk away. Brent jokingly smacked him in the back of the head and sat back down in the beat-up lounge chair to finish the sandwich he'd made earlier.

*****

Matt smiled and waved through the open window as he stood at the porcelain urinal in the garage. The onlookers waved back and saluted him with their drinks. One of the girls blew him a kiss and another mooned him, drawing hoots and applause, and like water being poured from a glass, he felt the tension drain from his body, and he was happy to be amongst his bros and away from Abby.

Matt stepped out from the darkness of the garage into the bright sunlight and took stock of his surroundings. He was dressed in blue jeans, cowboy boots, his red 4th of July Hawaiian shirt with a hibiscus flower print, and dark Ray Ban sun glasses. He was looking good.

There's no prettier place on earth then the Great North West, he thought as he cut a path through the crowd. It was 82 degrees and sunny, and to the south was Mount Rainier, which was always an awesome sight to behold no matter how many times he'd seen it before. To the north was Mount Baker, still capped with snow, to the west, the Olympic Mountain Range and to the East the Cascades. He could never quite describe the exact color of blue the sky was over this part of the country. He'd heard it described as blue-blue, deep-blue, gray-blue, rich blue, aqua-blue, cobalt-blue, violet-blue and a myriad of others, but there was no doubt that no sky on earth was bluer or richer than the canopy of blue that stretched over the tall firs from mountain top to mountain top, in all directions, over the Great Northwest. A gentle breeze blew in from the west and carried with it the scent of salt air from the Puget Sound, which was just a few miles away.

After scrutinizing the lay of the land, and waiting until after Abby had said her hellos and had walked off, he headed over to offer the obligatory greeting to the host, his Uncle Bill.

Someone had cranked up the tunes when the Eagles started singing, "*I was runnin' down the road tryin' to loosen my load, I had seven women on my mind...*" and in the few minutes that he'd been there, the party had stepped up three notches.

"Where's the beer," he said, stepping up to Brent and his uncle.

"Hey Matt," said Brent, offering his hand as Matt walked up. Matt took it, and catching Brent off guard, pulled him close for a *manly* type hug, which was more of a bump/push-away sort of thing than a hug.

"Good to see you, Bro. Damn good," said Matt, backing away but still holding tight to Brent's hand.

"Well don't start crying ya faggot," said Brent, smiling.

"Just didn't want you to feel neglected," replied Matt.

"Neglected? Hell, boy, while you been in the garage playing with yourself, I've been out here making time with your ol' lady," Brent said, giving Matt some good o' boy shit. "She's saving the last dance for me, but said to wait until you were passed out before hooking up with her."

"She's for sale, dude," said Matt before thinking.

"Shit, boy. If I want her, I'll just take her," said Brent, sneering into the sunlight, keeping the joust alive.

Before it went any further, Uncle Bill stepped up and laid a hand on Matt's shoulder. He knew these two guys loved each other like brothers; the problem was they often fought like brothers, too. Matt turned to greet his uncle, and Brent smiled and sat back down.

"Hi nephew."

"Hi Uncle Bill; looks like another good one," said Matt, refocusing after his "awkward hello" to Brent. "The pit is looking as hot as the women, and I'm starving. Where's the beef?" he said, as he reached down and opened the cooler and helped himself to an ice cold Bud. "Damn," he said, taking a long drink, "nothin' better than beer chilled on ice." He finished it in one long drink, crushed the can, and tossed it up against the side of the house where there was already a pile of empties stacking up.

"We got choices," said Uncle Bill. "We've got a load of salmon, thanks to the brothers from the peninsula, and we've got a ton of beef from the Lane County clan for the die-hard carnivores in the group," nodding his head towards Brent, who was tipping a bottle of beer straight up.

"Well, that'll be me too then," said Matt, fetching another beer. "Hey, there's Montana," he said looking past Uncle Bill to a group of cowboys at the far side of the yard. "Jesus, he hasn't been here for three years" he said, excusing himself and moving off before Uncle Bill had a chance to tell him that Montana had shown up with friends that Uncle Bill didn't know and hadn't invited.

CHAPTER 4

Montana was standing with a group of cowboys and cowgirls. The men were dressed in traditional cowboy shirts, scarves, hats, boots, and Levi jeans. The women were all wearing cowboy hats, had long hair, and were dressed in Levi mini-skirts or short-shorts. They sort of looked to Matt like a troupe of Silver Spur square dancers. Montana was waving excitedly for Matt to come on over and join them.

Matt was barely thirteen when Montana got him drunk on Jack Daniel's whiskey in celebration of his losing his virginity to Rose. He recalled the agony of puking his guts out on his first whisky drunk, and when he saw the bottle of Jack Montana was dangling down by his side between index and middle finger, he pointed to it and stuck the middle finger of his free hand in his mouth and faked puking. Matt had never acquired a taste for the harsh Tennessee whiskey, and to this day the smell of it brings back upchucking memories.

He couldn't remember much of what went on after the whiskey took affect but had been reminded of his stupidity, more than once, by his uncle, who had found him around 11 p.m., sprawled out in the back yard with the empty bottle lying next to him. His uncle had left him there to sleep it off, and the next morning when Matt came around, wet from the due, sore from the hard ground, deathly sick with his first hang-over, and smelling like puke, Montana was gone.

His uncle had found lots of extra chores for Matt to do that day, and when the sun finally went down and Matt had come slithering back into the house ready to collapse, his uncle simply said, "you're not old enough or smart enough to drink, Matt. Don't do it again." Matt knew by his uncle's tone and the glare in his eye that he was dead serious.

Montana's name didn't come up in conversation until after the next 4th of July party when he hadn't shown up. When Matt mentioned it in passing conversation, his uncle simply said, "Montana stepped over the line, and I told him it would be better if he stayed away for a while." And that was that. Matt had only seen him a few times since, but no matter how his uncle's feelings had changed towards Montana, Matt still liked him; even in spite of the conversation he'd overheard between his uncle and Brent a few weeks back.

He'd parked his truck out front of his uncle's house instead of in his usual parking spot next to the garage. He had just washed it, and he didn't want it all dusty when he got off work. He had walked, undetected, around the side of the house and out to the garage and was about to open the door when he'd overheard his uncle talking to someone.

"I think one of us needs to go down there for a visit," he was telling Brent. The tone in his uncle's voice caused Matt to wait and listen before barging in. After all, good information was good ammo. That's what he'd been taught by both his uncle and Brent.

"So what's up?" Brent asked Uncle Bill.

"From what Jake tells me, Montana has been showing up quite a bit over the past several months. It was no big deal in the beginning but since he's been showing up on a regular basis, he decided to mention it." Matt held his breath waiting for the punch line, but it was Brent who spoke next.

"Actually, he's been coming around my place more than usual too. I'm not too concerned about it, though, just figure he's shuffling more pot than usual. Business is good is what I'm thinking. What's the real problem? What else did Jake say. bro?"

"He said Montana always comes up to the house to let him and Karla know he's there but never hangs around for a cup of coffee or any chatter. He said he got an uneasy feeling last time he was there. Like something was wrong, maybe. Couldn't quite put his finger on it, just said he acted sort of suspicious."

"Well hell bro, that can be from smoking too much skunk. Ain't no big thing," said Brent, not hearing anything too extraordinary. "Probably dealing pot," he said, faking a big inhale off a fake twisty. Matt stayed silent and listened, but he figured like Brent; no big deal. It certainly didn't make Montana the kind of criminal that should to be put behind bars; hell, there are a lot worse offenses than shuffling a little pot. Matt put his hand on the door knob and was about to open it when his uncle started up again, in the same concerned tone.

"There's more," said Uncle Bill. "At first, Jake never thought anything of it but he's not stupid either, and one evening before dark he strolled down to where he figured Montana might be camping to say hello and to snoop around a bit."

"Yeah," said Brent. "And?"

"Well, he was greeted by a dark-skinned man with an assault rifle who ordered him to put his hands in the air and not move." Again, there was a long pause. "It seems Montana was pretty close by because he showed up as soon as he heard the commotion.

"What the hell, pot dealers are...?" started Brent, but was cut off by Uncle Bill.

"Montana quickly put the guard at ease, but the whole ordeal scared the hell out of Jake. He told me the man with the gun was not Mexican. Said he was Middle Eastern."

"What the fuck is Montana doing hanging with rag-heads?" asked Brent, now more concerned. Matt couldn't see, but knew Brent's mannerisms well enough to know he was scowling in deep thought. Uncle Bill hadn't used cultural slurs since he'd started raising Matt, but it didn't mean he didn't agree with Brent's description.

"One more thing," said Uncle Bill, "and this is the capper. Jake told me Montana didn't invite him to stay and chat, but instead turned him quickly back towards his house and said something like, 'thanks, Jake, but we're fine. No need to check on us again, okay?' Jake said it sounded more like an order or a threat than a friendly gesture." Matt had heard enough and opened the door.

"Hey Brent, how's it going?"

"Good Matt; and you?"

"Good," answered Matt. "I didn't know you were coming to town today, but it's always good to see you, bro. What's up?"

"Well, kid, you don't need to know everything," answered Brent in his usual challenging way. "But since you're so damn nosey, I am here to talk to your uncle about getting a new propane generator for my property."

"Sure thing," Matt said, a bit pissed that they hadn't trusted him with the information on Montana. Matt was already on edge from listening to the news and hearing about the state of current affairs in the country, and was in no mood for Brent's bullshit, so he walked over, hung his coat on the rack, and got busy. Brent and his uncle left the garage together, leaving Matt with questions.

Now, as the memory spiked through his brain, he concluded that perhaps it was a bit strange, but maybe it was just Jake's imagination running away with him. Hell, Montana is okay; and so what if he *is* shuffling pot. Hell, maybe he didn't want Jake to know what he was up to; and Jake was definitely mistaken about the dark skinned guy being Middle Eastern. Hell, Montana wouldn't be hangin' with some damn rag-head.

Montana was a friend, he reminded himself and deserves the benefit of doubt, and besides, Montana and his Uncle had history. Good, funny, story-telling history. And in spite of what he'd heard about Montana that day outside the garage, he was still stoked to see him.

*****

When Matt stepped up to Montana, his feelings of elation at seeing his old friend were suddenly crushed like so much shit under his boot. There were new faces in the crowd, and one of them stood out like a biker at a formal wedding party. Taliban, rag-head, Al-Qaeda, Islamic terrorist, all flashed like a bolt of lightning through his mind, and was compounded by the sudden recollection of the conversation that he'd overheard between Brent and his uncle about the Middle Eastern guy down in Cave Junction, and wondered if this was him. He felt his heart rate ladder up, and it took all his effort to remain civil. He wanted to react; pinch someone's head off, but he needed to know what the hell was going on. He was a warrior in training, after all, and information was power.

He had a hundred questions, like why did his uncle let this guy in and what was the connection between him and Montana? Why hadn't his uncle given him a heads up? Why wasn't he told? He suddenly felt betrayed on all fronts, and the urge to fight almost overcame his reason to stay calm.

"I see you're still packing that stainless steel Colt," Montana said, before Matt had a chance to swallow. And quick as a fly taking flight before being smashed, Montana pulled the tail of Matt's Hawaiian shirt back, exposing the stainless steel .45 Colt Commander that was strapped to his belt. Matt's hand flew to Montana's wrist with equal speed and wrenched it away with a twist that forced Montana half way to the ground in pain.

"What the fuck you doing shit-head," Matt said, turning him loose. His tone was cold and his eyes were so penetrating that it brought everyone to a standstill. The silence was as contagious as syphilis on a sailing ship full of whores and rum-soaked sailors. But Montana, determined to prove his loyalty to Moalim, ignored Matt's reprimand and continued with his disparagement.

"No offense, hotshot," he said, still writhing with pain. "I saw the reflection when you got out of your truck. It makes for one hell of a target when the sunlight hits it just right. They might be pretty, but they are the bull's eye of a target. Think about it," he said, smirking and offering Matt the bottle of Jack. Matt was boiling. He didn't like being talked down to—not by anyone. "How about a drink for old time sake, Matt?" offered Montana, holding the bottle of Jack out towards Matt.

"No thanks, Montana, I have a beer. It's a party, Montana," he said, standing defiantly within inches. "Lots of us are carrying our *trophy* pieces. Look at Brent," he said, more to make a point as to who his *real* comrades were than to make a point regarding shiny weapons. He then shifted his penetrating stare from Montana to the foreigner, and Montana quickly turned to Moalim and put his hand on his shoulder.

"This is Moalim," he said. "Moalim, this is Matt," he said, tilting his head towards Matt. "He's Billy's nephew," he said, tilting his head in the direction of Uncle Bill. Matt was furious! He felt the whole conversation a mockery, and his comment and gesture regarding his uncle was rude and disrespectful.

His Uncle and Montana certainly have history—good history, but that was then and this is now, and once Matt decided he didn't like someone it was damn near impossible for him to change his mind, and Montana had just stepped way over the line of acceptable bullshit.

Moalim, after a moment's hesitation, and with a face as hard as marble, and the stare of a rattlesnake, slowly raised a limp hand for the introductory handshake. Matt snickered at the gesture and slowly shook his head from side to side. He wanted to show the intruder right there and then five different ways to take him down with a hand shake, but instead he turned his head back towards Montana.

"That was rude, Montana—and disrespectful to both my uncle and to me," he said with as much calm as he could muster. He fought the urge to draw

43

his weapon and shove it into Montana's open mouth and give him some unsolicited advice about courtesy. His mind went reeling in the ensuing silence, and he felt the sudden need to get away from this asshole and his Middle Eastern buddy, before he lost it.

Matt had never shot a person, but being a hunter and a trained survivalist, there was little doubt in his mind that he could kill a human if it came to it. He'd been taught by the best and had been through training courses and exhibitions that were held so far out in the woods that even the bears got lost. His Uncle had taught him about guns and gun safety, but Brent had been his official weapons' instructor. When Matt decided to start packing, Brent had given him a long course in the use of weapons and had advised him on protocol. His first three hour lesson revolved around the axiom: "Don't draw your weapon—in fact don't pack a weapon at all if you don't know for sure that you can use it without hesitation." Every time he strapped on his gun, he wondered if today would be the day that he would be tested; and, standing in front of Montana at that very moment, an odd sensation came over him; he wanted to draw his gun and shoot both Montana and his new buddy right between the eyes.

He looked at the dark skinned cowboy with the peculiar looking knife with the wide, curved blade and made his decision.

"Excuse me," he said, turning to stare at Montana for an uncomfortable moment, after which his gaze fell again on the Arab cowboy, "I have to go leave a shit," he said turning briskly, and bumping into his uncle who'd just stepped up next to him. "Assholes," said Matt, loud enough for them all to hear.

*****

Uncle Bill had a full head of long gray hair that he kept tied back into a ponytail. His 6'-0" frame was not as solid as it once was, and at 200 pounds he'd developed a bit of a paunch. He didn't do much to try to reclaim his youthful physique; instead he was trying to accepting old age gracefully. He was, however, unwavering in his belief that, *it is better to have a gun and not need it, than to need a gun and not have it,* so he always carried. "I don't have to be that tough anymore," he'd told Matt awhile back. "The fuckers get too far out of line, I'll just shoot 'em." And although he'd said it jokingly, Matt knew damn well he'd meant it.

His face was tanned and lined like old leather, and he'd gotten used to a life of regimented certainties. He worked, he got paid, and he paid the bills. To relax, he read spy novels. He'd settled down when he took to overseeing his nephew's upbringing and never went back to the gypsy lifestyle of a wonderer. His love life was sporadic, at best. If he came across the right woman and there was chemistry, okay, otherwise he was content with just being good old Uncle Bill.

He'd been concerned ever since Montana showed up with his new sidekick and the other cowboys he didn't know. He didn't have sentries posted like Brent had at his place, so they just walked in, and since there were always new faces in the crowd, nobody but Uncle Bill ever noticed if someone uninvited was in the crowd. He figured anyone not invited would have to be pretty stupid, or have a death wish, to walk in on the outlaws from Lane County, and the cast of other characters that now occupied his back yard. He'd decided to put off a confrontation for a while to see what developed. Maybe he could find something out about his frequent trips to Cave Junction. Sooner or later, however, he would tell Montana that he was no longer welcome—not today, not next year, not ever.

"What's up with Matt," asked Montana, eyebrows raised, palms up, bottle of Jack still between his fingers, watching Matt walk away. No hello. No how you been? No introductions. No nothing, thought Uncle Bill.

"Well, Montana," began Uncle Bill, slowly picking his words with purpose, "Matt's been on edge lately, and like me, he doesn't like to be surprised with new faces of people who were not invited," he said, eyeing each of Montana's dressed-up cowboy friends, and then resting his eyes intently on Moalim. "You know the drill, Montana," he said, looking back at his old comrade. My place, my party, my rules, and I'm not impressed that you had the audacity to show up with a bunch of uninvited wanna-be cowboys without checking with me first." Moalim and his hired help stayed still as granite.

Montana did not blink, nor did he offer an explanation. Instead, he looked down at the hard dirt ground and moved some pebbles with the toe of his boot. When he looked back up, he was still looking towards the garage where Matt had just entered and had closed the door behind him.

"You didn't even come over and say hello when you arrived—you just moved in like you owned the place." He waited. "I would think that a kid who was brought up in a Catholic orphanage would have better manners than that. And...."

"Do you want us to leave?" Montana asked suddenly, interrupting his host. Uncle Bill was furious at the blatant disrespect, but if he slapped the impudent smirk off Montana's face it might just start a brawl. He always believed a good fist fight was good for attitude adjustment, but he didn't want to start something that was bound to be more than just a good old fist fight. It would be, he knew, a serious rumble and more than a few would get hurt—real bad!

"Yeah, Montana, I think it would be wise if you left." Montana finally looked at his old traveling buddy, but his shiny black eyes were like doors to a steel vault—nothing could be read in them except perhaps contempt. Finish your beers and hit the road. And Montana," he added, "you're not welcome here anymore." Montana shrugged as if it was no big deal, and the gesture reaffirmed to Uncle Bill that his decision was solid.

"Yeah, sure," said Montana tossing his empty beer bottle a few yards away into a metal barrel, which made a racket that sounded like a bomb going off in lieu of the silence that now encompassed this small area of the camp. "We'll head out right away," he said, contemptuously reaching down into his cooler and retrieving another beer.

Anyone else would have left then, thought Uncle Bill, but Montana, for some reason was pushing—flexing his muscles, demonstrating that he really didn't give a damn about the rules. What a moron, thought Uncle Bill, he's outmanned five to one. "Yeah, no problem; we'll start packing," said Montana, handing the open beer to Moalim. "Right Moalim?"

"Yes sir," said Moalim, spitting off to the side. "We don't want to be someplace we are not welcome. That is for sure. There are other places, further south, we can go to celebrate your independence day," he said, grasping Montana's shoulder.

May as well have spit in my face, thought Uncle Bill, as he turned and walked back towards the pit, thinking that kicking some ass might help relieve a shit-load of tension—to hell with the consequences—remembering that sometimes it's better to ask for forgiveness than to ask for permission.

"Mind if we finish our beers," one of the cowboys said loudly.

Uncle Bill did not *really* want a battlefield in his backyard, so he ignored the question and kept walking. On second thought, he stopped, turned around, and took two unhurried steps towards the one he figured was the mouth.

"Finish your beer and hit the road," he said, standing firm and staring him down, poised to lunge. When there was no further comment, he turned and walked back to the pit.

Brent was standing with the heal of his hand on the butt of his pistol, and Lip had his hand behind his back gripping the piece that was tucked into the waist band of his pants. Tiny stood next to them with his hands on his hips in a rather challenging manor. You didn't fuck with Tiny simply because of his size.

"What the hell was that all about?" asked Brent, when Uncle Bill stepped up to the pit.

"It started with Matt flipping out on Montana and his gang of shit-heads. It ended with me telling Montana and his gang of party crashers to leave, sooner rather than later," said Uncle Bill, reaching into the cooler to retrieve a much needed beer and the bottle of Jack.

His life had been pretty mellow the past ten or fifteen years. He wasn't used to confrontation any more, and he hoped that the guys didn't notice he was shaking, just a bit.

"Doesn't look like they're in too much of a hurry," said Lip.

"I told them to finish their beers and head out. I should have told them to hit the road now, but I saw you outlaws over here ready to start spreadin' lead and decided to give them a few minutes," he said, opening the bottle of Jack and taking a big swig, following it with a half a can of ice cold beer. "Let's just keep an eye on 'em until they leave. Won't be long, I'm sure," said Uncle Bill, wiping his mouth on his sleeve while staring in the direction of Montana.

"Maybe I should go over and help them pack," offered Brent, smiling.

"Yeah, what the hell, I could keep you company," offered Lip.

"I should probably tag along," said Tiny, "because there's way too many of them for just the two of you skinny bastards," he said, serious as a broken leg.

"I handled it, boys," said Uncle Bill, shaking his head. "Have another beer and chill. They'll be gone real soon." Suddenly he remembered the last thing the Arab cowboy had said; something about partying *further south*, and wondered if he was alluding to Cave Junction.

"Hey Brent, what do you know about Montana's new friend?" asked Uncle Bill, getting all serious again. "Hell, I didn't even know Montana was going to show up."

Brent, who was upending another beer, lowered and tossed the empty to the ground next to one of the coolers, before answering.

"After what you told me a few weeks back about Jake and Karla and Montana showing up at their place on a regular basis, I started asking around," said Brent, sitting back down in the relaxer. "No one at my place has ever seen Montana show up with any rag-heads, only babes and other Mexicans." Uncle Bill noticed while Brent was talking, that Montana and his gang had started milling around, picking up this and that and stuffing the same into their duffle bags. "Hell, Montana's camped at my place more than a few times a year," continued Brent. "He's never caused any trouble, and he always has good pot, so I didn't see the harm. Sure wonder what he's up to, though?"

"Who knows, but I would keep an eye on him if he ever shows up back to your place, again. I get really bad vibes from that bunch. Even the chicks," said Uncle Bill.

"Yeah, sure," said Brent, sort of shrugging it off. "Let me know if there's anything I can do to help with Matt," he said, changing the subject. "I'm pretty good at smacking people upside the head, myself," he said, giving his buddy a playful smack on the back of his head and then jumping back, hands up in defense.

"I'll get you for that," said Uncle Bill, smiling and pointing his finger at his friend. Brent took off, beer in hand, strutting off towards a group of gals on the other side of the lot, which brought a good gut guffaw from Lip. Tiny just stood watching the whole thing unfold without saying a word.

As Uncle Bill stirred the fire, he thought back about how he and Montana had first met, and how he'd changed since way back then. As he rearranged burning logs in the pit, he remembered the good times when they were both blowing in the wind; and one time in particular when they were witness to a million migrating tarantulas crossing Highway 10 in southern Texas. It was a long, *long* time ago.

*****

Matt stepped into the garage and closed the door. He'd been taught that indecision and hesitation could be deadly; however, the degree of the immediate threat and the ramifications of actions taken had to be calculated before action could be taken. Is there a real and imminent threat or is it just angry posturing, for example. This sort of analysis is a learned talent for most; for people like Brent, however, it was inherent. When facing down Montana, Matt had calculated the ramifications of his actions and had decided that it was not the time or the place to battle.

He went to the window behind the urinal and looked across the yard to where his uncle was talking to Montana. And after Uncle Bill turned and walked away, Montana leaned towards the Middle Eastern cowboy who then turned and looked towards Matt, and laughed. You fucking jihadist asshole, thought Matt, you don't fool me for a second.

Still on edge, but feeling better, Matt left the garage and headed for the cooler for another beer. After shaking off the ice water and popping the top, he went to the empty relaxer and plunked himself down, lifted one leg over the arm and took a long pull off his beer. His Hawaiian shirt was unbuttoned, exposing his .45. He took a deep breath and exhaled.

"Having a good time?" he asked Tiny who was sitting in the relaxer next to him.

"Always have a good time on the 4th," he said. "It's un-American not to.

"Sure the fuck is," said Matt, leaning forward to click beers with Tiny who was strong as an ox but mellow as a baby kitten; unless pushed. A few years back, Matt saw him grab two of his biker brothers and slam their heads together, just like on TV. Afterwards, Tiny stepped back and brushed his hands together as if brushing off dirt, and said, "That's the end of that shit." It was really funny. Not to the two leather clad drunks who were lying on the ground rubbing their noggins, but everyone else got quite a good laugh out of it.

"Looks like Montana and company are gearing up to head out," he said to his Uncle, who was putting a metal grate on top of the cinder blocks he'd arranged around the pit.

"I told them it would be best if they left," said Uncle Bill. Matt pondered for a moment and took a swig of beer.

"I can take care of myself, Uncle Bill. I don't need a baby sitter anymore," he said, tight jawed.

"Didn't have a lot to do with you Matt," his uncle said, which was partly true. "I went over when I noticed a problem, sure, but it was Montana and his group of dickheads that got themselves evicted. Number one—none of those boys and girls were invited, and Montana knows the rules. We can't have people around we don't know if we want to have a good time with family. Right?"

"True," sighed Matt.

"I was going to tell you about Moalim and the others when you got here, but before I had the chance, you spotted Montana and took off," he said, straightening the grate. "And besides, I wanted to check them out to see if anything odd was going on." Matt wanted to say something about the Cave Junction thing, but held back because he didn't want to let on that he'd been eavesdropping. It wasn't the right time.

"Well just the same, Uncle Bill, I can take care of myself," he said again, taking a swig of his beer. "I can't believe the nerve of Montana bringing that fucking asshole to the party," he said, staring in the direction of the cowboys who were now heading off towards their trucks. Fucking *rag head* he almost said, but at the last moment changed it to asshole, as he remembered a conversation he'd had with his uncle a few weeks back that had turned ugly when he'd casually referred to Arabs as *rag heads*.

"Why do you call them that?" Uncle Bill had asked him.

"What's the big deal," Matt said defensively. "Brent calls them diaper heads, for Christ's sake."

"You-are-not-Brent," his uncle had said sharply, emphasizing each word. He then began to lecture Matt on why people should not be judged by the color of their skin or their culture, or how they dress. Matt had heard it all before and became agitated with his uncle's didacticism. "Have some damn respect."

"I'm not a kid anymore, Uncle Bill, and I don't need another damn lecture on political correctness. I thought we had the same ideas about those Islamic jihadists' bastards," he'd said to his uncle. "We both know exactly where their loyalties lie—they want us all dead!"

When Matt was younger, he wouldn't have considered taking such a boisterous stand about anything, but he was damn near thirty, had his own place, and made his own money—he was an adult, for Christ's sake. "I don't need a fucking lecture, and I don't give a damn about what they say in the media about how all they want is a better life! Every damn one of them is loyal to the ideology of jihad! They are being allowed to rewrite our history, change our culture, and undermine our religion! We aren't even allowed to learn about American Heritage in school anymore because it's offensive to Islam! Damn, Uncle Bill, I even heard that *The Three Little Pigs* has been renamed *The Three Little Carpenters* in order to not offend Islam!" Matt had been screaming and remembered the exact instant it all turned ugly. Uncle Bill had jumped up from his chair so fast, and had come at him so quickly, that Matt had actually thought his uncle was going to punch him in the face.

"Shut the fuck up, and listen to what I'm saying," he'd ordered, stepping right up in front of Matt and jabbing him in the chest with his rock hard index finger. "You've been way over the line for the past few months, and it's affecting, not just you, but everyone around you. And quite frankly, Matt, you've turned into someone no one wants to be around. Not Abby, Eric, Brent, even me," he said so close to Matt's face that Matt could feel the heat from his uncle's breath. "It's no fun to be around someone that's always pissed off. Moaning and complaining like some celibate housewife—and your language of late is worse than gutter language. Fuck this, fuck that, fucking assholes, rag heads, bastards, mother-fuckers!"

It was at that point in the lecture that Matt had quit listening. He didn't move. And although he gave the appearance that he was listening, his mind had rolled on down the tracks a hundred miles away.

Uncle Bill did not move away, and his voice did not soften. "We are all aware of what's going on in the world today, but going off half-cocked is only going to get you into a whole lot of deep shit," his uncle had said. "You hear what I'm saying?" he demanded, leaning even closer to where they were almost touching noses. "Calm down, for Christ's sake," he said not waiting for an answer. "We are not at war with every single person who isn't white or American or Christian. Shit, Matt," he said stepping back and lowering his voice. "You act like you're about ready to start shooting people." Matt stood stone still listening to an *Uncle Bill Lecture*, something he'd not had to endure for a very long time.

Matt wanted to strike out at his uncle for not seeing the world as he saw it, and instantly flushed red. Matt knew how much bigger he was than his uncle and for a brief moment he had considered physical confrontation. *And that thought* is why the memory had remained so clear in his mind. He had actually considered striking out at the person who had saved his life; the man who had sacrificed his own freedom to give him a home, an education, a career. He felt sick at his tyranny, but his stance against what was right and what was wrong in the world had not changed, and al-Qaeda, whatever their façade, was the enemy, and of that conviction, Matt was unwavering.

The lecture had ended as abruptly as it had started. There was no manly hug, no handshake, no agreement, and although the work day was not over, they both went their separate ways. The next day at work, the subject of politics, the state of the union, crime, and the like was avoided like a downpour in April. Conversation, what little of it there was, was cordial and strictly business.

As he sat in the lounge chair thinking about that blowout a few weeks past he pondered on what his uncle had told him. Maybe he was right about people avoiding him and not wanting to be around him, and maybe he *was* acting like a jerk, like Abby says. Maybe my language is abusive, and it's true that I am indeed wound tighter than a double overhand knot; and maybe I am consumed with hate; but it is well directed hate, he concluded with an arrogant nod of his head and an twisted smirk.

He sat up on the edge of the chair, took another deep breath and let his arms dangle and his shoulders slump, there's good reason for the way I feel, and that's just the way it is. Those bastards will not take my country without a fight, he confirmed to his reflection in the top of his beer can.

"I'm off to get another beer," said Tiny, placing both of his giant hands on the arms of the relaxer for leverage and pushing himself to a standing position. "Want one?"

"Yeah. Sure. Thanks. Actually, bro, bring me two," Matt said, smiling up at Tiny.

"Good idea," said Tiny, nodding his fat, sweaty head which reminded Matt of a 'Bubble Head.' "I'll take two, too," he said, walking off.

As Tiny disappeared around the corner of the house, Matt began thinking about his language and decided that maybe he would try to clean it up. No promises and no guarantees. Smarter, less hyper, and less spontaneous might be wise. He felt good, again.

"Here's your beers, bro" said Tiny, handing two cold ones to Matt. "I'm off to harass some cowboys," he said smiling. "Guess it won't be Montana and that gang, though, looks like they've rolled up their gear and hit the trail." He waited a long silent minute before walking off towards a group of cowboys he recognized as, good-old-boys, from past events.

*****

Abby strolled casually towards the group of outlaw women on the other side of the yard. Everyone looked pretty darn happy, eating, drinking, laughing, and carrying on with nothing on their minds but partying and having a good time. The women postured with attitude, sexy pin-up-girls, and the men were ruggedly handsome. The 4th of July party was an excuse to dress-up, and all the women took special care to look as provocative as they possibly could, and it was no different for Abby.

This morning she had taken extra care primping for the *skin-dig*, an epithet from the first years when a bunch of the biker chicks shed their tops in the hot afternoon sun. Abby thought about it a few times, but she is just too shy.

Her *girls* are all hers and ample enough to create a darn nice eye-catching cleavage. She hasn't had children and gravity has not yet taken its toll. Today, for the first time, she is braless with nothing more to cover her twins than a thin white tank-top that leaves very little to the imagination. *What the heck, and Matt being an ass*, had been her rationale. Her blond hair contrasts nicely against her dark summer tan, and the large silver loop earrings, a present from Uncle Bill, dangle just above her shoulders and are the perfect accessories. Her shorts are not exactly camel-toe tight, but damn close.

This morning when she'd met Matt to go shopping, he hadn't said a word about how she looked. She hadn't really expected he would after the altercation the day before, but still, "you're looking good little momma,"

51

something he used to say often, may have eased the tension. She shook her head, tossing Matt from her mind.

She looked around for Eric and saw him standing with Rose and a group of girls whom she recognized. She spotted Matt who was still sitting up by the pit. She flashed on the conversation she would have with Uncle Bill when the time was right about Matt flipping out on the lady in black earlier that day. Dang! she thought, maybe I better try something stronger than Root Beer. Maybe a shooter or two of tequila will get my mind off Matt and his issues.

She continued to walk towards the small gang of women who surrounded Eric. She liked them all, except for Rose, a rumored nymphomaniac, who was always rubbing herself up against any man within reach. Today she had glommed onto Eric who was enjoying every bit of the attention he was getting from her.

She'd met Eric at the university, and at the end of the first semester he'd worked up enough courage to ask her out, but by then she had already hooked up with Matt. They shared a business class the second semester and developed a brother/sister relationship and often get together for lunch and to study. It was no big deal, and it didn't bother Matt in the least. After all, Eric was a computer geek and nothing more than a study buddy; he was not a threat. And for reasons that God only knows, Eric and Matt, different as night and day, had become good friends.

A few days ago, Eric had called Abby to tell her that he'd been invited to the 4th of July party by Uncle Bill for a job he'd done for Brent. Abby was surprised and then delighted as Eric outlined the events that led to the invitation. He had been as nervous as a high school graduate getting ready for the prom and as excited as a kid on his way to Disneyland.

One of the boys, now, she thought laughing to herself, as she approached the pack of erogenous women. Eric was dressed in jeans, slip-on deck shoes with no socks, and a pull-over shirt with a collar with a little alligator stitched over the upper left chest pocket. I guess nobody told him how to dress, she thought, smiling a huge smile and shaking her head at how out of place he looked, which reminded her of her first 4th of July party four years ago when Matt had joked about the hierarchy of men over women.

"Yep, men are men and women are women in this here world, darlin', and that's the way we like it. No mam, no room for women libbers in this here world," he said, winking at her. "Nope. None at all." Back then, Matt was a fun and exciting person to be around; weekend motorcycle trips, camping, car shows.

Abby scrutinized, for a moment, the pack of women dressed in leather mini-skirts, tight shorts, and halter tops, and wondered if any of them had regular jobs or children. She didn't know much about any of them, or any of the men, for that matter, though she couldn't imagine an imposter or a bad seed among them. She'd heard rumors, though, of a few miscreants who'd been taken to *the woods where even the bears get lost*, never to be seen or heard from again.

She was an outsider, and she knew it. Maybe I should make more of an effort? Invite a few of them over for lunch or tea. *Tea*, she thought, and chuckled aloud, embarrassing herself as a cowboy whom she recognized as Slim, a real honest to goodness cowboy from Arizona, who rode in rodeos for fun, walked straight towards her, causing her to stop in mid stride. He side-stepped her in what looked like a country western dance step and ducked under the branches of an apple tree, tipping his hat.

"Howdy, Abby; you're looking mighty fine today, mam."

"Howdy, right back at ya, Slim." He didn't stop to talk, but Abby was certain he'd made the effort to walk close enough to check her out. *Howdy* was just an excuse, and it made her glow. She noticed that he looked more bow-legged than the year before.

*****

As Abby closed in on the gang of scantily clad, half-naked girls, she felt a twinge of jealousy at the attention being showered on Eric by Rose. Rose was hugging Eric's upper arm between her breasts, half hiding it in her ample cleavage, forcing his hand to dangle just a touch away from her crotch. From the smile on his face, he was obviously enjoying himself very much, even though he was quite out of his element. Just like *my* first time here.

Four years ago, she had been a regular girl from a good middle class family, but since she'd started hanging with Matt, she had changed. She came to realize that there was another way of living besides getting married, having babies, and attending neighborhood Tupperware parties. Camping, music, motorcycle rallies, car races, spontaneous outings, and trips to here and there, none of which could be done easily with curtain-climbers in tow. She now preferred the James Dean, living on the edge, type of man. She liked scootin' around on the back of Matt's Harley Davidson Road King and going to car shows in his truck. She liked shooting guns and was even thinking about going hunting. Still, she never really felt like she fit in, maybe because she started this way of life late in the game, whereas a lot of these folks are second generation and have been at it all their lives.

Her thoughts returned to the lady in black and how lucky she was that the whole confrontation stayed verbal, because Matt was ready to blow. What used to be just hateful feelings had recently turned into hateful words, and his hateful words are now on the verge of turning into hateful actions. Heck, he could explode today, she thought, wondering what had happened to make Montana and his buddies leave. *Enough, already!* It was time to say hello to the tramps that had been eye-balling her from the other side of the yard.

*****

53

As Abby walked up to gang of outlaw girlfriends, she thought again about how absurd it was to think that any of them might want to come to her house for tea, and it was this thought that caused a huge Cheshire cat grin to appear on her face. Lotus, a good looking black girl who was chunky in all the right places, had been watching her for the past five minutes.

"What's so damn funny, Blondie?"

"I was just wondering if any of y'all wanted to come over to my place for tea sometime," she said, laughing, "And it struck me as funny, because y'all don't look like tea drinkers to me, that's all," she said, using her best southern drawl.

"Well just what do we look like to you, girlfriend," Lotus asked, hand on hip, "hoes?"

"Well," replied Abby, "now that you mention it—but good looking hoes," Abby said straight faced. They all burst into loud laughter, which drew stares from the guys and the first, "show us your tits," call-out of the day, which the girls ignored. Abby had figured it out long ago that flippin' shit, as they called it, came with the territory.

"How about trading in that kiddies drink for a beer, girlfriend," said Lotus as soon as she quit laughing.

"Root Beer?" said one the girls, wrinkling her nose.

"I've been thinking something a bit stronger is due." She knew from past experience that this gang of wenches would have one or two bottles, at least, stashed close by. She also figured she had better loosen up before she became a character in a story at next year's party. Maybe I should get a tattoo, she thought, admiring some of the art work on display.

"Name it girl, we got Jack and Tequila.

"Tequila!" declared Abby, shoving her fist in the air.

"Right here, girlfriend," said Lotus, reaching behind her and lifting a bottle of Hornitos, 100% Pure De Agave tequila from the table, unscrewing the cap and taking a big swing. "Rock and Roll Forever!" she hollered, and handed the bottle to Abby who grabbed it robustly and gulped down an enormous swallow, which immediately produced a devil-may-care attitude.

"You got it, girlfriend," Abby said, holding the bottle out towards Eric. "Rock and Roll, Forever!" she hollered.

"Hey Eric, she said, ignoring Rose. "Looks like you're having a good time, *boyfriend*," she said, deliberately pushing buttons.

"What?" snorted Rose; "one man ain't enough for you? You got to hit on this boy, too?" she said, pulling Eric even closer.

"Cat fight, cat fight", said one of the girls, muting the words with her fist. Eric, sporting a huge asinine grin, leaned silently into the cushiony softness of Rose's chest.

"Unlike some," replied Abby, still holding the bottle out to Eric, "one man at a time is my motto, and Matt does just fine." What a crock, she instantly thought. But before Rose had a chance to respond, she added, "I was just saying, Rose, that my friend Eric, here, looks like he's having a good time, that's all. No problem."

"Yeah? Well. We *are*, darlin'," said Rose, squeezing Eric's arm tighter to her boobs, forcing his hand to brush against the hem of her turquoise skirt. Abby thought, yep, I am definitely smarter than some.

Eric, having a beer in one hand, had to pull loose from Rose to get the bottle of tequila that Abby was shoving at him, and when he did, Abby gave Rose a quick mocking grin.

"You better watch your step, girl," said Rose, glaring at Abby.

"Cat fight, cat fight," repeated the girl who'd said it before. Abby just smiled. She felt tough enough right then to kick the shit out of three Rose's.

"Say when," she said, glaring back at Rose, realizing that it was the first time in her life she ever tried to start a fight.

"You just better watch it, that's all," repeated Rose, grabbing the bottle from Eric who was on his way to na-na land. Rose took a big swig and handed it to the tall Amazon standing next to her, who was staring down at Abby. The older woman, who looked like she'd been rode hard and put away wet, took a giant swig from the now half empty bottle and shoved it back at Abby.

"Drink up," she said in a challenging way. Abby waited, staring at her and her outstretched hand. Silence ensued. "Here," she said again. "You're the one who ordered this. Have another hit, bitch," she said, waiting for Abby to take the bottle. Abby knew it was common for the girls to call each other *bitch* in good humor, but this was clearly not humor, and although she was feeling omnipotent, the Amazon was way out of her league. She would probably give Tiny a run for his money, so Abby chose wisely to ignore the slander, hoping it would not make her look like a coward. She remembered Matt telling her that a bottle could be used as a weapon, so she grabbed the bottle with a side-swipe motion and tipped it to her lips in a quick smooth ballet.

"Thanks," she said, handing the bottle back to Lotus.

"Hey Abby," Eric slurred, "where you been? Have you met these fine ladies?" he said, stumbling a bit before Rose could steady him.

"We've all met," said Rose, grabbing his arm and leading him away. "Let's go say hi to the urinal," she said, talking baby talk as she led him off towards the garage.

"You be careful now Eric," Abby called after them.

"Don't you worry your pretty little bleach-blond head about Eric, sweetie. I will be taking real good care of him today *and* tonight." She put an emphasis on *tonight* that induced ooohs and aahs from them all.

"Looks like Eric has the next 24 all planned out for him. Nothing to do but follow Rosy," Lotus said, bumping Abby with her lusty hip and smiling. "You aren't jealous are you girl?"

"Not hardly," she said, looking up at Rose's amazon friend.

"Could it be true that you need two men to satisfy your white-girl lust, like Rose says? Who's the hoe, now, bitch," she said, drawing more laughter from the girls.

"Two?" retorted Abby, scowling her eyes together. "Two?" she said looking at Lotus, "Two? Hell, I could handle twenty boys his size. Men, darlin'; I need men, not boys. Men like Brent Chandler," she'd said before she could stop her tequila soaked brain from yakking shit.

"Uh-oh," said Lotus, "trouble in the love nest?" she said, referring to Matt. Abby was feeling no pain but was still conscious enough to wish she hadn't mentioned Brent.

"I was just saying that Brent is a hunk, that's all. And you don't need to go yakking your mouth about girl-talk—y'all."

"Hell, girl, my lips are sealed," said Lotus, dragging her fingers across her lips like she was zipping them closed. "Hell yes, you can trust me," she said, winking at the girlfriends.

*****

It was after 9 p.m. and the party was in full swing. The summer sky was not quite dark; no stars, no moon. Smoke from the cooking pit floated on a gentle evening breeze, reminding Abby of home.

She spotted Uncle Bill across the yard by the garage talking to Brent and decided it would be a good time to bend his ear. By the time she wove her way to where they were standing, Eric had joined them, still quite wobbly, but drinking Sprite. Rose was nowhere in sight, which was good. Eric appeared small in stature compared to Uncle Bill and Brent, as they stood in front of him, telling him a secret. She stepped close enough to hear what they were saying, and waited for an opportunity to interrupt.

"She's my neighbor," said Uncle Bill, obviously feeling no pain and in good spirits, "has been since I moved here. She's a nice girl, Eric, but she's pretty liberal with her favors, if you know what I mean," he said, grinning mischievously at Brent, who was snickering. Eric wobbled, and tried to focus. "She's been around the block, so to speak. Never kicked her boots off with me, though," continued Uncle Bill, suddenly serious as a preacher. "No sir," he added, shaking his hands back and forth in the stop position. Brent rubbed his mouth to keep from laughing.

"Yeah, me neither," Brent finally said, busting out laughing.

Eric took a swig of his Sprite, tilted his head, and shifted his weight from his left foot to his right foot and crunched his eyebrows together.

"She hangs mostly with the bikers," continued Uncle Bill with his lesson in love. "Being a loose woman, Eric," Uncle Bill said, now laughing, "she's not really wife material or steady girlfriend material, for that matter, but she's a damn good woman—and, Eric, she's a friend of the family, so treat her right," he said bending over, holding his stomach.

"And one more thing…."

"How dare you infer that my betrothed is a whore," slurred Eric.

"A damn good whore, though, said Brent, throwing his head back and guffawing loudly. "And who says a whore don't make a good girlfriend," he added, leaning into his buddy and giving him a shove with his shoulder. "I agree about them not making a good wife, but what woman does?" he added, still laughing. "As soon as you tie the knot they tie a knot around your balls and try to change you into something you ain't. Stay a bachelor, Eric. Love 'em and leave 'em wasn't coined by some dummy, and that's a fact."

Earlier, Abby had happened upon a very drunk Eric and Rose stumbling through the gate from Rose's place. Abby figured they were also emerging from Rose's boudoir. They were holding each other up, professing their love, like love-sick teenagers, to anyone who would listen. It was pathetic.

"I don't care what you assholes think," said Eric. "I love her, and I'm warning you, keep your distance, knaves." He was bending slightly and shaking his finger at them.

"Eric, we told Rose to make sure you had a good time tonight," said Uncle Bill, smacking Brent in the chest with the back of his hand. "You're not supposed to fall in love with a girl of the night, Eric. They're…."

"Shut your filthy mouths, scoundrels. I will here no more of this treachery," said Eric, hoisting his Sprite into the air like a pirate's sword.

Abby, after hearing the conspiracy behind the coupling of Rose and Eric, wasn't sure if it was funny or appalling, but they were so animated, so drunk, so hilarious that she concluded, with a chuckle, that the whole thing was really funny.

She felt bad about interrupting them, but what Brent had just said about women tying a knot around men's balls, and his outlook on marriage, and the rest, caused the aura around her idyllic man to fade just a bit. She imagined the three of them walking around the yard together, arm's slung over each other's shoulders, staggering here and there, spilling beer, and yakking shit. Not!

"Hi, guys," she said, stepping up. "I've been waiting to get you alone" she said, looking at Brent but talking to Uncle Bill. As soon as the words spewed from her mouth, she realized that she too, was a few shades into the wind. "What I mean is," she said, not making excuses for her blunder, and with a seriousness that required attention, "I need to talk to you about Matt," she said turning to Uncle Bill.

She felt like a party crasher, as both Uncle Bill and Brent sobered up, wiped the grins from their faces, and stood a bit taller at hearing the concern in her voice. Eric had his arms crossed over his chest, still as a statue, the last of his Sprite spilling onto the ground.

After hearing the details about the lady in black, Uncle Bill and Brent looked at each other, simultaneously raised their eyebrows and shook their heads. She had definitely brought them down. Eric just stood there, head bowed as if in prayer. Maybe he'd passed out—standing up.

"He's heading in a bad direction with a loaded gun," said Uncle Bill."

"Yeah," acknowledged Brent, "but he does have some valid points about what's right and what's wrong in this fucked up world. But you're right, both of you, he's looking for trouble in all the right places, and sooner or later he's going to find it. Do you want me to talk to him?" asked Brent.

"You know," said Uncle Bill. "I've been thinking about just that. I've had a go at him more than once, maybe it's time he hears it from someone else." He was nodding his head, agreeing with himself. "Yeah, would you do that, bro? Say what you need say to set him straight because he sure as shit ain't listening to me."

"You got it, Bro. I'll be all over him like...," he looked at Abby and said, "ants on honey," instead of his usual, *stink on shit*.

"Good," said Abby, "he is very close to losing it, and I don't feel comfortable around him—I *can't* be around him, in fact" she added. "Today was the last straw," she added, softly.

*****

Eric's brain had drifted off to someplace more exciting, and he was not paying any attention.

"Seems like he's obsessed with people from the Middle East these past few weeks," said Abby. "He thinks they're all terrorists; doesn't matter where they are from, they are all terrorists." Uncle Bill and Brent looked at each other but didn't say anything. Abby had heard some of the details about the incident between Montana and Matt earlier and figured they were all on the same page, expect for Eric, who was still not paying attention. "Eric! Get your head on straight, and I don't mean the one in your pants," she scolded. "We are talking about your friend here. He needs help, for crying out loud. He thinks the United States is about to fall to terrorists or some such crap!"

Eric turned to face Abby. His look of surprise quickly turned into a Cheshire cat grin that said a thousand words.

"I think I better go talk to him," he slurred.

"No don't!" said Uncle Bill and Brent in unison. Abby squeezed her lips together in a straight line and shook her head.

"We will take care of it," said Uncle Bill. "What you need to do is to watch out for him when you guys are out and about. Brent is going to talk to him real soon; until then, we all need to watch out for him. Any sign of trouble, call me immediately. Like Abby says, no telling what he might do if he's pushed." Abby remembered Eric telling her about the trip to Brent's and was about to bring it up when Eric started in.

"Actually," he slurred, "he scared the heck out of me last week on the way out to your place, Brent." He was looking at Brent, trying to be sober. "He stuck his gun out the window at some Mexicans who cut us off; scared the heck out of me. I really haven't seen him since, actually. Don't need that kind of shit."

"Why didn't you tell me?" demanded Brent. "You should have said something." Uncle Bill's eyebrows shot up. "After all the dust settles, friends stand by friends and when they are in trouble, they interfere, one way or another," lectured Brent, rather loudly, which seemed to sober Eric up just a little, forcing him to step back a step.

"Dude, I did say something to him," he said, timidly, "and I didn't even know you back then. And besides, like you all said, Matt's been on edge for more than just a few weeks," he said, in his own defense, seemingly more sober. "And besides that, as long as I've known him, he's been very opinionated about what's right and what's wrong. I figured he was just having a bad day. I told him never to do it again, guys," and looking at Abby added, "and gals or should I say gal? Or girl? Or wooomaaan?" he said, staring down at her cleavage and sporting a sloppy grin.

"Good god," said Abby, "he's been here ten hours and he's already turned into some kind of an outlaw clone." It was funny, but the way she'd said it was serious, so Uncle Bill and Brent restrained from laughing—just barely.

"Oh boy," said Uncle Bill, finally. "Thanks for telling us. And Eric," he said, gripping his shoulder hard enough to make him wince and turn to look into Uncle Bill's eyes. "Let us know immediately if he does anything at all that you figure is too out of line. You have a good sense about that, right?" he said, not wanting to sound condescending but wanting to be clear as water. "I mean, if it ain't by the book, *your* book, let us know. Do you understand what I'm saying, Eric?"

"Yes sir," he said. "Sure. Okay. I'll keep an eye on him," he said, rotating his shoulder after being released from Uncle Bill's vice-grip. "Where is he now, in fact? I haven't had any chance to chat with him all night. I need to tell him about my true love Rose," he said, raising his eyebrows and backing away; a renewed silly-ass Cheshire cat grin plastered to his face. Uncle Bill knew it didn't really matter if Eric mentioned this little palaver. The sooner Matt got the word that the posse was on his trail the better.

*****

Before Eric had backed three steps away, a biker chick smashed through the crowd, knocking them both to the ground.

"Kick some ass, Cindy! You can do it, girl," came a voice from the crowd. Abby, thought somebody was starting a fight with Eric, but when Lotus jumped into the fray and started pummeling the biker chick, she quickly realized that Eric was just a victim.

Lotus grabbed Cindy's hair, punched her in the mouth and then grabbed her halter top and yanked it down to the girl's waist, exposing her breasts to the crowd of cheering onlookers.

"Cat fight," yelled someone, as the circle of crazed onlookers multiplied. Eric had somehow scrambled out of the way and had regained his upright position and was yelling and cheering right along with everyone else. Abby heard one guy yell, "get her Lotus, come on Cindy, rip her top off." *Boys*, thought Abby.

Uncle Bill let the rumble take its course for a few minutes before stepping in; after all, everyone likes a good cat fight; even more than a wet t-shirt contest. As soon as it became apparent the Cindy was no match for Lotus, he grabbed Lotus by the hair and started pulling her off the biker chick, but not before Lotus had a chance to smack Cindy one more time on the side of the head, eliciting more cheers.

As Uncle Bill pulled Lotus back, the biker chick reached up and grabbed hold of Lotus's blouse, and ripped it clean off her back, exposing two black, mammoth boobs, which gave Lotus the renewed adrenaline to pull free from Uncle Bill and attack Cindy again. Uncle Bill lunged and tackled the fighting feline, and rolled her to the ground, coming to a halt in a perfect missionary position.

Brent grabbed Cindy by wrapping his arms around her, not really caring what he grabbed hold of, which just happened to be her tits. Although he was just trying to help stop the fight from escalating, the biker chick's old man, Snake, didn't see it that way.

"Hey, let go of my old lady's tits, you shit head," he yelled jumping into action.

He came up behind Brent and punched him in the side, forcing him to let go of Cindy who immediately tore into Lotus, who was trying to wrestle loose from Uncle Bill. Uncle Bill was now laughing so hard that he had to let go, and just as the two girls got hold of each other again, Matt stepped in to help pull them apart, and as if on cue, the back yard came alive with flying fists, kicks, beer baths, yahoos, grunts, groans, and the brawl was on.

It was the warriors who finally broke it up, but not before some noses and ribs got bruised and busted. The whole battle had not lasted more than ten minutes, but it seemed to Eric and Abby, who had backed well out of the away, like it had lasted a whole lot longer. As the scrappers were pulled apart, coarse words ripped through the darkness of night.

"Fucking bitch ripped my top," yelled someone from the crowd.

"Asshole cowboy bit me," someone else yelled.

"Scooter – trash - fucker kicked me in the balls," yelled another.

"Fucking skin heads…."

It was Rose who stepped up with two bottles of unopened booze. One bottle of Jack and one bottle of tequila.

"Here, everyone needs a good snort or two after a good fist fight. Shake hands, now. Kiss and make-up," she said gaily, pushing her chest out and pulling her chin in. Abby flinched, thinking someone was surely going to pop her in the mouth. Instead, her little performance, as mother to them all, had quite the opposite effect. The bottles of liquor were taken and passed around, bloody handshakes were exchanged, bloody heads were nodded, but Abby did not hear any apologies, nor did she see anybody kiss and make-up. The crowd applauded when Lotus and Cindy, tits still a-floppin', hugged. "Lesbo action," someone yelled, and the party was back in full swing, and Abby had new respect for Rose.

*****

At three in the morning, most of the rowdy bunch had crashed or had passed out in sleeping bags, tents, and lean-tos that had been set up in all corners of the yard, under tables, next to trees, and against the fence. The music had been turned down so low it could only be heard if you were standing next to a speaker, and voices were soft, slurred, and groggy.

The 4th of July party was winding down. But in the farthest corner of the lot, the *newbies* and the *young-bloods* partied on, laughing and passing around a bottle and a twisty.

Abby was not interested in sex, but Matt had intentions. In the basement bedroom of Uncle Bill's, she breathed a sigh of relief when he'd passed out as soon as his head hit the pillow. He wasn't much of a drinker, and tonight he had had a few too many.

She lay awake wondering what Brent was doing. She thought briefly about Eric and remembered seeing him being led through the gate that separated Uncle Bill's house from Rose's house next door. Friggin' kids was her last thought until the smell of bacon frying on the fire-pit outside her window drifted into her room and woke her. It was Sunday morning, July 5th.

*****

A few of the nomads were drinking hair-of-the-dog, but most were just laying around listlessly drinking tankards of hot, black coffee, hoping it would clear their heads and praying that it would ease the pain. The men, with mussed hair and wrinkled clothes, looked old and worn, and the women looked just as bad. Matt was right about how everything looks better at night, and it reminded her of the old cowboy song about how *the women all get prettier at closing time, they all begin to look like movie stars.*

Towards noon, the men began exchanging handshakes and hugging the women. Women were hugging women and promising to keep in touch, and then it was on down that long lonesome highway, as the worn out gang of outlaws slowly moved on to points unknown with promises of meeting again, same time, same place, next year. Everyone, as if on cue, left around the same time, leaving quite a mess for Uncle Bill to clean up.

"It's the price you pay for having the luxury of our company," said Tiny, as he fired up his Harley. "I'll see you at your place," he hollered to Brent, as he and Lip pulled out onto the dirt road leading away from Uncle Bill's.

Matt and Abby left Brent and Uncle Bill sitting in the lounge chairs and headed for home around one. They were helping with the clean-up, but Uncle Bill said, with a warm, fatherly smile. "I will do it, and I will enjoy it, so get the fuck out of my yard, will ya?" He watched as his nephew climbed into the cab of his truck, and when Matt closed the door, his uncle walked up to the door and said through the open window, "Let's make it a four day weekend. Take tomorrow off. Stay home and rest up. What do you think? Sound good?"

"Sounds great if I'm getting paid," said Matt, smiling.

"No work no pay," replied his uncle. "You know the drill, a day off is the pay. You in?"

"Damn straight," replied Matt. "Sounds good."

"I have some errands to run, and I'll be in your neighborhood," said his uncle. "How about I drop in around 10 for a cup of java?"

"Yeah. Sure," Matt said, reaching for the ignition. "I'll be there."

Matt and Abby went their separate ways when they arrived back at the apartments; each to the sanctuary of their own space. Abby told Matt that she needed to get ready for work the next day and needed time to wind down. Matt didn't argue. He needed some downtime, too.

*****

Matt set the cooler on the table, got a Sprite from the fridge, sat down on the couch, and switched on the tube. He'd had a good time at the party, hanging mostly with the warriors who were all super conservative survivalists who believed like he did, in God, country, apple pie, and, *buy more bullets.*

His last thought before falling asleep was a proclamation made by Prof, a biker with a Ph.D. in political science who had bailed from the system when he'd had all he could take of the politically correct format that had engulfed the world of academia, like the Asian flu. "Be prepared," he'd slurred, "because in the end, Herbert Spencer's ubiquitous phrase, *Survival of the Fittest,* will become the battle cry for every man, woman, and child—good, bad, and otherwise. *So sinister and so devastating will the future be, that it will invoke Darwin's Theory of Natural Selection."* Matt smiled and fell fast asleep.

*****

After everyone, including Brent, had gone their separate ways, Uncle Bill sat in the silence of his back yard and pondered another year gone by, another good party, and another year closer to becoming worm bait. Matt and his issues briefly flashed into his mind, and he hoped that Brent could get through to him.

Menacing gray clouds from the west moved ever closer, encroaching on the canopy of the blue skies of twilight; looks like rain, he thought, as he fell asleep in the old, dirty, and stained lounge chair.

*****

When Montana and his gang left the party, they drove back to the safe house where Moalim gathered them all together in the living room. He stood in front of the gang of clueless revolutionaries and gave them their final instructions.

"You have all been briefed, and you all know what to do and when to do it," he started. "You have everything you need; sticks of dynamite, bags of dynamite wired together, and six car bombs capable of taking out bridges, highways, and electrical grids. The revolution is close at hand," he shouted to a loud and excited crowd.

Montana had not heard jihad referred to as a revolution before, and wondered if this naïve band of terrorists knew the true cause that they were about to fight and die for. His suspicion was soon put to rest.

"Your country will soon be back into the hands of the people!" he jeered, shoving a fist into the air. Applause and fist banging once again rocked the room.

"After you have destroyed your targets, find a place to hole-up and wait for my call. If you are successful, I will tell you where thousands like you are going congregate to vote on a new form of government. You will hear from me within two hours of our marked time. Remember, comrades, there are thousands just like you, doing exactly what you are doing, at exactly the same time, so do exactly as we have planned. Follow the design without compromise. Let nothing stand in the way of the revolution," he hollered, this time jamming both fists into the air. "Viva, viva, viva the revolution," he hollered.

"Viva, viva, viva the revolution," they chanted, probably not even knowing where the well-known war chant had originated.

This is so bizarre thought Montana, nodding his head to the chant. Moalim is the Charles Manson of this misguided band of youngsters, and they are blindly following him into what they believe to be a revolution to take back their country from greedy politicians and an overspending government. They don't have a clue! There isn't a place to congregate after wards; there will be no phone calls, he knew. These people were nothing more than pawns—disposable pawns, at that. It's insane and ingenious at the same time, he thought, thrusting his hand into the air, joining the chant. Moalim looked over at him and smiled. They were on the same page.

"We have a big day tomorrow," Moalim said, after they'd settled down. "We *all* have a part in this and we are *all* expected to carry out our tasks *on time* and without *any* mistakes. There can be no excuses. Each of us has a small mission, and the success of the revolution depends on each small mission being carried out to perfection."

Montana wondered if the "we" Moalim mentioned meant that he and Moalim had a mission, as well, or if Moalim was just using that as motivation. The more he thought about it, the bigger the plot became. There must be hundreds of Moalim/Manson generals around the country. How many had he brought across the border, he wondered.

"Get some rest, my friends. Tomorrow is going to be a very busy day. Viva, viva, viva the revolution," he chanted one more time.

As Montana and Moalim left the house, the chant grew ever louder— *viva, viva, viva....*

*****

That night at the hotel, Moalim told Montana about *their* part.

"In the morning, we are going to meet with Sahib, you remember him? He used to be my body guard."

"Yes, I remember him. What ever happened to him? All of a sudden he just disappeared."

"He has been training recruits in Portland—a different kind of recruit; suicide bombers, you call them. There are some targets that require a one way ride, and Sahib will be one of those drivers. He has chosen to be with Allah on the day of the beginning of jihad against the United States."

"Allah be with him," was all Montana could think to say, not knowing if it was proper or not.

"Thank you, Montana. That was very kind," he said, taking a drink of water. "We will be driving a car loaded with explosives and a very short timing device, which I will leave on the ramp to the 520 floating bridge. You will follow and pick me up. We will then meet with Ali, Abdul, and another man who will have another car bomb for us to park on the on-ramp to Interstate 90 on our way out of Seattle."

"What's going to happen to Sahib?"

"He will meet a comrade on the east side of the bridge. They have two more car bombs—the bridge will be destroyed." Damn. It's really going down, thought Montana, realizing again the reality of what he'd been a part of for ten years. "Those of us who will continue on to Cave Junction will meet south of Seattle, you, me, Ali, and Abdul Aziz. We have a well-guarded and very secure safe house, where we will stay and wait for damage reports. After the jihad has started, we will leave for Cave Junction. Do you have any questions, brother?"

It was the first time Moalim had ever called him brother, and it made Montana feel like he was really a part of something. He was in all the way and he felt good.

"What about the other car bombs and the dynamite packages you left with the cowboys. What are they going to be used for?" Montana had already figured out the answer to this, but he wanted confirmation.

"They and thousands more 'expendables' like them," he said, emphasizing expendables, "will deliver their packages to electrical power stations, power relay stations, major power lines, bridges, police stations, fire stations, railroad depots, truck depots, loading docks; anything that will hinder or stop the flow of traffic, electricity, and communication."

"What do you mean by expendables? You told them you were going to contact them and tell them where to meet?"

"You saw those idiots, Montana. Most of them were homeless and the rest have no ambition other than finding the money for another jug of wine or another crack fix. They will destroy their targets, and if they live, they will have to learn to survive. There are no free rides."

"But they are expecting...."

"They are expendable, Montana," he said raising his voice. If they die, they will be with Allah, Insha'Allah. Some must die for the greater cause; you must know that. They are soldiers sent into battle by commanders who know that most of them will die; Normandy, Iwo Jima, to name just a few of your own great victories. Do you see?"

"Of course," he said, nodding his head in agreement. "Of course, I see."

"Leadership is not for the weak hearted," Montana; you need to learn to think with your brain and not year heart; be more objective, if you will. Do you understand?"

"Of course I understand. I'm just wondering if I'm expendable, too."

Moalim let out a loud heinous laugh that rocked the seriousness of the discussion—it sounded devilish, unnatural, and far away.

"Everyone is expendable, even me," he said

"Well that's reassuring," said Montana, taking a deep breath through his nose. And like water rushing over a broken damn, all his insecurities flooded back into his mind, bringing back a weariness that made him tired.

"So, as I was saying, began Moalim, "there will be no way for supplies to get in or out of the Great Northwest, for example, and it will be the same with every major city in the country. No communications, other than cell phones, and those will soon become useless without electricity to charge them. Eventually, it will come down to survival; each man, woman, and child for themselves; it will be neighbor against neighbor, friend against friend, brother against brother—anarchy will be the call of the day, until someone offers a better way; and that, my friend will be us. Are you ready for all that is ahead, Montana? Are you ready to become part of a new system?

"I'm ready brother," he said, quickly extending his hand to Moalim.

"It's going to be a great victory, Insha'Allah," he said.

"Insha'Allah," Montana said, in reply, and Moalim smiled.

"We have a busy day tomorrow," said Moalim, as he walked towards the bathroom, leaving Montana alone at the table.

CHAPTER 5 – PART 2

Matt slept like a hibernating bear until 9:30 p.m. when suddenly he was yanked from the hands of the sandman by the pounding of his heart. *Don't move, don't panic, breathe deeply through your nose and exhale slowly through his mouth, regain your natural rhythm.*

His can of pop sat untouched on the coffee table and the TV was on the news channel. He rolled off the couch, picked up the warm can of Sprite, and slouched his way into the kitchen to put it back into the refrigerator. What the hell was that all about, he wondered.

He stepped up to the window for a look. Trees were bent and swaying in the raging wind; and dirt and dust and leaves churned and danced down the street in a doomsday ballet. Gray and black clouds broiled in the sky and the air had taken on a murky brown tint; a sure sign that a storm was imminent. He pulled the cord and closed the blinds as it started to rain. It was time, past time, to hit the rack.

By the time he'd finished showering and getting ready for an early night, it was fifteen minutes into the 10 o'clock news. The anchorwoman wore a mask of heavy make-up, and was talking about a stalled car on the 520 floating bridge.

> *...police and a tow truck are on route to clear the lanes; commuters should keep to the left and expect delays. Due to the weather, there is an unusual number of stalled cars around the Puget Sound area tonight, so slow down, turn up the radio, and drive safe.*

> *In other news, four armed men, illegally in this country, who were stopped from carrying out an attack at Fort Wright three weeks ago, will be in court tomorrow for bail hearings. They have all been assigned court-appointed attorneys....*

Why do we spend tax payer's money on trials for scum bags who are caught in the act, he pondered, rubbing his temples. If they are caught with their hand in the cookie jar, then they are guilty. Why not just execute the bastards, immediately, and be done with it—seems like a good deterrent to me. I wonder how many more of the fuckers are in this country. Lot's I'll bet. He thought about Montana and his new sidekick, Moalim, and wondered what country he was from, and if he was a terrorist.

He wondered how attorneys could live with their consciences and concluded that they didn't have a conscience. Maybe guilty verdicts should include attorneys. Maybe if the *alleged* is found guilty and sentenced to death, his attorney should be sentenced to death, as well. He'd concluded a long time ago, that some criminals deserve no trial and no mercy.

As the painted anchorwoman was wrapping up the story on terrorists-trials and court appointed attorneys, the electricity suddenly went out, cutting her off in mid-sentence. No big surprise and no big loss, he thought. The news had been so horrific lately that Matt felt better off not watching it, at all. It put him on edge, raised his blood pressure, and generally just pissed him off.

How is it, he wondered, thinking about what the news lady had just said before the lights went out; how is it that a foreigner can come to this country, commit a crime of terrorism, and then get a court appointed lawyer, compliments of the Americans he was trying to kill. Something is very wrong with that scenario.

It was very dark, and except for the rain splattering against the side of his apartment, it was also very quiet, and the wind had died down to a breeze. He let his shoulders sag and relaxed his muscles. He slumped in his chair, closed his eyes and had just started to fall asleep when a huge crash of thunder, a bang so loud and so close that it sounded like Thor himself was pounding on his door demanding entrance, jolted him to an upright position, and for the second time in less than an hour his heart pounded inside his chest like a sledge hammer slamming railroad spikes.

"Jesus," he said, holding a hand over his thumping heart, waiting for his apartment to light up from the lightening flash that would certainly follow. He waited in vain, however, as there was nothing more, just the one booming explosion that shook the walls and the floors and probably the entire planet.

*****

The electric clock on the shelf had stopped at 10:25 p.m., and although night had fallen, the darkness inside his apartment seemed deeper and blacker than usual. The familiar light that usually shone through the cracks of the Venetian blinds from the street lights outside, and which cast motionless silhouettes on the walls and ceilings, was missing. It was more than dark; it was black. A creepy chill cater-pillared its way up his back as a car sped down the street outside his apartment, casting an eerie light show on his living room wall.

Although his apartment complex had frequent power outages, this seemed different for some reason. It was eerie, and his heart continued to pound.

It was an explosion, not thunder; that's why there was no lightning, he concluded. Maybe a transformer blew, he reasoned. He slowly reached for his Colt, which he always carried these days; even into the bathroom when he showered; he never opened the door, day or night, without gun in hand, hanging at his side, or concealed behind his back, a habit he'd started a few months back when a young woman had been attacked, beaten, raped, and robbed in Seattle, when she opened her door at 2 o'clock in the afternoon to a guy dressed in a brown delivery uniform. Like his uncle always preached, *it's better to have a gun and not need it, than to need a gun and not have it.*

Gently, he pushed his chair away from the big, sturdy, and battered table that served as his eating place, reading and writing desk, and odd job work-bench. He quietly stood and listened for anything out of the ordinary.

Like a cat on the prowl, he snuck past the wooden plant shelf, lightly brushing his bare arm against the various vines that wound back and forth, up and down, and around the wooden crates from which the stand was made. He crept past the sagging book shelves that held three times the number of books and magazines they were designed for, along with tools, clocks, car keys, and *things*. Rain was suddenly pounding the side of his apartment and sounded like a million pachinko balls falling into a metal pan. But yet, it was unusually quiet; quieter than he'd ever heard it before. He turned the corner into the kitchen.

Sliding his index finger along the nosing of the counter, he followed it until he met the outside wall of the apartment, six feet away. He stepped up to the window into cold rain water that that had blown in through the open window, and had puddled onto the floor. He pulled the draw string to open the mini-blinds. It was as dark outside as it was on the inside, and it had quit raining as quickly as it had started—typical in the Great Northwest.

*****

The window faced a main thoroughfare that ran east and west and provided a view of the rundown strip mall across the street, where on weekends, skate boarders tested their skills on chipped concrete steps and scraped steel railings. During daylight hours, Barker's Corner was a place of business, but under the cover of night, it became a hangout for gang-bangers dealing the latest high. New graffiti covered old graphite and was splashed here and there with shapes of geometrical secret symbols that abstractly resembled letters. Irritated shop owners fought a losing battle, splashing on white or gray paint trying to hide it, but instead of discouraging the nocturnal artists, the new paint left odd looking patches that made good, clean canvas for the next round of vandalism. Street lights, traffic lights, and the night-lights in the strip mall were out, making it look like a ghost town silhouetted through the rain from the bright headlights of passing cars.

The ominous feeling that he'd felt a few minutes earlier when the lights first went out went up a notch when he realized that there were no lights, none whatsoever, shining on the horizon to the south. This was strange indeed because it meant the outage was not just local. During past power outages, Matt had always known it was a neighborhood thing because he could still see lights on the hillside to the south. Tonight, however, there were no lights to the south—it was as black outside, in all directions, as he'd ever seen it.

He stood at the window squinting out into the darkness. The rain had completely stopped and the canopy of clouds had cracked open to reveal the depths of the universe beyond and the billions of stars that were, just moments before, hidden from view.

On any other night, cars would still be speeding up and down the street; tonight, however, they prowled, slowly and cautiously without the aid of street lights and signal lights. He suddenly realized that there was no traffic on I-5, which he could see from his window. This too, was very odd. After twenty minutes, he made his way back to the table to wait it out. One-thousand-and-one, one-thousand-and-two, one-thousand-and-three.

He realized that he was being very quiet for no particular reason, and concluded that being quiet in the dark was inherent to darkness itself. After twenty minutes, he rose from his chair, tucked his gun into his waistband, and, began making his way to the emergency supply closet to fetch his transistor radio.

The tiny linen closet in the hallway had been transformed into an emergency supply closet and was filled with survival necessities: guns and ammunition, water, camping gear, some canned and dehydrated food supplies, greenbacks, a little gold and silver, and his passport. Most of the gear was packed in a sturdy back-pack that was a bit heavy, but not too heavy for quick retrieval and a quick get-away, if and when the need arose. He was as prepared as anyone could be in the city, and better prepared than most.

Matt pulled open the narrow door and retrieved a powerful mini-flashlight and transistor radio and returned to the table. When he switched on the radio to the pre-set emergency broadcasting channel, he was rewarded with the crackling sound of static. That's no good, he thought; no good at all. He sat in the dark and continued to turn the dial, seeking information.

He tried to focus, but his head was pounding with hangover pain. He took four ibuprofens and gulped them down with a glass of ice cold water. For now, there was nothing he could do but search for a voice on the radio that would tell him what was happening. Vibrations from the crunchy static on the radio resonated through his body, and in the quiet darkness, his uncle's words, as if he were standing right next to him, replaced those of the anchorwoman's on the 10 o'clock news.

"Calm down, son, you're going to have a stroke, for Christ's sake." Matt smiled, and took a deep breath of air, held it, and exhaled slowly through his mouth. After repeating the ritual several times, he did, indeed, feel more relaxed, and although it was late, he reached for the land-line telephone to call his uncle and was not surprised to find no dial tone.

He moved cautiously through the darkness to his bedroom at the end of the hall, just past the supply closet, to fetch his cell phone. He punched in speed dial number one, and Uncle Bill picked up on the first ring.

*****

Uncle Bill had been on an urgent call from Brent and was about to call Matt when his phone, which he was still holding in his hand, rang.

"Uncle Bill?"

"Matt? What's up? Is everything okay?" he said anxiously."

"Yeah; Fine," he answered. Matt looked at the lighted dial on his watch and realized it was already midnight. "Sorry to call so late. I didn't' realize it was already the witching hour. Did I wake you up?"

"No. It's okay. I was awake. What's going on?" he asked, with a bit of urgency.

"The power is out again," said Matt. No big deal, but it's sort of strange because it's out to the south as far as I can see, as well. In fact, there isn't a light to be seen anywhere in any direction. Even the traffic on I-5 is damn near non-existent. First time I've ever seen it like this. Is the power out at your place?"

"Yeah, it's out here too," he said, exhaling loudly. "I was talking to Brent just before you called. The power is out up at his place, too, which is not surprising. But he had a call from Tiny up in Bellingham and the power is out there as well." Uncle Bill paused to inhale and exhale. "Brent said it was strange that the power was out here and so far north as well, so he called a friend in Portland and the power is out down there, as well." Uncle Bill knew that what he was telling Matt was probably causing his nephew's heart to race, but he had to be told so he continued. "Both Tiny and his buddy in Portland said loud explosions were heard just before the power went out. He said he would make some calls back east and let us know what he finds out. He also said he was going to dig-in and advised we do the same. I was just getting ready to call you."

Brent's stronghold in Monroe, WA, would be the first stop when and if it ever became necessary to evacuate the city. The evacuation plan, painstakingly put together by Brent, Uncle Bill, and Matt over a long period of time, was known simply as *Plan Alpha*, or just, *The Plan*, and was privy to a chosen few. There was no 'Plan Beta.' *Plan Alpha* contained a packet of typed instructions, maps, and guidelines on what to do and what not to do in case of an emergency, and how to get out of the city when and if the shit hit the fan. It was all hypothetical, of course, but it was a survival plan, and anyone with a lick of sense knew that a survival plan of some sort was mandatory.

"I was just drifting off when an explosion rocked me off my chair. At first I thought it was thunder but then thought maybe a transformer; but now, after what you're telling me, I'm thinking bombs," said Matt. "Sounded like it was right out in the front of my apartment; rattled everything, even the walls. Man." said Matt, fumbling for something substantial to say. "This doesn't sound good at all. It's a good thing the cell phones are still working. "Do you think we need to pack it out of here? Should I wake Abby up and head for Brent's?"

"I think it's real strange Matt, but I think we need to wait and see what Brent finds out. Let's not panic, but let's be ready." Matt listened with attentive concern. His uncle's words were robust, but his voice was shaky. "Certainly someone knows something," said Uncle Bill, now sounding spent, as if his energy had suddenly drained like the last of the sands in an hour glass. "Let's just stay cool and wait," he said softly.

Inside, Uncle Bill was not cool, at all. He was as shook as he'd been in a very long time. He feared the worst, and his gut feeling told him that the US was under some sort of attack, but he didn't want to add fuel to the fire by telling his, already on the edge, nephew what he really thought—not yet. "Hell, it could be a west coast thing. A power grid or a power surge may be all that it is," he said, knowing in his gut it was a long shot at best.

"We'll know soon enough," stated Matt with conviction. "No sense in borrowing trouble, I guess." Matt wanted to say what he was really thinking; *the fucking bastards have struck again,* but because his uncle was obviously shaken, he didn't want to stress him out any more than he already was. After what his uncle had just told him, Matt knew the situation was probably worse than just a power outage and he knew his uncle probably knew it too, but given the implications, neither was going to say it out loud—yet.

"Yeah, said his Uncle. It's pretty strange, alright, but let's not jump to conclusions. Let's wait until daylight and for Brent to call back. Can't be anything too serious, right? We got a roof over our heads, fire in the stove, and wood in the barn. Just be glad it's not winter," he added softly, sounding more troubled than Matt had ever heard him sound before.

"That's a fact," Matt finally said after a short pause in the conversation. "And like you said, it's probably no big deal. Strange, but no big deal," he said, picking up on the new tone the conversation was taking; a lighter, don't panic, tone. "We'll check it out in the morning then. Better hit the rack, I guess. By the way it was another great 4th."

"Okay then. Talk to you later, and thanks for checking on me. I'll let you know what Brent finds out as soon as he calls. But unless it's earth shattering, I won't call until tomorrow. Best save the batteries in the cell phones until we find out what's going on."

"Okay," said Matt, "talk to you later." He then pushed the button that disconnected the line. I should have put my cell phone on the charger when I got home, he thought. Should have bought that damn car-charger, too!

After hanging up, Matt punched in speed dial number two for Brent, but the line was busy. He then punched in speed dial three for Eric, not sure what he was going to say, but panic mode was not an option. There was, however, reason for serious concern. And being prepared was an absolute. Eric picked up on the third ring. It was 12:20 a.m.

*****

"Hey Eric, how's it going, buddy? Are you still up? Is your power out?" he asked, at shotgun speed. Matt pretty much figured that Eric's power *was* out, and since tomorrow was probably a work day for Eric, he'd most likely been in bed for hours and wasn't going to appreciate being woken in the middle of the night. He also figured Eric was still pissed at him, since they didn't have much to say to each other at the party. But issues with their camaraderie would have to wait. Eric needed to know what was going on so he could get ready in case the worst case scenario became reality.

"Hey Matt! Buddy! Yes, I'm still up," he answered cheerfully, as if he hadn't heard from his friend in years. "Hell yes, I'm up. In more ways than one, if you know what I mean," he whispered loud enough for Rose to hear. He sounded to Matt like a kid in grade school telling a secret. "Life is great and I'm in love!" Eric shouted into the phone. "What's going on?" Eric said, with some hesitancy. "Is everything okay? Why are you calling so late? Is anything wrong?" he asked, suddenly sounding very serious. The information Matt had, although urgent, could wait a few more minutes. Besides, he wanted to apologize to his friend for the way he'd been acting lately.

"All is well in my empire, Eric," he said. "I was awake and wanted to talk to someone, and who else to pester but my bro?" he said. "By the way, man, I'm sorry for freaking you out the other day on the way to Brent's. I've been on edge."

"You said a mouthful there, dude, but since I'm in such a generous mood tonight, all is forgiven. Apology accepted, but ya better watch out or I'll get my new commando buddies to kick your butt," he teased. "Dude, what a party! Thanks for inviting me. It was great!"

"You're welcome, bro," said Matt, "it was a good one indeed. By the way, are the lights out over there?"

"Yeah dude, it's darker than heck outside. We are surrounded by candle light, though, so all is well in my love nest. There is a bluebird on my shoulder," said Eric, with a giggle. "We went out on the balcony a while ago for a look and couldn't see a light anywhere in any direction. Figured a transformer blew, more than one, actually, because we heard quite a few blasts. Lots of stars, though," he giggled. "Some drunk probably hit a power pole and a transformer blew up and caused some sort of chain reaction. Or maybe it's a *terrorist attack*, Matt—do you think?" He did not wait for an answer. "It's pretty quiet; sort of eerie, actually."

Eric Erickson was a talker. *It's the Erickson curse*, he'd told Matt one day when he'd realized he'd been rambling.

"It's very quiet and very dark here too—eerie is just the word I was thinking, too." Matt paused for a moment, but there was no further reply. "Hey," said Matt, seriously. "I was talking to my uncle a while ago and he'd been talking to Brent. Brent says the lights are out all the way from Bellingham to Portland. Seems that...." Eric cut him off.

"That's a drag, dude, but don't bring me down. It's no big deal, I'm sure."

"Maybe not, bro, but better safe than sorry. Do you have your *Plan Alpha* kit handy?"

"No, but no sweat. It's around here someplace. But don't worry about it, Dude. I know all the power going down seems suspicious, especially to you, but it is not a terrorist attack, pal, I promise. I'm sure there is a rational explanation. Go to bed, Dude. Get some sleep."

Matt could tell that Eric was someplace else, and that no matter what he said, Eric was not going to get on the wagon to survival. Not tonight, anyway.

"Okay, bro. Sounds good," said Matt. "I just wanted to let you know what was going on. Sorry to call so late. I just wanted to say hello and check to make sure you were okay in the dark, all by yourself."

"Hey, I'm better than okay, bro. I'm in love!" Eric blared into the phone with joviality. "I am great because I've got the lovely Rose Beneli right here to protect me," he answered. "In fact, dude, she is cuddling me between her 44s as we speak. Says I need some long overdue nurturing." Matt heard Rose in the background.

"If that's Matt Lovell," she said, "tell him I've become a one man woman." Matt heard what she'd said, smiled into the phone, and shook his head and thought, that'll be the day.

"Matt" said Eric, laughing, "Which is bigger, do you think, your .44 or her 44s? A play on words from a computer geek, thought Matt. Not bad, even if he didn't have a .44.

"Damn, bro, one 4th of July party, and a few hours with Rose, and you've turned into an outlaw. Got the lingo down and all," he kidded. Eric ignored the comment and changed the subject.

"If the 'trons," short for electrons in geek language, Matt had learned, "are still not flowing in the morning, I won't be going to work, but I will be barbequing on the deck around noon." Eric had a large deck overlooking a jumbo size pool at his up-scale condo. It was a relaxing place to hang and always provided nice eye candy. Real nice. "Why don't you grab Abby and come on over, unless you're going to confession to pray for your sinful soul," he joked.

"Thanks, Eric. Sounds like a good time, but I'll have to see what's going on; because this blackout could be much worse than just another power outage."

"Man," said Eric, sounding exasperated at Matt's pessimism, "the economy is strong. All is well. Cheer up and quit being so darned negative. Jeez! You're ruining my mood and bringing me down. Go to bed, I'll talk to you later."

Matt heard Rose in the background, "See ya later, Matt," she said in a sing-song voice.

"Okay lover boy, have a good one," said Matt. "I'll catch up to you in the morning." Matt pushed the button on his cell. As he watched the light fade out on the dial, he checked the battery indicator. It was at about forty-five percent. The first real inconvenience of not having electricity dawned on him for the first time, and he kicked himself for not plugging it in when he'd first gotten home, as he usually did.

He got up and walked to the kitchen window and pulled the blinds apart to have one last look before hitting the rack. It was still as black outside as he'd ever seen it. Not even a car was on the road. It was uncanny. He thought about Eric, and how he was too much of a yuppie to take any of this seriously. He thought about Abby; sweet Abby, who was mostly in the same boat as Eric. He wondered how people like them would survive a state of anarchy. They won't, he concluded, unless they have friends to take care of them.

*****

Montana, Moalim, Ali, and Abdul sat in a room lighted by battery powered camping lamps. They had caused destruction like the west coast had never seen—like the western world had never seen! And now they waited for the reports.

"This is 87, *mission accomplished*; this is 432, *all went as planned*, this is 347, mission accomplished." Moalim had his phone on speaker and as the bombers reported, the numbers were taken down and matched with the master target list. 418 was the Deception Pass Bridge, 28 was the Hood Canal Bridge, 532 and 533 were the Narrows Bridges, and on it went until early morning.

Montana concluded that more bombings were planned over the next few days, which Moalim later confirmed; however, they would not be involved with any more attacks—not now, at least. Their new prime objective was to secure the Lassiter Ranch in Cave Junction, and since the major Interstates were on the targeted lists, they would be taking the back roads all the way. They would take two vehicles, Matt and Moalim in one and Ali and Abdul in the other. They would take turns driving and sleeping and stop at secure relay stations, as Moalim had called them, for food, lodging, supplies, and gas.

"Where is the gasoline coming from for the trip south?" asked Montana.

"One of the objectives last night," Moalim said smiling, "was to hijack gas tankers and deliver them to the relay stations; should be a few in Cave Junction by now," he said, nodding his head.

The strike had been fast and unexpected and the destruction was wide spread and complete. Highways, railroad tracks, power stations, bridges, telephone switching stations, government offices, cell towers, airport access roads. The targets were everything and anything that had to do with transportation and communication, and the destruction was so vast, that it had indeed brought the country to a standstill.

CHAPTER 6
JULY 6TH - LYNNWOOD, WA

Pounding thunder jolted him throughout the night. When he woke at seven o'clock, he quickly stood and pulled aside the bedroom curtains. The parking lot below was dry and the sun was shining, but the power was still out. The unsettling feeling in his gut was still there, and he felt it necessary to be very quiet in fear of disrupting some unseen presence. He walked softly into the kitchen and peered through the slits between the blinds. The streets were deserted. No cars, no buses, no people, and no newspaper on his front porch. He was convinced his country was at war and that the enemy had fired the first shot.

Matt knew that a blackout from Portland to Bellingham was *not* just a coincidence. He flipped open his cell to call his uncle but there was no service. And then he remembered the pounding of distant thunder in the and wondered if instead of thunder it was explosions.

This is the real deal, he said to himself, and suddenly felt a chill that tightened his skin from head to toe. He wondered if he should wake Abby and head for Brent's or to his uncle's, and then remembered that *The Plan* specifically states that his apartment, being the most central to his uncle, Abby and Eric, and closest to the exit route to Brent's, was the meeting place in the event that emergency evacuation became necessary. He flipped open his cell, still no bars. He tied his transistor radio, but there was only static. He had no choice but to wait for someone to show up with some news. He stared blankly out the window at nothing particular and wondered what he should do next—don't panic and breathe.

He concluded that the thunder he'd heard in the night was actually explosions. The bastards probably used car bombs and expendable suicide bombers. Hell, everyone who reads the papers or watches television knows what a car bomb can do. We could be isolated already, he thought, and was glad that he'd filled up both gas tanks on his truck on the way home from his uncles. He went back to his bedroom and dressed in blue jeans and a t-shirt, strapped on his cross-draw holster and slipped his .357 into place. He wore it exposed, not caring about gun laws or cops. If he was right about the country being under attack, he needed to be ready. He needed coffee, too, which he had already planned to brew on the barbeque. He went to the front door and stepped out onto the balcony of his small second story apartment.

He had a new tank of propane and there was meat in the freezer that could and should be cooked; one, because the electricity was out, and two, they could eat it on the way to Cave Junction, which he was sure would be very soon.

He fired up the barbeque and set the black, soot-stained, percolator coffee pot off to one side of the grate and sat down to wait, checking the service on his cell every few minutes. He was not so calm, but chose to think of it as being on the high alert, instead of being anxious.

Around 8:30 a.m., he witnessed the first sign of life. A neighbor lady, whom he did not know, stepped out onto the sidewalk below his balcony wearing a pink fluffy bath robe. She looked up and down the streets and then turned to go back inside. When she saw Matt, she smiled and said, "Another day off. Good." And then she disappeared back inside her apartment, totally unaware of the impending doom lying just over the horizon. Someone must know something. He tried his cell, but still, there was no service.

A lone jogger jogged by, and then a group of bicyclists, hunched over low handle bars and dressed in bright colored competition spandex, sped by, peddling hard, reminding him of *The Tour de France.* Soon, a few power walkers, pumping their arms and looking stupid marching in time to the music coming from their I-pods, waited for their turn to cross at the dead signal light. No one, it appeared, was too concerned about the black-out. Are they all stupid? They must have heard explosions—probably thought it was thunder. They must have heard news from their friends or relatives before the service went dead—maybe not.

The drivers of the few cars that were on the road were trying extra hard to be courteous by driving more slowly than usual and taking their rightful turn at the traffic light in orderly fashion, treating the intersection like a four way stop. There were always the few impatient "honkers," however, who leaned on their horns as they rode the bumpers of the cars in front. There is usually a good reason for road rage, he concluded.

He was monitoring the barbeque grill when he heard one of his neighbors below on the first floor say to someone else; "It's sort of like camping out."

"Yep, I guess it is," answered the other. No one seemed to know the extent of the outage and they didn't seem to care. From the looks of things, the power outage seemed to be a bonus—an extended weekend. The inconvenience of the power going out was nothing more than just that—an inconvenience. It was an acceptable tradeoff for another day off.

While he waited for the coffee to percolate, he wondered if the electricity was out in Cave Junction. Maybe Abby has heard something? He tried his transistor. Static. It was 10:30 a.m. and the sun was shining brightly through dissipating clouds, but it was still extraordinarily quiet. He wondered why his uncle wasn't there, or Eric. He was anxious, but not panicky. He willed the coffee to be done, and in short order the smell of fresh brewed beans filled the morning air, which drew Abby out through her door with cup in hand.

"Good morning, Matt. I see the power is out again," she said, with a smile. Coffee sure smells good," she said. Abby always had a smile on her face in the morning, and she always greeted him with, "good morning." No matter what had happened the day before, he could always count on her smile at first greeting. Matt got irritated with people who said, "Not 'till I've had my coffee," and who contorted their face in such a way that it reminded him of someone trying to leave a shit.

"Good morning right back to you, Abby. Would you like a cup of mud?" She nodded, and he poured her a cup, and then tossed three T-bone steaks onto the hot grill and paused to listen to them sizzle. He looked up as two cop cars sped by with lights flashing but sirens at rest. Not too unusual, he thought. "Yeah," he finally answered, "the power went out about 10:30 last night." Her tanned legs looked real nice in the morning sun. She was wearing a red silk robe that stopped just below her crotch, and she was barefoot; her hair was mussed, just right. He decided not to tell her anything, yet.

"I went to bed early and slept like a log," she said. Matt caught her looking at the pistol strapped to his hip and was pleasantly surprised when she didn't say something like, "expecting a war?" She went back to sipping her coffee and enjoying the morning sun and another precious day allotted her by the Almighty. Abby had faith.

"Did you hear the latest," she finally asked? Matt's head snapped up to listen. "I heard on the six o'clock news last night that people with electric cars are going to have to pay a higher income tax because they don't buy enough gas at the pumps to pay their fair share of taxes that go for highway maintenance."

"Oh. Yeah, I heard that," he replied, flipping the steaks with a little more gusto than intended. "It's so fu..., wrong," he said, checking his language. "They pay extra for a hybrid to save gas and help the county wean itself from the oil teat of the black monster, and they get burned by the feds for it. Go figure. I wonder how they're going to charge their batteries with the power out," he said smirking. She gave him a half-hearted smile over the brim of her coffee cup and closed her eyes as she took a sip.

Although she was older than Matt by more than a few years, she looked especially good today. Her blond hair was shining in the morning sun, and her blue eyes sparkled, and her was radiant and glowing. Her red silk robe clung to her body revealing, perky nipples, and breasts that still defied gravity. She seemed to have a glow around her head. Could be a good day for a poke, he thought, smiling a flirtatious smile at her.

"Forget it," she said, reading his mind and turning red.

Despite the war he'd confabulated in his head, he was suddenly feeling pretty damn good; better than he'd felt in a long time. The coffee was starting to give him the energy jolt he needed, and the white clouds of thick smoke from the old Webber carried the unmistakable smell of beef cooking over an open flame, which was always intoxicating.

"Have you heard from your parents lately?" he asked. "Did they celebrate the 4th?"

"I haven't talked to them in a week or so. I'm going to call them in a little while."

"Tell them hi for me," he said, trying to think of a way to say: *Come and tell me if you get through and if their power is out*, without sending up red flags.

He didn't want to tell her what he'd heard from his uncle because he didn't want her to worry. His personal feelings about what was going on were all speculation, he'd finally admitted to himself. He would wait to hear something concrete before telling her anything at all. He needed to be sure. He felt good. He felt in control.

The steaks smelt good, and he was cooking enough to last a few days. He had already decided to toss a bunch of chicken on the grill after the beef. Chow for a week, he thought. Maybe I'll take some over to Uncle Bill. Maybe I'll swing by and see Eric and his new squeeze—scope out the eye candy. Despite what he felt in his gut, he was calm. He was ready to move-out at a moment's notice, but for now, he would have to wait.

"Would you like a steak?" he asked Abby, who seemed preoccupied with thoughts of her own.

"No thanks," she said, looking up from her cup. "I'm going to fast today. Purge some of that delicious food from the weekend," she said, with another put-on smile. Purge was a disgusting word to Matt, and some of the glow that was around his neighbor quickly dissolved like the smoke from his barbeque. "But thanks anyway," she said. "I'm just going to hang and wait for the electricity to come back on. Read," she added.

"Okay then, how about another cup of coffee?

"Can I get a cup to go," she asked, perkily?

"Sure," he said, reaching for the pot. A few silent and uncomfortable moments passed before she headed back to her apartment. She turned and waved and said thank you as she opened her door and disappeared inside.

Matt reached for his cell just as four more cop cars sped by. When he looked off into the distance, to the south, he realized that the cell towers with the red flashing lights were gone. He had to squint to make sure they were actually gone and not just hidden in the trees—not easy to spot when the beacon lights are out. They were definitely gone, and quick as spit, he was wound as tight as a kimono on a Geisha girl. He tried his phone, and still there was no signal; and still, there was nothing he could do but wait.

*****

He took a deep breath as he plunked the largest of the T-bones on a plate and sat down on the wooden bench on his balcony, draping one leg over each side, setting the plate between his knees. He cut a good chunk of the fatty part from the end, stuck it in his mouth and started chewing. As he chewed, he wondered again, what the hell was going on. Where the hell are the cell towers, he wondered, squinting off into the distance, and could only come up with one answer. He knew about emergency Portable Cell Towers, PCT's as they were called, and wondered if they would be deployed.

The neighborhood was coming to life, and because everything was shut down, more people than usual were milling around. Neighbors were chatting with neighbors, dogs were doing their business, and owners, because they were in view of other neighbors, were cleaning up the mess. Cars were moving, people were walking, crows were squawking. But it was still very quiet, despite all the activity. It's like the Twilight Zone, he thought, watching the street for his uncle.

*****

Abby settled into the folds of her overstuffed couch, tucked her feet up under her butt, and wrapped the blanket around her shoulders, letting it fall to cover her body and legs. She picked up her cell phone to call her mother in Cave Junction and found she had no signal, which she simply attributed to the power outage. She would try again later.

She sipped her coffee and thought about when she'd first met Matt. She'd actually met Uncle Bill and Brent long before ever moving to Lynnwood and meeting Matt. Uncle Bill and her parents had history.

*****

Karla, a blue-blood hippie, if there is such a thing, is a bit on the heavy side and wears tie-died skirts and blouses, no bra, sandals, and love beads, and is as dedicated to her husband as a soul mate can be. Abby smiled at the thought of how her mother still gets giddy when she's around her dad.

Her father had built a "no pressure" business, as he'd called it, after moving to Cave Junction. He designed and maintained web pages for small business in the Illinois Valley. He worked from a modest office he'd built in the loft of the barn and earned a bit more than just enough to get by, and that was fine—no pressure, no hustle and bustle, no hassles from his clients. Abby was Jake and Karla's love child.

Abby longed for love like theirs. "Finding a soul mate is a matter of fate," her mother had told her. "Sometimes it happens fast, like with me and your father. For others it takes time and a great deal of patience. Most people, however, never find their soul mate at all. But it doesn't mean a married couple can't be very happy.

Abby thought about the picture that hung over the fireplace in the living room in her parent's home. Theirs was a ferry book love story. She hugged her knees which were now tucked tight against her chest. The story had been told a hundred times and it was always the same, and it always brought smiles to the faces of eager listeners.

"Where was this picture taken," or "is that you guys?" was all it took. They would look at each other with a sparkle in their eyes and begin the tale of Woodstock, 1969.

Abby recalled the picture had been taken by a journalist who was covering Woodstock. He was filming the Jefferson Airplane, who had just finished their number one hit, White Rabbit. The Airplane was leaving the stage and Joe Cocker was getting ready backstage to begin his session. There were some technical difficulties switching over some of the gear, so the announcer, filling in the time, yelled out, "anyone want to get married?" and Jake and Karla, who'd met the day before and had not separated since, and without even looking at each other or consulting one another, fired their hands into the air, waving them around franticly to get the MC's attention. When they realized they were totally in tune with each other, they raised both hands and started jumping up and down, and their love dance did not go unnoticed by the MC. "Well come on up and let's get it done," he bellowed to the applause of 200,000 thousand witnesses.

Jake grabbed the stranger standing next to him and asked him to be his best man, and Karla grabbed a girl standing next to her to be her maid of honor. It was a fast ceremony, orchestrated by a home-grown minister, and it was over in minutes. It had lasted long enough, however, for it all to be caught on 8mm tape by the journalist. The story had been splashed over the tabloids of every newspaper in the county. The stranger that Jake had grabbed to be his best man turned out to be Uncle Bill.

It's all so surreal, thought Abby. But it was true. Such a great love story, she thought, squeezing her knees up to her chest and feeling warm and fuzzy. She thought about the picture of her very young mother and an equally young father dressed in hippie garb of the 60s, long hair, naru shirt, and love beads.

After they returned to society and to the hassles of life in the city, they contacted the newspaper that the journalist had worked for and requested a copy of the footage. They didn't get a copy; instead, they got a framed picture and a wedding card signed by the crew of the paper. That's so cool, thought Abby, as she sat in the glow of the memory. The picture over the fire place was their only wedding picture.

Abby had known Uncle Bill all her life; as far back as she could remember. He had come to New York shortly after she was born, and he'd held her when she was a baby and had shared in her parents' joy. She remembered remembering Uncle Bill for the first time on her sixth birthday. He had come to New York to visit and had brought with him a huge, pink stuffed poodle for her birthday. It was one of those memories you can't quite put all together, but a good memory, just the same. He'd shown up many times as she was growing up, but he was mostly a name and a face—a friend of her parents.

*****

Her parents, together with Uncle Bill, purchased 250 acres in Cave Junction, Oregon, when property prices were still within reach, and as soon as the Lassiters retired, which was before they turned 55, they headed straight for the solitude of their own Garden of Eden on the Illinois River and never looked back.

They lived in an Airstream trailer during construction; first the power, then the well, then the septic system, and then the house, garage, and barn. The fresh air of the great outdoors worked its magic on them like an elixir, or the fountain of youth, and the years faded from their faces, and their bodies became solid and strong, like their new home. Uncle Bill paid his share and more; calling it a house warming present, he paid the entire bill for the barn the garage and guest house. When it was finished, the Lassiter ranch was pretty much self-sufficient.

Water was not a problem. They had a well that was hooked up to a generator. There was also a hand pump which they never used but had the foresight to install when the well was put in.

Food was not an issue either. They raised a few beef and a few pigs and sixty chickens; one chicken dinner a week for the whole year was the plan. Variety on ways to cook the birds was not an issue for Karla; she was a genius in the kitchen.

Uncle Bill introduced Brent to Abby's parents back when they first bought the property. It was Brent who had taught her father how to hunt. She remembered seeing her father all dressed up in camouflaged clothing with a painted face, beaming with pride as he told the story about how he'd bagged his first deer. "He's a natural," bragged Brent. Her father had always talked about hunting but never had the time or anyone to show him the ropes until he'd met Brent. Brent had told him that there was enough game in that area to keep him in meat forever and that he ought to learn to hunt. A plan was hatched and Brent went down and stayed with the Jake and Karla for a week and taught Jake everything he needed to know about hunting, and more. They had become friends despite Brent's rough and ready ways. That was a long time ago, and now her father is loading his own shells—who would of thunk it, she smiled. Brent was as hot back then as he is now, she smiled.

Heat was not a problem on the ranch, either. The wood stoves they had chosen were suitable for cooking as well as supplying heat. They had a buried propane tank that powered, via the generator, 'preferred circuits,' like the well, and the outlets that supplied power to the television and radio. Hot water for showers was produced using a special connection from the wood stove to the hot water tank. As far as being able to live off the land, they were in pretty good shape. They, too, were survivors.

The world had changed from the world that Jake and Karla had helped to liberate in the sixties and seventies. Abby remembered talking to her parents about some of the recent hate rallies in Seattle and comparing them to the love rallies her parents were a part of. Unlike the hateful liberals of today who gather at funerals of dead soldiers and taunt the bereaved by shouting slogans like "your kid deserved to die," and "God hates you," the liberals during Karla and Jake's day shouted slogans like *make love not war*.

Liberals of today had taken on a whole different aura than the flower child liberal of the 60s and 70s, and in Abby's opinion, it was no longer good to be considered a liberal. "It's the bleeding-heart liberals," Matt had preached, "who keep this country from moving forward." In many cases, she agreed; in others, she did not.

She remembered becoming indoctrinated into the gang of outlaws and learning about their ideals regarding politics and survival. They were a rough crowd, but once she had become part of the circle, their rough and tough façade began to fade until they became regular folks; rough and tough, they were, but good people just the same.

Their arguments about what was wrong with society were valid and Abby had no problem seeing their points of view. She had no problem with locking away the bad guys forever, even executing the real bad ones. She couldn't pull the trigger, but she could be on a jury that said yes to a death penalty. But if she had her way, there would be no more guns and no more wars. After all, she was a second generation flower-child.

It was shortly after she had moved into the apartment next to Matt that she was made privy to *The Plan*. She wondered why her parents never told her about it. Maybe they didn't want to *freak me out*, she thought, smiling at one of her mother's favorite phrases. Anyway, it was a no brainier that if something crazy happened, she would head back home to the woods. When she learned about *Plan Alpha*, she was surprised to learn that her home was the destination for others, as well as herself. She and Matt had gone over *The Plan* for 'when,' according to him, and 'if,' according to her, worse came to worse and they had to get out of the city, alive.

The Plan outlined what should be done if someone was downtown when bombs started going off, or a squadron of airplanes started crashing into buildings, or poisonous gas was released? Should you try to get home or should you find the quickest way out of town to Brent's, which was the first stop on the way to her parent's property in Cave Junction. She shook her head as she thought about how Matt had started carrying two gas masks in his truck. Abby did not like thinking about Armageddon or the end of the world. It was too bleak—too final. Survival was one thing; the end of the world was something altogether different.

She remembered Matt saying, "once the electricity goes out the apartment building is as unless as trying to pick butter up with a hot knife." These days it seemed he was looking forward to anarchy. She didn't think he realized what he was wishing for. She'd read enough to know it wouldn't be good. It wouldn't be good in any sense of the word.

Their differences aside, common sense dictated that if a national catastrophe did occur, the city was a graveyard waiting to be filled. She couldn't remember if she'd learned this or if she just knew it, but there was no doubt in her mind, that for her to survive, the logical place to go would be Cave Junction.

She got up and walked to the kitchen to warm her coffee in the microwave, then remembered the electricity was out. She considered going over to Matt's for a refill but just as quickly decided against it. She wanted to be alone with her thoughts.

She remembered a phase she'd gone through when she had called her parents by their first names, Karla and Jake, instead of mom and dad. She smiled. It was a phase her parents patiently waited for her to outgrow. How lucky I am, she thought, to have such wonderful and loving parents. She liked being in their company. She liked it when she was a kid and she liked it when she'd become an adult. They were always there for her—always encouraging. Even when she'd decided to quit college because she saw a better way to achieve her goals, they had supported her. They had told her numerous times that she was a blessing to them, but now, as she sat in the comfort of her apartment, she thought about how blessed *she* was to have *them*.

*****

Matt took his plate into the kitchen and put it into the sink and then went back to the balcony to wait. He sat down on the bench and leaned back against the rail and instantly dozed off in the warmth of the sun. It was 6 p.m. when he awoke to the loud blaring horns of a fire truck racing by with an emergency medical vehicle speeding close behind. Everything must be okay, he thought—cops racing by, fire trucks, emergency medical vehicles. Maybe Eric was right when he said, "I know all the power going down seems suspicious, especially to you, but it is not a terrorist attack, pal, I promise."

Matt got up and went into the kitchen for a glass of water, and returned to the bench on the porch. It suddenly dawned on him that the reason it was so quiet was that the constant buzz of electricity zipping through the wires overhead was gone. The word madness crossed his mind as he thought about the movie Frankenstein. He reached for his cell phone and punched in his uncle's number.

"Hi Uncle Bill, I've been trying to get hold of you, but I couldn't get a signal until now! The cell towers to the south are gone, Uncle Bill. They are just plain gone!"

Skipping formalities and small talk, Uncle Bill started right in. "They probably have some ECTs in place. Listen, Matt, I talked to Brent for a few minutes earlier, and he's digging in. Says a friend up that way with a short wave radio told him that there were fires burning in Seattle, Chicago, LA, New York, Houston, all over the country. Do you see smoke to the south towards Seattle," he asked.

"Yes. There are some smoke plumes, but nothing that looks like hell on earth. Not yet anyway," he said as his heart began to race. "It's true, then, we are under attack. Why the hell are we still in the city Uncle Bill?"

"The rumor is that an unknown terrorist organization has engineered attacks all over the country." Matt quickly stood up wondering if what he'd heard was correct. The whole country was under attack! Is that what he'd heard? He needed to stay rational and not panic. It was a rule of survival. "We are waiting to hear if our government has a plan."

"This is real bad, Uncle Bill," said Matt, in as close to a conversational tone as he could muster. "But I think we need to pack it up and get going. We can wait it out at Brent's. I've already seen trucks and vans, packed to the hilt, rolling east towards the mountains. Looks to me like a lot of people already know what's going on and are getting out of the city. Maybe they know something we don't."

"I think we should hold our ground tonight, Matt, and see what the situation is in the morning. We really don't know enough to head out...."

"They're blowing up the country, Uncle Bill, what more is there to know?" Matt said, adamantly

"I know we have a plan, Matt, but we need more information. I think we should wait out the night and get ready..." Matt did not like what he was hearing. He fully expected his uncle to say, "let's roll."

"I am already, *ready*, Uncle Bill. I have been for a long time," he said curtly, looking at his rifles and the pile of ammunition stacked next to the door.

"I know you're ready, Matt," said Uncle Bill, sounding on edge. "But think about it. We haven't heard anything official from the government, yet."

"How are *they* supposed to contact us, Uncle Bill, mental telepathy?" He began pacing, waiting for an answer. "Since when have you started putting your trust in the government, Uncle Bill?" Matt took a deep breath and sat down to listen.

"It would be best to just dig in for a few days before heading to Brent's, that's all."

"You just said the night, now it's a few days?" scorned Matt, standing up to pace again.

"I think we need to wait and see what the government does, Matt. They must be broadcasting somewhere." Matt felt like he was going to lose it. "This is the USA—we have the technology, the forces, and the man power to pull this all back together. I know it's not good, but in a few days, it could all be back under control."

"Why are you stalling, Uncle Bill? We can be at Brent's in a few hours tops, and we can wait it out there. The longer we stay in the city, the harder it's going to be to get out—you know that!" he said, exasperated. "It's pretty obvious what's going on. Why are you stalling?" he demanded.

"We need one more day, at least, Matt. We need to know what action the government is going to take. We need at least one more night."

"I don't like it," said Matt. This is the real thing, and I think we should go, now. Worst case scenario is we come back. But if we are caught in the panic of the city, we could have a real hard time getting out," he said.

Matt didn't like what his uncle was suggesting. Didn't like it one damn bit, but knew he was arguing a case he was going to lose. He had a choice. He could leave without his uncle or he could wait it out.

"Matt...."

"Maybe one more night could work," Matt said, not letting his uncle continue the argument he'd already won. "I can defend my place unless someone sets fire to it. If I have to...."

His cell lost its signal just after 8 o'clock. He didn't know if his battery had gone dead or if another tower went down. He figured the worst, but what he'd last said is what he would do—he would wait out the night.

He flipped open his cell phone to call Eric but there was no signal. He went next door and tapped on Abby's door, but there was no answer, and he decided not to wake her. She would need her rest for what lay ahead. If he had to, he would break her door down, but tonight he would let her rest.

Plan Alpha clearly states that the first meeting point will be my place. He hoped Eric had read the whole document and hadn't just tossed it aside as so much bunk. From Matt's house, they would head to Brent's. From there they would head to Cave Junction. They would travel in a caravan, as there is safety in numbers. He expected they would be on their way by noon tomorrow, tops. He checked his magnum, set out a few more candles and dragged his foam pad into the living room where he would spend the night. He tried his cell one more time, but still there was no signal.

Don't wait around for a person who may not be coming was one of the orders in *The Plan. Save yourself, and we will all meet in Cave Junction.* That was the long and the short of it. Eric's no dummy, he'll figure it out. He thought about Rose and was pretty sure she did not know about *Plan Alpha*, at all. But Rose was with Eric and Eric would not leave her behind. It was as good as it was going to get.

By the time he'd finished setting up camp in his living room, checking to see what was going on outside a half dozen times, drinking two beers, trying the radio and checking his phone, again, the dark canopy of night was creeping over the horizon, heading in his direction. It was late and he decided to hit the rack. He tossed his sleeping bag onto the pad and crawled in, only to get up thirty minutes later to peep through the blinds to see if anything new was going on outside.

*****

Abby tried calling home again and was happy to hear her mother's voice when she picked up on the 4th ring.

"I've been thinking about coming down for a visit," said Abby, after saying hello and how are you. "These guys, especially Matt, are driving me nuts. All he talks about is how bad everything is. His latest kick is how messed up the judicial system is and how terrorists are going to strike again. I need a break," she whined, imitating a young child. "And Matt's language is so hateful, these days," she continued in a more serious tone. "So dark. So scary. It's depressing. Ass-hole this, scum-bag that, fucking foreigner needs to learn the language, and on and on and on. It's driving me crazy. I mean, we are all aware of the troubles in the world, but he is so—dark." Abby realized she pretty much jumped right into bitching and felt bad. "I'm sorry about the language and the bitching, Mom; but I'm at my wit's end, here."

"That's okay, sweetie. Tell me more," Karla said.

"I suppose I'm a bit on edge. I know the world is not perfect, but is it really as bad as Matt makes it sound? Even Uncle Bill says he's out of line and on the edge. He's talked to Matt about his attitude *and* his language. Told him to calm down. You know Uncle Bill," she said, "he doesn't hold back. If he's got something to say, he's going to say it. Matt says he's getting soft, though. Says his uncle is getting too complacent to see what's really going on. He hasn't said it to his face, but he's said it to me." Her mother listened without interruption.

"I mean, I hate hearing about it all the time; but it's not even that, particularly. It's more about how he says it. He is so full of hate! So venomous! He carries his gun all the time just waiting for someone to cross him so he can shoot 'em, it seems. On the 4th when we were at the store getting supplies for the party at Uncle Bill's, he screamed at some lady dressed in an abya for parking in a handicap spot. I actually thought for a minute that he was going to hit her." Abby was on a roll. Venting. Letting it all out without seeming to take a breath.

"I'm sorry Mom. I don't mean to bother you with my problems. I can handle these *boys* just fine, really. I just needed a shoulder to cry on for a few minutes. I'm fine, really," she said, reassuringly. Abby suddenly remembered she hadn't mentioned the power outage. "Hey, mom, I forgot. Our power is out again."

"Number one, Abby, you can always 'vent' to your mother, darlin'. Never think you have to hold back or that you are bothering me. Okay?" she said. "I will give our old friend, Uncle Bill, a call, if you like. I won't tell him you said anything; I will just give him a call to see how he is and I'll let you know what he says. Okay? And we'll just keep it between us girls, okay?" She paused. "And about the power being out, it's out here too, but it's no big deal. It goes out all the time in the country. So, I'm guessing it's just a coincidence."

"I suppose your right," answered Abby. "And yeah, it would be good if you gave Uncle Bill a call. He's always asking how you and dad are doing."

"It sounds like you could use a break from the city, Abby," said Karla, changing the subject. "Why don't you come down for some R&R?" her mother said, using a phrase she'd picked up from Brent on one of his many visits. "Oh, and by the way, Montana was here a few weeks back. Said he was heading up for the party. Did you see him?"

"Yes, I saw him. Seems he and Matt got into some sort of argument and Montana left early. Matt probably pissed him off about something."

"Montana came up to the house," Karla continued, ignoring the sarcastic tone of her daughter's comment, "and asked if he and few friends could camp out down by the river. He's such a nice and polite young man. Your father went down to see them but told me they were busy and so he didn't stay. He seemed a bit on edge when he came back, but he didn't say anything." Abby wasn't really paying close attention and changed the subject without commenting.

"Some R&R really sounds good, Mom, and like I said, I've been thinking about it. I'll start making plans."

"Good then, when do you think you can come down?"

"How about if the electricity is not back on by tonight, I head out first thing in the morning?" she said. "I'll tell you all about the party when I see you. It was really fun. In fact, even if the electricity does come back on, I'm on my way. What the heck, I'm the boss," she said brightly, "so I can take my vacation whenever I want, and now is a good time. I can only stay a week, but expect me in three days. I'll call when I'm on the road."

"Sounds good, sweetheart. And Abby, try not to worry too much about Matt. I'm sure Uncle Bill and Brent will get him back on track."

It was a nice thought but obviously her mother didn't really grasp the magnitude of the situation, and Abby didn't want to bother her anymore with her problems—not on the phone, anyway.

"Okay Mom. I love you. Say hello to Dad. I better save my cell batteries in case the electricity doesn't come back on right away."

"I love you too, Sweetheart. See you soon, be careful and enjoy the drive.

CHAPTER 7
JULY 7TH - LYNNWOOD, WA

Morning came too early for Matt. He woke from a restless sleep with a jolt, raised himself to a sitting position, and squinted at the lime green hands on his Swiss Army watch. It read 6 a.m. The face on the small digital clock radio on the bookshelf was blank, indicating the electricity was still out. It was very quiet, and he could smell smoke from a cigarette wafting in through his open window. He stood up, stretched, and grabbed his cell. He thought about Eric and flipped open his phone. No signal. He was anxious to hit the road.

He thought about work and realized that there would be no more working on cars. Not for money anyway. No one would be going to work. It was over. The reality and implications of the past few days were hitting home. It would be a long, long time before any sense of normality was reestablished. He was now in the business of survival. *Survival Incorporated*, he thought, smiling. He would have to bring Abby up to speed today, Eric too, if he could reach him.

At the very instant that Matt walked back into the living room, a loud thumping sound startled him half out of his boxers and sent shivers down the entire length of his body. He hit the floor before he realized what the vibrations were coming. Helicopters, and it sounded like one was landing on the roof of the apartment. WHOMPH, WHOMPH, WHOMPH, WHOMPH.

He ran to the front door and yanked it open so hard that it got lose from his grip and smashed into the wall. What he saw was something out of an old black and white John Wayne war movie. He froze and stopped breathing at the site of all the giant helicopters that were flying low overhead. WHOMPH, WHOMPH, WHOMPH, WHOMPH.

There was not just one, but dozens of helicopters stretching from one end of the horizon to the other. They were dropping something that looked, at first, like confetti, but within seconds, Matt realized that leaflets were floating to the earth by the thousands. He ran the length of his balcony, down the steps, and out onto the wet lawn to retrieve one.

This is nuts! Maybe he was still asleep? And he commanded himself to wake up as he'd done so many times in the past when he was dreaming a dream he didn't like. It was so…surreal. His gut told him what the flyer as about, and hoped that there was still time, and that there was still a way out of the city, and that the world was not about to end.

The vibrations from the thumping blades of the helicopters brought neighbors out of their apartments, still clad in their skimpy and wrinkled night clothes. They pointed to the skies, and then scrambled to grab a leaflet. They read in silence as the helicopters became smaller and smaller and eventually disappeared over the treetops. Some people screamed in horror while others scurried back into their apartments and slammed and locked their doors behind them.

Matt stood in the street and looked at the open door of his apartment and then to Abby's door and wondered how she could sleep though the commotion. He stood where he was, clad only in his boxers, and read the message sent via carrier pigeon in the form of helicopters. *How are they going to contact us?* The question he'd asked his uncle last night had been answered.

THE CURRENT STATE OF EMERGENCY IS RED!

FELLOW AMERICANS

Thirty-one hours ago at approximately 1:30 a.m., Eastern Time, The United States of America was attacked by an unknown enemy.

PLEASE DO NOT PANIC. STAY CALM AND STAY HOME.

Homeland Security reports multiple and simultaneous attacks throughout the United States. Electricity is out across the nation, phone lines are dead, and transportation has ceased. Please stay in your homes today and give your government a chance to work. The streets must stay clear.

PLEASE DO NOT PANIC. STAY CALM AND STAY HOME.

With your cooperation,
this state of emergency will be resolved within a few days.

DO NOT PANIC. STAY CALM. STAY HOME.

No nuclear bombs or dirty bombs have been detonated and no gasses or chemicals have been detected. Stay together, America. Help each other. Those with, please help those without. We will keep you informed.

DO NOT PANIC. STAY CALM, AND STAY HOME.

It was almost 8 a.m. and Abby still hadn't come out of her door. Matt bolted for the stairs leading back up to the second story and ran the ten yards to Abby's door and pounded loudly. The message was clear: don't panic, stay calm, stay home, but it was not working for him; he was on the verge of panic, and he was definitely not calm, and he was certainly not going to stay home.

*****

Abby swung the door open but held it tight in one hand. Raggedy from sleep, she squinted into the bright sunlight, and clutched a blanket tight to her throat, shielding her body.

"What's wrong? What's going on," she said, breathing hard and still half asleep. "Jeez, I must have overslept. What time is it? I should be on my way by now," she said still squinting. "Where are your pants? What's going on?" she asked again, this time with concern.

Matt wondered where she was supposed to be on her way to, but no matter because whatever her plans were, they just changed. An air-raid siren started blaring somewhere in the distance. She looked past Matt and saw dark clouds of smoke off in the distance, towards Seattle, billowing hundreds of feet into the air.

"Oh no," she said, her eyes opening wide. "Has there been a plane crash?" Matt saw that she was looking over his shoulder, so he turned to see what she was looking at, and then he remembered that she knew nothing except that the electricity had gone out.

"It's not a plane crash, Abby," he said, turning back towards her. "The US is under attack by terrorists," he said, with enough urgency that Abby looked away from the smoke and into his eyes to see if she could detect some heinous joke in his demeanor. "But it's going to be alright," he quickly added. "I've talked with Uncle Bill. We are implementing *Plan Alpha*." The silence that had engulfed their world for the past few days was now shattered by a plethora of *noises*: babies crying, mothers wailing, men shouting, sirens blaring, and dogs barking.

"Oh my God," she said, bending over as if she might be sick to her stomach. She held the blanket tight to her throat and slowly backed into the morning darkness of her apartment. Her face contorted into an ugly face of terror and her hands flew to cover her mouth, letting loose of the blanket and stumbling backwards until she fell onto the couch next to the television. Naked expect for her white panties, she curled into a tight ball and wrapped her arms tightly around her legs and began rocking back and forth. She began to shake like a wet, cold puppy dog.

"It's not true, you liar," she hollered. "You fucking liar! I'm going to my mother's today! I overslept, that's all. I'm going home," she wailed.

Matt snatched the blanket from the floor and moved quickly to her side and laid it around her shoulders. He sat next to her and put his hand on her shoulder.

"Abby," he said with as much calm as he could muster, "It's going to be alright. I have talked to Uncle Bill. We are going to leave for Brent's in a little while. You need to be strong and get ready." His voice was shaky, and he felt weak all over.

"How do you know this is a terrorist attack," she screeched. "I talked to my mom just last night. I'm supposed to be on my way to Cave Junction today. I need to call her. I need to pack and get going."

"Everything is closed, Abby. Remember? The electricity is out—you can't even buy gas." He told her about the helicopters, and then he showed her the flyer and pointed out that it was from the White House.

"Read it to me, please," she said, sobbing. She was bent over and tucked into a little ball. When she heard the words, she lost control of her bladder. "I need to call my parents." she said, barely audible and still bent over.

"You need to get up and get ready, Abby. I'll help you. Come on," he encouraged, standing up and extending his hand.

"Matt," she said, not looking up at him. "I need some time to process this. Please. I'll be alright in a few minutes."

He wasn't sure he should leave her like this, but he had things to do, himself. He would be close by—next door—it would be okay, he concluded.

"Okay, Abby. I'll be next door if you need me, but you need to get up and get ready to leave?" After a few moments of silence, Matt walked quickly towards the door, but stopped when he reached it and turned around.

"I told you this was going to happen, Abby. I told everyone. You need to get up and get your things together. Orders from Uncle Bill are that you are to come to my place."

"You heard from Uncle Bill? Did he hear from my mom and dad?" she asked, turning her tear stained face up towards him, ignoring his pleas to get up and get ready. She did not remember him telling her, just minutes ago, that he'd talked with his uncle. She was on overload—probably in shock, he concluded.

"We were cut off before I could ask. Some of the cell phones are working, but the land lines are all down. Like the flyer said, it's the same everywhere. It's so surreal," he added, "thousands of simultaneous attacks—just like I said it was going to happen." She didn't move and she didn't say anything. Her head dropped. "It's happening, Abby, and we need to get ready to leave," he said, reaching for the door knob.

"I can't leave right this fucking minute, Matt," she screeched. "I need to try to get through to my parents. I need to pack some things. Go home! Please! I will come over in a while." She didn't want to hear any more "I told you so's." And she sure as hell didn't want Matt to know she'd peed her pants. "My doctor," she'd explained to Matt the first time that she'd wet her pants in his presence, "said it's an emotional overload issue brought on by extreme stress."

She wanted to call her parents and talk to them in private. She was not in the mood to listen to anything more Matt had to say. Even the sound of his voice was grating on her nerves.

"Please Matt, go. I need to call my parents." He didn't bother telling her, again, that the cell phones were out.

"I'll go, Abby, but like I said, I talked to Uncle Bill, and he told me to tell you to get ready and for you to come to my place. That's the bottom line, Abby. That's what needs to happen. He will be here real soon, he lied, and when he gets here, we will be leaving."

"I need to call my parents," she screamed.

"Okay. Okay," he said, laying one of the flyers on the table next to her door. "Do what you have to do and then come over. Keep your doors locked and don't open them for anyone except me," he ordered. "I'll keep an eye out and come back in a little while to check on you." He then stepped out and pulled the door closed behind him, and then quickly, and to Abby's dismay, he stepped back in.

"I'll bring a gun over in case...."

"I don't need a damn gun, Matt! Please just leave! If I need something I'll scream! I'll be fine! I'll come over when I'm ready!"

*****

Somewhere a hundred miles to the south of the mayhem in Seattle, Montana and Moalim pulled off the county road onto a winding dirt road. A mile on, around a stand of thick pines, they were met by a dozen or so men with some real nasty looking weapons pointed at their trucks—more specifically, at their heads. It was a camp, of sorts, with a handful of large green tents erected in no particular order. The second truck pulled in behind them and quickly pulled around Montana and came to a sliding stop, raising a dust cloud that all but obscured the big 4x. Ali and Abdul jumped out to the cheers of their comrades. Moalim joined them, but Montana hung back, feeling a bit out of place amongst the foreigners, who were all speaking in a language Montana recognized as Arabic.

"It is a great success," Ali said, switching to English and looking over his shoulder at Montana. "We have succeeded in Phase I, and Phase II, anarchy, has already begun," he yelled, shoving his fists into the air. Another round of cheers, shouts, and bursts of gunshots rocked the camp. Men were dancing and flinging their arms in the air and shaking their weapons.

Ali turned to Abdul and to Moalim and signaled for them to follow. He then looked at Montana and paused for such a long time that Montana wasn't sure that the next thing that came out of Ali's mouth might be, "kill the infidel." But instead, Ali motioned for Montana to come to his side, and as he made his way to the threesome, the troop of men began whispering to each other and pointing at him, and looked on with suspicion.

"We owe you a great deal, Montana," he said into his ear. And then he turned to the crowd. "This man is a hero and should be treated as such. Some of you may recognize him as the man who brought you across the border. Feed him and treat him as a brother." At that, he, Abdul, and Moalim walked towards one of the tents and disappeared inside.

*****

Matt stopped outside of his door and checked his watch. It was already 9 o'clock, and he was as anxious as he'd ever been in his life. He stood for moment and looked at the skies in the distance. The dark clouds of smoke were thicker than they had been earlier, and now he could smell it, as well. Traffic on the streets had increased to parade proportions. People were fleeing to who knows where, ignoring the government's petition to stay off the streets. This is getting worse by the minute, he concluded. Where is my uncle and where is Eric, he wondered tight lipped, kicking the railing. His cell phone was in his hand, he flipped it open and noticed his battery was nearly dead and his signal strength was weak—only two bars, but it did show a signal, and that was a good sign, and just as he was about to hit his uncle's speed dial number, his phone rang, which made him jump, damn near off the balcony.

"Matt!" yelled Uncle Bill into his ear. "Are you up? Are you seeing what's going on? Have you seen the flyers?"

"Shit, Uncle Bill, it's crazy over here. You don't know. You live in the 'burbs. I'm in the city. People are panicked. It's happening; just like I said!" As soon as he'd said it, he'd wished he hadn't, so he continued quickly. "There are helicopters everywhere dropping leaflets from Homeland Security. We're under attack! We need to get the fuck out of the city," yelled Matt into the phone." Talking to his uncle, he became more anxious and rattled than he was when he was talking to Abby. "Pack your truck and head to Brent's...."

"Matt," yelled Uncle Bill into the phone, cutting him off. "There's no time. The phones could go out any second. Stay home Matt. Get Abby over to your place and be ready to move. I'll call or come over soon. Stay put. I'm counting on you, Matt. I need to make some calls. I need to talk to Brent." Matt did not want to "stay put," he wanted to get going. He didn't want to stay home or stay calm or sit and wait. His heart was pounding so hard he had to sit down on the bench.

"What are you saying, Uncle? We need to move, now! I'll grab Abby and meet you at Brent's..."

"Matt. Please! Calm down and listen for just a minute. We need more information. We don't know the conditions in Monroe. Maybe we have to make a new plan. We need some time. Please. Do this one more thing. Do it for me, please." Matt was anxious, but he was not panicked, and he immediately switched gears. What his uncle was saying made sense. They did need to know if the route was still open. *I will stay calm,* he willed.

"Right. Of course, Uncle Bill. We need more information," he said, calmly. Do what you need to do, and I'll get Abby and be ready. We haven't heard the last of this, though," he added. "A second and a third wave could be executed at any time. Maybe germs or chemicals the next time and the targets will be the populated areas. These bastards are only beginning..."

"Matt," his uncle interrupted again. "We need to save our batteries. I need you to get Abby and bring her to your house; Eric too, and if Rose is still with him, her too—keep trying to call them, don't leave your apartment. I'll get back to you as soon as I can. Soon. Real soon. Just stay put?" It was more of an order than a request. "It would be best if we travel together...." Matt cut him off.

"Yeah, I know. Okay Uncle Bill," I'll get Abby and bring her over and wait for you to show up or call. Don't wait too long, Uncle Bill. This is real serious shit; we are under attack, for Christ's sake!"

"I'll be there or get back to you real soon," said Uncle Bill, and hung up.

*****

Uncle Bill was on the phone to Brent the second he hung up with Matt. Brent answered and skipped all formalities.

"Hey bro," his friend answered in his usual laid back voice, "it would appear that the kid was right. You guys better pack it up and head out to my place—no time to wait—the sooner the better. We can figure it out from here." He was talking as if it were just another day. But Brent always was a cool character; nothing much ever really ruffled his feathers. If he raised his voice, however, whoever was the target was already in over his head.

"Brent, have you heard any news from anyone?" Have you heard from Cave Junction?"

"No good, bro. I tried just a few minutes ago. The phones are down. But the fliers said the phones and the electricity were out all over the country, so it's not a big surprise. Keep in mind, too, that they have outages down there all the time, so who knows for sure if Karla and Jake even know what's happening."

"Have you heard anything about local conditions?"

"Not really. In fact a friend from the Redmond area called and read me the flyer around seven. We are too far out in the boonies for special delivery like you city dwellers," kidded Brent. Uncle Bill could tell Brent was trying to lighten the mood, but Uncle Bill was not laughing. He was not a warrior like Brent, he was an outlaw and he wasn't used to all this war crap. A fist fight was one thing, guns, bombs, and war was something else altogether.

"Pack it up and hit the road, and bring Matt, Abby, and that computer geek, Eric, with you too," ordered Brent, "and if Rose is with Eric bring her too. We can always use an extra...cook," he said. "There is no time to waste, my friend. Hell's chariot is on the way."

"I understand, but I need to hang tight a bit longer. I have some loose ends to tie up." He didn't give Brent time to comment. "Shit, this could be a one-time hit, Brent. I want to believe that there won't be another wave of attacks," he said thinking out loud. "Matt thinks there will be more hits and maybe next time it will be chemicals or germs. Man. This is a hard one to figure. Maybe I should send him and Abby on ahead?"

"Screw your tools, your house, your clients, and everything else, brother. Pack the tools you need to work on the truck and hit the fucking road. Nothing is worth anything anymore. The most valuable commodity you have is you, Matt, and Abby." Nothing else except water, weapons, ammo, and gasoline is worth a shit, dude. It's all gone—it's all over. A new world is on the horizon, bro." Uncle Bill didn't want to believe it. He didn't want to just walk away from his home, his comfortable life, his business; he didn't want to believe that his government couldn't fix this.

"I have some things that have to be taken care of before I leave. Damn! He said angrily. If I get a hold of the fuckers that started this, I'll cut their throats myself. This is fucking bullshit!"

"Understood, comrade, but you need to get your priorities in order and get a move on. Get the hell out of Dodge."

"I need to get my ditty bag together, get my truck loaded and dig up thirty pounds of gold," he said, as if he were talking about mowing the lawn.

"Holy shit, man; you never told me. You actually got thirty pounds of gold? Where the hell did that come from?" he asked. "Never mind, just toss it in the truck with the rest of your shit and get moving. How much is it worth, anyway?" he asked as an afterthought. "It could come in mighty handy to barter with," he said.

"Who knows what it's worth now; maybe nothing, maybe something; last week it was worth almost three-quarters of a million dollars, so I can't leave it behind," answered Uncle Bill.

"Holy shit, dude. Pack it up, strap on your piece, sling your shot gun, pack your rifles and ammo and hit the road. And grab the kids," he added, pressuring his friend.

"It's going to take some time, Brent. But if anything more happens, I will send Matt and Abby on ahead, and I will catch up to y'all later. I don't want to hold them up any more than I already have. But," he added, "traveling together is safer right now, I'm sure of that. I also believe Matt can hold out another night. You taught him well, Brent," he said, thinking out loud, realizing that he was rambling.

"Don't stroke me Bill. The good thing is that he's on the second floor. He has an advantage there, but if a gang of thieves wants something he's got, like his truck, they could probably hold him off long enough to take it. And," he said without pause, "if you don't mind my saying so, you need a reality check, brother. It's over—another night in the city is not clear thinking. You need to head to the country." Uncle Bill didn't like hearing what he didn't want to accept. He'd become contented. He'd built a home for himself and Matt. What was so wrong with not wanting to lose it all?

"I'm just thinking out loud here, bro," said, Uncle Bill, ignoring Brent's observations. "If this is a one-time attack," he started, "and if it doesn't get any worse, then bailing out and losing everything to looters may not be necessary." He was pacing in circles in his garage.

"Hell, bro," said Brent, "you need to keep a few things in mind. One, it's a lot worse out there than you are admitting. You're fooling yourself—you have already lost everything. And even if there are no more attacks, there is going to be fallout from the lack of law, supplies, power, shelter, water, gasoline. The flyers from the feds pretty much said it all. Reading between the lines, I would say it's a whole hell of a lot worse than what they are saying. Water is going to be worth more than your gold real soon, Bill. And in the city, armed gang bangers are going to start collecting collateral sooner rather than later. Liquor stores, gun shops, sporting-good-stores, and private residences have already become targets, according to my sources. The National Guard can't take care of it all, and besides, the men and women in the guard will soon be thinking about the safety of their own damn families."

Brent was talking fast and loud, and Uncle Bill was listening. Certainly, his oldest and dearest friend was more up to how to get through this than he was. Matt, for that matter, was more knowledgeable than he was about these sorts of things.

"We are all going to be targets," continued Brent. "It's going to get real ugly real fast, so don't wait too long. I don't want to have to come and save your ass," said Brent, spinning the cylinder of his .357 on his pant leg. "Like Matt said, it's just the beginning. Tell Matt to get Abby and keep her close. If I don't hear from you, I will be expecting you. Get moving, brother, and like I said, the sooner the better." But Uncle Bill had already made up his mind. He was going to wait another night to see what the government comes up with—digging up the gold was just an excuse, and Brent probably knew it.

"Okay, Brent, we will hold out and hide and watch until tomorrow." There was a very long silence.

"Don't wait too long," said Brent, and then hung up.

Was he really putting possessions before the safety of his family as Brent and his nephew had suggested? Was he thinking rationally? He knew he should probably go, but wasn't there time to see if the government could handle this? He *was* concerned about his house and his tools and the hundred thousand dollar '40 Ford coup in the garage, and he did need to dig up the gold buried beneath his feet. His hand moved down to the .357 that was holstered on his hip and he removed it and peered at it as if he'd never seen it before. It was one of three matching weapons, all with matching ivory handles and all with names engraved in cursive. He holstered his weapon, and quickly began to dig in the only place in the garage that was dirt. In the pit.

*****

Abby sat with her knees tucked up under her chin, blanket still wrapped tightly around her. She reached for her cell phone that was plugged into the recharge wire on the same table that held the television. She remembered thinking when she'd plugged it in that the power might come back on during the night. Dazed, crying, and in shock, she punched in her mother's number on her cell and waited, not realizing there was no signal.

She was a wreck by the time she gave in to the realization that the phones were not working. She began to shake all over again. She couldn't think rationally about what to do, but finally concluded that she needed to go to Matt's. Maybe he's heard from Uncle Bill again, or Brent. Maybe he's heard from her parents. It was enough to get her moving and get her mind off the end of the world.

She got up and went to her bedroom to get clean clothes, and then to the bathroom to take a hot shower. She stripped down and stepped into a very uncomfortable, cold-water shower, instead. She was glad that it was summer.

She retrieved her backpack from the closet and packed it with two changes of clothing and tossed in all her bath supplies, emergency medicines, vitamins, combs, brushes, and the like. She was careful not to be too girlish about what she packed. No photos, no perfume, no stuffed animals. Just the necessities, she kept reminding herself. It's what Matt had taught her and it's what is written in *Plan Alpha*.

"This is not a nightmare. I'm wide awake and it's happening," she said to the hallway mirror. "I am packing to escape the city because worst has come to worst." She saw the tears running down her cheeks before she felt them, and she slumped to the floor, crying, confused, scared, and alone. She had either passed out or had fallen asleep, because she suddenly came to. Her first thought was of Matt. Has he left me? Has he gone without me? A new wave of terror engulfed her, and she jumped to her feet. I have to get to Matt's.

*****

Matt was standing on his balcony, looking and listening. It was past noon, and the sun was almost straight up. He had not yet seen or heard from his Uncle and the cells were still down. Over six hours had gone by, and he was getting very antsy and very worried. He didn't know what was going on with anybody—not Uncle Bill, Abby, Brent, Eric, or Abby's parents. He was as much in the dark as when the power first went out Sunday night, and he didn't like it. Waiting was not his strong suite. His truck had long since been parked under his balcony, where he could keep an eye on it. There was not much more he could do.

He reasoned that Uncle Bill could take care of himself. If he needed to, he would load Abby into the truck and head to Brent's on his own. That's what *The Plan* says to do, and that's what everyone would expect him to do. Uncle Bill knows the score, and he could leave a note. He was packed and ready to go, and it was getting late, and it would not be good, he knew, to be on the road, alone, at night.

There were already abandoned cars on his street blocking the flow of traffic. There were people hurrying down the sidewalks in all directions with luggage and bags in hand. Some were heading east, some west, some north, some south, and some were actually just walking in circles. It's beginning to look like a war zone, he thought. He retrieved his cell phone from his shirt pocket to try his uncle for the hundredth time.

*****

Abby walked to her door and set her backpack down. It was 3 o'clock, and she was as ready as she was going to get. She thought about her scrap books and her pictures and her stereo and furniture. Her car. What could she do? Nothing. Nothing but go to Matt's.

When she stepped out onto the balcony, she saw vacated cars everywhere, heading all different directions, parked on the lawn, in the street, on the sidewalk. She saw smoke from fires that she couldn't see, and she could smell creosote in the tainted air. It looked like the pictures she'd seen on TV of the devastation left behind from hurricanes and tsunamis, and again she shivered from head to toe.

She saw that Matt had moved his truck onto the lawn below his balcony and wondered what the manager was going to say about the deep tire tracks he'd left in the lawn. Then she realized that there were probably no rules covering a national emergency. There probably wasn't even a manager any more. No more rent to be paid, either, she thought, as another chill ran through her neck and shoulders. No bills, at all, in fact. No job to go to. She thought about her store and all the books. It would all have to be left behind, just as it was stated in *The Plan*.

The little money she had in savings was not accessible, and she held little hope of ever getting it back—what good would it be, anyway. Money, as it pointed out in *The Plan*, would probably be worthless. There was no place to go to buy groceries. Or water. Or gasoline. Although she had read it, it never sunk in—she'd never given it any real consideration. It is horrible. What she was looking at was a living nightmare.

She wondered how those without the benefit of a Matt or an Uncle Bill were going to survive. She thought about the old people and was overcome with grief. She certainly had a better chance of making it out of the city alive than most, and for that, she was grateful. She'd been so stupid, and now she may die.

Her thoughts moved back and forth between what was happening now and the way life had been before Sunday night. She thought about going over to the 7-11 to get something to eat, and as she stood and stared in the direction of the store, she noticed two hooded figures quickly stepping out of the broken glass door with plastic bags full of whatever, and running around the side of the building to a waiting SUV. "Looters?" she said quietly at what she was seeing. Her breathing quickened, as if keeping pace with the long strides of the runners. My God! Looters! They are looting the store! She turned to knock on Matt's door when she heard voices coming from the apartment below.

They were talking very softly and Abby felt guilty about eavesdropping, but it didn't stop her from moving closer to the railing to hear better what was being said. Her heart was beating like that of a hummingbird as she watched the SUV by the 7-11 speed off down the road.

"We need to stay here like the flyer says, Mandy," she heard a young man say. "The government knows best. Your parents will be doing the same thing, and they will be expecting us to be doing the same, too. It will okay; we just need to wait it out. Those helicopters will be back by the end of the day with news that it's all over, you'll see. Please try to quit crying. I love you, Mandy. I won't let anything happen to you or to sissy. I promise."

The voices were coming from the young couple with the new baby girl that had moved in just last month. Abby had spent enough time with Matt to have heard all possible scenarios, and she knew the power outage and the destruction and the warning from the government was probably just the beginning. It was odd, she thought, how when all of the different scenarios were being brainstormed and discussed by her outlaw friends, that she hadn't really paid close attention. Now, however, she could recall almost every conversation, every word, and she knew that staying in the city was a death sentence. She wondered why the government would tell the people not to leave their homes and to stay inside. They must know that they are condemning them to death by telling them to stay home. Maybe they figure the smart ones will leave and those that don't...well, survival of the fittest, she guessed. Darwin's gene pool will tighten up.

The streets still had traffic, although vehicles stacked high with possessions had to zigzag between abandoned cars and rubbish. She reached for Matt's door when she heard more voices. A crowd of people were gathering outside on the lawn a few doors down. She stepped up and leaned on the railing to look over the side to see what the commotion was about.

The general gist of the conversation was that buildings were burning, radio and television stations had been blown up, trains were derailed, airports were closed, car bombs were exploding, freeways and highways were pock-marked with giant wholes left by car bombs, power sub stations had been destroyed, cell towers were toppled, and of course there were major traffic jams on all roads leading into and out of the city. She could not choke back the tears—she was losing it again. She tried desperately to breathe normally, but felt she was hyperventilating. Just then Matt's door flew open, scaring her to her knees.

"Abby, you're here. I'm sorry," he said, reaching down to help her up. "I didn't know you were out here. I was just coming to check on you. Are you okay, Abby?"

"Did you see the looters over at the 7-11?" she asked, pointing with her thumb over her shoulder as she staggered to her feet. She was shaking and scared to death, but she was trying hard to keep it together. Seeing Matt and his truck gave her a feeling of safety, but every time she let her mind wander to things like hospitals with no electricity, people without groceries or food, or heat, she had to choke back tears. It was a nightmare, and inside she was scared to death, not just for herself, but for everyone.

"What looters? Where?" demanded Matt.

"They're gone now. They looted the 7-11 a few minutes ago and then drove off." She didn't wait for Matt to answer. "Matt, I can't get hold of my parents," she said, moving directly in front of him, blocking his view. Her eyes were red from crying and her face contorted, as the flood gates opened once again. She flung herself into his arms where she hoped to find some comfort. Matt held her for a few seconds, and patted her back as if she were a child, and then he gently pushed her away, keeping hold of her shoulders.

"Abby, Uncle Bill called earlier this morning and he told me to get you and to stay put until he called or showed up. I haven't heard from him since, and I'm concerned. I haven't heard from Eric, either. I think it would be better if you came over to my house. Your folks have my number, and if they get hold of Uncle Bill or Brent, they will let us know. Come on, get your things," he said, letting go of her shoulders.

"I am not going anywhere," she screeched, backing away from him. My parents may be trying to call. I have to stay home," she screamed, tears rolling freely down her cheeks.

"Abby. Please. Be reasonable. This is not the time to become independent."

"What the hell is that supposed to mean, you fucker! How dare you think I can't take care of myself! I have a car. I know the way to Brent's, and I know the way to Cave Junction. Don't think I can't take care of myself, you…"
She stopped short of saying *bastard*, but it was what she was thinking.

"I know this is bad. I know you want to talk to your parents, but there is strength in numbers, Abby. Bring your cell. You know the land lines are out," he said, reaching out to her. "If your folks are trying to call they will call your cell, right?"

"Yes, of course they will," she said, perking up. "Sure, what difference does it make if I am at your apartment or mine," she said, looking up into his eyes. "I don't feel very good, Matt. I need to sit down. Can I come in?"

"Of course," he said, stepping aside to let her pass. She went to the couch and laid down, instead, and Matt put a blanket over her. "I'm glad you are here, Abby. I have everything we need. All we have to do is pack the rest of the supplies into the truck, and we can be on our way to Brent's. Are your bags packed?"

"Yes," she said, barely audible. "They're by my door."

"That's good Abby; I'll get them. Everything is going to be okay. Rest if you can. It's going to be a long ride to Cave Junction," he said, hoping it would give her something positive to think about.

How can he say that, she wondered? How can he be so sure that everything is going to be alright? The looting has already started. What's next? Murder! Rape! Please God, let me wake up.

*****

Abby wondered if Matt would still be concerned for her if it weren't for Uncle Bill's relationship with her parents. A new wave of tears welled up in her eyes, and she turned on her side with her face towards the back of the couch so when Matt returned, he wouldn't see her crying. She wished Brent or Uncle Bill were here. Even Eric would be more of a comfort. *Eric!* "Where is Eric," she screeched when Matt came back with her backpack. "Where is Eric?" she demanded again as if Matt were keeping it a secret. "Why isn't he here? He knows about *Plan Alpha*. He's supposed to be here. Where is he?"

"I don't know Abby. I couldn't get through to him. Damn, woman" he said, "I've been trying, Abby. He's probably on his way right now. Maybe he stopped for a damn burger. I don't know."

"He should have been here by now. Go look for him. He's our friend."

"Abby. He knows what to do. He will be here. Please try to calm down. How about a Valium?" He didn't wait for her to answer, but instead unzipped a zipper on one of his backpacks and withdrew a small amber bottle filled with pills. Pouring half the contents into his hand, he withdrew one small yellow pill. "Here," he said holding it out. She knew what valium was, but she'd never used it. Never needed too, but she snatched it out of his hand as if it were a magic pill that would fix everything. "I need water," she demanded.

"We need to find him," she insisted, getting up from the couch and heading towards the kitchen. "Don't you care about him?" she said, pushing past him. Matt took a deep breath.

"He knows the way here, and to Brent's, and to Cave Junction. There is traffic flowing, and he has a brand new 4x SUV," he said, trying hard not to swear, for whatever reason. He knows the route we are taking. Abby! *We can't leave!*

"I've got to go look for him," she said, pushing by him, again, walking briskly towards the door. "I'll find him. Don't worry Matt. I'll find him," she said, sincerely and reassuringly. "You wait here for Uncle Bill, and I will go get Eric."

"I can't let you leave, Abby. Uncle Bill told me to knock you out if I had to, but under no circumstances were either of us to leave."

"You really would hit me, wouldn't you, you bastard." This time she didn't hold back what she'd wanted to say earlier. What she'd been thinking the past few weeks.

"Yes, Abby, I will. Now sit the fuck down and shut the fuck up. I need to think." Abby obeyed.

*****

It was 5 p.m. and still there was no word from anyone. Matt made a point of trying to call Eric and Abby's parents in front of her so she could see that he was trying. He had lost patience with her.

The battery in his cell was nearly dead. Brent has a generator; I'll charge it when we get there. If Abby gets too much more out of control, he would duct tape her to a chair. He laughed to himself. She hadn't said a word since he'd told not to. Maybe the valium was kicking in. His cell rang at 6 p.m.

"Matt!"

"Uncle Bill!"

"Matt. I have been trying to get through for 2 hours. I almost jumped in the truck and came over, but I can't leave yet. Looters have already hit Rose's place next door because no one is there, but I scared them off with a couple of shots from the 12 gauge. The good news is, as bad as it is, conditions seem to be stabilizing—the cells are working off and on. I spoke briefly with Brent, but he still hasn't been able to get through to Jake and Karla. He also said that the National Guard is everywhere, but roads are still open and they were pretty much just watching and leaving people alone. How's Abby?" Before Matt could answer, he had to get out of ear shot of Abby and needed an excuse to step outside.

"You're breaking up, Uncle Bill. I'm stepping outside." He looked at Abby and was glad to see that she was staying on the couch. She was looking at him with anticipation, however. He gave her a hand signal that meant just a minute, and she stayed where she was.

"She's pretty upset. Hysterical, actually," he said, as soon as he was out of ear shot. "I gave her a valium. She wants to go looking for Eric, but I took her car keys without her knowing. I threatened to punch her in the jaw if she didn't sit down and try to recompose. She's in shock, I'm sure. She is pretty shook up, Uncle Bill."

"You need to convince her to stay at your house tonight...."

"What! We need to get the fuck out of here before we're trapped— before dark," he yelled into the mouthpiece of his cell, not believing what he'd just heard. "Stay here another night?" he repeated.

"Matt. Please listen. We don't have much time. We need to think rationally. You are pretty secure where you are. Brent said you have an advantage on the second floor. And there is only one way in." Matt was pacing the length of the balcony, ready to explode. It was too much. No Eric. They weren't leaving today, and Abby was off her rocker, and he, himself, was vibrating with each beat of his heart. He needed to get going. "I am okay here," his uncle continued, "I have enough fire power to blow up a city block, and every door and window in my house is booby trapped. Can you hold out one more night?"

"What is your problem, Uncle Bill? What is so fucking important that you are putting us all in jeopardy?" Matt was pulling no punches. He wanted to move.

"It seems the attacks have subsided...." This time Matt cut *him* off.

"Yeah, but things are going to erupt again at any minute. The 7-11 across the street was just looted. There are cars abandoned and smashed up, all up and down the road. People are running in every direction to who knows where, Uncle Bill, and I know this is not over! Not by a long shot. I can feel it. It's not safe here, Uncle Bill! The next attack could be with gas or germs. I was right about the whole thing to begin with, and you know it," he shouted. "We need to get the fuck out, now!"

"Stop shouting at me, God damn it! We need to hold out one more night! Please listen," he said, more calmly." Shit, thought Matt, I'm going to have to babysit him, Abby, and Eric, too; if Eric ever shows up, that is.

"Matt. I have thirty pounds of gold that I still need to dig up out of the garage, he lied. By the time I'm finished, it will be dark. It's better I think, to travel to Brent's during the day. First thing tomorrow we will head out. I swear to God, first thing tomorrow. I Promise." Matt's phone bleeped a low battery warning. "We need the gold to barter with," he said, pleading his case.

Gathering all the calm and patience he could muster, Matt said: "I don't like this, Uncle Bill; I don't like this one fucking bit! And, my phone just bleeped a low battery warning, so if we are disconnected again, you will know why."

"We need to stick together, Matt. All of us. There is strength in numbers."

"What do you want me to do?" Matt finally asked.

You can start by getting ready to head out.

"I'm packed and ready to go—I already told you that. I have been for two fucking days. My truck is below the balcony where I can keep an eye on it."

"Good. How about Abby?"

"I just told you...."

"You need to get her packed and ready. Lie to her if you have to. Tell her we're leaving tonight. You both need to be ready."

"I will do it your way, Uncle Bill, but don't patronize me," Matt said slowly, emphasizing what he was saying. I have already told you, I have it all under control here. Abby is on the couch and her things are here. All we have to do is get in the truck and go." What his uncle had said about the gold just dawned on him as if he were hearing it for the first time. "What do you mean you have 30 pounds of gold? Is that for real? Where did you get it?" His phone beeped again, and then went dead. Matt snapped the lid closed and went back inside. It was 6:08 p.m. He had a mission. Even if it wasn't getting the hell out of Dodge.

He sat down across from Abby.

"That was Uncle Bill. He talked to Brent. No one has heard from your parents. Could be the cell towers are down in that area and they don't have any idea of what's going on. Probably no PCTs out there," he said more to himself than to her.

"What's a PCT," asked Abby.

Portable Cell Tower," Matt said. "Could be they don't have a clue as to what's going on, he repeated. Uncle Bill told us to dig in for the night and that we will leave first thing in the morning. Abby didn't answer. Instead, she laid back down on the couch and rolled over, facing the back. Matt got out some supplies and fixed a tuna fish sandwich. He got out some cold steak and chicken from the ice chest to snack on. He wondered if Abby had eaten anything today.

He went to the couch and gently shook her shoulder. She turned over and opened her eyes.

"I'm ready," she said without preamble, and started to get up.

"We're not leaving yet, but you need to eat, Abby. It's not much but you need to keep your strength up." He set the plate on the coffee table next to her along with a bottle of water. She tightened her lips and looked at the food as if it were a plate full of worms and bugs.

"Thanks," she said softly, reaching for the water.

*****

Okay, he thought, she's here where I can keep an eye on her. If we have to leave, we can be out of here real fast. He sat down at the dining room table where he could keep an eye on the front door, Abby, and his truck on the lawn below. He watched Abby as she picked up a piece of cold steak and bit into it like a starving dog. "Do you have any salt and pepper," she barked, dropping the steak back onto the plate as if it were garbage.

"You're pushing Abby," he said, picking up the salt and pepper shaker from the table and taking it to her. "You better chill because I am about to the end of the line, here." She ate her food like an animal and did not say another word.

After an hour of silence, Matt told her that his uncle had called.

"You told me."

"Sorry, I didn't know if you heard me."

"Why wouldn't I hear you, Matt? You were sitting right in front of me."

"I just want to make sure we are on the same page, Abby. That's all. No need to bite my head off. I am trying to take care of everything, here. I'm trying to stay calm, and you are not helping with your attitude. Uncle Bill is stalling our get-away, and I don't know why," he confided. "I think we should have been out of here way before this. I don't know where Eric is, and I haven't heard from Brent." His thoughts were running together as he thought out loud. He needed to talk to someone rational, and it was not Abby. "What I do know," he continued, "is that we are all in this together. So it's no good to be fighting each other. We all want the same thing. We all have the same goal. Survive and get out of here alive, and get to Cave Junction—this is serious, Abby." Abby got up and started for the kitchen, and when she passed Matt, she said, "thanks for the dinner," and then she picked up his plate and carried them both into the kitchen. It was a start.

"I'm sorry, Abby, that we haven't heard from Jake and Karla. But they're in the county. They have supplies and water. They are probably fine. Do you want another valium?"

"No."

"You should try to sleep, Abby. I will wake you if anything changes." He was looking at her sitting on the couch, staring blank-faced at the wall or nothing at all. She turned her head slowly towards him.

"I figure *you* need some sleep," she countered. "I am not sleepy so *I* could keep an eye on things," she rebutted.

"I'm okay," he said, thinking he could not trust her. He didn't know if she would leave or fall asleep or what, but he couldn't trust her. I can booby trap the door, he thought, but who will watch the truck? The alarm system was set to go off with the slightest of vibration, and the red blinking warning light on the dash was a good deterrent. If the alarm did go off, he could be on the front porch, shotgun in hand, pretty damn fast. It might be okay, he reasoned, and after a minute he said, "Thanks. I could use some shut-eye." He smiled at her, and yawned.

"Good," she said. "I'll go leave a pee, first," she said, and headed towards the bathroom. Matt took the opportunity to fix a string to the door and to the lamp. He was looking forward to some sleep. When Abby returned, she laid her head down on the arm rest of the couch, and before Matt had finished cleaning up and getting ready for a much needed power nap, she was out. Matt looked at her sleeping, mouth open, and thought, fine lookout you're going to be. He placed a chair in front of the door and then put a vase on top the chair, close to the edge. Any movement at all and the vase would fall. He covered Abby and lay down on the pad in the middle of the room and was asleep.

*****

Matt woke and looked at his watch. He'd been sleeping like the dead for four hours. It was unusually quiet, and he was tired. Just as he was nodding off again, he heard a light knock at the front door. He turned over and picked up his gun and pulled back the hammer. He rose from his pad, slowly, and inched his way towards the door, staying to one side. Again, the knock, this time a bit more aggressive. Matt's grip on his .357 tightened as someone tried the knob. Matt pointed his gun at the door and inched towards the window next to the door to see if he could look between the cracks of the Venetian blinds to see who it was. Maybe it was Eric. The door knob moved again and this time there was the sound of a key being inserted into the lock. He took a chance. "Get away from the door unless you think it's a good day to die," he yelled, waking Abby who sat bolt upright. He figured if it was Eric, he would yell out. But no one spoke except for Abby.

"What's going on?" she yelled.

"Quiet!" he said, softly. Matt knew when people walked past his door. He could feel the vibration in the floor of the rickety old place, and there was no movement outside. Whoever was out there was not going away. Someone hit the door hard, trying to break it in. It startled him, and he stepped back. He aimed high in the door and pulled the trigger. A long flash of light blasted out the end of the barrel, and the smell of gun powder filled the room. Abby shrieked and pulled herself into a ball, holding the blanket close to her mouth, stifling back a scream.

The *boom* from his .357 was deafening inside the small apartment, but it did the trick. Whoever was outside started running. Matt moved to the window on the other side of the door and pulled the blinds apart just enough to see two men dressed in hoodies running down the steps, two and three at a time. He moved the small barricade from in front of the door and quickly stepped outside and took aim. They could come back, he thought. My truck is right there. He fired another round at their heels as they bolted around the corner and into the darkness.

Before going back into his apartment, he noticed that Abby's door was wide open. He took a small flashlight from his pocket and went to have a look. Her apartment had been sacked. Couches were turned over, drawers and cupboards were open. And the refrigerator, he noticed, was open and empty. There was clothing and books and papers scattered on the floors. The looters had hit her house, and neither of them had heard a thing. He closed the door behind him when he left. He looked down at his truck and could see the red warning light on his dash board flashing a reflection in the cab and believed it was the reason it had been left alone.

"What's going on Matt?" she whined loud enough for him to hear from the front porch. Matt came back into the apartment and closed and locked the door before answering her. She was now sitting up, on her knees, on the couch. It was the first time he'd shot at a person, or towards a person. He thought about Abby's apartment being looted and it was unnerving. What would have happened if she'd been home, he thought. She probably wouldn't have checked to see who it was. She would have just assumed it was me or Eric. He was shaking, and he was glad that the light from the candles was dim.

"It's okay," he said. "They're gone. Go back to sleep." He didn't want to tell her about her apartment because he knew she would want to go look. He went to the table and sat down. He was wide awake and concerned about his truck—their only way out—their only transportation. Abby had a car, but if they had to go cross county, it would be useless.

"Did you just kill someone Matt," she hollered.

Matt lifted his head and looked at her in disbelief. The dark shadows cast by the candles gave her an eerie appearance. She is going to be worthless, he thought.

"No, Abby, I just scared them away. Maybe I should have killed them, though. What they were doing was wrong and they are dangerous. Even after I warned them, they were still intent on breaking in. Yes," he said, "I should have shot them. Go back to sleep, I don't think there will be any more trouble tonight, so go back to sleep." Abby didn't argue. She curled up into the fetal position but did not close her eyes. Matt got up and blew out the candles, and the room became black and quiet and smelt of gun powder and candle smoke.

It was 4 a.m., and Matt was up wandering around. He checked on his truck and then covered Abby with the blanket that had fallen onto to the floor. He went to leave a pee and then tiptoed into the kitchen and peered out the tiny window to see if the world was still there.

A thick fog, engulfed in the blackness of dawn, suddenly glowed with lights from an oncoming vehicle, and within moments, a convoy of army trucks emerged from the dense haze. They disappeared as quickly as they appeared, back into the fog, leaving a trail of red taillights streaming into the mist. Seconds later, two jeeps appeared, and then another shot up the street going in the opposite direction. What the hell, he wondered.

Just as he was getting his sleepy brain around what he'd just seen, two more jeeps heading in opposite directions stopped in the middle of the road right outside of his apartment, where the drivers exchanged some words before speeding off to unknown destinations. What's going on now, he wondered? He waited and watched, but there was no more action. He sat down at the table and rested his head on his arms and dosed.

A few hours later he was rocked by the blaring voice of a man being amplified through loudspeakers. The initial blast from the powerful speakers jolted him to a standing position, causing him to bump his knee, and his heart to pound like a freight train hitting the joints in the tracks. He noticed, before disappearing into the kitchen, that Abby was also wide awake and in a sitting position. She had the blanket pulled tight around her neck, and her eyes were bulging. She was not smiling and did not say anything, for which he was grateful. Outside in the street, an army truck like the one he'd seen a few hours earlier, was moving slowly up the road.

"Marshall Law is in effect as of now," dictated the man with the microphone. *"There is a curfew effective immediately. All stores, businesses, and public transportation facilities are closed. Electricity is out in all locations. Gas stations cannot pump gas. Land line phones are out. Do not leave your homes. In case of emergency seek help from a neighbor, but do not drive—stay off of the streets.*

"Something else has happened," Matt said loudly. "The second wave; just like I said! I better try calling Uncle Bill," he added, not talking to anyone in particular, even though Abby was now up and walking towards the front door. The message outside continued as Matt grabbed his phone and caught up to Abby as she was pulling the chair away from the door.

"Stay in your homes. No one shall be driving any sort of rig on the streets," ordered the man adamantly. *"Stay off the streets. The National Guard has been given orders to remove all vehicles from the streets by any means*

necessary. You must stay off the streets so the United States Government can do its job."

"What's going on," whined Abby, as Matt flipped open his cell phone and opened the door all in one quick motion. His phone, he remembered, was dead.

"Give me your phone, Abby. Hurry!" Abby quickly reached into her pocket and retrieved her phone and handed it to Matt, who had his hand out waiting. It was off. Good, he thought, and pushed the button to power it up.

"Marshall Law is now in effect," he told her. "It's not good," he added, opening the door and stepping onto the balcony, half expecting to see his uncle pulling up next to his rig. "Something else has happened. It's escalated!" he shouted over the blaring of the bull horn, as he punched in his uncle's number. Abby didn't reply.

"Do not panic. Use your emergency rations and boil your water before you drink or cook with it. I repeat; a curfew is now in effect. If you are already out on the streets in your vehicle, return to your homes immediately. Stay off the roads or you will be removed with force. Looters will be shot without warning...."

Matt punched the final number into Abby's cell. His uncle answered before the first ring completed.

"You hearing this?" Matt hollered into the crackle of the phone.

"Loud and clear, Matt. We don't have much time. Stay there and be ready to move. Stick to *The Plan*. I'll be there as soon as I can. I'm leaving right now. I tried calling Brent, but I couldn't get through. I'm on my way," he said, and then hung up.

"Get ready Abby," Matt said, standing close to the railing, watching the convoy as it rolled slowly by. It was 6:30 a.m. "Uncle Bill is on his way. He should be here in less than thirty minutes. "Abby! Get moving. Get dressed," he ordered more loudly, not realizing that she had never *undressed*. "We need to load the truck, *now*," he said, sternly. "We're heading out." He would leave with or without his uncle at 8:30, and proceed with *Plan Alpha*. It was *The Plan*.

Instead of going for her backpack, Abby went back to the couch and sat down. The blanket was pulled tight around her mouth, exposing her nose and eyes, only. "Abby!" Matt said again. "Get up!"

"You don't need to scream at me, Matt! I hear you! What's going on?" she screeched. "I am dressed," she screeched, pulling off her blanket to let him see. "What's going on?"

He was at the end of his patience with her and he snapped.

"You just heard the fucking message, didn't you? The National Guard is driving up and down the street telling everyone to stay home and off the street. Uncle Bill is on his way." Matt could tell by the look on Abby's face that she didn't fully comprehend.

"How can we leave if the National Guard is ordering everyone to stay off the streets?" she asked. Matt was about to yell at her again when she stood up, and holding the blanket tight, she walked towards the bathroom without another word.

At 8 a.m., Uncle Bill still had not arrived. In the distance, he could hear The National Guard continuing its warnings, but nothing seemed any worse than it was earlier. He wished his uncle would hurry. "He should have been here by now," he said aloud. He was anxious to get out of the city. "Where the fuck is Eric," he said, not expecting an answer. Abby stepped out onto the balcony next to him.

"I thought your uncle was on his way. Where is he?" she cried. She was standing next to him with the blanket draped over her shoulders and clutched to her throat. She was using it as a hanky to wipe her red eyes and runny nose. She was in a pathetic state, and her blubbering and whining was irritating to him. She looked like someone he'd never seen before—like a street urchin hooked on heroin, and he was—repulsed.

"I don't know," he said harshly, "but *The Plan* says, if he doesn't show by 8:30, we are to leave without him and head to Brent's."

"We can't just leave," cried Abby, fresh tears running down her cheeks.

"Abby!" he said loudly, without consideration to her worries or cares or state of mind. "We have a plan, and procedures must be followed," he said as if talking to a child. "After 8:30, if my uncle is still not here, we must assume he is no longer headed in this direction—whatever the reason is irrelevant. Maybe the roads are out. Maybe he had a flat tire. Maybe he's dead," he said, exasperated. "What he will be doing and expecting us to do as well, is to take any route we can find to get to Brent's. It will do us no good to wait or to go looking for him. It's all part of *The fucking Plan*," he barked. "I thought you read it—two hours after the call telling me he is on his way to my house, if he is not here, we are to leave without him. Now snap out of it and join the team. I don't have time for this crap," he yelled. Abby looked at him for a moment, then turned and walked away without answering. Matt had too much on his mind to try explaining any more. He was wound as tight as the recoil spring in his .45. He was glad Abby hadn't wanted to go back into her apartment to get something she'd left behind.

The message continued to blast from the loud speakers and then repeated as the trucks slowly moved up one street and down another. Like an echo, he could hear them blaring out of synchronization in all directions.

Matt stood on the front porch thinking that maybe he's caught in traffic. Maybe the National Guard trashed his truck. Not likely, he concluded. Where the hell is Eric and Rose?

*****

Across town, Uncle Bill was throwing the last of his bags in the back of his truck, listening again to the repeating orders blasting from the loud speakers warning anyone who was driving on the roads to get off the roads and into their homes. The part that stuck in his mind was, *"if you are already out on the streets in your vehicle, return to your homes immediately."* That was their ticket to Brent's. They would make their move as one of those already on the road but heading home. It is time, he concluded, to get out of the city. He jumped into his truck, saluted his garage, and turned the ignition, but the truck did not start. The battery was as dead as flattened road kill.

*****

Moalim was driving the lead truck and there were two more trucks behind him, six riders in all. As they sped down the back roads towards Cave Junction, they left chaos and destruction in their wake, firing randomly at shadows in the streets and tossing sticks of dynamite at structures that were close to the road, leaving more panic and more destruction behind them. It was part of the plot, that after the first wave of attacks, to keep on striking, no matter how insignificant the targets are. They were only a few of the thousands of killers causing chaos and mayhem, and as Montana squeezed off a few rounds into the windows of a passing car, he wondered if there was a heaven and a hell. If there is, he thought, firing a few rounds into a house they were passing, he knew his final destination.

*****

While Matt waited, he thought about how harsh he'd been with Abby, and decided to go over *Plan Alpha* with her one more time, hoping that if he talked to her gently that it might bring her back into the fold. She was sitting on the couch, wiping her red eyes and runny nose on the blanket.

"Abby," he started gently, "I'm sorry I snapped at you, but I am just as much on edge as you are. I don't know where my uncle is. He should have been here by now. I don't know where Eric is either. He should have been here yesterday. I am just as worried and concerned as you, but we have to follow the procedure in *The Plan*." She looked up at him and waited for him to continue. "We are going to leave in twenty minutes with or without Uncle Bill and Eric, he repeated for the umpteenth time. "Everyone will meet at Brent's." For a minute, she didn't answer or argue.

"Let's just go straight to Cave Junction, Matt. Why stop at Brent's at all? Why do we have to wait any longer? Let's just get on the freeway and go. If the army stops us, we'll just apologize and head for the back roads. They can't be everywhere," she whined.

"Didn't you hear anything I just said, Abby? We are going to leave in twenty—no, make that fifth-teen minutes," he said, checking his watch. "And we will stick to *The Plan*. We will follow the route Uncle Bill is going to take to get to Brent's unless it's not passable. Eric will be taking the same route. Maybe he's already there; or maybe one or both of them are stuck on the side of the road, that's why we follow the same routes," he said, as if explaining to a small child.

"You think Eric is already there" she asked looking up at him.

"Maybe," he said, knowing it was probably not true unless he'd gotten there since his uncle had last talked to Brent. When he'd finished explaining, he opened the door, grabbed the cooler, stepped out onto the balcony and headed towards his truck. Abby picked up her pack and followed him out the door, and after tossing the last of the bags into the truck, they returned to the balcony and waited. Jesus, he thought, I wish Uncle Bill would get here. Damn! Where the hell is Eric and Rose?

It was 8:35—five minutes past evacuation time. They stood on the balcony and watched a line of jeeps speeding west towards the Puget Sound, swerving to avoid the broken down and abandoned vehicles on the road.

He felt comfortably odd standing there with his holstered magnum hanging off his belt, like a gunslinger in the old west. He was on high alert and was anxious to hit the road. He had heard the announcement about getting off the road if you were already on it, and knew there was only a small window of opportunity to get to Brent's. After a certain amount of time had passed, the excuse would no longer be believable, and the National Guard would do whatever they had to do. He envisioned a pile of cars and trucks piled one on top of the other, like in a rusty old junk yard. He would wait until 9 o'clock and then he and Abby would leave. If the feds push cars off the road, he wondered, where will the people go? It was probably a bluff.

If he had to, he would throw Abby down and tie her up. She was his responsibility. At least until he hooked up with his uncle. Suddenly he saw it. An out-of-place camouflaged 4x pick-up truck sandwiched between two government trucks. "Uncle Bill!" He yelled, pointing.

"Where?" she hollered.

"There," he pointed again.

He felt like someone had just poured a bucket of cold water over his head, as a rush of relief flushed through him. He'd never been happier to see anyone in his life. Uncle Bill's turn signal started blinking as he pulled out of the formation. He swerved hard to the right and jumped the curb and skidded to a halt next to Matt's truck, below the balcony. Matt guessed his uncle had simply told the army cops that he was on his way to my house when he heard the message about the curfew. He was a gutsy fellow, a good bullshitter, and a damn welcome sight to see.

*****

Uncle Bill piled out the door of his truck and slammed it shut behind him. He took the stairs two at a time until he stood directly in front of his nephew. Damn, he looks haggard, thought Matt—old, he thought.

"Good God, Uncle Bill, can you believe this shit?" Matt said, giving his uncle a hug, still thinking about how rough he looked.

"We've got to get going," Uncle Bill said, without answering. "It's not good Matt. These guys," he said, indicating the last of the convoy, "didn't tell me much, but they did tell me that power was out all over the country, and one of the older guys flat out told me that I should be heading in the other direction, meaning towards the hills and out of town. Sorry I'm late," he added, looking at his watch. It was 9 o'clock. "I had to put a new battery in my truck." He was talking to Matt, but he was looking at Abby.

"My neighbor has a friend who has a friend who told him that all the branches of the military, as well as the National Guard, were called into active duty two days ago—many, however, are not responding. He said there were fires burning and looting everywhere, including private homes." He wanted to tell Matt that there had also been reports of killings and rapes and that there were dead bodies in the streets, but he didn't want to say it in front of Abby. Besides, they would see for themselves soon enough. "We need to leave immediately. If we're stopped, we say we're heading *home* to Monroe. Tell them we were up in Bellingham at Tiny's, and that we were on our way to Monroe when we heard the news." He looked at Abby who had not moved from the railing of the balcony.

"Abby, you will ride with me," he said. It was not a request. He could tell she was in shock, just as Matt had said. He also figured Matt had probably not given her much nurturing—it wasn't part of his persona. "Eric will ride with Matt," he said, looking around. "Where the hell is Eric?" he demanded, looking straight at Abby and then at Matt, knowing the answer before the words finished blurting from his mouth.

Abby didn't answer. Instead she opened her arms and took two big steps toward Uncle Bill, tears pouring from her eyes like water over Niagara Falls. Uncle Bill looked over her shoulder at Matt and rolled his eyes.

"It's going to be alright, Abby. You need to trust me and Matt. We are going to Cave Junction to stay with your parents until this thing is over. First, though, we need to get to Brent's. Are you packed and ready to go?"

"I'm not a child," she said pushing herself away. "You don't need to talk to me as if I were a child. I am packed and ready. My bag is already in the truck. Are we going to go get Eric, first?" she demanded. She had wet her pants and did nothing to conceal it.

Uncle Bill who was dressed in black jeans, black T-shirt, camo vest, and hiking boots, pulled a familiar map from his back pocket, exposing his long barrel .357.

115

"Abby," he said, putting a gentle hand on her shoulder. "We need to leave right now. Eric will have to get to Brent's on his own. He knows what to do, and he has this same exact map," he said, holding the map out for Abby to see. "He's probably already moving. He may already be there," he said, smiling at her. "He's a smart guy, but we can't wait for him and we can't go searching for him. We have a very small window of opportunity here, and it is closing fast. We need to leave right now."

"Okay, Uncle Bill. I'm ready," she said, wiping her tears and her nose on the blanket.

"I will need you to navigate," Uncle Bill told her. "You will read the map and tell me the route. We can be at Brent's in an hour, hour and a half tops if the roads are clear, and with the Guards warning everyone to stay inside, there's a good chance ninety five percent of the people will be doing just that. We have a small window here," he repeated, "and we need to get going before it closes." He put his hand behind her back and guided her towards the trucks, being careful not to step on the blanket she'd become attached to, and was dragging on the ground behind her.

"Let's move," he said, looking over his shoulder at Matt.

"Okay. Good. Let's go," said Matt, closing the door. "Everything here is as secure as it's going to get. Let's hit it." He pinned a note to the door that simply read: Eric, follow Plan Alpha.

Uncle and nephew quickly checked the straps holding down the tarps over the beds of the trucks by giving them a tug before climbing into their cabs. Abby and her security blanket were already in the passenger seat of Uncle Bill's truck, waiting. A moment later they were speeding down the road heading for Brent's.

*****

Uncle Bill handed Abby the map.

"We need to get to Highway 2, and I figure we should go the back way. What do you think?" She took the map, but did not look at it.

"Yeah. We should go the back way. The route is via 524 through Thrasher's Corner and Maltby. One ninety-sixth to 522 to 162nd Street to 203. We can cross the river there," she said, in a monotone voice. She knew the route by heart because that's the route he and Matt always took. "Take the next right onto 196th," she said, and Uncle Bill turned hard without stopping. He glanced into his rearview mirror and saw Matt hot on his tail.

"Abby, if we get stopped, let me do the talking. Don't say anything, okay?"

"Of course. I know my place," she said, turning her head in his direction, smiling with her lips but not her eyes. Uncle Bill was real concerned, but it would have to wait until they got to Brent's. "It's good you memorized the directions, Abby." He didn't want to sound patronizing, but he wanted her to talk. It would be good medicine.

"I'm sure you know the way too, Uncle Bill, but thanks just the same."

The roads were pretty deserted; at least so far, but there was a smoky, brown haze that smelt like electrical wires burning. On the left, they passed a fast food joint with all the windows broken out. There were two cars overturned and still smoldering from fire that had consumed them. Uncle Bill wondered if it was an act of vandalism or if the Guards had made good on their threat. Whatever the reason, it was foreboding and it added to the uneasy feeling that was already living in his gut. Abby pulled the blanket over her nose and stared.

It was uncanny how the streets and parking lots were deserted. All of the shops had broken windows, and there was merchandise, garbage, and litter strewn everywhere. The survivors will survive, he thought. Good, bad, right or wrong, the strong will survive.

Uncle Bill accelerated to sixty, speeding past the convention center, slowing briefly at the dead light signals at the intersection leading to the freeway going south. The on-ramp was blocked by the National Guard. "Damn," he said, looking quickly at one of the soldiers who was holding a rifle across his chest, hoping that one of the four jeeps ready for pursuit did not speed out after him. He kept the truck moving and the guards left him alone. Matt followed close behind.

"They've got the freeway blocked off," said Abby, twisting in her seat to get a better look at the army vehicles and the soldiers standing guard. It was 9:30 a.m. Maybe she's coming around, thought Uncle Bill, but guessing, probably not.

"I am so scared," said Abby, choking back tears. "I don't know how my parents are or if they even know what's going on."

"Your parents are probably fine, Abby. They are used to power outages out there in the country." Uncle Bill caught a glance of Abby out of the corner of his eye. She looked so shaggy and unkempt and sad that he wanted to pull over and hug her, but there wasn't time. They had to keep moving—nurturing would have to wait. "It's going to be okay, sweetheart. You have to trust me," he said, concentrating on the road ahead. Hearing himself say the words aloud gave him a boost in confidence, as well. "We'll see them in a few days."

*****

Matt followed closely, matching his uncle's speed. There wasn't much traffic and people were nonexistent except for a few ghostly figures darting in out from between buildings and lurking in the shadows. Most of the population, he figured, were hiding behind locked and barricaded doors because they had no place to go. Most of them would parish. Trash and paper twisted and fluttered in the warm summer breeze and reminded Matt of yet another old black and white *Twilight Zone* episode he'd seen.

The caravan of two came to another freeway entrance, it too was barricaded by army trucks and guards, but none of them took out in hot pursuit, either. So far, so good. Getting to Brent's may not be as tricky as he'd thought. He hoped Eric was alright, Rose too.

About the time he was settling into driving and feeling somewhat at ease, they came to an intersection where he fell into line behind his uncle in a short line of cars, trucks, and vans. It was a road block. There were men wearing uniforms with no identifying patches. Not good, thought Matt.

He watched as one guard cautiously approached the truck in front of his Uncle. The guard had his gun drawn and was flanked by a guard who had his rifle leveled straight at the driver's head. After thirty seconds of verbal exchange, and a quick look into the windows and the bed of the uncovered truck, the guard waved him through. It was a good sign. Next, it was Uncle Bill's turn, and Matt rolled down his window and leaned a bit to hear what was being said.

He watched as one of the guards talked to his uncle, while the other guard held a rifle pointed menacingly at his uncle's head. Another pointed his rifle at Abby, while yet another started loosening the ropes holding down the tarp, lifting it a bit to see what was concealed beneath. It was very intimidating and very threatening. Matt wondered if they might be looking for someone or maybe explosives.

"Keep your hands on the wheel," ordered the guard. "Passenger," he said gruffly, "put your hands on the dash board." The guard waited for them to comply and then continued. "There's a curfew in effect right now and you are not allowed to be on the road," he bellowed in a very stern voice.

"I know," said Uncle Bill, "and I'm sorry. We heard the announcement this morning, but we were already on the road driving down from Bellingham. This is my niece," he indicated, with a nod of his head, making sure not to move his hands from the wheel, "and that's my nephew behind us," he said, nodding over his shoulder. "We are trying to get home." The guard listened. "Will we be able to get through?" asked Uncle Bill with the concern of a lost tourist.

"Show me your registration and license?" ordered the guard without answering. Shit, thought Matt, wrong address. He quickly recalled that the guards hadn't asked the driver in front of his Uncle Bill for his papers. Uncle Bill promptly provided the requested documents from the sun visor and waited.

"Is this your current address," the guard asked?

"No sir. We live in Monroe now. I just haven't had the chance to get it changed yet. We've been in Bellingham visiting friends, and we headed out this morning about five. We got wind of the announcements to head home about six and that's what we're trying to do," he said, peering up at the guard.

The guard stared at his uncle for a few seconds, looking like he was deciding whether to call him a liar and drag him out of the truck and beat him, or let him go. Matt watched as the guard bent down and looked over at Abby and hoped she stayed silent.

The guard then looked at his comrade who was shoving the corner of the tarp back down over the supplies. When the job was finished, he gave the boss man a nod of his head.

"Okay then, you guys get going and stay home once you get there. Am I clear?"

"Yes of course. We just want to get home."

"Move out," he shouted, stepping back from the truck and waving his uncle across the highway. After he passed through, the boss man stepped menacingly in front of Matt's truck and held up his hand in a gesture that unmistakably meant stop. The boss man's buddy now had his rifle pointed at Matt. It was scary as hell.

"Keep your hands on the wheel," he yelled, stepping closer. "Where are you going and what are you doing out on the road," he demanded, pointing his weapon straight at Matt's face.

"That's my uncle and my cousin, he said. "We were in Bellingham and now we are trying to get home." He could barely get the words out and breathe at the same time. He had never had the business end of a weapon pointed at him, and it was scary as hell; even though he believed they would not shoot him unless he did something really stupid. They were so damn serious and intimidating; they would scare the hell out of anybody.

"Move out and stay off the streets," he ordered, waving Matt through. Matt let out the clutch and his truck lurched and the engine stalled. His heart was pounding so damn hard he thought he might need to rest a second and take some deep breaths, but quickly turned the ignition key, instead. The power house under the hood roared to life, and in the next instant he was speeding across the intersection.

He picked up speed to catch up with his uncle who had slowed to wait for him. Just as he pulled up behind his uncle a helicopter flew low overhead blaring out the same message that they'd heard earlier. I sure hope Eric has found his way, thought Matt, quickly looking up. Him and Rose, that is.

They continued on 522 with no more interruptions. When they got to 162nd Uncle Bill hung a right. It was a shortcut to 203 that would take them across the Skykomish River. A mile past the river they turned left up a county road to an area known as High Rock, which was Brent Chandler's stronghold.

Uncle Bill stopped in front of the four-inch steel cow-gate that blocked entry to Brent's property. The gate set back twenty feet off the county road which ran parallel to the Skykomish River. Pine trees as tall as the Space Needle crowded the road in all directions allowing bolts of sunlight to penetrate the thick forest, like the rays shining through the stained glass windows of the Sistine Chapel.

The country air smelt pure and clean compared to the burned air in the city, and Matt breathed in deeply, replacing the polluted air in his lungs. The quietness in the country could be found no other place on earth. It was the *quintessential* quietness.

They used a password to get past Brent's camouflaged. Matt spotted Tiny talking with one of the guards, and right behind them he caught sight of a movement in the trees of a well camouflaged. If he hadn't moved, Matt would not have seen him at all.

The cow-gate swung open and the guard waved Uncle Bill and Abby through, and then Matt. As he followed his uncle up the pitted, dirt road, a labyrinth of switch backs made for slow going, he thought about Eric and hoped he was already here. Off to the sides of the rutted passage, small clearings served as encampments for *guests*. If the tenants were around, they were staying out of sight. He thought about how hard it would be to guard the perimeter, and then remembered Eric and the mission they'd been on a few weeks past when Eric installed surveillance cameras.

When they reached the cabin, Uncle Bill turned his truck around so that he was facing downhill. Matt waited until his uncle was parked and then followed suite. There were people milling around outside the cabin that Uncle Bill had never seen before; some in fatigues, some in street clothes, but all had a suspicious look in their eye that read, "who the fuck are you?" The serenity that he'd come to expect in the country had been replaced by a fortress of guns and attitude.

"Are you okay, Abby?" asked Uncle Bill. "Would you like to sit in the truck for a while?" He wasn't sure how to say it, but he figured she wouldn't want to walk into Brent's with wet pants. He also figured if she cleaned up and changed her clothes that perhaps she would feel better. "Brent has a shower with hot water, something we have all been without for a few days, and I am looking forward to getting clean," he said, being careful not to make an issue of her accident. "Would you like to take a hot shower?" he asked, gingerly.

"I think I'll just sit here for a while. A shower sounds good, though. Thanks. Uncle Bill," she said quietly with head bowed, "would you get my backpack out of Matt's truck for me, please?"

"Sure Abby, no problem. I'll let you know when the bathroom is clear."

"Thanks."

"Abby," he said, when he got back from Matt's truck with her pack. "If there is anything at all that you need. Any questions that you have, you only need to ask. You are like a daughter to me, Abby," he said, reaching in and gripping her shoulder. "I hope you know that you can lean on me if you need to—any time, for anything, anything at all." He leaned close and gave her a kiss on the forehead. "We're going to be okay, and I will do everything in my power to get you and your folks back together as soon as it's physically possible—a few days, I hope. Promise."

"Thanks," she said, sniffling back tears and smiling.

Matt was standing in the road waiting for his uncle and Abby to join him. When his uncle stepped up beside him, he realized Abby was staying in the truck.

"Is Abby feeling better?"

"I think so," answered Uncle Bill.

Just as they reached the steps that led to the covered porch, Brent emerged from inside, looking like Wild Bill Hickok, himself.

"The guards at the gate called up and told me you were here. It's about time, and it's damn good to see you, brother," he said, giving Uncle Bill a hug. You too, Matt," he said, giving him a handshake and hug, as well. "Where's Abby and Eric?" he asked, looking over at the trucks. "I see Abby, where's Eric?"

"Eric never made it," said Uncle Bill. "And we only had a small window of opportunity so we couldn't wait. We were hoping he was already here."

"No such luck," said Brent. "Damn, I sure hope he's all right, Matt. He seems like a good guy. Keep the faith," he said, nodding his head.

"He doesn't know the password to get past the guards, so maybe you should let the guys at the gate know that a computer geek named Eric might show up," said Matt.

"Will do," he said, flipping open his cell phone. Hope he's alright," he said, again. "How about Abby? How's she doing?"

"A little shook. A lot shook, actually," answered Uncle Bill. "She's still in shock. I think a hot shower will help, but she wants to sit in the truck for a while and get her thoughts together." Matt raised both eyebrows and nodded.

"No problem. The shower is free. and the fire is burning, so she can clean up any time."

"Good. I'll let her know in a little while," said Uncle Bill.

"Let's go inside to the table where we can talk," said Brent, turning towards the door and pushing it open.

*****

Abby took a clean pair of pants from her pack and set them on the empty seat next to her. Uncle Bill's words were comforting to her. She felt better than she had since Matt woke her up with the news of the attacks two or three, or was it four days ago? After a few minutes, she adjusted the rearview mirror for a look at herself. Her long blond hair was twisted, tangled, and oily. Her face was dirty and tear- streaks that looked like wondering rivers ran to her chin, and down her neck. She was mortified at how raggedy she looked.

She looked around and saw no one close by, so she very quickly unbuttoned her pants and slipped them off, panties too. She grabbed a clean pair of jeans and had them on in seconds flat. She opened the door and stepped out, taking the wet clothes that she had bundled into a tight wad, and placed them into the back of the truck, under the tarp, and placed her backpack on top. She would wash them out when she took a shower.

When she first looked towards the cabin, she saw no one, but when she looked the next time, she saw someone on the roof with a rifle, looking in her direction. A guard, she thought. Hope he had a good show. He's pretty far away, and probably can't see much from there anyway, she started thinking, and just as quickly thought, so who gives a shit. She was glad and relieved to be at Brent's. They were finally on their way.

She poured some water from a plastic bottle, and soaked the corner of her to wipe her face. It felt really good. The smell of smoke in the air reminded her of home. The morning fog that hung near the ground on the west coast was fading away, and the sky, the blue skies of the Great Northwest, were beginning to show above the tree tops. How odd it was, Abby thought, that it's so beautiful up there in the sky and so horrifying here below. God's earth had little to do with man's earth, she concluded.

I wonder if Brent has heard from my parents. I wonder where Eric is. God, she prayed, please let them be okay. When she looked back towards the roof of the cabin, the guard had disappeared. She stuffed her wet clothes into a plastic bag and put the bag in her pack, and then walked to the cabin and sat down in one of the wooden chairs on the porch, not quite ready to face the outlaws on the other side of the door.

*****

Matt knew his way around Brent's like he knew his way around his own apartment. The two story post and beam construction consisted of a kitchen and living room on the main floor, separated by an eating bar. A trap door in the floor of the kitchen led to a cellar where food and water was stored. The bathroom was behind a stone wall. On the living room side of the stone wall was a sturdy wood burning stove that could double as a cook top. On the door to the den off the living room was a 'Keep Out' sign posted in bold letters. The door was usually shut, but today it was open, exposing computer monitors and security monitors that lit the darkened cave in hues of green and gray; it was eerie and out of place, thought Matt—sort of like a secret room, behind a secret door in a science fiction movie. On the opposite wall, there were two large gun vaults that housed Brent's private stash of weapons.

The living room had a large rectangular wooden table which was the gathering place. A few wooden chairs lined the walls, but there was no couch or easy chairs. If you wanted to sleep, you went to your tent or to a room; sleeping was not allowed in the living room. The cabin seemed bigger on the inside than it looked from the outside.

"The news is not good, gentlemen. None of it," began Brent. "We don't know who's behind it, but from the reports coming in, here's how it went down. The war began at 10:30 p.m. Sunday night when the power went out. Car bombs caused most of the big damage, but there are numerous reports of hundreds, if not thousands, of individuals targeting any and all infrastructure that would stop the country from moving forward; this includes the destruction of transportation depots like truck stops, train stations, bus stations, airports, electrical sub stations, power lines, highways, bridges, government buildings, to name a few. We don't know if there will be another strike or not, but if there is, we expect it to be in the form of chemicals. Let's pray that that does not happen, gentlemen, as it's much harder to dodge gas than a bullet. We haven't heard of anything more."

"No word on who's behind it," questioned Uncle Bill.

Matt didn't wait for Brent to answer.

"I bet I know exactly who's behind it," he said, with composed intensity. Brent and Uncle Bill both turned to him at the same time, and Uncle Bill raised his hand in a hopeful gesture that might stop his nephew from starting in on one of his, out of control speeches, but before he could stop him, Matt started with his hypothesis.

"My guess is that over the years since 9/11, al-Qaida has been planting terrorist in our county and assigning each one of them a target and a time to carry out one massive, simultaneous strike." He looked at Brent, and then he looked at his uncle, and when neither of them said anything, he simply added, "It's what I think."

"You could be right, kid. You've been right so far," said Brent. Uncle Bill nodded in agreement and was pleasantly surprised at his nephew's calmness while explaining his theory. A theory he'd put forth on a number of occasions but in tantrum form.

"I need to get my maps from the truck," said Uncle Bill, getting up from his chair.

"I'll go with you."

"Me too," said Brent. "I could use some air, and Abby's probably ready for the shower, and I need to turn the heat down on the stove. It's hotter than hades in here," he said, racing for the door as if the place was on fire.

"Yes, it damn sure is," said Matt, almost knocking over his chair in his hurry to get outside.

Abby was still sitting in the chair on the porch, and when the door opened, she jumped up as if she were not allowed there.

"Hi Abby," said Brent, giving her a quick, paternal hug. "The bathroom is open; have at it. I'll tell everyone to stay clear of the house until you come out again."

"Thanks, Brent. I'll be quick."

"Take your time, Abby. The water is heated by the wood stove, so it won't run out."

"Thanks. It's good to be here," she said. "Have you heard from my parents?"

"No, Abby, I haven't. I'm sorry, but I wouldn't worry too much about your mom and Jake. They are used to hardships and can take care of themselves just fine." Abby leaned over and picked up her bag and stepped inside the cabin and closed the door.

"No one is to go inside until the lady comes back out," ordered Brent to a guard who was standing close by.

*****

Matt, Uncle Bill, and Brent walked to where the trucks were parked and talked about how Uncle Bill, Abby, and Matt were going to get to Cave Junction, when they were going to leave, and what they were going to take, how they were going to keep in touch, and when they would meet again. They gathered up the maps and talked about alternatives and hypotheticals until Abby came out of the cabin.

"Boy that felt good," she said, approaching the guys but speaking to no one in particular. She was smiling for the first time in days.

"Glad to hear it, darlin'," said Brent, smiling but hurried. "We need to talk for a few more minutes and look at a map, inside, so make yourself at home, Abby, but don't wander too far off. Like your uncle says, 'it ain't safe in these here woods, and there's a pervert behind every tree,'" he said, smiling. "Let's step back inside gentlemen," he said to Matt and Bill and started for the door of his cabin. "Hey Abby," he said, stopping and turning around, "one more thing." He looked at Uncle Bill and Matt. "I think it's time to drop the "Uncle" part of Uncle Bill," he said, with a serious tone. "It's not good for the enemy to know that folks are related; gives them an advantage. From now on, you are just friends traveling together."

"No problem, here," said Uncle Bill. It will be just fine with me to drop that handle for a while," remembering how it all started when Matt had come to live with him.

"No problem," Matt said smiling at his uncle—I guess," he said, wiping a pretend tear from his eye.

"I'll try," said Abby.

"It's especially important for you, Abby, to distance yourself in that way from these guys. You're just a hitchhiker or a neighbor heading south. No destination, and no specifics, just south—maybe because you have friends in California that you are trying to track down. Y'all can discuss the details later, but keep it simple."

"I'll be careful," she said.

"Good. Okay then. We have business to discuss," said Brent, motioning to Matt and Bill to follow him into the cabin.

Uncle Bill was tired and wanted the briefings to end. He knew the drill. He'd studied the maps, and in the end, the only plan was to get going and play it by ear. Naturally, they would stay as close to the route as possible.

"No one knew for sure what roads are open or closed or destroyed or fenced off by landowners protecting their own," said Brent before they'd had a chance to sit down. "If the cell phones work out in the country is something that has to be tested. *Plan Alpha* has its good points, for sure, but the real test will be trial and error." Uncle Bill was worn out. He wanted to set up camp and check on Abby and talk with Matt. He wanted to get away from all these people and all the confusion. I need my space, he thought—I miss the sanctuary of my garage.

*****

Suddenly the front door flew open. Abby burst through followed quickly by Tiny who had a body draped over his shoulder. He plopped Eric down in a chair and stepped back. At first everyone just stared.

"Eric needs help," Abby screamed. "Don't just stand there. Get him some water or something." Her outburst set in motion a triage of energy. One was fetching water, another a blanket, and another a medical kit.

"He showed up at the gate," said Tiny, "and I brought him up in the ATV." He stared down at the skinny, ragged kid he'd met a few days earlier and said, "Damn, I hope he's okay." Eric looked as if he'd been dropped out of the back of a fast moving truck, which turned out to be not too far from right.

"Eric," yelled Matt, grabbing his friend by the shoulder and forcing a glass of water into his hand. "What the hell happened to you? Eric!" Eric rolled his eyes and tried to focus. He took the water and drained the glass and then took a deep, shaky breath and lowered his head until his chin rested on his chest.

"Rose is dead," he said, so quietly that everyone had to strain to hear.

"What," said Uncle Bill?

"Rose is dead," he repeated. "We were at my place last night getting ready to come to your house, Matt, when someone knocked on my door. I thought it was one of my neighbors, so I opened it. I'm in a gated community for Christ's sake." His shoulders started humping as he began to cry. "I'm so sorry," he said between heaves. "There was nothing I could do." Abby went to his side and took his hand. "Oh, Eric, I'm so sorry."

"I loved her, Abby. I really loved her." No one moved or said anything for a long time. His clothes were torn and dirty and he was covered in blood from his head to his feet, making his story all the more pitiful.

"Eric. Tell us what happened," Brent finally said.

"I opened the door to see who was there, and all of a sudden it just slammed into my face. Two big black guys stormed in with guns, demanding money and my car keys. They knocked me down and started kicking me. I gave them everything they asked for, Matt. My car keys my money, everything," he said, looking up at Brent through tear filled eyes.

"What happened to Rose, Eric," asked Uncle Bill.

"They were laughing and talking about taking her with them as a door prize, and when one of them reached out for her, she slapped him hard across the face and then attacked him. He shoved her away and she fell and hit her head on the corner of the fireplace hearth." He burst into a new wave of tears and Abby put her hand on his shoulder, and he reached up and squeezed it, and they cried together. "She was shaking, Abby, and I thought that she was trying to get up, but when I reached down to her, I could see…into her head, and then she was still. She didn't move. It was the most blood….The most horrible thing I have ever seen." He began crying uncontrollably, and between sobs and breaths, he looked up at Abby. "Her eyes were open and she was looking right at me, Abby—I thought she might be alive so I tried shaking her…."

"It wasn't your fault, Eric," said Matt, putting his hand on Eric's shoulder, again. Except for the sobs escaping from Eric and Abby, the room was silent, as the news of their friend's death settled in on those who knew her best.

"How did you get here, Eric," asked Uncle Bill.

"I got a ride from the army."

Brent cocked his head sideways, scowled his eyebrows and said, "What?"

"When the black guys saw Rose's head split open they freaked out and ran. I ran after them not even knowing what I would do if I caught them. They knew where my car was because they ran right to it. They must have been watching me. Maybe they lived on the property; I don't know. When they got to my car and started to unlock the door, I stopped. I couldn't do anything, Matt. I was afraid!" He cried more loudly.

"There was nothing you could do, Eric. There were two of them and they had guns. It wasn't your fault. There was nothing any of us could have done in the same situation." *That's why I always carry a gun*, he wanted to say, but didn't.

"When they started driving away," Eric continued. "I didn't know what to do, so I chased them into the street; I ran after them but they just kept getting further and further away. Finally I had to stop and just stand there. I didn't want to go back to my apartment. I couldn't follow them. I didn't have my phone, so I just stood there," he said, choking back more tears. "I don't know how long I stood there before the National Guard came along. I told them what had happened. They didn't even go after them, Matt. They just let them go." He wiped his finger across his nose and stared at nothing.

"What happened next, Eric?"

"They took me back to my apartment and they covered Rose with a blanket. I told them we were trying to get to Monroe, and they told me they had a convoy going out that way, and that I could hitch a ride with them. They said they would take care of the body. It was so horrible, Matt. Brent, I am so sorry. I should have tried harder. I couldn't save her. I'm sorry," he cried.

Brent picked up the bottle of Jack Daniels that was sitting on the table and handed it to Eric.

"Eric. Out here, when something horrible like this happens, we find comfort in the arms of Uncle Jack. Here, have a pull. It will calm your nerves. It wasn't your fault."

What kind of bullshit is that, thought Matt. *Comfort in the arms of Uncle Jack?* Jesus. Eric took the bottle and finished off the last three fingers as if it were water.

"I've got to step outside for a few minutes, Eric," said Matt. "I'll be right outside the door if you need me. I'm glad you're here bro, and I'm real sorry about Rose. I know it's hard, man, but try to pull it together; we need you." Matt stepped through the door and Uncle Bill and Brent followed. Abby stayed with Eric.

Once outside and away from the front door, Matt said: "Can you believe that shit? Rose dead and Eric almost killed."

"Yeah," said Uncle Bill. "Jesus." Again, it was quiet for a long time as uncle and nephew tried to take it in. And again, it was Brent who finally broke the silence.

"Count your blessings, and look at the bright side, kid," he said, walking off down the road towards the front gate. "Your friend is alive" he said over his shoulder. The comment, like what he'd said to Eric about 'comfort in the arms of Uncle Jack,' seemed cold to Matt, and when he looked at his uncle, he saw that he was scowling.

*****

Abby waited and listened patiently to the outrageous story of Rose's untimely death one more time. She didn't want to hear about it again, it was too awful. She blocked out the gory parts and thought instead of a something she needed to do, and when she figured he was stable enough, she excused herself.

"Will you be okay here by yourself for a while? I'll go find you some clothes so you can get cleaned up—Brent has a really nice shower."

127

"I don't know. Yes, I guess. Yeah. Sure. Go ahead." Abby re-positioned the blanket that she'd put around Eric's shoulders.

"I'll be back soon," she promised, but before closing the door, she looked back; Eric had his head on the table and was sobbing so pathetically, that tears once again filled her own eyes, as well.

Eric was smaller than most men, and she didn't have anything that would fit him, which meant she was going to have to go on a scavenger hunt. She started down the dirt road in search of clothing for her friend. She saw that Uncle Bill and Matt were setting up camp, but she was a woman on a mission and did not stop.

"Everything okay?" hollered Uncle Bill as she walked by at a brisk pace. "Is Eric better?"

"Yes, Eric is better. He's going to clean up," she said, keeping her pace.

"Hey Abby," said Uncle Bill, catching up to her. "Where are you going?"

"I'm just walking. I'll be back in a few minutes," she said, turning back towards the trail. "I need some air."

"That's fine Abby, but don't wonder too far."

"I know," she said, gruffly, as she hurried off. Thirty yards down the road she came across a small campsite.

"Hello," she said, stopping to address the dark-skinned woman who was sitting near a small fire. The woman, older than Abby, but young, looked at Abby with suspicion, and before answering, she looked down at the ground beside her, and Abby's eyes instinctively followed her gaze to the huge revolver resting beside her. "I've got one just like it," Abby said, "but I left it back at the camp," she said. The Mexican woman smiled a knowing smile and Abby took it as a sign to continue. "Can I talk to you for a minute?"

"Sure," she said. "Me and my friends Smith and Wesson here could use some female conversation. Would you like some coffee?"

"Actually, I would. It sounds really good right about now. But I'm sort of on a mission. I have a friend who just arrived and he's in pretty bad shape. He was beaten up pretty badly trying to get out of the city. Everything he had was stolen…."

"I saw him being carried up the road a while ago. What can I do for you?"

"Well," started Abby, not knowing quite how to ask. "I noticed you are about my friend's size; he's not a very big guy," she said smiling. "I was wondering if you had an extra pair of pants and a shirt that I could buy. His shirt and pants are torn and all bloody." The weathered woman burst out laughing a feminine but mocking laugh, which made Abby feel very uncomfortable, wondering what she'd said that was wrong.

"I don't have any 'extra' anything," she said. "I do have a pair of pants and a shirt that I'm not wearing right now. But buy them?" she said, starting to laugh again. "Buy them with what, American dollars or Mexican Pesos? Don't you know that money is worthless, girl? I have no use for money," she said, nodding towards the fire, indicating for Abby to have a look. Around the edges of the small pit were half burned American and Mexican bills of all denomination.

Abby felt foolish. She knew money would be worthless, but it had slipped her mind. God, can it really be that bad, she thought, staring first into the fire and then back at the woman, swallowing hard at the realization.

"I don't have anything of value. I had to leave everything behind," said Abby, suddenly realizing that everything in her apartment was probably gone by now, too. She was racking her brain trying to think of what she could trade.

"I heard that you are heading south. I want a ride," the dark skinned woman said bluntly. "I need to get back to Mexico; to my family."

"Yes," said Abby, looking into the woman's dark brown eyes. "We are heading south, but I don't know if there's room. We have two trucks and four people."

"Well," said the Mexican, stirring the fire with her stick. "That's the price for the clothes."

"I don't know," said Abby, thinking. "I'll have to ask...."

"I have one more thing to offer," interrupted the pretty Mexican woman, tossing back a blanket that was lying next to the fire covering her sleeping bag. Abby looked down to see a fine looking, but short rifle. "I'm a warrior. I know how to shoot, and I know how to fight," she said. Abby's eyes lit up. We could probably use some more help, she thought.

"I'll go ask," said Abby. "I'll go ask right now, in fact. My name is Abby," she said, leaning over and extending her hand.

"Hello Abby. My name is Juanita. It's nice to meet you."

"Same here," said Abby, smiling. She liked Juanita and felt she would be a big help on the trek south, and female companionship, as well. She excused herself and hurried off to talk to Uncle Bill and Matt. When she came close to the campsite, she heard Uncle Bill and Matt talking. Matt was sitting on a stump, head down, listening to his uncle. She hesitated, and then waited, in the shadows.

"I understand why you feel that way, Matt. Lots of people distrust, even hate, anyone from the Middle East. But do you really think they're all bad? Matt thought for a few moments before answering. When he did, it was with the steady and firm voice of a man with convictions—no ranting, no raving, just a calm response stating his point of view.

"You know, Bill, I have thought about this for a long time. I have often wondered if I was crazy or if I was becoming a bigot, but the answer is always the same. No. I'm not crazy, and I am not a bigot, and I have good reason to distrust every damn one of them, and yes, I do think they are all bad, and I don't trust any of them. It's like I said earlier, I think they're all part of an elaborate plot to bring down the US. I just can't seem to give them the benefit of the doubt."

Abby thought it was odd to hear Matt call his uncle, *Bill,* instead of Uncle Bill. She also realized that Matt was *talking*, not screaming or ranting. He was just sharing his opinion with his uncle. When she thought more about it, she realized that his foul language had waned, as well. He seemed to be calmer since this whole thing started. More mature. How odd, she thought.

"Okay, Matt. You have a right to your opinion, and I have a right to mine."

"Fair enough," said Matt.

"Here is what I think," said Uncle Bill smiling. "I think we can and should be suspicious and leery of everyone we don't know, especially now. In fact, I think it's prudent. Profiling is a good idea, right now. But let's be smart about it, too. We can be suspicious and leery but avoid confrontation. Who knows what they know that could be beneficial to our own survival. If we can pass as a group of friends just trying to survive, I think we have an advantage."

"Well, we don't want to look like a bunch of pussies or easy targets either, Bill. We can't look weak. We won't last a day on the road if what I suspect is happening out there is really happening," he said. When Abby heard that, she wondered how it could be any worse. "People we run into need to know that we are prepared to defend ourselves, *with our lives,*" he emphasized. "They need to know that we are armed and dangerous. Damn, look what happened to Eric, for Christ's sake. Can you believe that? Rose is dead and he could have been killed, himself. It's a miracle that he made it here, at all," he said, changing the subject.

"It's amazing that he's alive," said Uncle Bill. Did you notice how Abby seems to have snapped to?" said Uncle Bill.

"Yeah, I noticed. And I'm glad—for both of them."

Abby didn't want to continue eaves dropping, now that the conversation was about her. And besides, she was on a mission.

"Hi Matt: Bill." she said, in the most gleeful tone that either had heard in quite some time. "I just ran into a girl named Juanita who has offered some clean clothes for Eric if she can hitch a ride south—I didn't tell her we were going to Cave Junction," she quickly added before someone yelled at her. "She's trying to get home to Mexico." Matt scowled and looked up at Abby.

"We can't take anyone with us, Abby. We're full up. Clean clothes for a ride south? I don't think so. We can find something for him to wear. I'll ask around. Is she Mexican?"

"Let me invite her over, Matt. She's a real nice woman and she has guns, and yes she's Mexican, but she knows how fight—she's a warrior and looks pretty tough. Like the warrior girls at Uncle Bill's party," she said in a sing-song voice—a voice Matt recognized as one she used in the past when she was trying to get him to do something he didn't particularly want to do. "I mean Bill's party," she said, correcting her mistake.

"Well good luck to her," said Matt, "but we have enough guns."

"We may be able to use someone like her," said Uncle Bill, raising his eyebrows and turning his head towards Matt, making it sound more like a question than a statement.

"Maybe," said Matt, after thinking a moment. "I guess we could invite her over for some coffee to *feel her out*," he said smirking.

*****

Uncle Bill, although laid back in his older years, had been around plenty in his younger years, and was no dummy. He knew that talk was cheap and that good intentions never got the Golden Gate Bridge built. He knew he couldn't count on Abby or Eric for the help they might need to get to Cave Junction, and the jury was still out on his nephew because he'd never really been tested. He hoped that when the going got edgy, that Matt would be up to the task at hand. A warrior would be a big advantage.

"Okay, Uncle Bill. I'll go get her," said Abby, getting up and brushing off her butt.

"Abby," said, Uncle Bill, "it was decided that everyone will call me Bill, remember? It's a security thing. If the bad guys know we are related, they will have an advantage. Please call me Bill from now on. Don't slip up, Abby. It could mean the difference between life and death.

"Okay Bill," she said, as she skipped off down the dirt road like Dorothy in the Wizard of Oz.

"She still ain't quite right," said Uncle Bill.

"She's still over the edge," said Matt, looking at his uncle watching Abby dance off down the dirt road.

*****

Back at the cabin, Eric, tired, achy, and dirty, had fallen asleep. When he woke, he felt better. Not good, but better. He believed in power naps. He felt out of place sitting there at the table draped in a blanket, more like a waif than a computer guru. The Jack was wearing off and he wished he had another bottle. He grew tired of waiting for Abby to return, and of the people who were wandering in and out asking him if Brent were there and then asking, "what the hell happened to you?" He decided to go outside and look for his friends.

*****

It was 6 p.m. and the tents had been set up next to the trucks. A chill was in the air, and the heat from the fire felt good. Something hot to drink would be good, thought Uncle Bill. But it would have to wait.

"I'm going to go check on Eric," he said, getting up slowly.

"I still have a lot of chicken and a bit of steak I barbequed a few days ago that needs to be eaten," said Matt. "Maybe he's hungry."

"Sounds good," said Uncle Bill. "Get Abby going on something when she gets back. Keep her busy." When he turned towards the cabin, he bumped into Eric.

"Eric," he said, reaching out to him. "I was just coming to see how you were doing. Are you feeling any better? Would you like something to eat?"

"I don't know what to do," he said, sobbing. "I have nothing. Rose is dead. My car's been stolen, and who knows what's left of my house and my stuff," he said, not answering the question. "How come no one cares that Rose is dead, Uncle Bill? It's like everyone is just saying 'oh well.'"

"Eric," he said, taking hold of his shoulders with a firm grip. "It's tough—it's very tough on all of us. Rose was one of the gang; we all liked her very much. We loved her. I've known her since she was a kid, and I am very shaken by the whole thing. I don't know what happened to her parents either, Eric, they disappeared. We all lost a lot, and we all had to leave everything behind. But right now, Eric, we need to think about surviving." He squeezed a little harder when it looked like Eric's thoughts were drifting—he wanted Eric to focus on surviving; he *needed* Eric to focus on surviving. "Everyone will have to pull their own weight." He would carry him for a while but soon he would have to do his share or he would be a burden and detrimental to them all. "Have you read the information we gave you in the packet about getting to Cave Junction?" asked Uncle Bill, changing the subject.

"No. Not really. I sort of looked at it. I'm sorry. I just never thought anything like this could ever happen. Jesus. This is a nightmare," he said, tears running down his face.

"It certainly seems like a nightmare, Eric, but I guarantee you that it's not—it's all as real as you and me standing here talking. We all have to pull together," he said, tightening his grip on Eric's shoulders, again; "for everyone's sake. We need everyone to be thinking rationally and we need everyone on the same page. You need to read the material in the book. We will be leaving for Cave Junction in the morning," he said, knowing that nothing had been set in stone as to when they were really going to leave. "We've been wondering if we should travel by day or by night. Maybe the sooner we get going the better. I want you to think about this, Eric, so we can talk about it later. Would you do that for me?"

He felt like he was talking to a kid and hoped that he did not come off as patronizing. *Jesus*, he thought. Abby and Eric were both adults, but neither of them had any idea how to survive without electricity, a microwave oven, and the connivance store on the corner. He figured it was the same with most young folks of their generation. They never had to work very hard to survive. Never had to get up at the crack of dawn to milk a cow or kill a chicken just to eat. That will all change. They will have to learn to survive or they will certainly

Out of the Gray Zone, Heading South

perish—no one will carry them for too long. The younger generation has grown up in a world that is not very savvy on survival, unlike many kids in other parts of the world. American kids are all so very, very naïve, he thought.

"Yeah, Uncle Bill," said Eric, brushing the wetness from his face with his bare arm. "I'll pull it together. Fuck, man, I'll try. I could sure use a shower and some clean clothes. Do you have any more whiskey?"

"Why don't you go over to the tent and ask Matt," he said, releasing his grip on Eric's shoulders. "He's really worried about you, and so is Abby. And Eric," he added, taking hold of his shoulder again, "you don't need to start talking like Matt, if you know what I mean."

"Yeah, okay. Sorry. It's just that...."

"It will get better," said Uncle Bill, turning him loose. He felt fatigue overtake his tense body like a cold wave from the Pacific Ocean slapping down upon him. He wanted to sleep. He exhaled a long sigh, wondering how all this was going to turn out. He needed to remember to tell Eric to call him Bill.

*****

At 7 p.m., Matt, tired and worn-out, had started dinner. He'd had very little sleep in the past four days and looked forward to the rest he would get in the security of Brent's fortress. He thought about the looting of Abby's apartment and wondered what would have happened to her if she had been there when it all came down. He realized he hadn't told anyone about it. Nor had he mentioned shooting a hole in his front door to his uncle. He was surprised, in fact, that his uncle hadn't noticed the bullet hole because the door was pretty splintered.

"Hi everyone," said Abby, prancing into the light of the fire as if she were arriving at a sorority party. "I want you to meet Juanita. Juanita, this is Matt," she said, pointing to Matt who quit stirring long enough to look up at the stranger and size her up: Mexican, five foot 8, 130 pounds, black hair, black eyes, big tits, and damn good looking. "That's Uncle Bill over there and that's Eric, our friend who needs the clothes," she pointed to each in turn. Uncle Bill got up, walked over, and extended his hand. Eric did not lift his head or acknowledge her.

"Sorry," Matt said, "I can't shake right now," nodding towards his cooking. He wondered if she was an illegal.

"Welcome, Juanita, to our humble campsite," said Uncle Bill. "We don't have much, but you're welcome to stay if you're hungry."

"Thanks," she said, gripping Uncle Bill's hand as hard as any man, and looking him in the eye. "I would like a ride as far south as you're going," she said, standing square in front of him. "I'm a warrior with *experience*," she said, with an emphasis on experience. She pulled her poncho aside exposing her pistol. "I also have a .223 rifle, a thousand rounds of ammo, and am rated as an expert marksman. I can live off the land, hunt, clean the kill, start fires without

133

matches—I'm a survivalist, and I am offering my services *and* loyalty for a ride south." She waited a moment before adding. "And I will throw in a shirt and a pair of pants for the kid," she said, nodding her head towards Eric.

"That's quite a resume," said Uncle Bill. "What's your story?"

"United States Army Special Forces; sniper, and search and rescue," she said. Matt looked up and wondered if he could take her. She peered down at him at the same instant with a look that sent a chill though him. The knowing look in her eyes was cold and sharp, and he felt like she had just read his mind and was silently saying something like, "don't be a fool."

"Well Juanita, those are some pretty impressive credentials, but I'll have to talk it over with 'the clan,' he said. He damn well wanted to take her along; even if Eric had to ride in the bed of the truck! There was no doubt in *his* mind, but he would have to talk to Matt because his nephew had issues with foreigners, and he didn't need any more problems. "It would be pretty cramped," he said, nodding towards the trucks.

"I understand," she said, "but don't take too long to decide. I've put the word out that I'm looking for a ride, and I imagine someone's going to take me up on it sooner than later, if for no other reason than to try and get into my pants," she said, smiling and winking at Uncle Bill, who went speechless for the first time in a very long time. Matt broke the silence.

"Chow's ready if anyone wants to take a chance," he said, looking up at Juanita with new interest. He liked her style and he liked her. She didn't appear to be much older than Matt, but older. He'd already made up his mind that she was going to get his vote. See there, he thought to himself, I'm not a bigot at all.

Abby went over to where Eric had flopped back against the tarps in the bed of the truck. Although his eyes were closed, tears ran down the sides of his cheeks and dripped into the folds of the tarp that pillowed his head. She nudged him until he opened his eyes.

"Eric, dinner is ready." She held out the blanket that she'd been carrying around with her for the past few days. "Here, take this until you can shower and shave," she said smiling. "Come on," she urged, turning around and walking back to the camp fire where she sat down next to Juanita and waited for Matt to dish out the slightly burnt steak and chicken. The first plate went to Juanita.

"Company first," he said, not knowing for sure if he should smile at her or not. He felt awkward around the warrior woman. After a ten minutes or so of chatter about current affairs, Uncle Bill was more convinced than ever that they needed the services of Juanita. He needed to solidify this deal now, before she left and was picked up by someone else. He caught Matt's eye and tipped his head towards Juanita, and lifted his eyebrows in a questioning way. Matt picking up on the body language and nodded his head in agreement.

"Settled then," he said turning towards Juanita. "We'd be happy to give you a ride south, Juanita." Matt nodded, and Abby smiled and clapped her hands, softly. Uncle Bill, Matt, *and* Juanita all turned to look at her, in wonder.

"Thanks," she said, looking at each of the three nomads, analyzing them each in turn. "You've made a good decision," she said, matter-of-factly. "Thanks for the chow, Matt." She picked up her back pack that was resting beside her and produced a pair of pants and a shirt. "Here are the clothes for Eric," she said, handing them to Abby instead of Eric who had since wandered into the shadows just outside the fire. "I don't have any spare panties," she said with a chuckle. Matt guffawed, Uncle Bill smiled, and Abby well, Abby was in deep thought and said nothing. "I'm ready to move out whenever you say," said Juanita as she walked off into the darkness. She's good, thought Matt, watching her until she was out of sight.

Eric was ordered to take a shower and change before hitting the rack, which he did, and was now sleeping, albeit a bit restlessly. By 10 p.m. they were all hanging with the sandman.

CHAPTER 10
JULY 10TH - HEADING SOUTH

Shards of bright morning sunlight pierced the maze of evergreens just before 5 a.m., and although the sunlight penetrated the webbing of Matt's tent, it was the smell of the campfire, boiling coffee, and sizzling bacon that roused him from a sleep void of dreams. He looked out through the netting and saw Juanita poking at the fire with a stick. A charred coffee pot sat to one side of the grill, and she was sipping from a cup with her free hand. She was wearing a black beret, jeans, and army boots, her dark hair was pulled tight into a pony-tail.

"Good morning," he said, walking up to the fire.

"Back at cha," she answered. "I had some bacon that needed cooking so decided to start earning my keep. Hope it doesn't poison anyone. Coffee's ready, too."

"Sounds great," he said, looking around for the latrine.

"It's over behind your trucks," she said reading his body language.

"I'll be back in a few," he said, smiling."

"You've got my permission soldier," she said, smiling up at him, displaying a black hole where a missing front tooth used to be. He stared for just a second before walking off towards the back of the trucks and into the woods. When he got back, he took a cup from a tree branch where it was hanging to dry, and poured himself a cup of coffee that was as black as his sleep.

"What's the plan?" she asked.

"Not sure yet. But I think we're heading out this morning. We're going to talk it over when Brent comes down. See if he's heard any more news." She had her tooth back in and he was curious as to how she'd lost it, but didn't ask.

"Word is you're heading to Cave Junction. Why Cave Junction?" she asked.

"Abby's folks live there," Matt said scowling. "They got property on the Illinois River." Juanita just nodded her head. "Who told you we were going to Cave Junction?" asked Matt. "Not many people know our destination."

"After I left here last night, I stopped by a campfire for a jolt, and I overheard something about Brent's friends and Cave Junction. Why? Is there a problem?" she said peering up at him.

"No problem. Just, well, you know. Loose lips sink ships, that's all," he said smiling.

"Cave Junction seems to be a catch phrase around here lately," she said.

"How's that," said Matt.

"The campsite next to mine belongs to an old friend of mine, and when I got up this morning, a couple of fellows were packing to leave. They must have come in sometime between the time I came up for dinner last night and the time I got back, and hit the rack pronto. It's no big deal, but since we're heading to Cave Junction, I thought I would mention it because the camp site belongs to an old friend of mine, Montana, and…"

"Was he here?" Matt interrupted, raising his voice. "Was Montana here this morning?"

"No, he was not here," she snapped. "Just a couple of his buddies."

"How do you know Montana?"

"Hey, what's your problem, mister? You and me, we just met," she said, standing up and facing him. "I'm telling you because there was a common thread, Cave Junction, for Christ's sake. The travelers were talking in Arabic, but I did catch the words, Cave Junction, so I thought I would mention it. Too many coincidences to let it slide," she said, recomposing herself. "So what's up?"

Matt took a deep breath, let it out slowly, and took a sip of coffee before answering.

"The short answer is that we don't trust Montana," he said. "Montana and my Uncle were traveling buddies for while—way back when. I've known him since I was about ten. But over the years, Montana has started stepping over the line. Doing things that are questionable; not following the code of the clan, so to speak. The bottom line is that he is no longer welcome at my uncle's."

"If you are talking about him shuffling weed, hell, he's been doing that for as long as I've known him, and I've known him for a long time. As far as I know, he's a hundred percent. At least he used to be. We traveled together for a while, in Mexico." She paused as if deciding on something. "In fact, I've stayed in Cave Junction a few times with Montana."

Matt was thinking about what she'd said, but for a change, he kept his thoughts to himself. He was concerned that the Arabs might be headed to Cave Junction but it was the knowledge that Juanita and Montana had once been traveling companions that peeved him.

"Do you know where his *buddies* were headed when they left?" he asked, more nicely.

"Like I said, all I could make out was Cave Junction." Matt didn't like the scenario she'd painted. It would be no good to run into that gang of shit-heads in Cave Junction. No good at all. He needed to talk to his Uncle.

"Terrorists bastards," he said under his breath but loud enough for Juanita to hear. She looked at him and was about to say something when the sound of someone moving caused them both to look in the direction of the tents, just in time to see Uncle Bill stumbling through the flap.

He stretched his arms and bent at the waist, and then he stretched again in all sorts of contortions. He smiled at Matt and Juanita as he walked up to the fire. Abby and Eric followed close behind.

"Good morning," said Uncle Bill, walking past them. "I'm going up to talk to Brent," he said, leaving Eric and Abby by the fire.

"Coffee is hot and black," said Matt. The cups are there," he pointed.

"Smells good," said Abby, yawning.

"Wait up, Bill," said Matt. "I'll walk up with you. Need to talk to you about something," he said, glancing at Juanita. After thirty minutes, Brent, Uncle Bill, and Matt emerged from the cabin, in that order. They stood on the porch for a few more minutes talking and then headed to the campsite, each with a steaming cup of coffee in hand.

"We're leaving A-SAP," Uncle Bill informed the small group that had moved up close to the fire. Eric was just finishing up a plate of toast and bacon. Abby was drinking coffee and eating a piece of bread with peanut butter on it. "Finish up and start loading up the gear," he ordered.

"What's up, boss," said Juanita, looking at Brent, rather than Uncle Bill.

"Some friends from West Seattle got through on the cell last night," he began. "It was a short conversation, a report actually. It's the first news we've heard in over 16 hours. They said that Seattle was deserted and looked like an Iraqi war zone. Fires burning everywhere, cars overturned, windows broken, and armed gangs of looters ducking in and out of the shadows and stopping cars that look like easy prey." He bent down and picked up the stick that Juanita had been using to stir the fire and began poking around the coals, thinking about what he was going to say next. "There is no nice way to say this," he began, looking up at Abby. "My contact said that there were piles of bodies burning in the streets." Abby's hand flew to her mouth, stifling a gasp.

"Why would there be dead bodies burning," she screeched.

"Hard telling for sure, Abby," answered Matt. "One answer would be that they are being burned because they are dead, and whoever is burning them is smart enough to know that dead bodies attract rats and rats carry fleas, and fleas carry plague, and we sure as hell don't need a damn plague to break out."

Her eyes were wide as she thought about another scenario that she'd never considered in the *end of the world scenario* that she'd painted in her head.

"I guess someone thinks there's a future," moaned Eric.

"Hey. He lives," said Matt, turning towards his friend. "Of course there's going to be a future, Eric. What the hell do you think this is all about," he said. "America will rise up stronger and better than ever—you can count on it, pal."

"Excuse me," said Brent, "I need to pass on more *ammo*," he said, smiling at Matt. "My contact said there were explosions all through the night—

the targets were bridges, highways, cell towers, train tracks, you know, telephone poles, and major roads, anything that will immobilize."

"We need to roll," said Uncle Bill, "and the sooner the better. Once the cities are empty, scavengers will start moving to the country."

"There's more," said Brent, holding up his hand to halt Abby who'd already started grabbing gear. "Cars and trucks are abandoned everywhere, lots are burned, others are burning or tipped over; looks like a tornado blew through," he said. "Make-shift campsites, people screaming…and dying." He paused for a minute before continuing. "There has been some contact with friends up in the Bellingham area, too; friends of Tiny's said Bellingham was damn near burned to the ground—killings, rapes, and piles of bodies burning in the streets." Eric moved up closer to the fire, next to Abby and to Juanita.

"We have decided that you should leave as soon as possible. We debated about traveling at night and traveling during the day and decided that you should head out now. You can re-evaluate the situation when you make camp tonight." He tossed the last drops of his coffee onto the hot coals. "Any thoughts?"

Abby looked at Brent but before she could ask, Brent said, "We haven't heard any more from Cave Junction, Abby, I'm sorry. If I had to guess, though, I'd say that your folks are probably in better shape than most." Abby, closed her eyes and nodded her head. When she opened them again, she walked over to Brent and gave him a long, tight hug.

"I am going to miss you, Brent. More than you know," she sobbed quietly in his ear. Brent smiled; not his usual lecherous smile, but an understanding smile that was unusual for him.

"Good luck," he said, offering handshakes all around. When he got to Juanita, he took her by the hand and led her over to where Matt was picking up some gear. "Take care of these people for me Juanita. They're my family. Matt told us what you told him this morning," he said, looking at Matt. "It was good information. Thanks. I also told him *and* Bill that I would trust you with my life." He took both her hands into his and peered into her eyes for what seemed a week.

Juanita didn't mention seeing Montana before the party, and decided to keep it to herself. After all, she'd just met these people, and she's known Montana for a long time. She would play it by ear.

"You can count on me, boss," and with nothing more to say, Brent turned her loose and started back towards his cabin. In quick order, the trucks were packed, the tarps tied down, and the gang of vagabond outlaws was ready to roll.

It was decided that Juanita would ride shotgun for Matt, and Eric and Abby would ride with Uncle Bill. Abby had shot plenty of guns, and oddly enough, she was a dead-eye natural with Uncle Bill's .357 at 25 yards; a daunting task, even for a pro. Abby rode shotgun, and Eric, useless as a spent cartridge, climbed into the small, narrow, and cramped back seat of Uncle Bill's king cab.

Uncle Bill led the way down the winding dirt road towards the county highway where they turned left onto highway 203. There was zero traffic, but off in the distance, and in the direction they were heading, smoke filled the sky as if the country side were ablaze.

*****

"This is the route," Matt said, handing the map that he'd tucked in the visor to Juanita. "As you already know, we are heading to Cave Junction." He didn't feel like going into the whole thing about *The Plan*, so he just let it go at that. "We're taking mostly back roads, but if we have to, we can four-wheel it. And, if we can make time by getting on a highway, we may do that, as well. At least that's *The Plan*," he said, shifting into third gear. "The red ink-lines mark the route," he said.

"Good," she said, "takes some of the guess work out of it."

They'd gone less than two miles when they came across three burned up cars that were still smoldering on the side of the road. He let off the gas for a second to have a closer look. There was no one around.

"I suspect that's just the tip of the iceberg," said Juanita stoically, taking a quick glance and then focusing again on the map.

"I guess you've seen plenty of this sort of thing, being a warrior and all," he queried.

"Seen my share in the Middle East; after a while you become calloused—another burned up car, truck, tank, town."

"Puts me on alert," he said, "heightens my senses."

"As it should, soldier; don't ever let your guard down, no matter how banal a situation may seem. I've seen five year old suicide bombers carrying bombs in a bread basket."

After a minute had passed, she turned her head towards Matt and said, "When I told you about those guys camping at Montana's this morning, it put you on edge. Word in camp is that you hate *all* foreigners, and I need to know where I stand with you. Do I need to watch my back, or do you have my back?" Matt didn't answer and he didn't look at her, either. "I'm asking because if you haven't noticed, I'm Mexican."

For reasons he couldn't explain, he felt shy around Juanita. And although he was a bit intimidated by her, he wanted her to understand how he felt. He also needed to assure her that he absolutely had her back. He kept his eyes on the road and his uncle's truck up ahead, and finally he answered.

"Well, I got this theory about them...."

"You mean about Middle Easterners, Mexicans, foreigners or all of the above," she said, not letting him finish.

"Yeah," he said, defensively. "All of the above, and as long as we're on the subject, don't leave out child molesters and litterbugs, corrupt politicians."

"I'm listening," she said, interrupting him again, "but try to stick to foreigners for now, we can explore your other hang-ups some other time."

"Look. I don't want or need a damn lecture, but I will tell you how it is," he said white-knuckling the steering wheel. "First of all, no matter how I feel about all of the above, I've damn well got your back same as I got the backs of everyone in that truck up there," he said, pointing fervently with the middle finger of his free hand.

"So far so good," she said.

"I'll tell you what I think, Juanita, but you have to quit interrupting me," he said, glancing quickly in her direction.

"Understood," she said, rolling down her window to spit. Matt picked up speed to stay up with his uncle. A sign post noted that they were close to the town of Dustin.

"I am tired of everyone giving me shit about how I feel about what's going on. I knew this was going to happen, for Christ's sake."

"Just skip the poor me routine and get on with your story," she said, "just the facts, soldier." She'd called him soldier a few times now, and he liked the sound of it. It gave him some sort of boost; made him feel like a warrior.

"You said you wouldn't interrupt," he said, scowling at her. Juanita was focused on the horizon, however, and didn't see him looking, so he took the opportunity to quickly scan her profile, and he wondered what she looked like without clothes.

"All Middle Eastern A-rabs are terrorists," he said, looking back to the road. "And I'm not too crazy about having the enemy in our camp. And as far as I'm concerned, Montana and his Arab buddy Moalim and whoever those Middle Easterners were that showed up last night are the enemy. From what we've heard, thousands terrorists struck at the same time all over the country the other night. Who knows what they have planned next. It could be germs or gas, and I don't trust any damn one of them and that's about it. I think," he quickly added, "the fuckers are trying to hijack my country."

Juanita adjusted herself as Matt waited for her to say something, but she was silent.

"Well," said Matt?

"Well, you might be right, but for the wrong reasons. And, some of your vocab needs adjusting; for one thing, all Middle Easterners are not A-rabs. In fact, if you call someone from Iran and Arab, you will have a fight on your hands. They are Persian; that's why on some maps you see the gulf between Saudi Arabia and Iran referred to as the Arabian Gulf by the Saudis and the Persian Gulf by Iranians."

"Well thank you for the history lesson, but let's try to stay on topic, Major," he said, jokingly. After all, he was trying to explain, not start an argument. He'd mellowed. For some reason this whole nightmare had relaxed him. "Damn straight I'm right," he said; then, "what do you mean, 'the wrong reasons.'"

"It's just a theory that has been going around the warrior camps, but some of it comes from some pretty tactically smart people."

"Well."

"In a nutshell, maybe the terrorists are working for someone or some organization with big bucks. Maybe they are doing the dirty work of mass genocide for something other than religious reasons. Maybe it's all about power and money." Matt was silent. It was a new and bizarre concept that caught him quite off guard. He didn't think Juanita was crazy, but what she'd said was outrageous.

"Genocide," he said, "against who?"

"Yes, why not? Eliminate the poor so the rich don't have to support them. It happens all the time."

"We are not exactly poor...."

"You *are* poor compared to the top one percent of your country, guaranteed; even affluent middle class and high middle class, even millionaires are poor in comparison to the money that could buy this kind of coup." Matt had heard a bit about the imbalance of wealth in his country but hadn't given it much thought. Figured it was an economic problem.

"Everyone is poor compared to the untouchables," he said, "it's an economic issue. Moving the work force out of the country, bringing in illegal aliens to work for wages below minimum wage, fair trade agreements, and so on."

"Wait," she said, checking her rear view mirror. "Before you go on and on, let me propose a very complex scenario for you; something much more complex than bad economics and myopia." Although she had once again insulted him, he just smiled, shook his head and let it go—sort of. Her theory was interesting at least, intriguing for sure, and if she was crazy, he needed to know that, as well.

"Damn, woman, you sure got a way with words," he said, letting her know that he was indeed hanging on her every word.

"Okay, how about this. Let's suppose the wealthiest one percent of this country planned this economic down fall that has made the poor poorer and the rich, extremely rich. If they are smart enough to pull that off; cunning enough to pull that off, under the radar, they may be smart enough to engineer a terrorist attack in the name of jihad, when actually it's, like I said, planned genocide carried out by, what you call, Arab terrorist, who haven't' a clue that they are being used."

"Damn," he said trying to take it in. "You mean a conspiracy against America using a whole nation of terrorists without their knowledge?" Lost in the discussion he'd inadvertently slowed, and when he realized it, he stomped on the accelerator to catch up to his uncle. Then, "like I said, that's the route." He thumbed towards the map that Juanita had sitting on her lap. "It doesn't mean that it is cast in stone, so if you have any suggestions we are always open to new ideas—that genocide idea is pretty out there," he said, as a shiver ran down his back. Juanita did not elaborate further, and it was not silent for long.

"We won't know much until we get down the road a bit," she said, glancing down at the map. "Your route looks reasonable, but who knows. Can't say I've been on all these back roads, but I've rolled down a few of them, for sure. My only suggestion is to take it easy at first. These dirt roads and hairpin turns can be slick as cows-come," she said. Matt laughed, and she continued. "It looks like the first town we come to is Dustin," she said. "According to the map, we will try to cross I-90 near Preston."

Juanita straightened up in her seat, set the map on the dashboard, and adjusted her .223 so that it rested more comfortably between her legs. She checked her rear view mirror and then glued her eyes to the road. Uncle Bill's truck that was leading the way like a cat with his tail on fire.

"By the way, have you heard anything from your family?"

"Word is, it's not so good down there," she said. "But then it never was so good in Mexico. Gangs and drug lords pretty much do what they want. Most people probably think it's just another day."

Matt hit some loose gravel on the side of the road, causing the truck to fish-tail just a bit.

"Keep your eyes on the road, soldier," ordered Juanita. "Hell, we got a whole fucking army hunting us down trying to kill us, you don't need to help them out," she said, in a very relaxed way, which Matt took as friendly jousting.

"I'll do the drivin', little momma, and you do the guardin'," he said, giving her a quick glance and a playful smile. "I've been sliding around these back roads for a long, long time, darlin' so you just hold on tight and enjoy the ride." Despite the situation, he was feeling good.

"I ain't your momma and don't call me darlin'," she said. "And keep your fucking eyes on the road.

*****

Uncle Bill drove while Abby rode in the passenger seat, staring out the window. Eric, still pensive, sat quietly crunched-up in the seat behind them. A gun rack hung in the window behind his head that held one rifle and one shotgun. They slowed to gaze at a pile of burned out cars. No one spoke. They just looked.

"Well Abby," Uncle Bill said, speeding up. "We are on our way to Cave Junction. How do you feel?"

"I feel better," she said, "thanks."

"How about you, Eric. Feel any better?"

"I'm so tired," he said. Abby turned to look at him, and Uncle Bill glanced at him in the rear view mirror.

"Sleep if you can, but first listen up," he said. "Abby, you're riding shotgun. There's a pistol in the glove box. If I tell you to get it, do it fast and without question. It's my single action .357 and you've shot it plenty of times, so you know how to use it. Eric, you can rest for a while, but sooner or later you're going to have to take a turn at driving." He was pretty sure that Eric would be useless riding shotgun. He wasn't even sure he could drive, but he had to give him something to think about besides Rose and the world coming to an end. "If I tell you to hand up a rifle, don't hesitate. Do you know which one is the rifle and which is the shotgun?"

"Yes sir, I know," said Eric. "The shotgun is on the bottom and the rifle is on top. But I've never shot either," he said, barely audible.

"Hopefully you won't need to, but we all need to be on the same page. We don't know what to expect, but we do know it's not going to be a Sunday drive, and from what we've heard, it's going to get worse, so we need to be alert—*and ready*! Here are some rules. Don't trust anyone. Don't tell anyone where we're going or where we've been; if you have to, tell them we are coming from Bellingham and we are heading south, and that's all. Both of you stick close to me and Matt or Juanita and hopefully we'll be okay. And one more thing, Eric, don't call me Uncle any more. Just call me Bill. It's a security thing," he simply said, not wanting to go into detail. "Any questions?"

"I've got a question," said Abby, not waiting for Eric to answer. "When are we going to get to Cave Junction?"

"A few days. Four or five at most, we hope. Like I said, we don't really know what we're going to run in to." His gut feeling was that he couldn't depend on either of them. After all, they were just kids and neither had ever had to endure any kind of discomfort, let alone any sort of combat. Abby, he thought, probably has never even watched war movies on TV—not many women did. She was more of a *Sound of Music* kind of girl. Eric probably didn't watch TV at all. Probably too busy playing computer games; after all, that was his job, and he seemed to love it just like he, himself, loved his job, rebuilding cars. They were both going to have to grow up fast. He checked the odometer; they'd gone only twelve miles and were almost to Dustin.

They smelt it before they saw it. Something was burning. Suddenly the truck was engulfed by a thick reddish-brown haze; around the next bend they came to the main drag of the small country town of Dustin—or what was left of it.

The *Welcome to Dustin* sign that hung on sturdy wooden posts at the outskirts of town and advertised the population at 4,500 was smeared with big white letters that warned, *Stay Out!* But there was not a single person in sight. Uncle Bill wondered how many of the 4,500 were still alive, and if the sign had been written by the good guys or the bad guys?

Smoke hovered over the land like a thick sludge, making it difficult to breathe; there were a few scattered fires still burning yellow, but mostly, all that remained of a community that was thriving five days prior were the charred skeletal remains of homes, vehicles, churches, and businesses, reminding him of pictures he'd seen of burned out towns from past world wars.

Burned out cars and trucks littered the streets, front lawns, and parking lots in such a jumbled mess that it appeared that someone had put them all in a big Mason jar and had rolled them out like so many dice. Why all the destruction he wondered. Why burn the town?

Abby held tightly to the dash with one hand, the other hand covered her nose and mouth with a rag she'd found in the glove box.

"My God! This just can't be real," she said, sobbing. "Maybe they're all dead," she said, tears running down her cheeks. Why would anybody burn down an entire town," she wondered aloud, as if reading Uncle Bill's thoughts.

It was hard not to slow down and gawk, but it was too dangerous, and besides, it was hard to breathe. He sped up, maneuvering around litter and debris of every imaginable kind; mattresses, TVs, chain saws, garbage bins, stones, glass, smoldering piles of who-knows-what. What was left of Dustin looked like old black and white war film footage from a past era.

He wanted to get through the town as quickly as possible and sped up even more. He stole a glance into his rearview mirror and saw that Matt was so close that he could see the expression of shock on his face. Eric was staring, wide eyed, mouth open, out the small window in the side of the truck. Uncle Bill heard the glove box open and quickly looked towards Abby. She'd reached into the cubby hole and had pulled out his magnum. He needed to stop and talk to Matt and Juanita.

"Guess I better keep this handy," she said, with a new voice—a voice of confidence and of authority. She was talking like a different person; she had morphed from a whining baby into a mature woman. She sounded totally together, and he wasn't sure what to think; he was sure, however, that he wasn't sure he trusted her with his gun.

"That's okay, Abby," he said, looking briefly down at the gun. "It's good to be ready." It was the best he could do for now. "You know the drill," he added. "You have put a lot of rounds through that gun, remember? It's a single action, Black Hawk revolver, so you need to cock it before you pull the trigger."

"I know," was all she said.

They were almost out of town and back into the county side when they came upon a truck going the other direction that slowed to a stop as they approached. The occupants looked rough and dirty and were staring, their faces covered with face masks of devils and skeletons. Nobody waved and nobody smiled, they just stared.

*****

Abby sat with the gun on her lap thinking about the past few days. She was still pretty shook up; who wouldn't be? Like Uncle Bill and Matt had said, no one knows for sure what to expect. She was still scared, but she felt a new calm as she fondled the gun on her lap and absorbed the comfort of the cold steel. The reality of the scene in Dustin had triggered the survival instinct in her, and nothing was more important now than getting to Cave Junction to take care of her parents. Not Matt, not Eric, not even Uncle Bill. A sudden feeling of urgency crept over her; if she had to, she would get there on her own. She suddenly remembered something that Matt had told her about survival. "Even anti-gun, single mothers with small children who grow flowers and wear aprons will become killers to feed and protect their babies."

She was familiar with the magnum and, as Uncle Bill had said, she had shot it many times; for a big gun, it had felt comfortable in her hand from the first time she'd picked it up. "A weapon should become an extension of your hand," Uncle Bill had told her, and that's exactly the way it felt right now. She thought about Eric, who was curled up in the back seat, and the nightmare he must have gone through the night Rose was killed. It was a hundred years ago—or so it felt. She thought about Brent and wondered if she would ever see him again. She thought again about her parents and quickly concluded that she was ready to do whatever it took to survive.

"No one's going to steel our water, by God, not while I've got this," she said, breaking the silence and looking down at the pistol on her lap. "Man, that was horrible," she said, again. A long and loud sigh, almost sounding like a cry, came from the back seat, catching both Abby's and Uncle Bill's attention.

"Are you okay, Eric?" she asked, laying the gun on the floor boards and then twisting in her seat. "How are you doing, Eric. Are you okay?" Besides everything else, he probably has a hangover, thought Abby, remembering how much he'd been drinking. Abby could never figure how drinking cleared the head of anything, *a temporary high that led to depression was the alcohol trip.*

"It's all just so surreal," he said. "I keep trying to wake up. Look, I even pinched myself so hard that I made little half-moons on my arm," he said, raising his arm to show Abby. It was the most he'd spoken since he was first carried through the door at Brent's.

"Don't do that anymore, Eric," she said, taking hold of his hand and squeezing. "It's real and we're all in this nightmare together. It's going to be alright, though. I'm real sorry about Rose," she said, "but we have to move on. We have to think about getting to Cave Junction. You're going to love my parents," she said, smiling. Fresh streams of tears ran down his cheeks as his face contorted into someone unknown. "It's going to be okay," she said again, squeezing his hand more tightly.

"Thanks Abby," he sobbed. "I will try to pull it together. I need to sleep. Is it okay if I sleep for a while, Abby?" he asked. "I'm sure I will feel better if I can sleep. Can I sleep for a while Uncle Bill?"

"Sure Eric, you can sleep. We'll wake you up if we need you. Grab that blanket there and pull it over yourself to stay warm." Eric covered his head with the blanket and became quiet.

"He's pretty wiped out," she said, "but I know him. He's going to be okay." Uncle Bill looked at her and smiled. "I think I am going to be okay, too, Bill. That was horrible back there," she said, for the third time, shaking her head.

Uncle Bill nodded and said, "Yes it was. Then he said, "I'm going to have to pull over pretty soon and talk to Matt. I want them to lead the way.

*****

Montana led the way and another truck followed. They pulled off into the trees about a hundred miles north of Cave Junction to relieve themselves, stretch, and talk, in that order.

"We have a plan," said Moalim. "We are going to meet up with a few more comrades outside the Lassiter ranch to plan our assault," he said. "We need to keep a low profile from here on out. We want to look like Mexicans trying to get back to Mexico. Have your papers ready, and your weapons locked and loaded."

"Are we going to kill them?" asked Montana.

"We may need them for leverage—but sooner or later they will become expendable," said Moalim with indifference. He waited for a Montana to say something, but Montana stood still as a lamp post, grinding his teeth and popping out his jaw bones. "I can see you still have a problem with this, Montana, and I can understand, so when the time comes, you won't have to do anything. Someone else will take care of it." Montana stuffed a bite of Hostess Twinkie into his mouth and said nothing.

"Have you ever heard of *Plan Alpha*, Montana?" Montana shrugged his shoulders, shook his head, and swallowed all at the same time.

"No. What is it?"

"It's a survival plan that I *borrowed* from Brent's place that outlines how to survive a major catastrophe—how to get out of the city alive. It's really quite well thought out," he said as an afterthought. "Being that it's survival plan, I must assume that it is meant for only a few select individuals, wouldn't you agree?" Montana shrugged and pushed the other half of the Twinkie into his mouth with his index finger and waited for Moalim to continue. "Who would you guess are those special people it was meant for, Montana?" Montana gulped down the rest of his Twinkie, instantly realizing the full implications of *Plan Alpha*.

"Probably Bill, since he and the Lassiters are best friends. Matt his nephew, and Abby the Lassiter's daughter. I don't know about Brent. Brent has his own stronghold," he said hurriedly. "I'm just thinking out loud here, but maybe you found it at Brent's because all of those people are family to each other."

"That means, Montana, that if they get out of the city alive, they will be heading here, and that's the only reason, my friend, that we will not kill the Lassiters the minute we see them. In a worst case scenario, we will need them to barter with."

*****

Uncle Bill pulled over a few miles south of Dustin and talked about the ruin they had just seen, and Juanita assured them that it was most likely going to be the norm at best.

"It will get worse and worse. It is already anarchical, but as the days go by there will be more bloodshed as people run low on food and water. It will be a survival of the fittest," she concluded.

"Survival for those who have the most guns," you mean, said Matt.

"It will certainly help, yes," confirmed Juanita. But we are a gang of five. If we encounter a gang of 20 or 50, we will be, well, tested."

"And that is exactly why I said we need to stay alert at all times," said Uncle Bill looking at Abby and Eric. "We are not on a Sunday drive. For example, we don't ever want to find ourselves boxed in."

"We should always have an escape route in mind," added Juanita.

They also agreed not to stop except in the case of emergency, and that Matt and Juanita should take the lead as they were more capable of clearing the way if it should come to that.

They drove through Novelty, Stuart, Still Water, Carnation, Pleasant Hill, and Fall City, all of which were in some stage of destruction. They turned up a county road that was almost as pitted as the dirt road that led up to Brent's place. Here, they found cover behind a stand of trees and pulled over for a quick stretch and a peanut butter sandwich. Uncle Bill checked his cell phone but there was no service. They piled back into the trucks and drove cross county via small county roads to Preston, where they planned to cross over I-90. When they came to the overpass, however, they were turned away by a heavily armed US military.

"Military presence is a good sign, don't you think," he said to Juanita, who didn't answer. They were directed to a side road that bypassed the overpass, by heavily armed military. A few miles down the road they came to highway 18 where the army was letting people cross over the small bridge without much hassle. Brent had warned them that this might happen, so it was not a big surprise. The army's mission, it seemed, was to keep the traffic moving and away from the *big* bridge, as it was tank sturdy and only one of two ways to cross I-90 for hundreds of miles. "No comment?" he asked.

"I'm on duty, soldier," was all she said.

*****

Matt looked into the rear view mirror and saw that his uncle was flashing his headlights, which was a signal to pull over. Matt down shifted and made a hard left onto dirt access road throwing dirt and gravel and a cloud of dust into the wind. Juanita grabbed hold of her rifle and slammed a hand on the dashboard for support

"What the hell are you doing?" she demanded.

"Uncle Bill wants to talk," was all he said, as he shoved open his door and stepped out.

"You could warn me next time," she said, jumping down from the 4x with rifle in hand.

"Sorry. Hey Bill, what's up?" he said.

"We better find a place to set up camp for the night," he said, to the haggard gang that had gathered around. "We don't want to be struggling in the dark." Abby pointed to some trees on a small hill down the highway.

"Maybe those trees will give us some cover *and* a vantage point," she said with some authority, pointing to a knoll of high ground more than a few miles down the road. Matt spun around so fast that he almost tripped himself. He didn't expect her to have any input, and where did she learn a phrase like, "vantage point." When he looked more closely, he realized she was holding his uncle's magnum down to her side.

"I'm feeling better, Matt," she said, in way of explanation, when she saw him staring at her with his mouth half open. "I'm over it," she said, "and I had time to read *Plan Alpha*. The section on finding high ground for camping and how it should be a vantage point." Matt just stared at her until Juanita spoke.

"I think we should take cover in the trees too," said Juanita. "Down here, we're sitting ducks, trees are good cover."

"Agreed," said Uncle Bill.

"Okay, then. Let's head for the hills," said Abby as if she were now in charge. Matt started back to his truck but his eyes were glued on Abby. How could she be a basket-case one minute and alert and making good sense the next?

Just then a Jeep came barreling down the road leaving a whirlwind of thick dust in its wake.

"Oh shit," said Uncle Bill, "let's move." Juanita walked quickly to the passenger side of Matt's truck and Uncle Bill walked to the side of his. The trucks were parked just at the right angle to offer some protection from what was surely coming.

"Eric, zip it up and get back in the truck. Now!" hollered Abby. Eric, hearing the anxiety in Abby's voice, quickly turned and raced back to the truck, falling twice before piling into the back of Uncle Bill's truck and ducking down between the seats, praying that the jeep just kept going.

"Keep you weapons at ready," ordered Juanita. "Don't point, but be ready to *shoot to kill*," she ordered loud enough for all to hear. Abby did not cock the single action magnum, but she did place her thumb on the hammer, Matt did the same. Uncle Bill and Juanita released the safeties on their rifles and held them across their chests, trigger fingers on stand-by.

*****

The small band of extremists arrived at the appointed place on time, Montana, Moalim, and Ali in the lead truck pulled to a stop, the second truck did the same. They were now only five miles from the Lassiter ranch.

"We need to wait another day before going in," Moalim said as they gathered around the front end of the Montana's truck. "The other members of our party were held up in a fire fight a hundred fifty miles back—evidently, someone wanted to *steal* their truck," he said, smiling. "None of our men were killed, but they will be quite late getting here. The unfortunate would-be thieves are now, what do you say Montana, *worm bait*?" This colloquialism drew puzzled looks from the foreigners, but Montana snickered and Moalim laughed. "What this means is," Moalim continued, "we wait another day before moving on the Lassiter Ranch. We will camp here tonight." He looked at the small band of killers and then turned and took Ali by the elbow, in a silent gesture of dismissal, and moved off, out of hearing range.

"Montana, you and the others set up camp," he said over his shoulder.

*****

The jeep with three passengers slowed just enough to make a sliding turn onto the dirt road. It lunged forward and skidded to a stop ten yards from the back of Uncle Bill's truck. An older male wearing an International Harvester cap was driving, a younger skinny male passenger with long shaggy hair, a headband, and a goatee was in the passenger seat, and a bald, unshaven, tall, rough looking character was standing behind the driver's seat, clasping an assault rifle to the roll bar.

"You folks are trespassing," yelled the driver, before the dust had settled.

"We just pulled over to talk for a minute," said Juanita, stepping away from the truck, rifle at the ready. "We aren't staying. In fact we were just getting ready to move out when you pulled up."

"Where you from?" asked the driver, in a rough tone, but with less hostility.

"Up near Seattle," said Uncle Bill, taking Juanita's queue and stepping out from behind his truck, rifle at ready. "We're heading south. We don't want any trouble. Sorry to have trespassed. We'll be on our way."

"What's going on up there?" asked the passenger in a surprisingly high pitched tone. "In Seattle, I mean. I guess the whole fucking town is on fire."

"It's about the same as everywhere else between here and there. Everything is burned down and deserted," answered Uncle Bill.

"Well there ain't no sense in trying to go much further tonight," he said changing tack; "hell, it's damn near dark," said the skinny guy in the passenger seat, who had taken charge. "You might as well follow us back to our place. You can camp the night and get an early start. Might be safer than being on the road—from what we hear, anyways," he said, with a hint of a smirk. Matt's neck hair stood on end and he was suddenly on high alert—he suddenly wasn't buying any of it and was getting ready to politely, but firmly decline when Juanita spoke up.

"Thanks just the same, she said, "but we're going to keep on rolling while it's still light. We're meeting up with some comrades, and we're running late." Good strategy, thought Matt, maybe if they think there's more of us, they won't bother following us.

"Suit yourselves," said the skinny guy but not giving the driver the nod do move. "Ya'll got plenty of water and food?" he asked, as if he would offer some if the answer was no. He was looking straight at Abby.

"We got plenty of water and food," she said, before anyone else could answer.

An eerie silence pursued, and while seconds seemed to turn into minutes, the sun dipped behind a mountain top, casting a chilling shadow on all. Matt's eyes moved from the passenger to the driver to the man in back and then back again. He was as ready to shoot as he'd ever been in his life.

"Well, the facts are," said Juanita, trying to cover up Abby's reckless, and dangerous reply, "we don't really have much of anything. We had to leave in one hell of a hurry, as you can well appreciate," she said smiling, trying to keep it light. "We've got just enough to get to where we're going—we hope." Silence pursued as the sun sank a bit further behind the peaks of the mountains. "I guess we'll be heading out then," she finally said, backing towards the trucks, nodding to the rest of the group to load up. "I'll walk beside Matt's truck until we're out of here," she said to Uncle Bill, not taking her eyes off the threat. "You lead the way. Pull up in front of Matt and make a U-turn to the left. Matt, you follow."

"Where ya goin', sweetheart," hollered the bald headed guy in the back of the jeep as Matt rolled slowly by waiting for Juanita to jump onto the running board of his truck.

*****

Uncle Bill didn't want to give a lecture, but it was necessary if they were going to survive. "Those were *not* good people," he said to Abby after they were back in the truck and back on the road.

"As soon as I said it," I knew I made a mistake, she said in defense. "I'm sorry. It won't happen again. It's just that they seemed so sincere, they caught me off guard."

"I can't make it clear enough how important it is that nobody know our status, Abby. It's absolutely a matter of life and death. Water in particular, if not already, will be worth its weight in gold."

He felt the need to reiterate even though he knew that she was going to get it from Matt and probably Juanita as well. Eric was as quite as a rock, but Uncle Bill could see him in the rear view mirror and knew he was paying attention. Maybe he's coming around.

"I don't want to lecture, Abby, but those guys were very dangerous. If we hadn't shown some fire power, we would probably all be dead right now. The two in the front had weapons on the ready behind the dash, for sure, and the guy in the back had a rifle in plain sight. We can't trust anyone. Who knows if they really have property or not, but I'm guessing they damn well don't. Do you understand what I'm saying, Abby?"

"Yes. I get it. I'm sorry. I'll do better," she said, quietly. "It's all pretty crazy. Water being worth its weight in gold; towns burning; killers everywhere. I will be more careful, I promise it will not happen again." After a few minutes of silence, she said, "It really *is* a matter of survival of the fittest and the most prepared, just like Matt used to preach," she said.

More than a few miles up the road, Matt pulled onto a dirt road that wound its way up into the trees.

*****

"Man, that was weird," said Matt, slowing to a crawl to keep the dust down from giving away their location. Juanita turned in her seat to see if they were being followed, and saw nothing obvious.

"That was not weird, Matt, that was bad," she said. "Those guys had bad intensions, soldier, and you better have a talk with your girlfriend," she added.

"You can damn well believe I will have a chat with Abby," he said. He felt the urge to mention that he and Abby were not really together these days, but it faded as quickly as it had surfaced.

"There was nothing good about that run-in at all," repeated Juanita. Matt pulled into some brush just inside the tree line. "This look good to you?" he asked, looking around.

"I need to check it out for other ways in and out of here. We need to do it right now," she said with an urgency that made Matt's skin tighten. "I don't think we've seen the last of those fuckers," she said, getting out of truck.

"We'll need guard duty assigned immediately," she ordered over the cab of the truck.

"I know all that," said Matt, climbing out of his truck. "I'm not stupid."

"It was rhetorical, Matt. Just saying the obvious confirms that we are on the same page for Christ's sake. Get on board, will ya," she said walking away.

"What the fuck is that supposed to mean," he said, hollering at her as she hurried towards Uncle Bill.

"I just told you," she said shaking her head.

Matt didn't like being talked to like that, even though what she'd said about confirming that they were on the same page made perfect sense. In fact, he did the same thing, himself. He remembered a few days back when he'd told Abby that he was just thinking out loud to make sure they were both on the same page.

"That was critical," she said loudly as she approached Uncle Bill. "Agree?"

"Agreed. Can we keep an eye on the road from here?" said Uncle Bill, looking in the direction that they'd come. "We need a quick check of the land and guard duty right now," he said, as if expecting trouble immediately. "I don't trust that bunch any more than I can see them."

Juanita looked at Matt.

"See how that works cowboy? Me and your uncle are on the same page. Try to keep up; we need you right now!" She was not kidding.

"I get it," said Matt, "and I'm on it." He was not used to anyone talking to him like that and his feelings were mixed. Focus, he thought.

After a quick but thorough look around, it was decided that they had a good vantage point right where they were, and being in the trees, they had cover from anyone passing by on the county road below.

"Do you think they're watching?" asked Uncle Bill.

"Affirmative," answered Juanita. "They know exactly where we are."

"Do you think we should keep moving?"

"It won't matter," she said. "They want everything we got, and they got nothing better to do than to follow us and wait us out. May as well make a stand here," she said, squinting towards the road.

"You mean get ready for a fight?" he said, not quite ready to believe what she meant. "Maybe they won't bother with us. Maybe they think we're too much trouble," said Uncle Bill. "They saw we were armed, for Christ's sake."

"Yeah right," said Juanita, turning to look Uncle Bill in the eye. "I'm sure they got a good reading on who's here including Abby, no offense, and Eric, who is not exactly a major threat, if you know what I mean."

"Just the same, they may not come after us," said Uncle Bill.

"Right, Bill, and pigs can fly," she said, squinting into the setting sun. "They're coming, I'll bet my life on it. The good thing is that we are on high ground which is a whole lot better than having them chasing us down the road."

"I agree," said Matt.

"Glad you're on board, soldier," said Juanita, giving Matt a nod. "We need to get ready for the worst," she said, walking towards the tree line, where she would have a good view of the road.

*****

Uncle Bill hurried to his truck to fetch his rifle. Abby, who'd been standing close by listening, started getting food out and getting water ready to boil. Eric walked around aimlessly until Juanita told him to sit down, out of sight. Each was in their own world thinking about what Juanita had said. Matt walked up to the top of the knoll to check escape route options, and after a look he walked over to where Juanita was watching the road.

"We will need two guards on duty all night," he said. "One watching here and one to watching the back side. Do you really think we are going to be in a fire fight?" asked Matt.

"If it was me, and I wanted what we have, I would strike in early morning," she said. "I figure we can expect them between one and three. "Do you think Abby is up for a first watch?"

"I don't know. Maybe. It would probably be better if she took a watch now rather than in the middle of the night if you think the shit's going to hit the fan after midnight."

"I think I can do it," said Abby, who'd stepped up behind them.

"Can't be no 'think I can do it' shit," said Matt, irritated at her interruption. "Either you can or you can't because all our lives depend on who's watching our backs."

"What I mean, Matt, is that I have never been on *watch* before, but I *think* I can do it. Who knows for sure what's going to happen. Jesus, Matt, you're such an ass sometimes." Matt looked at her with mouth open ready to retaliate, but she started in again before he had the chance. "Sure, I can do it. I see something I yell for *you*. Right?"

"Well, sort of," said Juanita, before Matt could answer. "Don't, under any circumstances, leave your post. If they're coming fast, shoot to kill and we will damn sure be her in a few seconds. "If you see them sneaking up, and if there is time, it would be better to alert us without too much noise so we can set up. We'll run a panic line from here to the tent so you don't have to leave your post. You can't leave this spot," she repeated, glaring at the young blonde. Matt took a deep breath and let it out slowly.

"I better get back to the back side," said Matt, walking away.

"Okay," said Abby, "I can do it, but it sounds like you expect them for sure. Are you expecting them to attack us for sure," she asked, looking at Juanita.

"Nothing is ever for sure, Abby, but I think there is a damn good chance due to the fact that we got two trucks filled with supplies, not to mention our guns. And, we probably don't look too threatening. I'm thinking the reason they didn't hit us this afternoon is because they wanted to regroup and maybe get more soldiers."

"Agreed," said Uncle Bill, sitting down next to Juanita. "I thought about it and concluded that you're most likely right. I don't like the idea of having a gun battle, but you're probably right. If they're coming, they'll probably wait until they think, that we think, there isn't a threat. I just don't like it, that's all."

"I don't like it either," said Juanita. "We don't know how many men they have or where they may come from or how big their organization is. And we're in unfamiliar territory. But this is our best defense. We play the hand we're dealt, and we play to win."

"Abby and Matt will take the first watch, and we'll take the second watch. Wake us at midnight, Abby, and I don't mean one minute after. Don't be thinking you are doing us a favor by letting us sleep in. If they're coming, and I think they are, we need to be ready. Do you understand, Abby, how important this is?"

"I understand, Juanita, and I won't let you down."

"For now, Abby, bring me a sandwich and a cup of coffee, Matt too. We can't leave our posts—not even to pee." It was an order, not a request—no please was included.

"Okay," said Abby, turning back towards the camp site.

"I guess that's it then," said Uncle Bill.

"That's it," said Juanita. "But I've been thinking." Uncle Bill waited. "I'm thinking that if they had a big force of manpower, they would have come back by now—while it was light. Makes me think their unit is light on man power."

"I'm not a warrior, but it sounds logical," said Uncle Bill.

"Either way," she said squinting out into the red sunset, "we'll be as ready as we can be."

At midnight, Abby woke Uncle Bill and Juanita to take over guard duty, and at 3 a.m., all hell broke loose.

*****

Five men, dressed in dark clothing, crept quickly and quietly through the night, being careful to stay hidden in the shadows cast from the light of the full moon. They had watched the nomads pull off the road from 5 miles back, and knew exactly where they were camped—just like Juanita had guessed.

When they got closer, they went to their bellies and slithered through the sage-grass like snakes, and crawled along silently, at a snail's pace.

Suddenly, Uncle Bill was blinded by two glaring flood lights shining into his eyes.

"Freeze mother-fucker or you're a dead man," ordered one of the men, loudly, and Uncle Bill froze. Between the dots before his eyes, he saw a man, just a few feet away, pointing a rifle at his head. "All we want," said another man, in a sing song voice, off to the side and barely silhouetted by the glare of the powerful spot lights, "is your water, your food, your trucks, and of course, your women," he said, laughing.

"Shut up, Hank," said the bandit holding the rifle on Uncle Bill. At that, three more men stepped into the light and started moving towards the tent and the trucks.

"We want your supplies and your trucks. Give it up peacefully and you will all live to see another day," he said. "Resist, and you will all die."

"The rest of you fucking gypsies get out here right now," yelled one of the bandits loudly, looking towards the tent and the trucks. "No funny business or gramps here gets it." The beam of one of the spot lights scanned the bushes, the tent, the trucks, and the surrounding landscape, while the other remained trained on Uncle Bill. "You got to the count of three," yelled the leader. "One, two...

Rat-a-tat-tat, rat-a-tat-tat, and before the echo had died down, three would-be-bandits dropped where they stood. At the exact same time, Abby rolled out from under Matt's truck, raised her gun and fired at the bandit holding the gun on Uncle Bill, hitting him square in the forehead, cocked her gun again and shot the other in the back of his head as he ran for cover.

"Holy shit," said Matt, coming up fast from the tent, gun in hand. "Jesus Christ, Juanita," he said, sounding stunned. "You killed them all," he said, obviously shaken. "You killed them all," he repeated, standing next to the bodies.

"No, I didn't," she said, looking at Abby who was holstering her weapon. "Don't fuck with warriors," she said, winking at Abby, as she quickly walked to each of the bodies to check for life. All five were dead and spreading fluids into the dirt. Matt stared, hypnotized, at the sheen of dark blood that was seeping from the forehead of one of the bodies.

"This one," said Juanita, standing close and looking down, "Abby plugged. That one too," she said, nodding to the guy with half his face missing. Matt quickly turned and faced Abby who was standing with her hands on her hips, chin up.

"Abby...?"

"I told you I was okay," she said.

It was unusually quiet. No birds chirping in the trees; no rustle of leaves in the early morning breeze; no one, it seemed, was breathing except for Juanita. Eric was sitting on the ground by the front of the truck, just looking.

"I had to take advantage of the moment," Juanita finally said to everyone and no one in particular. "If we would have given up our weapons," she said huskily, "we would all be dead—I guarantee it." She stood looking warily down the hill for anything suspicious. "Keep this in mind for when it happens again. Sometimes, you have to shoot first and ask questions later."

"Jesus," said Uncle Bill, still rubbing his eyes. "I didn't even see them until they stood up."

Everyone looked at him, but said nothing.

"We need to move out," ordered Juanita. "If they got buddies..."

Uncle Bill did not wait for her to finish. "Kill those fucking flood lights," he ordered, walking off towards the trees.

Abby walked slowly towards the dead bodies lying on the ground. She wasn't hysterical and she hadn't wet her pants. She was just looking curiously at something she'd never seen before. Dead men killed with bullets.

Eric moved up next to her but said nothing. He was looking down at one of the bad guys and the flood light that lay beside him. He bent down, picked it up, and turned it off, and for a few moments, it was as black as a well-diggers butt.

"Nope," Juanita said quietly to Matt as she bent down and shut off the other flood light. "I couldn't take that chance, cowboy—it's better to strike first." Matt was still staring down at the dead men lying in the dirt.

Juanita stood up and pulled a hand full of shells from her jacket and started reloading her rifle. "Snap to, boys and girls," she yelled, rolling the faceless man onto his stomach with her foot. "And remember, if at all possible, always check your kill to make sure they are dead," she said, looking around. "We can't take them with us, and we sure as hell don't want them shooting us in the back, so *always* shoot to kill."

"Well cowboy, *we* just saved your life. And *we* are women, and I'm a Mexican besides," said Juanita. Matt couldn't tell if she was smiling or ridiculing him for not being on the front line. In the moonlight, her silhouette looked alien. He didn't respond and he didn't say anything more to anyone— not to Juanita or to Eric, Abby, or to his uncle. He just started picking up camp, getting ready to head out.

The dead men were left where they fell and the trucks were loaded, and and two outlaws, two warriors, and one space cadet were bouncing over rough terrain, down the side of the hill with lights off, driving by moonlight in less than ten minutes.

A memory from the past came to rest in the forefront of Matt's mind. Something about killing is nothing to take lightly or something close—it was Brent who'd said it, he remembered. He wondered how Abby felt about killing someone. Damn, he thought, she was the girl next door, the one who crocheted doilies and had pretty tea cups. She used to go out of her way not to kill a bug seeking shelter in her house, and she just killed two men.

CHAPTER 11
JULY 11 - ON THE ROAD

Eric was driving Uncle Bill's truck and Uncle Bill was riding shotgun. Abby was in the back seat bouncing around but sleeping soundly. Matt and Juanita were in the lead. They stayed mostly on the back roads, and when they came to towns, they either drove straight through them or skirted them, but they never stopped for any reason. Black Diamond was destroyed. Smoke still wafted from fallen buildings. Like the previous towns, it also appeared to be deserted.

"I wasn't prepared for anything like this," said Eric once they started rolling.

"No one ever is," said Uncle Bill, trying to sound confident. "Hell, those guys could have killed us all—and it was my watch. We can only do the best we can do and that's it." Uncle Bill felt bad about getting caught off guard, but worse, he felt bad because his charges could all have been killed. He had to get over it—he had to buck up. The kids needed him to be strong. Juanita was right about what she'd implied. If it weren't for her and Abby they would all be dead. He shook his head when he thought about what sweet little Abby had done and wondered how many other non-violent people would become killers in the name of survival. "It's so primitive; so primeval, so basic," he said finishing his thoughts aloud. "It's absolutely a matter of survival of the fittest; it's also a matter of who has the most fire power and who is willing to kill to stay alive," he added, nodding his head, agreeing with himself.

"It's true, but you and Matt and Brent were ready for all this. I just never believed the U.S. could be brought down like this," said Eric. There's no law—it's pretty much each man for himself—anarchy, just like Matt said it would be. The US is supposed to be the strongest most powerful country in the world. This was not supposed to happen."

"To be honest, Eric, I never expected this to happen either—not like Matt and Brent, anyway. Sure, we had supplies stashed, and we had a plan, but I hoped it would never happen. I expected hard times because of the bad economy. Gangs, crime and all that, but I never really expected anything like this." He was rambling, but it was good therapy—for both of them.

"I guess I'm pretty lucky that I know you guys," said Eric. "Otherwise I would probably be dead by now." He was silent for a few moments, and Uncle Bill figured he was thinking about Rose, same as him. "I should have paid more attention to what Matt was telling me about being ready. I just never thought anything like this could happen," he repeated.

"Matt can be pretty intense sometimes. It's been hard to listen to his ramblings lately, but he's a good man and he knows how to survive, so you shouldn't hesitate to depend on him. He thinks a lot of you, Eric. In fact, he didn't want to leave the other day before you got to his place, but our window of opportunity was closing—it was my call to head out."

"I understand, now. But you know what? I've never even been camping before the other night at Brent's. In fact it was the first time I have ever slept outside. First time in a tent, first time eating over a campfire, and first time I can remember not having a shower every day or brushing my teeth or changing my clothes. And, I never saw a dead person until Rose was killed. And last night...man! We are all very lucky that Juanita knows what she knows. And Abby," he said more quietly, "My God, Bill, Abby killed two people!" He stopped talking and concentrated on the road.

He seems to be coming around, thought Uncle Bill.

*****

Matt led the way as they drove south on back roads, taking much more time then they'd wanted. In some places, wrecked cars and trucks and sometimes a downed tree or telephone pole blocked passage. If they could, they would four-wheel around, or in the case of the tree or pole, get out the chain saw and get after it, while Juanita kept guard. It was weird.

Communes had sprung up overnight—big communes, some with hundreds of tents. Most of them were pitched well off the side of the road and were well-guarded by denizens of armed citizens sporting demeanors that read, stay away or die. Probably what was left of the small towns that had been destroyed, thought Matt, trying, like *they* were, to survive another day.

Sometimes the only way from one side of a small town to the other was through town where there were still gangs and thugs lurking in the shadows, waiting for opportunities. They'd begun seeing dead bodies hanging from trees with signs around their necks that read, looter, or rapist, or killer; some of them were stripped naked and some of them were women. There was also the occasional twisted, dead body laying alongside the street, like so much garbage. Gun fire and explosions in the distant had become a common sound, and the smell of smoke and gunpowder was common, and is places floated like smog over the ground.

The back road he was driving on got rougher and windier and Matt had to slow down. He realized that he was not as prepared for the reality of anarchy as he had thought. A long sigh escaped his lips as he thought about how bad this really was, and how much worse it was probably going to get; but, he was more prepared right now than he was before last night. He was learning from Juanita, and as much as he had problems with authority, he was learning plenty from her.

He'd read plenty and heard lots of stories from Brent and his buddies, but living it was something altogether different. He was witnessing anarchy, firsthand. People were turning into savages. Money and social status meant nothing; everyone was in the same boat. Everyone was fighting to stay alive;

indeed, he thought, stepping hard on the gas pedal, be careful of what you wish for.

They were making better time as they neared Tenino, Bucoda, and Centralia. There were a lot of vehicles moving—mostly small convoys of no less than four or five. He thought about the possibility of hooking up with another group heading south, but held his thoughts and his eyes on the road.

Outside Longview there was a traffic jam. Vehicles were lined up waiting to cross the Lewis and Clark Bridge. Here, like the roads to Fort Lewis, the army had a strong presence.

"I guess the government is letting up on people wanting to get out of town. I suppose it's more prudent to guard bridges and major roadways than small towns and cities," said Matt, breaking the long stretch of silence. "It's a good sign, I think, that the army has a presence." He was hoping for confirmation, but heard only the sound of wind blowing through the open windows.

When it was their turn to cross, the guards, rifles pointed threateningly at their heads, just waved them through. A huge sign that could not be missed, read:

KEEP MOVING!
DO NOT STOP OR YOU WILL BE SHOT!

"These guys mean business," said Juanita. "At least their letting us cross. I was concerned about this," she said, looking at the river below. "Probably better to let us pass than to have angry mobs protesting. They can't shoot us all," she said, looking all around. Matt looked over the railing and saw that government vehicles and troops were present on the beaches of the Columbia River, as well.

For an unknown reason, he thought about the new family that had moved in to the apartment below his him in Lynnwood. He wondered if they were still there or if they were dead or if they had tried to leave. He didn't think they stood a chance. He couldn't help but wonder if people got hungry enough, would they start eating each other. And he thought about the mother and the father…and the baby.

"You said a mouth full there," he answered, getting his mind off cannibalism.

He made a command decision to stick to the major roads for a while and see how it went. They sped south hitting speeds of 80, 90, and a hundred mile an hour. They stopped on a side road in Goble to check the map and have a sandwich. They were out of the trucks long enough to pee, stretch for a minute or two, and switch drivers, and then they were back in the cages and moving again, all within twenty minutes time. Uncle Bill took over driving for Eric, and he and Abby switched places. Uncle Bill took the lead.

161

They headed cross country to Pittsburg, passed Buxton and skirted Beaverton, McMinnville, and Corvallis moving as fast as they could through what was left of the small towns. The traffic thinned as they sped past Harrisburg, Junction City, and Eugene and all the way to Elkton where highway 38 and 138 come together. The destruction didn't seem as bad here, but it was still deserted. It was 4 p.m. and they had made good progress but it was time to start looking for a place to camp.

*****

On a back road, near Elkton, they came upon a barricade of sawhorses draped with yellow tape blocking passage into a large open field off to the right. Armed civilians dressed in flannel shirts and other garb, typical of farmers, stood guard. Beyond the barricade was a large encampment that resembled county fairgrounds, minus the long narrow stock pens that house goats, chickens, and pigs. At first Uncle Bill thought it was just another commune, but this one was different than the others.

There were many dozens of people milling around tents, lean-tos, and small camp fires, there was even what appeared to be a big-top circus tent off in the distance. It looked like a Viking encampment, complete with dirty little urchins running freely about, playing at games that children play. A very large army tent sat twenty yards the other side of the gate. A line of people stood in front of the entry flap, waiting. Above the flap there was a 4x8 sheet of plywood with big black letters splashed on the surface that simply read, 'store.' The store was guarded by men with rifles. These men, however, were dressed in military type clothing and looked like warriors.

His intention was to drive on by when he realized that the road that continued on past the circus was also blocked by a barricade and guarded with sentries. Deep ditches on both sides of the road had been dug, which would force them to stop. He slowed to a crawl to give himself time to think.

"Damn," said Uncle Bill, looking into his mirror to see where Matt was and damn glad to see that he was on his bumper. "What the fuck is going on," he said, not addressing either Abby or Eric.

"Looks like a big family reunion," said Abby, flipping open the loading gate on the magnum and spinning the cylinder slowly, click, click, click, to make sure all six chambers were loaded. It was a habit she'd quickly picked up since watching Juanita reloading her rifle last night. She was as cool and calm as he'd ever seen her.

"I don't like it," said Uncle Bill.

"Perhaps it's a community of survivors that's pooled all their resources. Just like what we're planning to do in Cave Junction," offered Eric, leaning into the front seat—"reminds me of the dark ages," he added.

When they came to the blockade, two of the farmer-guards stepped out into the road and flagged them down while a few others stood close by at the ready—all were armed but kept their weapons pointed away from the travelers. Uncle Bill drove slowly, driving onto what was left of the shoulder, indicating, he hoped, that his intent was not to stop but to continue on down the road. He rolled down his window and pointed to the road and signaled that he wanted to keep on going. The farmer stepped in front of the truck, and unless Uncle Bill wanted to run him down, he would be forced to stop.

"Be ready Abby. Keep your gun down, keep your thumb on the hammer and keep it pointed at my window so this shit-head won't miss it. And be careful for Christ's sake. Don't do anything unless I say so. I'll do the talking," he said as he coasted to a stop. "We're not getting stuck in this rat-hole, and that's that." The farmer-guard came around to the driver's side of the truck and addressed Uncle Bill.

"Y'all together?" he asked, pointing to Matt's truck which had stopped a truck length back. Because Uncle Bill's truck sat high off the ground, the guard did not need to bend down to see Abby who was indeed pointing the business end of the .357 right at his face with confidence and no wobble.

"Yes," answered Uncle Bill. "We are passing through. We don't want any trouble."

"There ain't no trouble here mister; not unless you start it," he said, keeping an eye on Abby. He took a step back and looked around at his comrades.

"Good then," said Uncle Bill, pushing the gear shifter into first. "If you'll stand aside, and move that barricade, we'll be on our way. The guard did not motion to the others to move the barricade, but instead he looked back at Matt's truck as if deciding what to do. Uncle Bill took the moment to look into his rear view mirror. Juanita had her .223 shouldered with the barrel resting on the dash. Still, the farmer stood his ground. Abby sat stiff in her seat, staring straight into the man's face, her finger dangerously tight on the trigger of the rifle.

"Where ya headed?" he asked, returning Abby's stare.

"We are heading south," said Abby, before Uncle Bill could answer. Eric flinched and Uncle Bill didn't move.

"Well," the farmer drawled, "we got a trading store. We need gas and water if you got any to trade; we have a pretty good supply of medical supplies, canned food, fresh deer meat, toothbrushes, that sort of thing. If you want to look around, we'll pull the sawhorses aside and y'all can pull in and park right over there." He pointed to a spot where a bunch of mismatched vehicles were parked in no particular order.

"Thanks just the same," said Uncle Bill, "but we'll be moving on."

"Suit yourselves," said the farmer-guard, finally moving aside. "Good luck to y'all and watch your backs—it's dangerous out there," he said, smirking a smile that revealed green scum on his teeth.

Uncle Bill pulled out slowly. Matt pulled up fast and was so close that to someone watching he might have been in tow. They drove fast for ten miles before Uncle Bill pulled over and quickly told Matt and Juanita about the commune, the store, and basically what was going on and what had been offered.

"We don't need anything," said Juanita, "except to get as far away from here as we can."

"I could use a toothbrush," said Eric, smiling.

"I don't think it's a good idea to go shopping," she said, not smiling.

"We could use some information, then," he rebutted. "Maybe they are just a bunch of farmers trying to get by. Maybe they have some useful news. Maybe some of them have come up the roads we are heading down. They didn't look so threatening," he added?"

"I'm telling you, those good ol' farm boys are big, big trouble," she said looking at Uncle Bill and then at Matt, ignoring Eric.

"I think Juanita is right," said Matt. "Nothing about that place looked right."

"I agree," said Uncle Bill. "We need to find a place to camp before it gets dark," he added, changing the subject.

"It would be better to keep moving," said Juanita. "These guys are not what they appear to be, boys and girls," she said sarcastically. "My guess is that most of these folks are being held against their will, if they know it or not. They've probably been lured in with promises of food and safe lodging, and then they're convinced to donate everything for the greater good of the many. Sound familiar? We need to get as far away from here as we can, and fast."

"Maybe up there," Abby said, pointing to a clump of trees on a small hill a mile or more further down the road.

"Looks okay to me," said Eric. "Could be good to stay close to this commune—maybe not," he quickly added, after Juanita gave him the, *what the fuck did I just say*, look.

"Y'all are looking for trouble if you go back there. I guarantee it," said Juanita, obviously agitated. "What I *can't* guarantee is that if you do go back there, that I can protect you. Understand, that you will be on your own."

"Let's check out the hill," said Uncle Bill, motioning with his head to load up.

"You're the boss."

Although Juanita was not so happy with the decision, she was in the middle of nowhere, and right now, the power of numbers was a plus. What could she do?

"Load up," she ordered.

*****

Uncle Bill found a wagon trail of a dirt road that led up to the trees that Abby had pointed out, pulled up about a hundred yards and stopped behind a small stand of Douglas Fir to consult with his clan. They were still a hundred yards from the trees at the top of hill.

"Looks like tire tracks going up but not coming down," said Juanita, squatting and rubbing her hand over the tread marks, trying to determine how old they were.

"Maybe the road goes on over the top," said Matt.

"And maybe not," said Juanita standing up brushing off her hands. "They're more than just a few days old."

"The sun is setting," said Uncle Bill, "I think we better check it out."

It was discussed and agreed to send one truck up to the trees with a white flag attached to the antenna while the other truck held back.

"If anyone is up there, they already know we're here," said Juanita. "And if they wanted us dead, it's an easy shot from up there. They could have killed us all by now, because we're sitting ducks standing out here in the middle of this fucking field," she said, from behind Matt's truck, at which Eric dropped to his knees behind Uncle Bill's truck. "So, either there isn't anyone up there, or they don't want any trouble, or they're hoping we leave." Eric slid into the passenger seat of Uncle Bill's truck, and scooted down until his eyes were level with the dash. "It's a crap shoot, but I'm guessing there won't be any trouble. Not from up there any way," she said looking over her shoulder back in the direction from which they had come.

It was decided, to Eric's dismay, that he and Uncle Bill would drive up with the white flag of peace.

*****

Montana and Moalim walked up to the front door of the Lassiter ranch as if they were just visiting and knocked lightly; there was no sense in storming the place if they didn't have to. Moalim stood to one side with his .40 caliber Glock at his side. He had no intentions of wooing the owners; he planned a quick invasion. When Jake opened the door, Moalim pushed his way in, grabbing Jake by the collar as he did so. "No trouble old man, and you and the missus will live," he said, shoving the business end of the pistol under his jaw. Montana followed close behind, and Ali came in last. The other three killers waited outside.

"Montana, what's this all about," pleaded Karla, rising from the couch.

"Stay put, old lady," ordered Moalim.

"Please do as he says, Karla—Jake. We need the use of your cabin for a while," lied Montana.

"All you need to do is ask," said Karla. "Why the guns? And please, mister, let my husband go. He's no threat. What do you want?" asked Karla, now with tears streaming down her face. "We saw you drive up, Montana. We

165

know you, so we put our guns down." She pointed to two rifles on the table. Where is Abby?"

"Go sit down next to your wife, old man, and don't try anything courageous or you will both die." Karla's eyes sprung wide with terror as her hands sprang to her mouth, stifling a gasp. Ali gathered up the rifles.

"What does he mean, Montana?" she asked, lowering her hands to the couch and moving forward, starting to get up. "Are you going to kill us? Oh my God, Montana, what's going on?" she begged. "Where's Abby?" she screeched.

"Jesus, Moalim, chill a little. Nobody's going to die, for Christ's sake." Moalim gave Montana a stare that penetrated the next county.

"Go outside Montana and tell the others we are in, and we are secure. Now!" he ordered loudly when Montana hesitated.

"Sure, okay, Moalim, but remember, we need these people alive."

"You've said enough, Montana," said Ali, with the voice of authority. It was the first time that Ali had addressed him directly. "Shut your mouth and do as you're told," he ordered, firmly, turning to face Montana with a deadly and menacing stare. It was at that moment, that Montana got the feeling that he was probably expendable.

"Okay, I'm going," he said, too embarrassed to look over at Jake and Karla.

"Have you seen Abby?" begged Karla, tears flowing like rivers.

"I told you to be silent," said Moalim, swiveling around and pointing his gun at Karla's head.

"Let's just do what they want," said Jake, taking hold of her arm and gently coaxing her to sit back. "It's going to be alright," he assured her.

*****

A shot rang out raising a cloud of dust five yards in front of Uncle Bill's truck. He slammed on his breaks; he was twenty yards from the top of the knoll.

"Stop right there," yelled the voice of an old man. "Get out of the truck and put your hands up." Eric slouched in his seat, and started mumbling. *Dear God, Dear, Dear God.*

"This guy is not a warrior," he said to Eric. Then with urgency, "Eric, pull your shit together; get out slowly, but stay behind the door, and for Christ's sake, put your hands in the air. We don't want this guy thinking we are trying to pull something."

After climbing down from the cab, Uncle Bill motioned for Matt and company to stay where they were for fear they might barge in like the cavalry.

"What do you want," yelled the man from somewhere behind cover.

"We are only looking for a place to camp for the night. We are heading south at first light," said Uncle Bill. "We can move on right now if that's what you want. We don't want any trouble." A long minute of silence followed.

"We don't want no trouble either, mister" came the shaky voice from the trees, but rest assured we are prepared and quite capable if it comes to it. Right now we have rifles trained on you *and* your friends down the hill.

"Whoever these people are, they are harmless," whispered Uncle Bill. Eric did not answer but was fidgeting like he needed to pee.

"We need some water. Do you have any extra water we can trade for?" yelled the old man.

Uncle Bill thought quickly and determined that they should be in Cave Junction by the day after tomorrow at the latest—maybe even tomorrow. He decided to take a chance.

"We can give up two gallons. Three tops," hollered Uncle Bill. Again, there was a long silence. "We got water mister, and we'll be happy to share it with you for a place to camp tonight," hollered Uncle Bill, again. "We don't need anything from you. We have our own rations. We just need a place to camp." More silence.

"Okay, then, you can come on up. When you get here, pull in behind the trees where you can't be seen from the road. Leave your guns in your trucks and get out so we can look you in the eye," said the hidden voice. Uncle Bill turned to face downhill and signaled Matt and the others to come up, and then turned back to the trees.

"You got yourself a deal," yelled Uncle Bill.

When Matt pulled up, Uncle Bill walked to the passenger side of his truck where Juanita was sitting and filled them in.

"Don't try and pull anything," yelled the man in the trees.

"Just explaining to our friends what's going on," yelled Uncle Bill.

"We leave our rifles in the truck," said Juanita, taking over, but we all carry a pistol, in our belts, under our shirts, in the back. If it comes to it, and I don't think it will from what Bill says, hit the dirt, roll, and shoot to kill. Is that understood?" she added, looking straight at Matt, who opened his eyes as if saying, what you looking at me for? It seemed they were all on the same page, for a change.

"I can't carry a gun," said Eric. "I would just shoot myself in the foot, or one of you." Matt looked at him and shook his head.

"Eric, you have to get over that. You…

"Now is not the time," interrupted Uncle Bill. "Eric, when we get up there, hang back and stay close to Abby and Matt. Juanita and I will go in first. I trust these guys and don't think they want any trouble. Just trying to survive in a world that's gone haywire, I'd say."

"Okay," said Eric, wide eyed and scared shitless.

Uncle Bill hollered to the man in the trees. "We're coming up. We will leave our guns in the truck. How do we know you aren't going to gun us done when we get there?" he hollered.

"If we wanted to kill you," the voice in the trees assured him, "we could have done it by now. We don't want any trouble."

"This guy is old," whispered Juanita to no one in particular. "He is not a threat. Okay," she said to the others, "let's go," and they piled into the trucks and started slowly up the last twenty yards of the knoll.

*****

"My name is Bill and this is Juanita," he said to the old man and the unarmed old woman standing slightly behind him. "That's Matt, Abby, and Eric," said Uncle Bill pointing towards Matt's truck. "Like I said, we are heading south and need a place to camp for the night. That's all. If you point your guns away, we'll move our trucks further into the trees so they can't be seen from the road and then we'll get the water you asked for."

"Get the water first," ordered the old withered farmer who was now standing in front of Uncle Bill, pointing his gun straight at his heart, while his wife, who was also old and withered, hung back, licking her dried-up lips.

Husband and wife both had white hair and wore clothes that were too big for their frail bodies. The old man was wearing a tan colored work shirt and his neck stuck out the top of the buttoned-up collar like a straw in a bottle of soda pop. The old lady was wearing a dirty, flower print dress. She was not as skinny as her husband, but wrinkled skin hung from her tired bones and wobbled when she moved. She had a pleasant smile. She looked like a grandmother who would be at her best in the kitchen cooking for loved ones.

"Put your gun down, Thomas," said the old lady. These are good folks. I can feel it. Y'all are welcome," she said with what was left of her southern drawl.

"Okay, Sam," he said, tucking the old 30-30 up under his arm as if it were a shotgun. "You better get your trucks in the trees, then. You can get the water after that," he said, turning away. "You folks make yourself at home, for what it is," he said, leaning his rifle against a tree.

Within minutes, the trucks were under the cover of a large stand firs. Uncle Bill undid the straps holding down the tarp of his truck and retrieved a jug of water and carried it over to the old man, who was watching his every move. Matt wondered, as he looked at the two pathetic old people, how they'd come to be living in the trees. Where's their home, he wondered?

"I'll give you a two more gallons before we head out in the morning."

"Thanks mister. Thanks a lot." The old man's lower eyelids drooped and the red flesh hung like a fresh wound, as it did on many older folks. He ogled the water as the precious gift that it was, and then scurried off towards his wife with the liquid gold.

"No problem, Tom. Glad to help," said Uncle Bill. He and his nephew watched as the old man handed the jug to his wife.

"I'm not drinking out of a jug, Tom. Please. Get me a cup," whispered the old lady. Uncle Bill looked at Abby and smiled. The cup that Tom provided was an empty tin can with the wrapper removed.

*****

After the two had their fill of water, Sam brushed back a stray strand of gray hair and smoothed her dirty apron. Juanita had walked around to where she could keep an eye on the road, leaving Matt, Eric, Abby, and Uncle Bill with the old folks.

"Our ranch is that way," the old lady volunteered, pointing towards the direction that the vagabonds had come from. "Other side of that small hill, right there," she said, continuing to point a crooked finger, squinting as if that would bring it into sight. You can't see our place from here, but it's real nice, and it's right over there," she continued, pointing in the direction of the circus the vagabonds had passed just a short while ago. Uncle Bill looked at Sam's husband who was sitting, leaning against a tree next to her, head down.

"We didn't even know there was a problem," she began. "Our power goes out all the time up here. It wasn't until the knock on the door and those bastards barged in bringing mud and muck from outside with no consideration at all." Her voice was crackling like a hot fire and was getting louder as her frustration grew.

"Now mother, we been through worse. We'll get through this too," said her husband, putting his arm around her shoulder. "They told us they were taking our house and that we should pack some food and water into the truck and get out. They gave us ten minutes. Fortunately, they hadn't checked the barn too closely and didn't find the guns I keep out there to ward off coyotes and foxes and the like," said the old man, reliving the experience. "I don't do much hunting any more, but I keep my guns cleaned and oiled." His story elicited silence. "Anyway, we packed what we could and started filling water jugs when they told us to get out and not to come back. What could we do?" he said, looking at his wife for confirmation. We had no choice—there was so many of them," he choked, head twisted sideways, away from the stares. "We were no match for those cowards; we didn't stand a chance."

"Indians, I think," interrupted Sam. "Not American Indians, neither," she said. "There just wasn't nothin' we could do. There was just too damn many of 'em," she said, looking up at Abby, who had tears of sorrow running down her face.

"Oh dear," said the old woman, getting up and going over to Abby. "Please don't cry sweetheart." She pulled Abby into her arms and hugged her, and gently rocked her from side to side.

"From what we've seen," said Uncle Bill, you're probably lucky to be alive."

"I guess," answered Sam as she let go of Abby, "if y'all consider living like a wild animal lucky."

"We're real sorry to hear about your home," said Uncle Bill in a low voice. "We'd like to help you get it back, but…"

"Don't you worry about that," said the old man, sitting up straight, taking charge of the conversation. "You and us together don't have enough fire power to do it. That band of cutthroats you had to drive through to get here is all part of their new empire. Don't you worry, young man, the United States Army will be along any day and we'll get our place back real soon, you can bet your last dime on that. Don't you worry about a thing," he said, patting his wife's shoulder. He then excused himself. "I'll be right back," he said. "Nature calls."

He walked slowly into the bushes, did his business, and then he stopped at his well-used farm truck and retrieved a fifth of whiskey. He stood in front of the small fire and took a swallow, and then he handed the bottle to Uncle Bill who took a small swallow and passed it on to Matt, who did likewise before passing it on to Eric who took a slug and a half before passing it on to Abby, who also took a small jolt.

After the bottle made the rounds, the old man took another swig and then passed the bottle to his wife who, surprisingly, took a swig as if she were quite used to it. When she finished, she took another swig before passing it on to Uncle Bill who passed it on Matt who passed it to Eric, who took the bottle and looked around at his new companions and took another gulp, causing bubbles to gurgle to the bottom of the upturned jug, before passing it on to a scowling Abby, who passed it back to the old man.

"Thanks," said Uncle Bill

"Yeah," said Eric—"took the edge off."

The old lady got up and walked, hunched over, one small step at a time towards their old truck, when she returned to the campfire she had an old flour sack full of who knew what, but looked as if it weighed more than she did.

"It would be our pleasure to have y'all for dinner tonight," she said, setting the bag down and looking around at everyone.

"It would be *our* pleasure," said Uncle Bill, speaking for everyone.

"It won't take long," she said. "I'll give a holler when it's ready."

Abby walked over to where Juanita was watching the road, and Matt started setting up camp with Uncle Bill. Eric sat with the old man and had another drink. Everyone kept busy and to themselves.

*****

"Come and get it," hollered the old lady gleefully, as if she were serving up a banquet. And although the meager meal consisted of only stew and crackers, she announced it with the pride of a master chef serving up Thanksgiving dinner. Matt could tell that she'd probably done it a hundred times in the past, and he pictured her hustling about in a warm, cheery country style kitchen. She announced it with so much gaiety in her voice that no one would have guessed that the state of affairs was apocalyptic, and everyone gathered around the campfire, except for Juanita.

The old folks joked with each other as they dished up plates for everyone. The first plate was taken over to Juanita, who would not leave her post—for any reason. "I wish the kids could stay longer," Matt heard the old lady say to her husband when she thought no one was listening. The comment tugged at his heart strings. Damn, he thought. It just ain't right. He wanted to go down to the encampment and start shooting. Kill as many of the bad guys as he could, but he knew that such an enterprise would be suicidal.

"That was real good," said Abby, putting her thin plastic picnic bowel and plastic spoon on top of the bowl that the old lady had set near the flour bag to be cleaned and reused. "Darn good, in fact, after what we've been eating," she said, smiling a labored smile at Matt.

There really wasn't much to talk about that wasn't depressing, so rather than break the mood, everyone just sat for a while, taking turns cleaning up this and that, getting ready to turn in. The fire was dying down and it was getting late.

"Let's go to bed," Sam, the old man said, helping his wife to stand. "You folks do what you need to do," he said, to the gang of travelers, leading his wife towards their tent. "You can stay as long as you like." And then, he suddenly stopped and put his free hand to his heart and grimaced. Everyone froze.

"Are you okay old man," asked Sam stopping and taking hold of his arm to look into his face.

"I'm fine; just a bit of heart burn from the whisky," said Tom, "his words wavering off into the dark void of night.

"Come along then, husband," she said, as they turned and disappeared behind the blue plastic flap of their tent.

Juanita hollered over for Matt to come and relieve her, and after she briefed him, she walked with purpose over to talk to Uncle Bill.

"We need to set guard duty and hit the rack," she said. "It's going to be a very long day tomorrow. We should leave at dawn," she said, flipping her rifle onto her shoulder.

"It could be a very long night if that gang of thieves decides that they want what we have," said Uncle Bill.

"We should grab a few hours, Bill, and then take the late shift. If those jerks come a knockin' it won't be until 2 or 3 in the morning—a repeat of last night."

Juanita seemed to be the only one with any energy left to make a plan, so it was settled without any discussion, just nods of confirmation. Matt would take the first watch on the front side and wake Juanita at midnight. Eric would watch the back side of the campsite and the rest would get some much needed sleep.

Uncle Bill was getting ready to hit the hay when the old man returned, still holding his hand over his heart.

"Would anyone have any antacids," he asked: "Seems the whisky is causing a fuss tonight."

"I got some in my bag," said Abby. "I'll get them."

"I overheard you talking about guard duty," said the old man before Abby came back. "I served in World War II and would be proud to take a turn. "I don't think Sam would be any good at it though, but I sure don't mind doing my share; served in World War II," he said again.

"Seems like you and yours could use some rest," said Abby, returning with the antacids and handing them to the old man. "We can handle guard duty, Right Bill?"

"Absolutely," he said. He wanted to ask the old man if there was something more wrong than just heart burn, but then he thought, what good would it do? "Thanks for volunteering Tom, now *and* back then, too, but you and Sam should get some rest. Like Abby said, we can handle the guard duty, but if we need you, you can damn well believe we'll give you a holler." The old man smiled and thanked them with a nod of his head and then he turned and short-stepped his way back to his tent.

*****

Matt sat watching the road and was thankful that there was no activity. He thought about the battle last night and wondered if there would be another one tonight—certainly Juanita thought so. He was damn glad to have a seasoned warrior like Juanita with them who probably looked at two day firefights as the norm—hell, she's probably used to firefights that never let up, he thought. Whatever her experience, it was clear that she knew what she was doing and that one battle was not the end of the war.

He ducked under cover of a tree where he had a view of the front access road and left a pee. Eric was supposed to be walking the back perimeter of the knoll. Matt was pretty sure he didn't know really what he was supposed to be doing. It was a steep, grassy slope down to the darkness below, and at night it looked like a bottomless pit. The incline, according to consensus, was too steep for a surprise attack, which meant if an attack came it would come from the front. If Eric saw something, anything at all, he was to alert the others immediately, and that's probably all that he understood.

*****

At around 11:30 p.m., just before it was time to change the guard, Abby walked over and sat down next to Matt.

"Anything going on," she asked, handing him a cup of coffee. "I couldn't sleep," she said, before Matt could answer. Matt took the coffee and interpreted it as a gesture of peace.

"Abby, I'm sorry about the way things have been going between us lately. It's been…." She cut him off before he could finish.

"Don't worry about it, Matt," she said, calmly. "I'm over it, and I'm over you," her eyes gleaming like steel balls in the moonlight, her voice as rock solid as a politician running for president. She hadn't meant it to sound spiteful, but it probably did.

"Gees, Abby, there's no reason to be bitter. It's been a hard week."

"It's been a hard year," she said, still calm. "But listen, it's okay. We had a good run, and I'm guessing, Matt, that it's probably okay with you too if we split up. You don't seem to be too happy these days, either."

"I'm sorry Abby," he said, sincerely. "It's not your fault, really. Maybe things will be better once we get to Cave Junction…"

"It's over Matt. I was going to tell you after the party but then all this happened," she said softly, waving her hand across the horizon.

"It was exciting for a long time, Matt, and I thank you sincerely for introducing me to a lot of really good people and for all the good times and good memories, but we both need to move on."

"Gee, Abby, I…."

"Wait, Matt, let me finish. I have to get this out in case worst comes to worst, if you know what I mean." Matt lowered his head and nodded in submission. It was true what she'd said, he was ready for a change too, but still, breaking up was hard to do, and it always carried with it some hurt, always. "This whole war thing has put a new perspective on life for me. You saw all this coming," she continued. "I was so naïve." He wanted to say something because he knew that she was probably hurting, but he could not think of any words that would due.

"We are practically brother and sister, if you think about it. It's sort of weird since we have been intimate," she said smiling, "but true just the same. Anyway, I really hope that we can stay friends." She was standing so close to him that he could feel her heat, and in the moment, he wanted to take her in his arms and hug her. "I'll go wake up Bill and Juanita," she said, turning away before he could respond.

As he sat and watched the road below, he pondered what Abby had said. It *had* been a good ride; a damn good ride and he had no regrets. And now Abby had cut him loose with no chance of reconciliation, it was over. Suddenly a few questions regarding love had become crystal clear to him. He loved Abby, but he was not *in love* with her. He could *give* his life for her, but he couldn't *live* his life for her. He loved her like a sister. It was solid and he felt good.

"Everything okay," asked his uncle who had walked up behind to him.

173

"Yeah, sure. Everything is as good as it can be considering the circumstances." He caught sight of movement by the tents and saw Juanita heading off into the bushes. "She's okay," don't you think?" Matt said, indicating Juanita with a nod of his head.

"Yeah. Sure. She's a fox," said Uncle Bill. "Way too old for you though," he added with a chuckle. Although Matt had been referring to her warrior talents, he decided to go with the flow.

"Hey, age doesn't mean shit when it comes to love. Brent told me so," said Matt, smiling.

"My buddy Brent gets love and lust mixed up. He uses the terms as if they were interchangeable. He doesn't know shit about love," laughed Uncle Bill. They both laughed and then as if someone had turned off the radio, they sat in silence.

"It's too bad about those old folks," said Matt, drawing a line in the dirt with a stick. They didn't have a chance. If they would have tried to fight back, they'd both be dead." His uncle just nodded. "I guess we were real lucky to have Juanita in the trees last night or we would all be dead, too. Don't you think?"

"Well, it would have gotten real ugly, that's for sure," said Uncle Bill, not wanting to admit to the possibility.

"She's not bad for a Mexican," said Matt, smiling at the ground where he was drawing nonsensical lines in the dirt with a stick.

"Hey, you're coming right along. Maybe there's hope for you yet," he said, slapping Matt on the back, after which there was another period of silence.

Matt considered talking about last night, but decided against it.

"Yeah. Guess I should get some shut-eye," he said. "One more thing, Abby broke up with me a little while ago; no need to go into the details but her reasons are valid," he said, looking over his shoulder. "I've been a real ass the last few months. I'm sorry."

"Hey, no problem, Matt, I knew you would come around. Sorry about you a Abby," was all he said.

"By the way, Bill, just because I like the Mexican chick doesn't mean I like the fucking Arabs." And he was as serious as a heart attack.

"You better get some shut eye, Son. It's going to be another long day tomorrow," he said, standing up and gripping Matt's shoulder. "We probably need to talk about a lot of things, Matt, but for now we need to stay focused. We need to get to Cave Junction and then we can rest and reflect."

*****

Before Uncle Bill headed to the back side of the camp to relieve Eric, he went over to where Juanita was pouring herself a cup of java.

"Looks good," he said taking a cup from the log next to the fire. "Get any sleep?"

"Slept like a drunken soldier," she said. "Could have slept longer but my, do-anything-but-go-to-the-store-for-you, military issue watch sounded the alarm to rise and shine, so here I am. And you?"

"In and out, but I got enough, thanks."

"Say Bill, why do you think those clowns back there let us pass today?" she said, after he poured his coffee. She looked out into the darkness pondering the reasons, waiting for his answer.

"Not sure," said Uncle Bill. "Maybe the guard didn't like the way Abby was pointing the business end of my .357 at his head," he said. "Or maybe he saw that you had your rifle pointing in the same direction."

"Well, like I told Matt, I think they're waiting for a better opportunity," said Juanita.

"Jesus," said Uncle Bill shaking his head. "I sure hope you're wrong. I'm not ready for a replay of last night. Too old for this sort of shit anymore," he said taking in a deep breath.

"Oh bullshit," said Juanita, smiling. "You still got it, and besides, you're the leader of the pack," she said, smiling a flirtatious smile at him. She walked a few feet away and looked towards the dark horizon towards the circus. "I'm sure they know where we are, though. I figure they have a perimeter, and I also figure they watch their perimeter as far as their spotting scopes can see. What do you think," she said, turning towards Bill.

"Yeah," he said. "Makes sense, for sure. Yeah. Damn." He took another deep breath and held it, and then let it out slowly. "They need to see what's coming, just like we do."

"I'm sure they would like to have everything we got. I think they want our trucks, our guns, and Abby. I think the rest of us are expendable."

"Hey, don't count yourself short, sweetheart," he said, walking up next to her. "You'd be welcome at my place any time," he said, returning the flirt.

"See," she said, smiling. "You still got it. You're not so bad yourself, you smooth-talking son-of a gun." They looked at each other, scanning souls with their eyes, both lost in their own thoughts that had nothing to do with war. When after a few moments it had become uncomfortable, Juanita lowered her gaze and turned away.

"I was really hoping to skirt another battle," he said—shit! "I suppose if they're coming it *will* be sometime soon," he said. "Maybe we should load everyone up and head out—take the old folks with us. Kids could ride in the bed. Shit!" he said again, as he continued to think out loud.

"We have the advantage up here," said Juanita, thinking out loud. "We can see them coming. No tall grass to hide in like last night. On the other hand, if they show up with a couple of dozen men," she added, it could get real nasty." There was a considerable pause as they thought about a way out. "I think we need to pack up now and head out of here overland, out the back side," she said, all in one breath. I scouted it ealier but couldn't see beyond the tree line down there, but it may be our best option. If we leave the way we came, they could be waiting. Do you think your trucks can handle the terrain out back?"

"Damn," he said again. "I was really hoping to get out of here without a problem. Maybe we should have driven further down the road before pulling off," he said glancing at Juanita, and glad that she didn't say, I told you so. "And yes, our trucks can handle that little hill," he said smiling. "I looked at it earlier with Matt and it looks doable, rough, but doable. Didn't see any other tracks so we may be the first, but the good thing is, it's all downhill," he chuckled.

"I think you made a good call last night, Bill. After thinking about it, they probably got their territory covered for ten miles in all directions. If anything, we made a good move stopping here," she said. "That's my guess, anyways."

"Did you see what they had down there when we drove past, Juanita? Hell, they had gas tankers and semi-trucks full of who knows what. Hell, they're building a new town any way they can."

"Just like your ancestors," said Juanita, smiling, "by hook or by crook, as the saying goes." And then quickly added, "That's just a saying, Bill, nothing personal, I assure you. We got some pretty greedy folks south of the border, too."

"No offense taken, Juanita," he said. "My only concern is getting Matt, Abby, and Eric to Cave Junction alive, and I'm counting on you to help make that happen. You're input, your experience, *and* your charm," he added smiling, "is very much appreciated. If I don't have a chance to say it later, thanks."

"Don't talk that shit, man. We are all going to get to Cave Junction just fine."

"Small talk is good, but action is needed to stay alive. It's 1:00 now," said Juanita. "We should start packing right away."

"Doesn't give Matt and Abby much sleep time."

"We all have to suffer, Bill. They can sleep when we get to Cave Junction. They can handle it. They're young," she said, smiling.

"Maybe the Metsker maps show a better lay of the land out back," he said, getting up to fetch a map. "Wish I would have invested in a GPS," he said shaking his head. "Always something."

"I'll go tell Matt and the others to start packing it up, and I'll wake the old folks, too," she said, moving towards the tents.

*****

"Mister," said the old lady to Uncle Bill when he walked past her tent. "Would you please check on Tom? That's my husband's name, Tom," she said, with a far away, unfocussed look on her face. Uncle Bill flashed on Tom holding his hand over his chest, earlier and a feeling of dread swept over him like a cold breeze off the Pacific.

"Is something wrong?"

"Well," she hesitated, "probably not, but Tom snores like crazy; has for the past fifty years; every night he snores. Tonight, he's not snoring. Could you check on him for me, mister? It sure would make me feel better if I knew for sure he was just tuckered out and sleeping like a baby," she pleaded.

"Sure Sam, I'll take a look."

He touched the old lady on the shoulder and stepped inside the tent. When he emerged a few moments later, Juanita was standing next to the old lady with her arm draped around her shoulder. "I'm very sorry," he said, looking into hopeful eyes. When Sam heard what she probably already knew, her gaze dropped to her feet, and for a second, Uncle Bill thought she might collapse, for she seemed to shrink in size right before his eyes. Thinking the worst is one thing, having it confirmed is altogether a different reality. Her shoulders sagged and she unhooked from Juanita and walked towards the tent. When she got to the flap, she turned to face Uncle Bill and Juanita.

"Thanks, mister," she said, looking at Uncle Bill with a blank stare. "I'd like to spend some time alone with my Tommy, if that's alright."

"Of course," said Uncle Bill. "We'll be right here if you need us. Would you like Juanita to go with you?"

"Thanks, but I'll be alright," she said, disappearing into the darkness of the tent.

"Damn," said Juanita, finally, we..." Before she could finish saying what she was thinking, a loud bang and a bright flash from the old folks' tent brought Eric, Abby, and Matt running.

"What the hell was that," hollered Matt looking at Juanita who was emerging from the old tent.

"We need to pack it up and get out of here right now," she said. "That shot is going to bring those fuckers running," she said, pointing in the direction of tent city. "And they will be here damn soon. Start packin' and don't be too neat about it. We need to move. Now!" she hollered, trying to get everyone moving.

"What happened?" repeated Matt.

"The old man had a heart attack and the old lady just killed herself," said Juanita. "We need to hit it right the fuck now," she ordered. Abby's hands flew to her mouth.

"No! She cried. "This can't be happening." She was shaking her hands in front of her as if she were shaking off excess water after washing them.

"She couldn't see the world ahead without him," said Uncle Bill, stepping up beside her. "We need to pack, Abby. Come on," he said, pulling her away and towards the campfire.

Matt was tearing down the tent and throwing gear into the back of the trucks when Juanita yelled, "here they come!" She was at the edge of the knoll, rifle to her shoulder.

"There's no more time Abby," hollered Uncle Bill. "Get in the truck," he ordered. He looked over at Matt who was already behind the wheel of his tuck and motioned to him that they were going to drive down the back side of the knoll. There was no other choice. Juanita popped off a few shots at the attackers before turning and running to the passenger side of Matt's truck. Eric jumped into the back seat of Uncle Bill's truck, and Abby flew into the shot gun seat.

"Okay," yelled Uncle Bill, jumping in behind the wheel, "let's roll," he hollered, bringing the big engine of his 4x to life, and in the next second he was bouncing down the backside of the knoll, heading into the darkness of unknown territory, leaving behind the two dead bodies of Tom and Sam.

*****

Matt gunned the engine of his truck and flew over the edge of the knoll as Juanita slammed shut the passenger door. He steered hard to keep his rig from rolling, and slid sideways before re-gaining control. He dodged trees and bushes and bounced over boulders, sometimes going airborne. From atop the knoll, the hillside looked smooth, but instead, it was a landscape of deep ruts and jagged rocks that caused his truck to bounce like an airliner in stage-10 turbulence. Juanita was leaning forward in her seat, holding on to the dashboard; the decent was to wild to glance behind to see if the killers were following. Matt's truck, although a modified four wheel drive, was not really meant for this sort of terrain or abuse, and he prayed that it would hold together.

Everyone in Uncle Bill's truck was being bounced around like so many Ping-Pong balls in a bingo machine. Abby managed a glance out the side window, but she did not have the muscle power to fight the inertia of the flying truck to look to the rear. Eric was wide-eyed, and hanging on for his life. When they got close to the tree-line Matt hit the brakes hard, but too late. The fence he smashed through was not a problem, but the river coming up fast was reason for concern. He cramped the wheel hard to the right and slid sideways, fishtailing but under control; he hit the gas, following nothing more than a narrow game trail, and hoping for the best.

"We can't outrun them!" hollered Juanita. We need to cross over to the other side. If they have troops up the road, we are being herded right into an ambush. We need to stop! We have to neutralize this from here!" she hollered, reaching for the door handle. Matt slammed on his brakes and flipped off his head lights, and Uncle Bill slid to a stop behind. Everyone jumped out of the trucks and quickly gathered between the hood of Uncle Bill's truck and the bed of Matt's. Juanita quickly explained the counter attack while bright headlights bounced around the country side like giant search lights panning the skies as the enemy bounced down the side of the hill in hot pursuit.

"It's our only chance," she said. "Split up, wait until they are close and then take a few quick shots and then move to a new location just as fast as you can. We have to stop these bastards here!" she reiterated. "Shoot to kill, maggots!" At that she ran towards the first set of headlights shining through the trees behind them. "Move!" she hollered."

Uncle Bill took the opposite side of the trail and was on a dead run. Abby and Matt followed a few yards behind. The space on either side of the game trail was narrow, not really a lot of room to spread out. Thirty yards up, Uncle Bill hit the dirt and took aim and fired at the vehicle that was now almost upon him, taking out the front windshield. The killers had sped right into their trap, unaware that their prey had stopped to take a stand. The Jeep spun sideways and went into the stream at a high speed and flipped violently onto its side, and instantly the woods erupted in a great fireball of light and heat. Matt and Abby kept moving.

Gun fire from Juanita's .223 racked the landscape as she let loose on a second 4x just coming over the top of the knoll, bringing it to a sliding stop. Matt and Abby kept moving.

The third vehicle, only twenty yards away, had skidded to a sideways stop, and from the glare from the fire of the first Jeep, Matt saw four men jump into the tall grass, two on each side. He crouched and ran towards them. Abby moved away from Matt and followed suit, and like a well-oiled machine in motion, they both dove into the deep grass and waited in ambush. Behind them they could hear gun fire, and as suddenly as it had all started, it stopped, and it became eerily silent.

Abby crouched, heart pounding, directly across from Matt. She was holding her pistol with both hands, waiting, thinking about nothing but her immediate mission. It happened quickly. Two men snuck straight into the crouched comrades, and when they were right on top of them, Matt stood and fired, cocked his weapon and fired again and two men went down. Ten yards away, two killers crouched at the sudden explosion of gun fire, but too late. Abby had seen them and knew exactly where they were. She stood and fired, emptying her gun into the last of the killers, and again, except for the crackle of the fire from the Jeep in the water, all was silent.

Juanita and Uncle Bill were there before the smoke from the magnums disappeared into the darkness of night.

"We need to get the fuck out of here," yelled Uncle Bill. Discussion will have to wait.

"We need to cross the river," hollered Juanita.

"Agreed," answered Uncle Bill.

Back near the trucks, Eric crawled up out of the grass from where he was hiding. As he ran up the road towards his friends, a single gunshot rang out

179

and he stood paralyzed, frozen in time, and in slow motion, he slumped to the ground. Matt drew his revolver and unloaded the remaining cartridges, fanning the hammer as fast as he could, into the half dead bandit that had been thrown from the Jeep before it caught fire.

"No," screamed Abby running to her fallen friend. Matt and Uncle Bill stood anxiously beside her as she tugged Eric into her breast and wept.

"I'm so sorry," said Juanita, softly, "but we need to move out right now," she said putting her hand on Abby's shoulder. "Come on Abby. Let him go. We need to move out." Abby laid Eric gently on the ground and stood up. "Whose kill was that," she demanded, remembering Juanita's tutelage. "Who didn't check their fucking kill," she hollered at her comrades.

"Stop it, soldier!" ordered Juanita. "There's no time now." Abby stood her ground as stiff as an obelisk.

"You assholes!" screamed Abby.

"Back off lady!" ordered Juanita stepping up and yelling right into Abby's face, and this time, Abby obeyed. Uncle Bill and Matt stood next to their fallen friend, and Juniata hurried Abby back towards the trucks and helped her back into the shotgun seat of Uncle Bill's 4x. Uncle and nephew picked up their friend and quickly followed. When they reached the trucks, they gently laid Eric under the tarp of Matt's truck, and just as quickly, started preparing to cross the stream.

Uncle Bill tied a rope around his waist and handed the other end to Matt, and stepped into the water. How deep the water was, they could not tell, it was too dark, but they had to know and this was the quickest way. After four steps, he fell, but he quickly regained his footing. He fell two more times, but each time he was able to stand again without much effort. The water never went higher than his waist. "Okay," he hollered. "Come across." Juanita jumped into his truck with Abby and turned into the water, and Matt did the same.

Uncle Bill's truck sat high in the river and was having no trouble crossing, but three-quarters of the way across, Matt's rig slid sideways in the current and got hung up in the rocks. Uncle Bill watched in horror as his nephew's truck began tipping onto its side. He feared the worst, and was about to yell to Matt to jump, when the truck leaned into a submerged bolder and brought it to a halt before it went over. Before Juanita made land, Uncle Bill was signaling for her to turn around so that the winch on the front end of his truck was facing back towards Matt. As soon as she was in position, Uncle Bill released the winch lock and headed back into the water with hook and cable.

In less than twenty minutes, Matt's truck was freed from the obstruction and was sitting next to his uncle's truck on the opposite side of the river. Dawn was spreading across the landscape highlighting the carnage on the opposite side of the river, ghostly visible through the mist and smoke of early morn. Minutes later, the two trucks, headlights off, began slowly maneuvering, off-road, through the trees heading, according to the sun, more west than south. Matt was out front.

When he finally came to a clearing, he turned his truck due south, picked up speed, and continued their escape away from the river and the county road, where more bandits surely lay in wait. Juanita sat silent and alert, which he took as a good sign and kept rolling, without explanation, as fast as the terrain would allow. If he made a questionable choice, he knew she would say so; they were on the same page, and he now welcomed productive critique for what it was and not as an assault on his character.

After an hour, they had not come across any more trouble, and the sun was up over the distant hills bringing with it a new day and leaving behind the horrors of night. They came across a path with two ruts that looked like they'd been made by a wagon train from the days of the old west. Matt decided to take a chance, as he needed to get further away, and at a faster pace. Again, Juanita sat quietly. He drove with talent, heading for what he hoped would be a safe exit. In ten minutes they were speeding south on a county dirt road; due south according to Juanita's compass. South to Cave Junction.

*****

As Matt negotiated the curves and bumps and holes in the unkempt road, he thought about the 4th of July party at his uncles. It was a distant memory—a lifetime ago, yet it had only been seven days since the party, and only six days since the lights went out. He thought about Eric lying in the back of his truck, and Rose, who had probably been tossed onto a pile with other dead bodies and set a fire. He thought about what might have happened between the two had they lived, and he wished he could stop and think and wonder why.

He and Abby had both killed another human being and have not even had the chance to digest it or talk about it. He thought about Juanita sitting silently in the passenger seat holding tight to her weapon, and wondered if any of them would still be alive if she were not along. Just as quickly, he thought— fucking terrorist bastards.

It was just past 11 a.m. when Matt pulled off to the side of the dirt road. He needed a rest, maybe some sleep. Everyone did. They found a good hill with cover and a view of the road, and parked the rigs. Juanita hopped out of the truck and went back to cover the tracks they'd left driving through the tall grass.

The view from the mesa was 360 degrees, and around the campfire it was quiet. No talk of the narrow escape or even about the killings. It was quiet and somber with each person hiding in the darkness of their own thoughts. In a little while, sandwiches had been made and passed around; soon after they'd eaten, the tired troupe began drifting off to sleep.

"I'll take the first watch," volunteered Abby, breaking the silence, and there was no argument.

*****

Abby let everyone sleep until 4 o'clock in the afternoon. The changing of the guard took only a few minutes, and in no time, Juanita and Uncle Bill were sitting by the fire watching through the trees in the direction they had come, drinking hot coffee. Matt was still sleeping and it was decided to leave him be. Abby lay down in the crushed grass where Uncle Bill had been sleeping and stared up into the tree tops, thinking about Eric's lifeless body lying in the back of the truck. Certainly it would start to decay soon, and smell. The thought brought tears to her eyes, and she rolled over onto her side and was asleep before the first tear hit the ground.

Uncle Bill and Juanita talked about the next day before setting up for the night. They agreed that they were in a good location, and that it was very unlikely that they would be discovered by anyone, friend or foe. They figured they could make Cave Junction by tomorrow evening if they got an early start and a good night's sleep.

"It was pretty amazing how everyone acted on instinct this morning," said Juanita. "It was as if we had discussed strategy."

"I know," said Uncle Bill, "it was a miracle, actually."

"It was pretty remarkable," she said. "I just wanted to say it."

"I know."

With that, Juanita got up and walked to the truck and got out a shovel, found a good spot looking out towards the distant hill, and started digging a grave. In a few minutes, Uncle Bill followed and shortly after that, Matt woke, and realizing what was going on, got up to help. Abby woke and sat up, but did not get up to help. She sat quietly sobbing, arms wrapped around her legs.

When Eric was at last laid to rest, Uncle Bill did his best at recollecting Eric's short life and his relationship to the outlaws. Abby cried for a while, then sobbed and then fell asleep again. Matt and Juanita went for a walk to scout the perimeter, and Uncle Bill made a new pot of coffee, and as he sat sipping a fresh cup, he wondered if Montana and Moalim were headed to Cave Junction—or perhaps, he thought, they might already be there. He thought about the cell phones but knew they would not work this far out in the country. He would just have to wait to see, and hope and pray, that his old friends were safe.

CHAPTER 12
JULY 12TH

The rain during the night had cleaned the air leaving it smelling crisp and fresh. It was the first night since leaving Brent's that any of them had gotten a good night's sleep. They woke in the morning refreshed, and Matt handed out beef jerky and hot coffee as they gathered around the small fire pit, and in short order, and without much chatter, they were on their way, driving through another round of rain, leaving behind Eric and the horrors of the past 24 hours.

Driving hard over a county dirt road, Matt led the way and Juanita rode shot gun. Abby followed close behind, driving Uncle Bill's truck. Ten miles down the road the rain suddenly stopped, and the clouds moved aside for the sun, causing the landscape to look like painted art work on a canvas. Steam and fog hovered over the grounds in the fields, and rays of sun pierced through the trees like thousands of arrows being shot from heaven. It was all so still, that it felt to Matt like they might be the only survivors left on earth. The air is dryer in southern Oregon, he thought.

Random memories popped into his mind for no reason and in no particular order, like the time Brent told him: "Don't take killing lightly, son. It's a load some can handle, others, it will drive crazy." I will be able to carry this burden, thought Matt, swerving to miss a huge pot hole. I am not a cold blooded killer; I killed in self-defense and to protect myself and my family, and for that reason, I will be okay with it, and I can do it again.

A week ago he'd been wishing for his world to change, and now that it had, he'd become acutely aware that the consequences exceeded the wish, exponentially. Be careful of what you wish for, he remembered someone telling him a hundred years ago.

He remembered suggesting to Eric that anarchy was the only answer, and now that he was in the middle of it, it was much uglier and more horrible than he'd ever imagined.

Defending yourself on a one-to-one basis is one thing, but protecting what you have against regiments of gangs is a different challenge all together. They would need more fire power, bigger guns, fully automatic weapons, and they needed troops.

The days and nights had melding together, and it seemed a long time ago that they were at his Uncle's party. He thought for a moment that maybe there was something concrete about the philosophy of metaphysics, and that maybe if he pictured a better world instead of the world he'd wished for, that a better world would be the reality and not this horrible nightmare where his friends get killed.

He was calm, and he drove on while the sun moved slowly a little higher in the sky with each mile, not caring at all how bad he felt that his friend Eric was dead; and Rose, the girl next door, who'd offered him lemonade but gave him something else instead, was also gone forever.

*****

"So, Juanita, where in Mexico are you from," he asked, thumping his thumbs on the steering wheel, wanting to get his mind going in a different direction.

"I'm from Monterrey," she answered. "It's a big town south of Laredo, Texas. "Do you know where it is? Have you even heard of it?" The way she'd answered seemed harsh and defensive and it raised his hackles. "Why you asking?" she snapped, turning to look at him.

"Just wondering. Damn, woman, I was just trying to get my mind off Eric and Rose and all the rest of the bullshit, that's all; what's the big deal? Maybe you swam the river, for Christ's sake," he said jokingly, working hard to keep his cool.

"You know that I was in *your* military, so how the hell could I be an illegal?" She didn't say it, but Matt felt she was about to add idiot or moron, and it tightened his jaws even more.

"Jesus, Juanita what the fuck is eating you? Got the curse today or something?" Juanita didn't answer and Matt gripped the steering wheel a bit more tightly and kept driving.

"I heard you were some kind of white supremacist," she finally said, her Mexican accent stronger than ever. "Maybe you got a problem with Mexicans like you got problems with Arabs. You some kind of fucking bigot," she blurted.

"What the fuck is eating you, for Christ's sake," he said, slamming the shifter down into third gear and stepping hard on the gas, and then back into fourth gear picking up more speed, fishtailing around a corner and throwing a cloud of dirt into the air.

Juanita grabbed hold of the dash and the hand grip above the passenger window, and rode it out, rifle resting between her thighs. She didn't admit it, but he'd hit the nail on the head. Women's hormones play nasty, evil tricks on them during the time of the *curse*, a term she'd never heard but certainly fit the bloody occasion.

"I got good fucking reasons to hate al-Qaeda-fucking-terrorist-bastards!" he blurted. "And free-loading Mexicans too, for that matter—and anyone else in this country that's here illegally." His calm had dissipated with the morning fog, and he was ready for a fight. Juanita put down the map she was studying and took a deep breath.

"What gives you the right to…."

"My rights *and* my freedom are at stake," he snapped before she could finish. "Immigrants come to this country for a free ride, refusing to learn *our* language, demanding that we change our system to accommodate their culture, their religion, learn *their* language, give them a handout, and all at the cost of billions of dollars in taxes to those of us who work for a living. Damn right I'm pissed and damn straight I've got a right!" he said, slamming the truck into third gear, and then back into fourth, again, a habit he'd developed and unconsciously practiced when he was irritated.

And the worst part is, senorita, is that they are so ungrateful and so belligerent that they use the very legal system that allows them to stay here, illegally, to demand their rights — they've got no fucking rights, Juanita— they - are – illegally - in - this - country." It was the first time he'd spouted off about this issue in a long time, and it felt good. He was ready for battle.

"You should think about what's wrong with your government instead of hating people for taking advantage of what your government does for them," said Juanita, more calmly. "How can you blame people for wanting a better life? I have been all over the world, Matt, and I've seen people living in slums that make your garbage dumps look like piles of gold. For the most part, the immigrants, illegal or not, are just trying for a better life. All of them aren't terrorists and criminals, but your news media makes it sound that way to keep myopic people on edge and afraid. Have you ever traveled outside your own zip code," she asked sarcastically. "Stupid question," she said to the wind. "If you had," she quickly added, "you wouldn't be so fucking ignorant."

"Who the fuck you calling ignorant!"

"Hey! You started it...."

"All I did was ask where you were from, for Christ's sake."

In his pursuit to discover the connections between Islam the religion, Middle Easterners, terrorists, Muslims, Pakistanis, Afghanis, Iranians, Saudi Arabians, Arabs, etc., he'd committed to memory events from the past that seemed to point directly to radical Islamic Terrorists from the Middle East for most fanatical activity here and abroad; whoever *they* were, they came in many guises and rallied under dozens of different names, one day loyal to this cause and the next day switching sides. He'd also read plenty of books on the subject, like *See No Evil* and *Invasion*, and had committed much of it to memory.

His list of events involving terrorism include, for example, Bobby Kennedy being shot and killed in 1968 by the assassin extremist, Sirhan Sirhan, from the Middle East; the Palestinian paramilitary terrorist group who killed eleven Israeli athletes at the 1972 Munich Olympics, and in 1979 the group of Islamist and Middle Eastern students who took over the American Embassy in Tehran and held 52 American hostages for 444 days, "Victims of terrorism and anarchy," announced President Jimmy Carter. In 1983, the US marine barracks in Beirut was blown up by an organization called Islamic Jihad, killing 229 American and French servicemen. TWA flight 847 was hijacked in 1985 at

Athens by a group of terrorists calling themselves the Organization for the Oppressed of the Earth. One passenger, A US Navy diver was beaten and shot, and his body dumped onto the tarmac. The other passengers were eventually released in trade for 735 Lebanese Shiite militant prisoners, by Israel. In 1988, Pan Am flight 103 was blown up with a bomb killing all 243 passengers and 16 crew members, along with countless people on the ground from falling debris; it is claimed that Muammar Gaddafi personally ordered the attack, and the list continues to grow and grow, and all this happened *before* 9/11. No, he thought, I'm not ignorant, not at all. How much evidence was needed to point the finger at a pretty solid prospect, he wondered.

"First, I did not say you were *stupid*, quite the contrary. What I said was you are *ignorant;* ill-informed as to what's really going on in this world." There was a pause, as his tightened grip on the steering wheel did not go unnoticed by Juanita. He slammed the tranny back into third. "Perhaps ignorant is a strong word, Matt, but really, I did not mean any offense. Hear me out," she said more softly.

He smirked, shifted into fourth, and indicated *go ahead* with a twist of his head. After all, he was just warming up.

"I am as sure about what I'm saying, as I'm sure all this is real," she said, moving her palm from side to side, indicating the landscape beyond the dirty windshield. "Pakistanis, Africans, Thais, Arabs, *Mexicans*," she added with emphasis, "and all the rest of the immigrant population in your country, for the most part, are simply seeking a better life. That's one group. There is another group here seeking political asylum after helping your government with some coup in some oil rich county or whatever. The point is, all the super powers do the same thing; they all promises a better life, or in the case of American invasion, democracy." She wanted to finish before he interrupted her. "And, guaranteed, Matt, your country is not the only one who works this way. If one faction in an impoverished country wants power because they know they have untapped gold or diamond mines, then genocide becomes a reality. Greed and power is what keeps all this going," again waving her hand from side to side.

A silence fell like a sheet, as she thought about how to proceed. She didn't want to argue, she just wanted to fill him in on some facts that perhaps he hadn't considered. Once he knew more about the corruption that controls the world, he would be more confused than ever as to what was really right and what was really wrong, and then, and only then, would be in the same boat.

Matt listened, thinking that maybe they weren't really on different pages, after all. Maybe they just had different ways of seeing the same thing, and maybe, just maybe she knew stuff he didn't. He would listen.

"Who is the terrorist, Matt, when a country is invaded for whatever reason and innocent men, women, and children are killed in the name of liberation? Your government has invaded and committed genocide, starting with the American Indians. They have also invaded countries like Iran, Libya, Panama, Iraq, the Philippines, Vietnam, and the list goes on and on. What do you think the innocent ones think, Matt?" she said rhetorically. "The farmer who is trying to get his crop in, the woman who is walking her children to school, the fisherman who is trying to pull from the sea a catch to feed his family. What do you think these people, Muslim, Hindu, Christian, Catholic or Buddhist, no matter; what do you think they think when they see the bombs falling, and the soldiers coming? Who are the terrorists in these scenarios, Matt?" She paused to take a breath and look out her window, and then in a soft quiet voice she said, "You need the facts—all the facts; you need to look at the issues from all perspectives before you condemn." They rode a long ways in silence.

"Okay then, are you feeling better," he said, in voice, not condescending, and not with judgment, but with a tone in his voice that seemed to indicate, that he was done arguing, and wanted to move on.

"Well, there is one more thing I would like to say, if that's okay." He nodded, with a put on smile, but he was getting damn tired of being lectured to. One-thousand-and-one.... "All Arabs are not terrorists, and all terrorists are not Islamic Jihadists or al-Qaeda. The majority of people, in all the countries of world, regardless of their race, religion, or politics, want peace. Not all Arabs are the bad guys?"

Matt did not answer, but he was thinking about what she'd said. Of course he knew she was right; he had always known, after all he was brought up that way. It's just that everyone that he knew, including his uncle, was in such denial of there being a problem, that it irked him to the point of martyrdom.

"Okay friend, I hear what you're saying, and I know that you are right. I will try, Juanita, to mend my wicked fucking ways," he said mockingly, but in jest, and hoped that his little bit of macho sarcasm wasn't enough to overpower his good intentions, and that Juanita would take what he'd said about trying, seriously.

"That's a start," amigo.

"Okay amigo, can we kiss and make up," he said, smiling a flirtations smile.

"In your fucking dreams, white boy," she said, with a straight face.

*****

Uncle Bill pulled the Metsker map from the glove compartment, opened it on his lap, and began tracing the route he wanted to take.

"The country around here is more mountainous. Could take more time than we want if we stay the course. Maybe I can find some short cuts. Maybe, Abby, we can be in Cave Junction by tonight." Abby glanced at him and smiled.

"That sounds great. Let's hit it," she said, stomping on the gas, causing the truck to fishtail. "Whoa," she said, letting up on the gas and slowing down.

"Easy there, Richard Petty," joked Uncle Bill.

"I know some of the back roads to my folks' place," she said. Let's switch places, and I'll look at the maps, and without waiting for a reply she slowed to a stop, jumped out and headed around to the other side. Uncle Bill did the same, and within a few seconds, they were heading back down the road, catching up to Matt. "Okay," she said, "I'll trace the roads I know in Cave Junction, back to where we are now, and see if there are any short cuts. Uhhh, where are we," she muttered, at which they both burst out laughing.

"Guess we will have to do some triangulations," he said. "I bet Juanita knows more about that than we do. We need to pull over and make a plan," he said.

"Agreed," said Abby, remembering the phrase she'd heard Juanita use. He flashed his lights at Matt and began slowing down. Matt found a spot behind some trees and pulled over.

"How's the gas holding out?" asked Uncle Bill, when Matt came back to his truck to inquire as to what was up.

"Main tanks running low but the auxiliary tank if full," he said, "so no problem. How about you? Is that why we're stopping? Do we need to syphon, or rather do *you* need to syphon, some gas from my tank?" he jokingly, and in good humor.

"I carry a good ten gallons more than you, nephew, so I'm good, too. We need to figure our approximate location," said Uncle Bill. "Juanita, do you have any idea where we are?" he smiled, and Abby laughed at the inside joke.

"I can figure pretty close," she said, taking the map that Uncle Bill was holding out to her. She looked around on the ground and found a good straight stick and pushed it into the ground. "I'll use this as a dial," she said, pulling a compass from her breast pocket.

"I'll fix something to eat," said Abby.

"I'll watch the road," said Uncle Bill. And Matt watched with admiration, as Juanita began to figure their approximate location.

*****

The sun was shining and birds were chirping; it was warm, and there was no immediate threat. It was more like a picnic than a mission of survival.

"Thank God for coolers," said Abby, pulling some bologna out of the watery ice. "I guess we should drain these things," she added, talking more to the cooler than to Juanita, who was the closest person to her.

"Save the water, Abby. It's messy, I know, but if we have to drink it, we can boil it," and Abby quickly replaced the stopper, halting the flow of murky water from spilling onto the ground.

"I should have thought about that. Man, this survival thing is hard to get hold of," she said, shaking her head.

"You're doing as well as any warrior I've had the pleasure to serve with, Abby. You came through for us all when our lives were at stake," said Juanita. When Abby didn't respond, Juanita figured she wasn't ready to talk about it yet, so she changed the subject. "We're getting pretty close," she said, folding up the map. "We'll probably be there tonight. I bet you're real anxious to see your folks."

"You have no idea. I miss them so much," said Abby, as if sharing a secret with a close friend. "I was going to come down for a visit when all this crap started up—man, I was a mess," she said, shaking her head, and flushing red. "I hope they're okay." She finished making the sandwiches at the same time that Uncle Bill walked up.

"Good timing," said Matt, reaching for a bologna sandwich.

"Dam straight," said Abby. "We are so in tune, we can read each other's minds," she said, laughing a loud at her clever response. Everyone stopped and looked around at their comrades for the first time in many days. They were a sorry looking bunch of vagabonds, for sure. They'd all been living in the same clothes they started with when their journey began; they were dirty and mussed and looked like street people; however, the thought of reading each other's minds brought a smirk to them all.

"I sure the fuck hope not," said Matt, thinking about Juanita, but not looking at her.

"Me too, actually," chimed in Abby, thinking about Brent.

"Just the same, we are in tune," said Juanita, thinking mostly about the mission.

"We are definitely in tune," said Uncle Bill, "and here's to the brothers from up north," he said, toasting a jug of water high in the air. "Here, here," they all said, more or less, in unison.

"We have an idea as to where we are," said Juanita. "If we head in this direction," she pointed to the map, "we should intersect with this road somewhere between here and here." She pointed to a road that led into the general vicinity of Cave Junction. "Abby probably knows the way from here."

There was no reason to doubt each other after what they'd been through. They were working together like a finely tuned machine. They ate quickly, not because they were in a hurry but because they were starving.

"Does anyone know where Montana was headed when he left the party," asked Abby. The question flew out of the blue and caught Matt and Uncle Bill off guard, as they'd made it a point not to talk about the possibilities in front of her.

"When I saw him and his buddies at Brent's before the party," said Juanita, "they mentioned that they were heading south. I figured that meant south of the border because Montana said he'd see me down south, and since he knew I was going to Mexico, I just figured that's what he meant."

"What!" said Matt. "You saw Montana at Brent's *before* the party?"

"Brent never mentioned that Montana was at his place when we were talking about it," said Uncle Bill. "You say he and Moalim were there—at Brent's?"

"Yeah, well I don't know who Moalim is, but Montana was there with some friends before the party, but Brent had already headed out the day before."

"I thought you said you didn't see Montana at Brent's," questioned Matt, quickly.

"I said he wasn't there the morning we left. Besides, what the fuck difference does it make?"

"Man," you had me freaked out there for a minute," interrupted Uncle Bill, seeing the whole picture. "Brent never knew that Montana was at his place, and you didn't know that Montana might be involved in terrorist activity. All you know is what Matt told you about the argument at the party."

"Correct."

Matt stayed silent, thinking that he'd probably jumped the gun, again. He smiled and tilted his head at Juanita, who did not return the gesture.

The conversation left Abby pretty much in the dark.

"What's going on," she asked. "Is there a problem, other than Montana and his buddies were making trouble at the party and that they were asked to leave?"

"Well Abby," started Uncle Bill, we don't know, but maybe they're heading to Cave Junction. We don't know." She needed to be told, and now was as good a time as any.

"Is that bad," she asked? "What's going on? Why are you so concerned about Montana? Have they done something? Tell me damn it, I have a right to know!" she screeched.

"Yeah, same here," said Juanita, giving Matt the evil eye.

"We don't know much, Abby, and we're mostly just guessing. We have no proof," said Uncle Bill. Abby stood up and started pacing, one hand on the butt end of the .357 that was now in a holster that was strapped around her waist like a gun-slingers outfit from the 1800s.

"We think that Montana might be involved in smuggling terrorists across the border. We also think that he may be using your folks' place as a stop over after crossing." He was about to tell her of the run in that her father had a few weeks ago with Montana, when she interrupted him.

"Oh shit," she said. "They're probably there," said Abby, starting to pack up the gear. "We need to roll," she said.

"Wait, Abby, we are only guessing…"

"When I talked to my mother just before we left Lynnwood," said Abby, "she told me that Montana had been showing up a lot over the past few months. She told me that the last time, just a few weeks ago, that my dad went down to say hello at their camp site and came back a bit distraught. But she didn't know why and my dad didn't say. We need to get moving," she said, tying down one end of the tarp on Matt's truck.

Uncle Bill told her what Brent had told him about her dad's run-in with Montana and his gang; not sparing the part about the assault rifle.

"Your dad told Brent that he thought that something might be wrong. "Said Montana was real stand-offish when he stopped in to see how the camping was going."

"We don't really know what they are up to, then," interrupted Juanita. "Just because they had a falling out with Matt and his uncle doesn't mean they're up to no good," she said, giving them the benefit of doubt. "Guess we have to wait and see."

"We aren't waiting," said Abby. "We need to get going. What I know, what my mother told me, what my father told Brent, and Matt's gut feeling is enough for me. We need to move out," she said, as if she were rounding up the wagons.

"Let's roll, then" said Uncle Bill, coming up to Abby. "Same people, same trucks, let's hit it," he said, tossing his rubbish into a plastic sack. "Matt and Juanita will take the lead."

"Do you want to drive, Juanita?" asked Matt before they climbed in.

"Sure," she said without hesitation. "It will be a welcome change. Thanks."

They drove for a long time without seeing anyone or anything, just more country and more bumpy dirt roads. Silent hours sped by as did the miles, and before they realized just how much time and space had passed, they were near Cow Creek. They were getting close.

*****

Montana, Moalim, and Ali sat on the front deck of the Lassiter ranch in the morning sun, discussing the next phase of their plan. The other terrorists were keeping watch in and around the property. Montana was still astounded at how such a seemingly small group of terrorist could bring the United States. to a standstill. Just as staggering was the fact that he was sitting with the master minds of the whole plot.

The Lassiters were allowed to move around, but were warned of the consequences for trying anything foolish. "And remember," Moalim had said, "Your daughter is probably on her way here, so if you don't want her *abused*," he said smirking a creepy smile, "don't be stupid."

And the Lassiters listened and they obeyed and they became prisoners in their own home.

191

"Maybe we should just kill these infidels and take the place now," said Moalim. "Why wait. They are going to die eventually, anyway?" Montana felt a twinge at the finality of the proclamation, and wondered, since he was not Muslim, if he was considered an infidel, as well. He glanced over at Ali, who was staring off into the forest.

"It's true, Moalim, but we will do it my way," countered Ali, still staring off into the woods. "If they give us trouble…well, we will cross that bridge when we come to it, as they say in Texas, right Montana." Montana felt that he was being tested once again and hoped that his anxiety about killing old friends did not show through.

"Like I said, Ali, I don't have a problem with it. I think, however, that keeping them alive for bartering power is logical. If Bill and Brent and the rest of that gang made it out of the city alive, they are headed here. They will be following that escape *Plan Alpha* that y'all copped from Brent's. If they got out of the city, and I'm betting they did, then they will be here."

"Okay," said Moalim. "How much problem can two old people cause us any way?"

"It's not the old folks that concern, me," said Ali. "We need this property for our headquarters. It's ideal in location and size and has everything we need to survive the upcoming chaos."

Montana sat looking off into the distance at nothing in particular. He knew that his old friend Bill would put it all together. If he didn't, certainly Brent would, and he expected that sooner or later they would show up in Cave Junction, and that when that time came, it would be kill or be killed.

"When will our reinforcements arrive," asked Moalim, addressing Ali, who had stood up and was leaning against a post, lighting a cigarette. It was the first that Montana had heard of reinforcements, and he wondered if they were the same group that he'd met at the first refilling station on the way down.

"They will be here soon," said Ali. "Two or three days. There is still work to be done in the cities. They will be here when their work is finished. Until then, we will have to do with what we have—we will have to stay vigilant." There were no more questions and no more talk. Ali stepped off the porch and walked towards the woods as Montana and Moalim sat in silence and watched.

*****

Close to Wonder, Uncle Bill told Abby to find a place to pull over. They were within a few miles of the property and it was time to make a plan. It was 5 p.m., and the sun was a yellow-white ball in the sky. It was warm and there was a slight breeze, but the air did not smell burnt like it did near the cities; however, there was a hint of smoke from a wood fire in the air—the sort of smell that comes from a wood stove or a camp fire that is inherent to life in the country. Early summer was evolving into mid-summer and Mother Nature, in spite of man's problems, was moving forward. Wild flowers were blooming, new leaves were growing, birds were chirping, squirrels were scampering, and they had even seen some deer. Maybe this is a good sign, thought Uncle Bill. Maybe the whole country will follow suit and come back to life, stronger than ever. He wondered what the government was doing.

"We need to go in on foot, along the river, and scout the area," said Uncle Bill, as he ate a peanut butter sandwich. "The question is who should go?"

"I can go," volunteered Abby. "I know the area and the river and the woods. This is my backyard. I should go."

"I think that Juanita and I should go," said Uncle Bill.

"I will to go with you, then," said Abby. "I know the area," she argued.

"Not a good idea," said Matt, wishing from the expression on her face that he'd let his uncle handle it.

"They're my folks, Matt. I have a right to go to my own home," she snapped.

"That's not the issue," said Uncle Bill, getting Matt off the hook.

"Don't patronize me, Bill," she said with an emphasis on *Bill*. "I've been through just as much as anyone here." I've been shot at, and I've killed. I lost one of my best friends and everything that I own," she said, turning towards Matt.

"I don't like it," piped in Juanita. "I think that I should go by myself. Makes better sense. I'm trained in this sort of thing and no offense, but I'm in better shape than anyone here. I will go, alone," she said, standing up and brushing off the dust.

"I think..." started Uncle Bill.

"I'm in just as good a shape as you are," said Matt, defensively.

"I'm not in..." started Uncle Bill again.

"Listen Bill, you need to stay here and watch after Abby. No offense Abby," she said, turning to face her, "aside from being a damned good warrior, you're the package."

"What do you mean, I'm the package?" she said, loudly. She jumped up, exasperated with everyone telling her what she could and couldn't do. She was ready for a fist fight. "Don't patronize me!" she yelled.

"You know what she means, Abby, so don't dumb up on us," scorned Uncle Bill. "And we are not patronizing you; we just want you to know how important you are to us." Abby closed her eyes and shook her head. "We are here and we are alive," continued Uncle Bill—just a little more time—please." Abby became quiet but did not sit down. She was pacing, thinking about her next move.

"In regards to the mission," started Juanita, "we should wait until dark."

"I agree," said Matt. "The river goes right by their property and Abby can brief *us*," he said, ignoring the part about what Juanita had said about going alone. "I promise I won't get you lost, Major," he said, smiling at Juanita, "or try to take advantage of you out there in the woods."

"That's the last of my worries turd; stay focused," she said, shaking her head and turning to Uncle Bill. "What do you think Bill?"

"After dark is probably better," he said, giving into the fact that he was going to stay behind. Abby said nothing.

"Okay, then," said Matt. "We wait. Agreed?"

"Agreed," said Uncle Bill. Abby stayed silent.

"Okay then, I'll get ready to head out."

"Me too," said Matt, and there was no further argument.

"There is a spot up the ways, a bit," said Uncle Bill. "It's a spot where me and Brent camp when we come up for R&R. It's right on the river. I think we should move up there now and settle in," he said, standing up to stretch. "It's not far, a few miles at most." No one argued, and soon they were back in the trucks moving slowly through the trees towards the river.

The camp site was very secluded, had good cover, a nice view of the river, but nothing else. The hours creped by as slow as a two-legged turtle, and everyone, tired, worn and on edge, stayed to themselves, pondering their own thoughts and drifting in and out of nap-land.

*****

Uncle Bill was exhausted and knew that if he relaxed too much, it would be real hard for him to get moving again. What Juanita had said about his physical condition was true. In some ways, he felt his useful days were over. Only a few more hours—a day at most, and it would be over, and his promise to his friends to keep their daughter safe would be behind him; That is, if all went in favor of the outlaws. He grinned at the thought of how ma and pa Lassiter were going to take the transformation of their sweet, darling Abby to warrior Abby.

He was looking forward to the warmth and friendship of his friends' home, a hot shower and a hot meal and a comfortable place to sleep. He thought about Rose and Eric and felt the worse about Rose because he'd known her since she was a child. He thought about Matt and how he'd changed in the past week. It would take time, he knew, before any of them fully comprehended what they had come through. There would be time to reflect without having to be on guard; a time when they could sit and talk without having to worry about someone sneaking up on them, trying to kill them. He hoped it all went well. Maybe Montana wasn't even here. Maybe they will be able to just run right up to the door and be welcomed with open arms.

Juanita was a true warrior—all business, level headed and always on task; he would be eternally grateful to her, because without her help, they would certainly have had a much harder time, and most likely, they would all be dead. It had not gone unnoticed how his nephew acted around her. He stopped short of calling it a mating dance, but knew the flirtatious signs. He would not mind, despite the age difference, if they hooked up. She would be a good equalizer for him—damn sure wouldn't be able to push her around; hell Juanita would probably kick the shit out of him, he thought smiling, if he pulled the shit on her that he pulled on Abby. He loved Abby like a daughter and was glad that she was moving on with her life without Matt. He also knew how she felt about Brent—odd, he thought, how things work out.

*****

Matt was soul searching. He thought it such a huge coincidence that what he'd been thinking about, and almost hoping for, anarchy and that it was really happening. He thought about Abby and all the good times they'd spent together, and he hoped with all his heart that they could remain good friends. Brother and sister sort of friends. He would still die for her if it came down to it, but he was not in love with her. He hoped she would be okay. He could not think about Eric and Rose. That would have to wait. Uncle Bill had saved him from an orphanage or worse, the streets, when he took him in after his mother had abandoned him. He loved him and needed to tell him so. It was on his short list of things to do. Juanita is really something, he thought, as his eyes closed and he drifted off.

*****

Juanita was always on guard, even if it wasn't her shift. War was war, and it was best not to take it personally, or get to emotionally involved with issues like who got killed—a soldier needed to stay focused. She'd come to care about Uncle Bill, Abby, and even Matt. Mostly, she finally realized, Matt was just thinking out loud when he was spouting off about terrorists. Probably just regurgitating what he'd heard from somebody on the six-o'clock news, or read in a book. He had a lot of it right, but he was naïve—he wasn't a dummy; he just needed to see more of the world. Maybe she would take him to Mexico with her, help him on his way. He needed to get back to the old adage, that you can't judge a book by its cover. Give a person a chance to prove if they are good or bad before condemning them to death. She had friends, close comrades, who were of Middle Eastern decent, and she would trust any one of them with her life.

When she first met Abby, Abby reminded her of the proverbial dumb blond. She was a follower, and although she probably believed in women's lib, she didn't act the part of a liberated woman. But she had matured overnight. She felt bad about Eric. She remembered Abby raging on about who didn't check their kill, and had intended to tell her that in the heat of battle, it's not always possible, but things were happening so fast, she never had the chance.

195

She probably figured it out for herself by now. She wondered what Abby's parents were going to be like, besides old. I hope they are okay, she thought, staring into the river. I hope my family in Mexico is alright, too.

*****

Matt woke from his power and squinted at the fluorescent dial on his watch. He jumped up, ready to be pissed if Juanita had taken off without him.

"Let's talk strategy, soldier" she said without preamble, sneaking up behind him, causing him to jump.

"I just woke up," he said, in defense of his edginess. Serious as the situation was, Matt couldn't help thinking about how good looking she was, even with a dirty face that was barely discernible in the moonlight. Wait, he thought, that's not dirt, it's paint.

"You got paint on your face," he said, knowing full well what it was. She reached into her vest pocket and pulled out a tube.

"Moon's still almost full; can't be too careful." Matt took the tube and applied some paint in the same pattern as Juanita's.

"How's that," he said, handing back the tube.

"It ain't a beauty contest, worm" she said, sticking the tube into her shirt pocket, and giving Matt a little smile.

"Okay, then," she said, breaking his spell. "Here's the way I see it. We don't know how widespread the destruction is; that is, is it just in the US or is it international? My guess is that it's not international, but from what we've heard, it would appear that it's definitely national." Matt nodded in agreement. "I also agree with your theory on how it all came down; that is, I think that terrorist cells have been set up throughout the county and that they all struck at the same time." Again, Matt just nodded, but inside he was very appreciative of her acknowledgement of his insight. "I also think that maybe there is a bigger power behind it all than Islamic extremists," she paused, "or whomever. Like I said, I think that whoever is responsible for the destruction may be an unknowing pawn in a much bigger scheme. We'll see." She was putting it on the table for Matt, confiding her personal opinions and thoughts; it was serious dialogue, which gave Matt a feeling of equality, which in turn, put him at ease.

"I've been thinking this would happen for a long time, but it's real eerie that it's really happening," he confided, straight faced and as serious as bee sting.

"About our mission," she said, getting back on target. "Do you have any problems taking orders from me?"

"I have no problems with you giving the orders," he said. "I've had some backyard training," he added, thinking about all the time that he'd spent with Brent. A week ago he called it combat training, now, after what he'd been through, he referred to it as backyard training. He hoped that Brent wouldn't be offended.

"You know more than most. You're strong and in good shape," she said, reassuringly. "And Brent had nothing but good things to say about your abilities. Your uncle too, has great confidence in you. They told me going in, that you've been on edge lately, and between what they said and what you've told me, I understand. I would like you to know, too, that even though I am one of those hateful and dreaded immigrants that you are always going on about, I don't like the fucking scumbag gang banger killers, or the law breakers any more than you do; Mexican, Russian, Korean, al-Qaeda or any of the rest. But we can talk about all that later. Now," she said, looking him straight in the eye, "we need to stay focused, and we need to have strategy going in." She was trying to put their differences behind them as well as put him at ease for the upcoming mission.

What we need to stay focused on, Matt, is that we are trying to deliver this gang of vagabonds, meaning you, your Uncle, and Abby to a safe haven. That is our mission and our priority—and our only priority. We don't have any time for personal vendettas against foreigners—we will stay focused. And one more thing, Matt, we don't know for sure that Montana and Moalim have anything at all to do with any of this, or even if they are here, for that matter. It's only speculation. Remember that if we run into them."

"Yes, Captain, sir...mam," he said, smiling and saluting. "I'll be real careful not to hurt anybody's feelings," he said. He felt like his old self. The Matt he used to be before he turned into a hater, and he liked it. "Just one thing, Juanita," he said with a serious tone. "You may not think that Montana is dirty, but I still do. I think that him and his Arab buddy are traitors—it's just a gut feeling, Juanita, but if I were you, darlin', I would keep them in your front sights and not take any chances if we run into them."

"Thanks, Private—I'll definitely keep that in mind." And at that, they decided on some hand signals and talked strategy.

Uncle Bill and Abby came up beside the small campfire where Matt and Juanita were drinking hot coffee to wish them luck.

"Okay then, it's time to move out. Stay a few paces behind me. Stay low and keep your eyes open. If you need to talk to me," she reminded him, "tap me. Don't speak. We are going to sneak up on the house like a cat sneaking up on a mouse, and only to assess the situation. Slow crawling and zero noise. Is that clear, mister?" Matt was thinking about an excuse to tap her on the butt since she was going to be in the lead.

"Understood, Captain," he said, and saluted again. Uncle Bill shook his head and Abby just looked. They both saw *the good old Matt* in his antics, and it was good.

"Cut the crap, soldier," she said, scowling. "Let's move out," she said, once again snapping Matt out of his adolescent day dream.

"I've been waiting for hours," he said, smiling at his uncle. "See you in a little while, Abby," he said, and when he approached her to give her a hug, she did not back away.

"Be safe, Matt, and hurry back," she said, turning him loose.

"Okay, we're off. It's 9:56 p.m. Everyone set their watches to 10 p.m.," she said punching buttons to change the hour. "I figure we should be back no later than 2 a.m. It's not even two miles, so it gives us plenty of time. If we are not back by two, give it another two hours before coming after us."

"Sounds sort of okay," said Uncle Bill.

"Yeah, but only sort of," said Abby.

"I don't expect any trouble. It's only a reconnaissance mission." said Juanita.

"We'll be fine," said Matt. "We'll be watching each other's butts," he said. Fortunately it was a common phrase and nobody gave it a second thought, except for him.

"What if…"

"We'll leave the *what-ifs* out of the equation," said Juanita, dismissing Abby's question and moving away towards the river. We *will* be back by 2 a.m. And Abby," she said, turning to her blond friend, "if all goes according to plan, you will be sleeping in your own bed tonight." Abby smiled and nodded. She looks good, thought Juanita, better without makeup, and a bit on the trashy side, and that revolver hanging in that cross draw holster, fits her well. "Remember too, Abby, we don't know for sure that Montana is even here."

*****

The going was as easy as Matt had anticipated. There were no houses along their path, no destruction like what they had witnessed over the past few days, just the woods and fresh air mixed with a hint of smoke from a distant camp fire or a wood stove. For now, they had left the world of anarchy behind.

The moon was not as bright as it was a few days ago, but still bright enough to light the way. They stayed close to the tree line that skirted the river, and in forty-five minutes they were twenty yards from Jake and Karla's ranch, hidden well in the trees and wild grass that surrounded the property. Fifth-teen yards behind them, the Illinois River raced silently on its way to meet up with the Rogue River, and eventually out to sea.

"Something is wrong," whispered Matt, squirming up next to Juanita. "Too many people, too many lights; Jake and Karla are country folks, early-to-bed-early-to-rise. We need a closer look."

"Okay," whispered Juanita, "I'll go, you stay."

"But you don't know what Jake and Karla look like," he said. "Maybe I should go?"

198

"Can't do it that way, soldier. I will go and be back before you know it. Thirty minutes tops. I'll belly crawl. And as far as what they look like, their old folks and they will look like old folks, not terrorists."

Just then a dog started barking. It stood like a statue near the front door of the cabin and was pointing in their direction. "Fuck," she whispered anxiously. "Back up to the river, fast; but don't make any noise."

Matt started moving as the dog began barking with more verve, and pulling hard at his leash, trying to break loose. The water was cold but they had no choice. He remembered what his uncle had said when this all started about being thankful that it wasn't winter. They moved carefully from one rock to the next until they found one they could crouch behind, sort of. The river was not real swift but swift enough to flush them down stream if they lost their hold, which could be a good thing, thought Matt, since it was the direction of camp.

Reconnaissance was not over, however. They needed more information. They ducked their heads under the water as a bright beam from a flashlight scanned the area where they hid. After a few moments, they rose slowly out of the water to just below their noses. Just a few yards away, on the edge of the bank, the dog continued his warning. It was tugging and pulling on its leash, wanting to be free to pursue its prey. After a few minutes, the man and dog moved up river to continue their surveillance. Juanita put her arm around Matt and lead him further downstream. They moved a little further out into the current, as well. "Can you swim?" she said, above the sound of the river.

"Yeah, I can swim."

"Don't unless I say so. And don't try to cross. Just get out far enough to drift with the current. Stay close together," she said when she let go of him.

"We still don't know if those are bad guys or good guys," she whispered. "Maybe they're neighbors come together for the sake of all...duck," she said, putting her hand a top Matt's head as a beam of light flashed over the rippling water.

In the moonlight, Matt could barely make out the silhouette of the guy holding the dog at bay. He had a cowboy hat on his head and he was about the size of Montana. Lying motionless in the cold water he concluded, for the first time, that he really didn't know if Montana was a terrorist or not; Moalim either, for that matter. Just the same, he would stick to the same advice that he'd given to Juanita. He would not let them out of his front sights.

"Look at the guy with the cowboy hat," he said quietly. "Does that look like Montana to you?" Juanita squinted, trying to keep from floating down river. "Can't tell from here," she said. "He's definitely wearing a cowboy hat, though." They lay perfectly still as the dog and the master had a look around. The river flowed nearer the tree line the further down river they drifted, and the dog and master were following the tree line—dog leading, master following, and within seconds, they were only ten yards away for each other; too late to make a swim for it without being detected. The dog was frantically barking, and the master was scouring the water and the beach with his flashlight, Matt and Juanita were submerged to their noses.

"Come on, Duke," said the guy with cowboy hat, there ain't nothin' here but squirrels and night time varmints. Damn, boy, can't y'all sniff out anything but varmints? Lucky for y'all it wasn't a skunk. Would of had to shoot ya. Now come on," he said, more loudly yanking on the canine's leash, at which they both turned and started back up to the cabin. Juanita gave it a couple of minutes before she and Matt crawled out of the water and up onto the bank.

"Damn," said Matt. That *was* Montana."

"It was Montana, all right," she confirmed, looking up towards the cabin. "Wonder what he's up to."

"You told me you used to hang with him. Thought you guys were tight," fishing but not wanting to sound like he was judging or accusing.

"We haven't been tight—ever, really. We just had a good ride for a while. One day I woke up and he'd become an jerk, so I split. We still don't know if he's here as a guest or as the enemy though," she said. "Come on. We need to get back."

"We still don't know what's going on inside or how many of them there are," protested Matt. "We need more info."

"That ain't happening grasshopper. We can't get any closer with that dog on guard. The next time he flares up, they will all come down for a real good closer look. Let's move," she said, crouching low.

*****

It was 1:30 a.m. when Matt and Juanita stepped out of the shadows and back into camp. Uncle Bill and Abby acted as if they hadn't seen them in years.

"You're not going to believe it Bill," started Matt ignoring the welcoming committee. "Montana was there, but we couldn't get close enough to see how many other people were there because of the fucking dog. But I'm guessing more than two because there were at least two trucks in the turn-around. All the outside lights were on and all the inside lights were on, too."

"Duke," squealed, Abby, "that's my dog. "He's harmless," she added, excited with the news.

"Yeah, that *is* what Montana called him, *Duke*," said Juanita. "He sure in the shit didn't sound harmless, though; he was so close to sniffing us out that he was practically slobbering on our heads."

"He just wanted to meet you," said Abby. "That's all." Juanita pulled off her wet over-shirt and as she did so, her wet t-shirt rose to just below her breasts leaving nothing to the imagination, except for what Matt was thinking.

"Did you see Moalim," asked Uncle Bill?"

"We couldn't get close enough. We need a different plan. But if Montana is there, we have to assume Moalim is there, as well, right?"

"Probably," said Uncle Bill.

"Did you see my folks, Matt?" asked Abby, a look of hope on her face.

"Couldn't see much of anything, Abby. Sorry," he said, peeling off his own wet shirt exposing his muscular torso.

"Well, we have to get up there," said Abby, stepping up to the fire. "I need to see my folks. And one more thing," she said. "As far as I know, Montana has never stayed up at the house, so what does that tell you? Something's not right, is what it tells me. And my folks *never* put Duke on a leash. Why would they. He's used to running." Abby had given them something to think about, so she waited a few seconds to let it sink in. "I'm very worried about my parents," she continued, looking at Juanita. "Maybe it would be better to go in while they're all tired after a long day?" she said, pleadingly. "My folks might be in trouble. Maybe their hurt?"

"I don't want to sound insensitive," said Juanita, looking around and then stopping when her gaze came to Abby, "but if harm was going to come to them, it probably already has."

"Maybe not. If Montana and his buddies are expecting us," interrupted Matt. "They may need Jake and Karla for bartering." He waited, thinking. "I don't like it either, but like Abby said, and as far as any of knows, Montana has never stayed up at the house. Right Bill?" he said, remembering his uncle's and Brent's conversation in the garage a hundred years ago.

"That's a good point," said Uncle Bill. "If he's at the house, they've probably taken over the place."

"Not necessarily," said Juanita. "Maybe there was trouble and they were invited for protection." Abby nodded her head in hope.

"I'm guessing there's trouble," said Matt.

"No! snapped Abby.

"We're not saying they aren't okay, Abby," said Juanita, resting her hand gently on Abby's shoulder. "We are saying that if Montana has moved into the main house, then he is probably calling the shots. He has no reason to harm your parents," she lied.

"Unless they tried to stop him," said Matt, and getting a dirty look from both Juanita and his uncle.

"I don't think they would," said Uncle Bill. "Could be that they told your parents that they were sent by me or Brent to make sure they stayed safe until we got here."

Matt was thinking, but this time because of Juanita's subtle warning about upsetting Abby further, he did not say the obvious. *If they have the man power to secure the site, why would they need to keep Jake and Karla alive? Hostages? Why? Why would they need hostages? What do they want to barter with us for? We got nothing they need. They will kill us on site.* Juanita was looking at him when he glanced over at her, and she was ever so slightly nodding her head as if she'd read his mind and was confirming his conclusion.

"How about this," offered Matt. "And Abby, please forgive us, but we need to think out loud." Abby sighed and nodded consent.

"That's fine, Matt, y'all think out loud as much as you like, and you can damn well expect the same from me."

"Good," said Matt, we wouldn't want it any other way, right Bill, Juanita?"

"Right," they confirmed in unison.

"Maybe," Matt started, "if they see us as a threat, and if Karla and Jake are still alive, they will offer them up in trade for us going away and leaving them alone. A gun battle, even a small gun battle is bound to get some of them killed. What if someone here is important to their goals? They can't afford a gun battle."

"Even if they give us Jake and Karla, that's no guarantee to them that we won't be back," said Juanita. Hell, even *we* know that we're not leaving without a fight, right?"

"I have to go along with that," said Uncle Bill. "And as much as I want to get in there, I think it's prudent to wait until the sun comes up. We can go at dawn. It's only a few hours off," he said. "Maybe we can catch them off guard if we go in at daylight before they're all up and moving around."

"Something's going on and I have to go see what it is," demanded Abby. "Don't try to stop me this time. I'm going home!" she said, standing firm, palm of her right hand resting on the butt of her magnum in what could have been construed as a threat.

"I don't like it," said Matt, coming out of the shadows where he'd gone to leave a pee. He had on dry clothes and his cross draw holster was anchored in front instead of his side. "We might be walking into a trap," he continued. Abby crossed them over her chest. "Let's consider a worst case scenario." He paused before going on. "Let's say Montana and his gang of shit-heads stormed in and killed your parents," he said, looking at Abby, and again apologizing. "If they have killed Jake and Karla, they will kill us on sight because they know if they don't, we will certainly kill them."

"Agreed," said Juanita, nodding her head.

"Certainly a possibility," said Uncle Bill.

"Probably? Possibly?" questioned Matt at his uncle's refusal to see the light.

"You think they're going to make us prospects in their little gang of vigilante, cutthroat terrorists? No way! he barked more loudly than he'd intended. He just as quickly came to ease before starting up again. "If they have killed Abby's parents, do you think they are going to tolerate Abby's emotions, or yours," he said, looking at his uncle. "Or mine or Brent's?" Hell no. If Montana has hooked up with terrorists, four more dead bodies are not going to matter. In fact, he will want us *all* dead because we are all a threat—period. Ain't that right, Juanita?" Everyone was staring at Juanita, waiting for her answer. "Well?" he said again to Juanita, staring wide eyed waiting for confirmation.

"He's absolutely correct. If they've killed Abby's parents, they will want us dead as well."

Everyone looked at Uncle Bill because Matt's objection was originally addressed to him, and they were all following closely, all thinking out loud, and all on the same page.

"I know," he finally said.

*****

"Beer, broads, and bullshit, whispered a voice from the woods. Don't shoot, *Uncle Jack's here*," ordered the same voice a bit more loudly. It was a lousy imitation of Jack Nicholson in the movie, *The Shining*.

Four nomads hit the ground rolling and came up with weapons pointed at the intruder, who had snuck, unnoticed, into their midst. None of them shot, however, and Matt instantly realized that it was *instinct*, that had kept him from unloading on Brent Chandler.

"You just about got your fucking ass shot off, Brent Chandler," Matt said, raising his gun towards the sky and releasing the hammer before holstering it. What the fuck are you doing sneaking around in the bushes like a damned Indian, anyway? You asshole! You scared the shit out of me," he said, going over to greet him.

"You're real lucky, dickhead," Juanita said scowling, "that I didn't put ten rounds into your pretty little face, mister."

Abby broke loose of her paralysis, holstered her weapon and ran to Brent, and jumped into his arms, locking her legs around his waist, knocking him backwards.

"Brent! I am so damn happy to see you," she wailed, clinging to him like a vine.

"It's been way too long, sweetheart—way too long, indeed," he said, smiling his flirtatious smile before lowering her to the ground.

"Damn good to see you, bro," said Uncle Bill, giving him a hearty handshake and a man-hug. "What are you doing here?" he said, getting right to business. But before Brent could answer, Uncle Bill continued. "Jesus, bro, you scared the hell out me. And to be frank, you're lucky one of these three outlaws didn't put a bullet in you," he said, waving his arms at his three companions. He didn't elaborate. The perils of their journey would have to wait. "I haven't heard that password in a long time, amigo," he said, leading his friend over to the campfire.

"After you left," began Brent, "I found there were some weapons and ammunition missing from my closet, along with my copy of *Plan Alpha.*"

"Oh boy," said Uncle Bill.

"You are going to want to hear this," said Brent. "With the help of my comrades here," he waved his arms towards the trees, and out of the shadows, on all sides of the dirty gang of outlaws, stepped thirteen of the most bad-ass looking warriors any of them had ever seen. "We were able to extract certain information from a certain someone who *was* a known associate of Montana's," he said with a knowing smile. "After trying your cell phone with zero success, I had no choice but to hightail it on down here and hope that I got here in time, which was not an easy task, as I'm sure you know. We ran into a circus sort of place that we had to sort of liberate," he said, smiling, "but that can wait. In my opinion you are most likely walking into a trap, partner, and that's why we're here."

Matt, looked around at all the warriors that had snuck up on them undetected, and nodded, thinking, these guys are real good.

"And," Brent continued, "I'm sorry to report, or not so sorry, actually, that that certain someone that we extracted information from can't be here tonight to tell you in person what a scum-bag Montana and his acquaintances are, but unfortunately he is no longer amongst the living—took a trip into the woods where bears get lost," he said smiling at Abby. "Probably worm bait by now," he said, smiling at Juanita and holding his gaze long enough that it made a silent, eerie statement to everyone around the campfire.

"What about my parents, Brent. Have you heard anything?"

"I'm sorry, Abby, we still haven't heard anything, but I am guessing since Montana is expecting you, us too, for that matter, that your parents are worth more to him alive than dead—but it's only a guess, Abby." Abby crossed her legs and sat where she was; a look of deep concern on her face.

"These are my brothers," he said, waving his hand in a circle indicating his posse of warriors. There are fourteen of us, we started out with twenty; six gave their life for the cause, and we are here to stop this before it goes any further," he said matter-of-factly. "You're not going to like what I have to say."

"I don't like it already," said Juanita, giving Brent a solid stare.

"Okay then," here's how it lays out." He took in a deep breath and walked closer to the small campfire and sat down. "Got any whisky," he asked? "Hey, where's the computer geek," he said looking around.

"He was killed in a skirmish last night, or was it early this morning or yesterday morning," said Abby. "He's dead, Brent. But Matt got the bastard who killed him. Eric wasn't even armed."

"Damn, Abby. I'm sorry to hear it. I actually liked the little guy. Real sorry to hear it."

Abby had gotten up to retrieve the bottle of Jack, "We are real sorry to hear about your fallen brothers, too, Brent. Here," she said, handing over the bottle to Brent who took it and then looked around at his raggedy-ass group of friends and said, "Out here, when something horrible like this happens, we find comfort in the arms of Uncle Jack. Here's to Eric and Rose and a few others we lost along the way." He saluted Uncle Bill and the gang of nomads and then his comrades and then took a good slug of the stout Tennessee whisky, after which he handed the bottle to Abby.

"Here's to them all," she said, taking a slug and passing it on, and after the bottle made the rounds and came back to Abby, she carried it over to one of the warriors.

"Thanks, Abby, but we have a job to do. But we'll all take a rain check on the offer," said the giant standing in front of her.

"You are welcome at our camp site any time, brother," she said, giving him a hug.

"Yeah, well, like I was saying," Brent started again. "As you already know, Montana ain't quite the guy he used to be. What you don't know is that he's got a smuggling ring going on out of Mexico, and I don't mean just ganja."

"Damn!" said Matt. "Smuggling in *a-rab* terrorists, I'm betting."

"Al-Qaeda terrorists," corrected Brent. "How the fuck many times do I have to tell you, kid, all terrorists are not Arabs and all Arabs are not terrorist." Juanita clapped three times slowly and smiled.

"Here, here," she said.

"I know that," said Matt. "Slip of the tongue, that's all. Hell, y'all know what I meant," he said in his defense.

"Please stay focused," said Abby, with a school teacher tone that got everyone to look at her. "My folks are in danger. Real danger, you guys. Maybe they're dead!" she said, sternly.

"Okay then," said Brent, we are sure that Montana and his gang has taken charge of Jake and Karla's place. I'm sorry, Abby."

"We sort of figured that," said Juanita. "We just got back from reconnaissance and saw Montana at the ranch. Couldn't get close enough to see how many others there were, but saw Montana, for sure."

"We know that, too," said Brent. "We observed you two *sneakin'* through the bushes making enough noise to raise the dead," he said with a chuckle.

Juanita's mouth fell open but she said nothing.

"You mean you were watching us watching them," said Matt, not trying to be funny, but garnered a chuckle from Brent.

"Yeah, that's exactly what I mean kid. We been here long enough to have scouted out the entire lay of the land and there ain't nobody else here but who's up there at the house.

"We need to go now," said Abby, looking around for support.

"But that ain't going to last too long," he said, ignoring Abby.

Brent got up and walked over to Juanita who was standing just outside the light of the campfire, holding her rifle across her chest. He stepped up so close to her that it would be impossible for her to bring her weapon around to a firing position. A tactical move he only used if he knew for sure that he could handle his opponent.

"I know you used to hang with Montana, Juanita," Brent said, looking straight and hard into her eyes. Matt suddenly realized that the warriors were watching Juanita like a hawk watching a rat. "When you cut it off with him a few years back, was that the end? Do you know anything about any of this? Are you still associated with him in any way?"

It was pretty direct and you could hear the proverbial pin drop. Everyone tensed, including the warriors, waiting for Juanita to answer the impromptu interrogation.

"Hey," said Matt, moving up to the fire, "you don't think…" Juanita cut him off with a quick glance and then stepped back a few steps but did not move her weapon. Brent moved quickly to the side allowing his warriors, who quickly brought their weapons to their shoulders, a clear shot.

"You're hurting my feelings, dude," she said, returning Brent's stare. "If I was still hooked up with Montana, I wouldn't have helped these gypsies here stay alive—I would have taken them out a long time ago."

"You needed a ride south," said Brent.

"I could have made my way here in any number of ways, including, killing them all any time I wanted and stolen everything they have." A silence followed that was so tense that it could be felt. "You're starting to piss me off, Brent," she said. Matt noticed the red in her dark cheeks and figured she was more than just a little pissed, and as far as he was concerned she had good reason.

"She's on our side, Brent. Lay off," said Matt.

"There is no question in my mind as to her allegiance," added Uncle Bill.

"She's a sister," said Abby. She saved our lives." Brent considered Juanita with one of his looks that penetrates the façade in search of the soul.

"Sorry, Juanita, I had to ask," he said, waving his men off. "The guy who gave up Montana's plans said you were in on it. His name was Mendoza."

"That little weasel," she said? She snorted out her nose, and forced a short laugh. "I guess I shouldn't be surprised. Well I'm surprised that he's still alive—or *was* still alive," she said correcting herself. "The guy was a dirty lecherous pig. He hung around like a dog waiting for handouts. Montana let him hang because he had contacts that bought major quantities of pot and cocaine. He hit on me a few times, and the last time I made him cry in front of his friends," she said, finishing her defense.

"Okay, Juanita," he said. "Sorry. You understand I had to ask."

"No problem, Major. I understand, and I would have done the same thing, sir."

"Okay, then," said Brent, here's the rest of the story. Jake and Karla are family to me, and this is bigger than just taking over their ranch. This place is part of a very large, nationwide conspiracy, and he is smuggling in terrorists just like Matt figured. And he's been doing it for a long, long time."

"We need to go now," said Abby, again, stepping into the light of the fire, and looking at Brent with pleading eyes.

"We're going Abby, but let me finish. You need to see the whole picture."

"Montana's been bringing in Islamic jihadist for about 10 years, now, and his buddy Moalim is one of the ring leaders, so we're pretty damn sure that Montana is taking his orders from him, and not the other way around. Do you see the implications here," he asked Bill.

"Why would Montana hook up with Jihadists," he asked.

"How about this," said Brent. "His real name is Juan Torres, son of an immigrant from Iran by the name of Mohammad al-Hadadi."

"Damn," said Uncle Bill, dumbfounded at the revelation.

"Yep," confirmed Brent, "and him and his gang-bangers, who are spread out all over the country, lit a match at the same time and, BOOM!" he said, moving his arms apart creating an imaginary Hiroshima mushroom cloud. "You were right about it all, Matt—lucky guess," he kidded.

"Their plan is to take over this country, they are still on the move, and they are still causing chaos."

"Why this country," asked Uncle Bill. "I mean, we are too big and too powerful."

"Right," said Matt. "They gotta be nuts."

"They want a country with enough natural resource to sustain on its own—as asinine as it sounds, they want a country that has it all—the richest country in the world; the good old US of A."

"That's crazy," said Uncle Bill. "It's impossible," he said, looking at Matt. "This was a fluke. It's unbelievable that this plot was not uncovered. How could they organize?"

"Internet, disposable cell phones, you name it—it's all very complicated, I'm sure. I can only tell you that it's been in planning for a very long time, and Jake and Karla's place have been part of an underground railroad, so to speak, to these fuckers for a very long time." He looked at Abby who was slowly turning the chamber of the magnum that she had claimed as her own. Each click of the cylinder, as it slid into place, echoed in the silence of the still night air. She was staring at Brent with a look so serious, that he locked onto her stare for a few moments, trying to analyze her possible thoughts.

"How do you know all this," asked Juanita.

"It's been checked out, comrade, and I guarantee you it's true as spit," said Brent. "The guy that was *persuaded*, shall we say, to give up the information," he said, smiling at his comrades, "had plenty to say. Said he was a born again Christian out of San Quinton and turned gang banger when he met Montana in LA. He told Montana that he knew guys in Mexico who sold, and that he'd met plenty of guys in the joint with contacts on the outside that wanted to buy. He was a natural for a guy like Montana who was making money smuggling weed. One thing led to another and Montana eventually fell in with Moalim and the rest is history. Seems they have a cell in Monterey, Juanita, and that's another reason I had to ask you about your relationship with Montana. Could be your folks are in danger, too," he said.

"That bastard," said Juanita, spitting into the fire. "That fucking bastard was just using me to set up a base in my home town. "I'm going to cut his balls off and feed them to him," she said. "As for my folks, thanks for the concern, but they only met Montana one time. They don't have anything to offer him or his kind. They live in a small village outside Monterey with a community well in the middle of the courtyard. I'm sure they are not in any danger from him."

"We need to go save my parents," pleaded Abby.

"We need Montana and Moalim alive," said Brent, addressing Abby. "Maybe the government doesn't believe in torture, but we need some information, and I guarantee you, sweetheart, the scum-bags will tell us what we need to know. One more thing," he said, "my guess is that your parents are alive and being held hostage because Montana et-al are stalling for time. If they can barter with us, for your parents, it will buy them a few days—maybe enough time for their troops to get here. Once that happens, they will have no use for them or any of us. I can guarantee you, because of the stolen Plan Alfa, they know we are all on our way. Their only hope is that their army gets here before we strike."

"Sounds plausible," said Juanita. And like you said, once that happens, it will be a damn war, trying to get the place back."

"Makes sense," agreed Matt.

"What are we going to do about my parents, Brent—when are we going to go save them?"

"Okay Abby. First, *we* aren't going to go get them. Y'all are going to stay here, and me and my comrades are going to do what we do best," he said. "You, Matt, Bill, and Juanita and one of my men will stay here. It will be over before you know it, but time is of the essence. We need to take this site before their reinforcements get here, which could be any time." No one said anything about waiting until daylight.

"Okay then," said Brent to his comrades. "If there is no further chit-chat, then let's move out. You know *The Plan*."

*****

It happened so fast that Matt wondered if it really happened at all. Was Brent really there? Had the last fifteen minutes been a dream? Was it all about to go down? After a few minutes he said: "I can't believe they snuck up on us like that."

"Ditto, soldier," said Juanita. "I must be losing it."

"You ain't loosing nothin', little momma," said Matt, giving her one of his seductive smiles.

"Chill maggot," she said, "we still have business to take care of." Abby and Uncle Bill were shaking their heads at the banter, and Abby smiled inside at the *dearism* that Matt had used; a dearism he used on her to make her smile on the outside. Will he ever grow up, she wondered.

The warrior that was left behind was still as a statue, standing just outside the rim of fire light from the small pit. Thirty minutes passed, and then there was a barrage of gun fire that lasted ten seconds and launched a million birds into the sky, adding to the ruckus, which in turn caused a hail of leaves to float silently to the ground; and then it became as quite as a church hall on Sunday morning waiting for the cleric to arrive. It was uncanny, at best.

"Mount up," ordered the warrior. "I'll ride shotgun with Bill, the rest of you follow in Matt's truck. Let's move," he said, heading to the trucks.

*****

When they came to the cabin, Brent was sitting on the porch, beer in hand. Two warriors were standing guard at the door, the rest were nowhere to be seen. Montana and Moalim were tied to a tree with duct tape and there were four corpses lying next to each other out front.

"Come on up neighbors," he hollered in his good timing voice, and they all hurriedly piled out of the trucks. "All is well. Jake and Karla have been expecting you."

Abby took off running, but Matt and his uncle just walked. It was over—for now, anyways. Juanita walked to the bodies to have a look, and then she put her full attention on Montana. He'd been knocked around, plenty, but it was nothing compared to what she wanted to do to him.

EPILOGUE

It had been three days since the Uncle Bill and his clan had arrived from up north. They were all rested and cleaned up, and their stomachs were full, and an *enchanted familial spell* now hung in the air, thanks in large part to the magic mothering of Karla.

The day after the battle to save Jake and Karla, an uncountable number of good-guy warriors were watching the perimeter. There were snipers and guards and hourly patrols. Surveillance cameras were in place and a command center had been set up in Jakes work space in the barn. The people and the property were as secure as Fort Knox.

The battle had been won, but sporadic reports received by Brent affirmed that anarchy was in full bloom in the cities. Thousands, if not millions of people were dead, tall buildings were tumbled like tinker toys, bridges were collapsed, and killing and thievery was rampant; the list of horrors was endless. But no faction, here or abroad, had stepped up and claimed responsibility for the strike that had brought the most powerful country in the world to its knees.

Middle Eastern countries vehemently denied having any part in the matter. One rather cryptic report, that seemed odd to everyone but the gang of vagabonds, put the blame on some unknown worldwide organization of billionaires that was using terrorist organizations to, unknowingly, fight their battles.

"I'm heading out this morning," said Juanita, stepping out the door and setting her pack-sack down, and leaning her rifle against the outside door jamb. "You girls are going to have to get along without me for a while," she said, looking at Brent and Uncle Bill.

"You clean up nicely," said Brent, getting a laugh from the others on the porch. Juanita smiled and everyone froze at the site of her missing tooth, to which she smiled even bigger, knowing full well that she had not put in her bridge.

"What's wrong, boys, cat got your tongue," she kidded.

"Your tooth!" said Uncle Bill, "your damn tooth is missing."

"Yep, lost it saving you girls' asses a few days back," she kidded, still smiling. "So hope you appreciate my tenacious dedication and my personal sacrifice, and can find a monetary way to repay me one of these days," still spreading the bull. "You know us warriors don't work for free," she said, making sure they all got a good look at her toothless smile.

"That reminds me," said Uncle Bill, getting up from his seat and going into the cabin and returning shortly with two, one-pound bricks of gold. "Here, maybe you can use this to barter with. I don't know if it's worth a shit because we haven't tried to use it yet. Could be worthless, but if it's any good, Juanita, you earned it and more. Thanks for saving my family's lives," he said, sputtering a bit on his words and covering it with a fake cough. "Damn pollen," he said.

"Jesus, Bill, I was just kidding," she said, gawking at the bricks he was shoving at her.

"Take them, Juanita, please."

"Thanks Bill," she said with no more objections, taking the bars and putting them into her bag.

"You're welcome, Juanita. Have a safe trip, and come back, if you want to. Hell, bring your folks if you want, we'll all be right here." It was a very generous offer, and it caused Juanita's eyes to water but not spill over.

"I've got to get down south of the border, if there is one, and check on my folks," she finally said, sniffling. "Indeed," she said, "damn pollen."

Everyone knew that she had to go sometime, but they weren't ready—who is ever ready for one of the family to leave. She gave them all a hug, Jake and Karla too, and then she turned to Abby.

"Y'all are in good hands, Abby. You have a great family here. I'll be back to check on *y'all*," she said mimicking what was so easily picked up when hanging with folks from the south. Abby jumped off the chair and quick stepped to Juanita and wrapped her arms around her in a hug of love, as tears fell freely down her cheeks.

"I'm going to miss you so much, sister," she choked out between sobs." Finally she stepped back but kept hold of Juanita's hands and looked hard into her eyes, and time went by. "You are my sister, Juanita, and I love you," she sobbed, "and you are always welcome here—for a day or a night or forever, our home is your home," she said turning to her mother and father, acknowledging eager confirmation from them both, after which she recomposed. "Damn girl, I don't think I ever thanked you for saving my life—how many times was it now?"

"A dozen at least," kidded Juanita, stepping towards her gear.

And a silent and gentle breeze followed her as she picked up her bag and slung her rifle and stepped off the porch and walked towards Matt where he was seated on a log a few steps away from the porch, drawing circles in the dirt with a stick.

"Hey soldier," she said, standing close with her legs spread in a perfect at-ease stance. "If you want to see Mexico, I could use a ride and someone to watch my back—if you aren't needed around here, that is," she said, looking back at Abby. Matt looked up in surprise from where he was seated with a smile as big as the Grand Canyon and eyes as red as Rose's lipstick; first at Juanita and then at Abby, who was smiling and nodding her head.

"You should go, Matt," said Abby from the porch. "You could use some time to discover the new you." She pulled her magnum from the cross draw holster hanging from her hip, and spun the cylinder. "I can take care of things around here until you *both* come back," she said, shoving the pistol back into the holster. "Besides, we have a small army of permanent warriors who's staying on to help us out. We'll be starting a new way of life here Matt, based on, *is it right or is it wrong*—sound familiar," she said, misty eyed. Matt smiled as he walked to the porch and took her in his arms for a good solid sisterly hug.

"I love you sister," was all that he could choke out.

"I think it would do you good to take off for a while, and you'll be in good hands." She smiled at Juanita and then gave them both another hug. "Thanks Matt, thanks for everything she whispered in his ear. I love you brother, so have a good trip and come back safely. This is your home now. Right here with all of us."

"Thanks Abby, I…" She cut him off.

"Hush," she said, with tears in her eyes. "No need for words, Matt. I have always known you were a good man with good intentions." At that, she backed away. "An asshole sometimes," she said, smiling a radiant smile, "but a good man." Matt turned to Juanita.

"I would love to see Mexico," he said. "Shotgun," he yelled.

"Well by god, your escaping my charms again," hollered Brent, breaking the ensuing silence. "I was thinking about making you my old lady and bringing you back to my place to cook and clean and take care of the basic domestic activities that a man like me needs," he said, gut laughing.

"Fat chance of that ever happening, shit-head," she said, smiling. "Can't be chained to no fucking kitchen sink; no offense Mrs. Lassiter, but it ain't my style. I got places to go and things to do," she said, knowing that she would return to Cave Junction for a visit at least; after all, she was a warrior, and her talents could be used to fight the bad guys. The government was still around someplace, and soon they would be mobilizing and they could use her talents and Matt's too, for that matter. It would be damn good for him to go through basic training, she thought smiling.

"Just as well," said Brent, "taming you would be more of a challenge than this old man is up to these days. I probably need someone who's at least half way civilized," he said, sneaking a glance over at Abby. Uncle Bill, Jake, and Karla sat quietly at the end of the porch, watching the future unfold. Montana and Moalim had been moved to the woods, and were nowhere in sight.

*****

Brent and a handful of warriors would head back up to Monroe where Brent would turn over command of his property to his buddies, and once he extracted the information he wanted from Montana and Moalim, out of view from the women folk, they would end up in the woods where bears get lost. He'd committed to returning to Cave Junction to be part of the new extended family of outlaws, which kept Abby grinning like a school kid.

*****

Matt had gathered his ditty bag and was handing out one last round of goodbyes. When he got to his uncle, he whispered in his ear; "I love you, Uncle Bill, thanks for everything."

"I love you too, Son. Take care and be safe," he said. When the backed away from each other, they both had tears in their eyes that spilled over.

"Dame pollen, they said at exactly the same time, bringing on laugher from all.

"Okay, then, sweet momma, "let's rock and roll," said Matt, jumping from the porch and heading towards his new traveling companion.

"I ain't your momma," she said, "and you already know I ain't too damn sweet. Shotgun!" she yelled, racing for the truck.

"Hey," yelled Matt in hot pursuit, "I called shotgun first."

THE END

ABOUT THE AUTHOR

LJ Sinnott was born in Everett, Washington, and currently resides in the Great Northwest.

Made in the USA
Charleston, SC
17 May 2013